M000312488

MYSTIC BONDS

PARANORMAL WORLD BOOK ONE

C. C. SOLOMON

CatDog Publications

Mystic Bonds is a work of fiction. Names, characters, places and incidents are either the product of the author's imagination or are used fictitiously, and any resemblance to actual persons, living or dead, business establishments, events or locales is entirely coincidental.

Copyright © 2019 by C.C. Solomon

All rights reserved; no part of this document shall be reproduced, stored or transmitted in any form and by any means without the express permission of the author. Nor may this document be printed or circulated in any form, binding or cover, other than that which it is published.

ISBN: 978-1-7336259-5-1

ACKNOWLEDGMENTS

Thank you to all my friends and family who supported my dreams. My beta readers, Diana, Montrez and Shay, who gave me so much feedback. My editor, Nina Gooden, for her great eyesight, help, and encouraging comments. My proofreaders at Yours Truly Book Services for their help improving my books. Morgan and Charlee who gave me their artists eyes for a cover.

FOREWORD

You can find information on prior books by C.C. Solomon on Amazon.

PROLOGUE

"That was the worst town visit we've ever had," Charles grumbled as he drove our gray SUV down the two-way street at a snail's pace, avoiding the rusted cars abandoned haphazardly on both sides of the road.

"It wasn't that bad," I replied, leaning my head on the passenger side window.

"They were little jerks. Reminded me of why I hated school so much."

I chuckled. "You were a nerd back then, I can understand that."

"Shut it."

I laughed even harder. "Kids, they were just kids."

"I've never seen that. It's kind of sad."

Years of doing bartering in different towns and this was the first time we'd encountered a village of only children. Well, they weren't all kids. The eldest were perhaps very early twenties. Just barely what used to be the drinking age of twenty-one. And apparently, people of that age would be kicked out of the town once they turned twenty-two. Ever since the world became a magical nightmare, us survivors were pretty low on trust. It was no surprise that a pool of children, a little under one hundred of them, had decided to come together and form their own more civilized *Lord of the Flies*. It was odd, but they seemed to have structure of some sort.

"They seemed very mature," I said.

"One of them called me a shithead."

"Yeah, but you did curse him out before that."

Charles cut his eyes at me quickly before looking back at the road. "He threatened to turn my head into an actual pile of feces. I mean, could he have really done that?"

I shrugged, still laughing. "He was a wizard so... anything's possible."

Charles shivered. "Like I said, that was a town of jerks."

"Who had a lot to barter with us, so stop complaining."

"Well, someone else can go next—" Charles suddenly stopped talking.

I turned to Charles. "What's-"

I didn't have to ask him what was wrong. It was suddenly very clear. To the left of us, a group of ten to fifteen people were scattered about an open field, seemingly running in terror.

They were running from something.

A monster that charged at them from farther down the field.

It was the stuff of nightmares. I'd honestly never seen anything like it. Not on TV and definitely not in real life.

It was over twenty feet tall. Normal sized, it could have been a dog.

A freaking dog.

It was covered in long, dark-brown, matted fur with a short bushy tail. I'm no dog expert, so I couldn't determine the breed. Maybe a Rottweiler. It had sharp, slobbery teeth and bright, red eyes.

And it roared.

The sound was loud and monstrous. I didn't have much experience with roars, so the closest I could compare it to was a bear. Definitely not a dog. The ground shook with the sound.

Some of the people running shot at the monster dog with rifles. No magic was used. They were regular humans. They didn't stand a chance. The bullets seemed to only annoy the dog rather than injure it.

I looked back to monster dog and saw it shaking its huge head, the kicking legs of some poor man hanging out of its enormous, bloody mouth. It widened its jaw again and gulped the man whole. It didn't take time to chew before it moved forward and chomped on its next victim.

I was no hero. I loved scary movies, but there was a limit to my fear level. I didn't like spiders, and I'd run screaming, butt-naked out of the house to escape a cockroach or a snake. Yet, something moved me to help.

"Stop the car," I shouted.

"Hell, no!" Charles yelled.

"We need to help them! They aren't paranormals. They'll all die."

"Amina…"

"Our parents didn't raise us to not help where we can."

"Damn it," Charles murmured as he slowed the car down and pulled off to the right side of the road. "That thing is going to stomp on this car, and then we're going to be dead."

"Stay here then," I stated, getting out of the car.

"Yeah, right," I heard him say as he opened his driver's side door.

I jogged across the street and stopped at the edge of the field.

"What are you going to do?" Charles asked, beside me.

"Something," I replied. I really didn't know. After all this time, my magic was still surprising me. I mostly learned

3

about what I could do through trial and error. That and just plain winging it. I would wing it now.

I reached out towards the massacre with my hands, pushing my magic through my fingers. I was at least fifty feet away. I wasn't thinking; just desperate to stop this monster from eating any more people.

"Stop! Please!" I screamed.

A sharp, head-splitting pain ripped through my brain, causing me to lose balance. I had to steady myself with outstretched arms. The front of my skull felt like it was breaking, and my vision blurred momentarily. My knees grew weak, and I stumbled a bit. Charles caught me before I hit the ground and steadied me.

The disorientation felt like it lasted for minutes, but logically I knew it was less time. Pain always came when I used this form of magic, and although I knew it was coming, it never failed to knock me back.

The monster stopped just inches away from an older, white woman who had fallen on the ground. Nightmare dog turned its head, which was the size of a monster truck, towards me.

"Sit!" I shouted. It was actually more of a question, but I said it with force, so that counted for something.

And the dog sat! However, head-splitting pain also returned. A wave of nausea came as well, but it was not long-lasting.

Having this momentary diversion, the woman got up and ran to a man nearby who was aiming a rifle at monster dog. The monster didn't move its attention or cloudy gaze away from me.

"What are you going to do now?" Charles asked.

"Going to send it back to hell where it came from."

How I planned to do that, I actually didn't know, but I decided to think logically. It listened to me when I told it to stop and when I said for it to sit so... "Die."

4

A barrage of pain attacked my whole body like every nerve was set on fire. I keeled over and cried out.

Fido tilted to the side and then toppled all the way to the ground with a earth-shaking thud. Its eyes stayed open but were now glazed over in a death stare. Its black tongue hung out of its mouth, and legs became stiff.

He looked dead to me.

The pain vanished as quickly as it had come.

I fell to the ground from the shock of it all.

It was a pretty uneventful battle.

"Is it? Is it dead?" called a man off to our left.

"Yes!" I shouted back. I sat upright and supported myself with my right hand.

"What are you?" asked the woman I'd saved from being dinner.

"I'm a witch."

"You're very strong," said the man beside her, his eyes wide.

I shrugged modestly. "I'm okay."

"You controlled it just with your voice. That's more than okay," said another woman. She squinted her eyes and walked towards us with cautious steps.

"She's a rockstar," Charles boasted.

"We could use power like yours," said the man on our left, walking forward.

"We're already part of a village, but if you need our help, we'd be happy to—"

"Barter," Charles cut in. "You can't be doing all these unpaid services, Sis," he whispered, placing a hand on my shoulder.

"We don't need to trade," said the other woman. "We just need your blood."

"Say what—" Charles didn't finish his sentence. I heard the sound of a gunshot from behind us. Charles arched his back and dropped to his knees.

I spun around, my hands out to attack with my magic. A bullet hit me in my shoulder, and I soon felt a sharp blast of pain spread through me. I stumbled forward but lost my balance and fell to the ground. My vision clouded, and I saw several boots walk forward before darkness washed over me.

CHAPTER 1

$\mathcal{I}$ wasn't sure where I was. It was dark. Nighttime. I was outside in a small park surrounded by streets, sidewalks, row homes, and what looked like a couple of mom-and-pop restaurants and bars. I was in a neighborhood. Perhaps in the city. What city, I couldn't be sure. Nothing unique to identify my surroundings popped out in the dark.

I sat down on a bench at the perimeter of the park under a lamp post. I looked ahead across the grassy field at a red, neon "Open" sign on the front of a bar sandwiched between houses. Music played off in the distance.

There was life around me. I could feel it, like a minor static on the skin. However, no one was outside, and I heard no buzz of human chatter. I couldn't tell how late it was. It was certainly too late to be sitting outside alone. Yet, I didn't get up.

It was summer, I think, by the feel of thick heat on my skin and the way I was dressed. I had on an all-white, A-line, spaghetti strapped dress that stopped at my knees. On my feet, I wore simple light-brown colored sandals that matched closely to my skin tone. My dark, brown hair was out in its natural curly state, grazing my shoulders.

I looked like bait for a predator.

A distant roar, like the sound of a lion, got me to my feet. I spun around, trying to locate the origin of the noise but had no such luck. This was a city; the roar of a lion didn't match the surrounding. Then again, neither did me standing out in the dark.

"It's just someone's TV playing too loudly," I muttered, wrapping my arms around myself. I wasn't cold, but I was certainly creeped out.

I was being naive, borderline stupid. Why was I out here? Could I be waiting for someone? Why didn't I know?

I listened for the animal call again, yet heard nothing but the music from the bar across the street.

I sat back down carefully, my bottom on the edge of the bench. The music was comforting. Odd noises didn't sound so bad when you had the baseline of an old, 90s-era song playing along with it.

Or so I told myself.

Something electric suddenly pricked the air around me. Goosebumps peppered my arms and made the fine hairs stand up. I heard a shuffling behind me to my left but didn't turn around, too afraid to see the source of what I assumed was the animal roar. The sound grew closer. Footsteps or paws crunched grass. A shadow appeared on the sidewalk where my bench and I rested under the street light. It was human-shaped.

"Mind if I sit next to you?" The voice was deep, male, soothing, and familiar.

I looked to my left at the source of the voice. A few steps in front of me now stood a man, perhaps in his late twenties, although age worked differently nowadays, so one never really knew how old another person was exactly.

He had a pleasant smile on his face and kind, light-brown

eyes, honey-colored skin, and short, wavy black, hair faded close to his scalp. He wore dark jeans and an untucked, white button-down shirt that covered his just shy of 6-foot, athletic frame. On his feet were black and white Converse that gave him a boy-next-door appeal. He was very attractive, and his smile, with full lips and the world's nicest white teeth, made his face almost glow.

He smiled like he knew me like he had all the answers and was excited to tell them to me. Ease settled in.

"Uh, yeah, sure. I'm sorry, do I know you?" I asked.

He sat down beside me.

Close.

I could smell his cologne. Like sandalwood and summer rain on grass with a tinge of something sweet. It was intoxicating.

He didn't answer, just tilted his head as if studying me. "I'm not sure. I feel like I've seen you somewhere before. Are you in business school?"

I shook my head. "Law school."

He nodded slowly. "Platinum Gym, maybe? I go there a lot."

I tried not to look him up and down, but it was evident from how his clothes laid on his body that he was fit.

However, I had no gym membership of any kind. I shook my head.

He squinted his eyes. "Dating app?"

I cracked a smile. "Now, that's entirely possible."

He stretched his hand out to me. "My name is Phillip Leal," he said. "I'm sure I must have swiped up for you. Well, back when that kind of thing existed."

I chuckled, shaking his hand. His hand was warm and surprisingly soft. "I'm Amina. Langston," I replied.

"Ah, Amina, Amina, yes, that name sounds familiar," he called out, slapping his forehead lightly. "Beautiful name for a beautiful woman."

9

There was charm oozing from him unaided by even words. I'm sure I blushed and was thankful it was dark and that my almond coloring was deep enough to hide it.

"So, what brings you out in the park, looking like bait, along with me?" I asked.

"Would you run if I told you I didn't know? Sometimes things get fuzzy here for me."

"You aren't the only one. Maybe both of us got hit on the head."

Phillip turned away and leaned back on the bench, staring up at the night sky. "Let's help each other then. Do you live in the area?"

Did I? I didn't know for sure, but the park felt familiar. "Yeah, I think so. Where are you from?"

He smiled again. "I'm from Philly but originally from the Dominican Republic. Came here when I was five."

Two places crossed off my list of where in the world I was. "So, we know who we are just not where or why we're here."

He gave me a lazy smile that made my stomach twist.I felt like a 13-year-old with her first crush. It was those damn eyes. They seemed to connect with me, showing a genuine interest that made me feel...beautiful. "How—"

He was cut off by another roar, still distant but just as distressing. It didn't sound quite like a lion-like I first thought. A bear? I looked at Phillip. "Please tell me you heard that. Hey, do you think maybe there's a zoo around here?"

"It's not from the zoo, but nothing can hurt us here." His voice was soft and fell over me like a protective blanket. "I remember, I remember," he whispered more to himself than me.

I sat back on the bench. Nothing made sense. Here I was in the dark with a stranger and not bothered by some random, scary, animal noises. Maybe I was drugged and didn't know it.

"I know it all seems crazy, but it'll make sense soon, it always does. You just have to remember." Phillip sat up straight. "I don't always remember. At least not at first. I have to keep talking, and then everything starts falling into place. I just need to ask questions. How's your brother?"

Clearly, I was losing my mind as well because I didn't recall telling him about my family. If we were close enough for him to know about Charles, then why couldn't I remember him? Who *was* this guy?

I squinted my eyes again and turned, fully facing Phillip. "I'm so confused. Have we talked before? I just don't remember." Statement of the night.

His smile left, and his eyes went serious. "You have a brother named Charles. He's got powers too."

I moved to the edge of the bench again. Was he crazy? Was I crazy? Nothing he was saying was registering. "Right, but how—"

"Did I know any of that? Because we've met before. You always forget until the very end. Which I can understand. I used to forget too. I don't know why I started remembering." He grabbed my hand in his and looked into my eyes, seemingly searching them. "Listen to me, Amina. I need you to remember me from now on. This is important. I'm Phillip Leal. It's important that we stay connected. I couldn't figure out how to get you to remember before, but I think I know now. I'm Phillip Leal. Remember my name."

The ground shook, and another roar bellowed with it. The shake was not strong and only lasted a second, but it was enough to disturb me. "Was that an earthquake? And what is making that *noise*? We shouldn't be out here," I shouted, wanting to get up and run to safety. Home. Wherever that was. Why couldn't I remember where home was?

Phillip leaned close to me and whispered words in my ear that I didn't understand. It wasn't Spanish.

"What did you say?" I asked as he leaned back.

"It's a spell that I hope works. You'll remember me next time. You'll remember everything we talk about when I see you again," he replied.

I didn't respond. I didn't know exactly what to say. I was sitting in a vacant park, at night, with a handsome but incredibly odd stranger, weird things kept happening, and I seemed to be the only one concerned about them.

"I'm so confused," I replied.

A soft smile crossed his lips. "I know, and I'm sorry. I know you so well now, and you still look at me like a stranger."

"I wish I could remember you. You seem like someone I'd really like to get to know." I leaned towards him. "Maybe inside, where it's safe? Then you can tell me what the hell is going on."

He sighed and looked around into the darkness of the park. "It's not safe anywhere. They want the gifts you have…"

I frowned. "Who's 'they?' What gifts?"

He looked up at the sky again, and I followed suit. There were no stars out, but the moon was full, giving some light to accompany the street lamps. "I thought I'd get through it, but it's not happening."

"Phillip, I have no idea what you are talking about." I touched his shoulder. "You gotta help me here."

He looked down at me. "You'll die if you stay where you are. You have to find a way to get out. And when you do, don't go alone. Never be alone. When you see the others, bring them with you."

Before I could ask him further questions, the streetlights flickered, and I heard an unsettling flapping of large wings from above. For me to hear the wings flapping, I knew it was something larger than a bird, but what? I looked up at the sky, searching, and saw nothing but the moon. A loud bird's screech thundered in my ears. I jumped up and turned around, looking into the darkness.

Phillip remained still.

"What the hell was that?" I yelled at him as if he had the answers.

Phillip stood up and sighed. "They're coming. I gave you some help. When you can, run."

I stopped searching around for the invisible bird thing and looked back at him. "What help? Run where?"

"To me." His brown eyes softened as he said that, and I was touched with an emotion I couldn't place.

I grabbed his hands. "We need to get inside; something's out here. There's a bar across the street where we can talk."

"I have to go, Amina." He brought my right hand up to his lips and kissed it softly. "And you have to wake up."

"Wake up? Huh? Where are you going?"

The roar came again, along with the bird's screech.

This was too much. "The hell!" I shouted in frustration. "We gotta get out of here!" I yanked at his hand, but he didn't budge. "Come on, Phillip. I don't want to stick around to find out whatever is making those noises."

"I'm near D.C. in—"

～

*M*y eyes opened to a dark room. I heard footsteps circling around me.

"Wake up, Sleeping Beauty," said a female voice. Curtains were pulled, and sunlight spread through the room.

I squinted, closing one eye against the bright rays.

My eyes still had a thin glaze of sleep over them, and I blinked it away to see my surroundings clearer.

"Did you sleep well?" The mystery voice asked.

I looked around the pale green room, filled with generic light wooden furniture. I was on a full-sized hospital bed under white sheets. Across from the foot of the bed was a small, flat-screened TV mounted to the wall. Off to the left of the TV was a door cracked open, revealing a bit of tiled floor. It was probably a bathroom. I turned my head to the window on my right. It was a bright sunny day. I could see tops of vivid green trees, so I knew I was a couple of floors up in a building.

"How do you feel?" said the voice, coming now from my left.

I turned my head and found a woman standing in front of me; she was white and in her early 50s with graying red hair and bright green eyes, laugh lines deepened at the corners giving away her regular pleasant disposition. I knew her all too well.

Joanie.

She was checking what I assumed were my vitals on a machine next to me. She then looked at the IV bag hanging off the hook; my right arm was stuck with the attached needle.

I opened my mouth to speak, lips dry and cracked. My throat felt like it was on fire, and my head felt like someone kept flicking me with their fingers in the middle of my forehead. "Like crap," I croaked.

"Let me get you some water, honey," she said and poured me a glass of water from a pitcher on the side table. "If I had some sliced lemon, that'd be even better."

I sat up slowly, still feeling weak, and took the glass. "It'd give this place a real spa-like feel," I replied, through sips of water.

Joanie scoffed. "Hardly." She sighed and put her hands on her slender hips. "Hopefully, they leave you alone today. You need to get your strength back."

I rolled my eyes. "For what, them to come back again the next day? I'd be better with them just finishing me off."

Joanie sucked her teeth. "Don't you talk like that, honey. There's always a better day coming. And you've got your brother here. You aren't alone."

They want the gifts you have.

Why had that popped in my head just now?

Suddenly, images of a handsome black man with kind eyes popped into my mind.

Phillip.

It was all a dream. One that I finally remembered.

"Feel up to going to breakfast? I can get a wheelchair if you need help. I think it would do you some good to get out of this room. See folk. See Charles."

I gave a deep sigh and tossed the sheets aside. I swung my sock-covered feet to the side of the bed, scooted to the edge and stood up. My legs buckled, but I leaned onto my IV pole and waited until I had my balance again.

"You need the wheelchair, darlin'?" Joanie asked, holding me up by the right arm.

I quickly shook my head.

When you can, run.

I needed my legs. "Just need to fully wake up."

Joanie nodded. "Take a shower, get dressed. Then we can walk over to the cafeteria. I'll be waiting outside."

"Thanks."

When you can, run.

I needed my energy. I was breaking out of here.

CHAPTER 2

$\mathcal{T}$he world had changed a great deal in the past nine years. One day I was a regular first-year law student, and the next, the supernatural just popped up. Our strange, new world brought with it nightmarish beings and changed a good portion of the human population into something different. We'd learned several theories about the supernatural and why many humans, like myself, were changed. Some unlucky souls transformed into monsters, leading many to believe that creatures such as vampires and werewolves had never been fiction but long-forgotten or hidden tales of history.

The most popular theory was that we had a special latent gene that was turned on when the supernatural came to life. Some people believed that we always possessed our powers, but they were suppressed by a spell that was then broken. Others thought we were exposed to something that made us change. Still more believed we were tested on unknowingly or given a bad vaccine at some point in our lives. It all just seemed like ideas one might read in the origin story of a comic book superhero. I, however, was less concerned with the how and more concerned with the why and the what.

Why now? What set it all off?

The supernatural popping up, in what I would soon learn to be a global event, was just the start of the horrors.

Electricity and technology went on the fritz and would only work again through magic.

Then there was the Sickness, as we called it. This disease came upon us at the same time as the supernatural and, although not airborne, did not take long to infect and kill the human host. It disguised itself as flu-like symptoms but very quickly progressed to something worse, resulting in bleeding from the eyes, nose, mouth, and ears, organ failure; blindness; dementia; and hearing loss. The Sickness came fast and hard, and there was no doubt that it was related to the supernatural event and possibly supernatural itself.

We always thought it would be the supernatural creatures that would end the world with nightmarish monsters and dark spells. However, the Sickness is what killed, in what reports would say years later, over fifty percent of our world population. It only affected humans without supernatural gifts, and nine years later, non-gifted humans made up only a little over thirty percent of our overall, decimated population.

I had been lucky in this new world, for the most part, regarding my safety. Having magic helped. Charles, who was gifted with magic over technology, became a treasure. He got electricity to work and the internet to start. I was a friend of social media and my smartphone, long before the world changed, and now it was the only source of learning about what was happening to our world and how to adapt. I found websites about witchcraft and practiced my own magic. Some years into the new world, I even met a woman who practiced witchcraft long before the world accepted such magic. She became my teacher until her death from a naturally occurring heart attack.

While I hadn't thought I was invincible—my teacher's

death reminded me of that—I'd thought I was safe. Until about six or seven months ago, when my brother and I had been driving down a road from a trade. We'd made the fateful decision to stop and help a group of regular humans from becoming a meal for what I can only describe as a giant dog. Although we saved the day, we'd been far from rewarded. Next thing we knew, we were being jumped by tons of other people in what we first assumed were abandoned cars. We were drugged and locked up in this place full of magical misfits.

I had been trapped in this hospital for over six months, I think. Time was hard to track here. Our days became monotonous. The building was more of a prison than a place of healing. Our daily routine made us weaker, not better. Wake up, eat, labor, give blood, rest. Rinse and repeat. Honestly, I was surprised to still be alive.

I stood at the perimeter of the hospital cafeteria, holding a tray of unappetizing looking oatmeal and a cup of tea, searching for Charles.

"Mina! Over here!" Charles yelled from my left, waving a hand in the air. He had a smile on his face.

Why did he look so damn happy? How could he have so much joy?

I walked over to the circular table and sat down next to my brother. Two other prisoners that Charles and I befriended were seated at the table, a man named Jared Hightower and a woman named Chelsea King.

"I'm telling you, Jared," Charles began, "When I get out of here, I'm going to make an interactive magic teaching computer game. I can probably even make it holographic and have A.I. That's the next wave. We're about nine years in, it's time for people to have fun again."

"If we get out of here, I'll help you with marketing," Jared snorted.

Charles frowned. "You think this is a pipe dream, don't you?"

"Any plans that don't involve killing the fuckers that run this place seem like pipe dreams to me," Jared replied, waving his spoon in the air.

I shook my head. "You have to have hope, or else what's the point?" I stated.

Charles pointed at me. "See, she gets it. How you feeling, Sis?" Charles asked, his smile turning to a look of worry.

"Alive," I muttered before putting a spoonful of oatmeal in my mouth. My throat still felt raw, mouth dry, and the food went down hard, trapped in my throat. I sipped on my tea to help it down. The liquid felt soothing and somehow calmed me. Tea had become a special treat nowadays. It gave a sense of normalcy.

"Well, I feel half-dead," Jared stated. He gave a loud yawn, squinting his dark-brown eyes. He was white with tanned skin, long blond hair, and a toned physique that supported his previous job as a Raven's football player in the Pre-world, what we called the time before magic. He looked twenty-something, but he said he was 35 years old. It made sense. Those who gained paranormal abilities aged differently. Once we hit our twenties, our aging slowed dramatically.

"Yesterday, they nearly killed me," Jared continued. "I had to get a healer. We have to figure out a way to kill them."

Jared always talked about killing them. We tried to hush him up with that talk, but he wasn't scared, and he was still alive, so we just let him go on.

"We can't win against them," Chelsea said, looking down at her food. She was a petite woman appearing to be in her twenties with long, thick, strawberry-blond hair and hazel eyes. "I haven't had a clear thought in almost a year. My powers feel like they've just up and gone."

Our captors were humans, we were now…other. What we were, the normal humans wanted to be, and they had found a way to use us to enhance themselves while keeping our powers turned off.

I'd seen people die, being experimented on and broken here.

"We're getting out," I said matter-of-factly, staring down at my cardboard-tasting oatmeal.

"Dream up an escape plan?" Charles asked, an amused look on his face.

I shook my head. "At the right time, we're just going to walk out of here."

"Well, if it were that easy we'd be free by now," Jared began. "Our kind helped these assholes keep us in here. Made up the damn drugs to mute our powers. And for what? To get better food, clothes? Who gives a fuck!"

Chelsea winced.

I shrugged. I felt a sense of calm I couldn't explain. I really had no plan, but I knew that we were getting out of here. Because of a dream? I couldn't help but wonder if I was losing my mind. If my being here all this time had finally broken me.

"Look at Sam," Jared said, shaking his head.

We looked over a few tables and saw a man who, in the Pre-world, was probably in his early 50s, but in this new world, looked twenty years older. His hair, long and disheveled, had gone totally gray before our eyes. He was thin, with lifeless green eyes and a full beard. His skin was ashen and pale. He looked like a sick Santa Clause. Sam sat, slowly eating oatmeal, lifting the spoon as if it were a heavy dumbbell.

"He's not going to make it much longer," Charles observed.

"Right," Jared stated. "So, what's the point of playing it safe? We die now, or we die later."

"Some of us aren't running to death that easily," Chelsea said with a bit of anger in her voice. "Some of us have hope that things will get better. That we will be rescued. We just have to keep living."

I smiled and patted her hand. "And that's what I plan for us to do." When I figured out a plan.

After breakfast, I wandered over to the garden area. The grounds were full of flowers and vegetables that we, the prisoners, put there and kept up. Our main job was to keep the facility going. Farming, tending to the cattle, cleaning, cooking, keeping the power functioning with our magic. We were, for the most part, off the grid and self-sustaining, despite the rest of the country slowly getting back to the way things once were.

I'd never had a green thumb before, but in this new world, my job was growing vegetables, fruits, and herbs. I got on my knees and checked on several spices of oregano, rosemary, and thyme.

I felt him coming towards me before he showed up. I always did. My skin tingled, and I had a queasiness in the pit of my stomach.

"Amina, you look well," he said. His voice was deep, and when he spoke, it felt as if my bones rattled in my body from the vibration.

I cringed and looked up at him. He had become my nightmare realized. His name was David Everett. He ran the hospital/prison. I wasn't sure if he had any unseen bosses, but visually he was it to all of us prisoners.

David was in his mid to late 30s, fit and tall, maybe 6'4, with short, dirty-blond hair, and blue eyes so pale they looked almost clear around the black pupils. He had a strong jaw with thin lips and a narrow nose. In another life, one might have found him attractive. However, he wasn't my type. In the Pre-world, I imagined he was a yuppie prick who worked on Wall Street and had an easy life. It seemed a bit unfair that in this new world, he would still be winning.

I didn't speak and continued to tend to the garden.

He knelt beside me, and my stomach clenched.

"Glad to see you've recovered."

I scooted away. "I don't want to have a conversation with you. We aren't friends. You aren't my boss. We don't need small talk."

"Amina, I'm sad you feel that way."

I faced him, frowning. "Cut the bullshit. I've been trapped here for six months. At no point was I ever confused that I was here on some extended vacation. You kidnapped me and my brother and all these people—"

"You're not people," David said, his voice tight with anger, eyes growing colder.

I balled my fist, holding in my own anger. "You hate us, but you want to be us."

He smiled, but the frostiness in his eyes remained. "Amina, we've had this conversation time and time again. It's getting boring. This is just us fighting fire with fire. We have no choice. Your kind murders us. I think we are being quite generous taking you in. I take care of you. I give you food, shelter, clothing. And in return," he reached into his pocket and pulled out a small vial filled with red liquid. Most of it was blood, probably mine. "In return, you give me this. Fair trade, no?"

I looked at him in disgust. "Funny, I don't recall needing your help. We were surviving; we were doing well. You weren't. We didn't need a damn trade."

He opened the vial and drank the liquid. I wanted to gag. I'd seen worse; I should have been stronger, but I wasn't. This place had taken a lot out of me. Almost every night, they took our blood, having found some way to make a blood potion to make themselves stronger that I couldn't figure out. Maybe it was magic as well.

David tapped the bottom of the vial, trying to drain it of all its liquid. I wanted to knock the vial out of his hand, but that would do no good in the end. He licked his lips, capturing any remaining serum, and gave a deep sigh, closing his eyes and smiling.

I shuddered. "You could have had this moment in your room. In private. But no, you're an asshole, so you sit here and do it in front of all of us," I spat.

He opened his eyes and turned to me as if just noticing I was there. "I really like your spunk, Amina. It kind of turns me on. You know, in another life, we'd probably be dating. I would never consider you in any romantic relationship now, of course, but it doesn't mean we couldn't be together in other ways." He smirked at me with lust-filled eyes, and I grimaced. "I could make life good for you here."

"As always, no thanks."

He looked me over in a way that made me want to cover up more. "You could have better food. More entertainment privileges. Alcohol. Get you off of labor. I could visit you tonight to...help you reconsider."

I looked away. "Pass."

"That's what you say now, but you'll change. They always do."

"I haven't in six months."

He gave a dry chuckle. "You've got a strong resolve. I think that's what makes you more interesting to me. But I will wear you down. Just like the others. I've been very respectful of you all this time. I've never hurt you or your brother, Charles. Remember that every time you turn me down."

David leaned over, and I recoiled, my lips in a tight line. He moved closer towards me and kissed me on the cheek. I fought the urge to immediately rub at my face.

"Everything okay, Mina?" Jared asked, walking over to me, a rake in his hand.

I nodded. "Nothing I can't handle."

David gave Jared an amused look. "And in case it wasn't, Jim, was it?"

"Jared," the werewolf sneered.

"Jared, what were you going to do?"

Jared tightened his grip on the rake but kept his eyes on David, rage brimming beneath the surface of his gaze.

David stood up. "On your knees, wolf."

"What?" Jared asked eyebrows gathered in confusion.

"Knees, get on your knees." David gave a smug smile.

"Is this necessary?" I asked.

"I'm waiting," David stated, ignoring my question.

Jared's lips tightened in a line, and he griped the rake so tightly his knuckles turned white. His emotions were written all over his face. He was contemplating. Not about kneeling down but about using that rake to stick into David's stomach. And David knew it. This request was a lesson. A lesson to show us who was in power. Because although Jared, as a werewolf, could have easily snapped David's neck, he couldn't do it now. Not while he was drugged and drastically reduced in power. And not right after David had ingested the special serum to make himself super-powered. It would end up in Jared getting hurt or worse.

"You wouldn't want me to hurt the lovely Amina, here, would you? She's your friend. You care about her. I would hate to damage her," David stated, a threat in his voice.

I glared up at David. Damage me? Like I was some sort of object. I realized he meant it as he said it. To him, we were not people. He would hurt me and think because I was paranormal, I could be repaired. He had no thought about the psychological damage.

I looked to Jared and slowly shook my head. He had to set his pride aside and give in just this once. We'd be out of here and we would have our revenge.

Jared jammed the rake into the dirt and got to his knees, holding David's eyes as he lowered down.

David walked over to him, lifted his left leg in the air, and knocked Jared in the shoulder with his foot. Jared fell back on his butt in the dirt, and David laughed.

"Good dog," he stated. He turned to me and winked. "Have a nice afternoon, Amina. You're doing good work in this garden. I think I'll have you cook something good for me tonight," he said, walking away.

I gave his back the middle finger.

Jared pounded the ground with his fist. "That fucker makes my ass itch. Son of a bitch thinks he can do whatever he wants."

"For now."

Jared got up. "You know, it's funny."

I stood up as well, wiping the dirt off of my cargo pants. "How so?"

"I used to be an arrogant prick. Thought I was the top of the food chain. Didn't acknowledge my privilege. Maybe this is karma for my selfish ways. Maybe for not thinking about people who didn't have the privileges I had."

I sighed. "Well, if it's karma for you, what is it for me?"

CHAPTER 3

A few days had passed since my dream of the mysterious Phillip, and I had lucked out so far with not having another blood draw. I still didn't have a plan of action yet, but when the drugs they kept us on wore off, I had hopes my mind would be a little sharper.

I looked out of the window of my room/prison. The evening sunset a warm, orange glow over the hospital grounds. Nothing creepy scampered across the lawn or flew in the air, but that was due to the protective ward surrounding the hospital grounds. For a moment, the world seemed…normal.

I wasn't really sure where we were, but I could tell it was in the suburbs or the countryside. The cities held the most supernatural mayhem. This was mostly because there were more people in a smaller zone. For instance, vampires liked the city. There were more people for them to drain, and it was easier for the vampires to get to them.

The rural areas were risky, too. Yes, it had the least amount of supernatural beings, but the ones it did have were the scariest of all. Usually, the big scary creatures that took blood, sweat, and tears to get rid of. Plant life that flourished and, you know, ate people. And were-creatures that liked to run wild and free and also…eat people. Sure, this stuff came to the suburbs but not as often and not as strong as it was in the country or city. The suburbs used to seem like boring meccas for families; now they were the ideal living situation for everyone.

I had to keep in mind outside threats when I escaped. Leaving would be difficult, and leaving at night would be risky, even after we got off the premises. I could see myself breaking free from these bloodsuckers only to face real bloodsuckers in the woods.

I heard a knock at my door. "It's unlocked…as always," I called.

Chelsea walked in. She looked ready to go to the club. She wore red lipstick, her hair was down and cascading over her shoulders, and she had on a short, green, bodycon dress with gold stilettos.

"Going to a party tonight?" I asked dryly, leaning back on my bed.

I noticed that she had a wrinkled shopping bag in her hand. She put it on the foot of my bed.

"They have fun here. They have a whole community in a part of the hospital we never get to go to," she stated, placing her hands on her hips. "There's a restaurant and a makeshift bar, and they have a rec room, gym, hair salon."

How was this answering my question? I raised an eyebrow. "Fascinating. What's in the bag?"

"Clothes." She reached in and pulled out a silver, one-shouldered dress that stopped at the knees. She dug back into the bag and brought out a pair of silver, strappy sandals.

"What is this for?"

"You. To wear and come with me."

I frowned and crossed my arms. "Go with you where? We are prisoners, not teens sneaking out the window to go to a club."

"You dress up, you go there, flirt a little. The more you flirt, the more you get. It'll make life better." She sat down on my bed.

"I'm missing a sentence here. Go where?" I asked again.

She sighed. "The restaurant becomes their bar of sorts. It's their entertainment at night."

"Got it. And so by flirting, you mean sleep with."

She gave me a patient smile. "You only do what you want to do."

"Chelsea, I'm not going to whore myself out for these guys and make it seem like things are okay."

Chelsea stiffened. "I'm not a whore."

I leaned forward and touched her hand. "Of course, you aren't. Look, these magic sedatives they have us on to keep us in line aren't allowing us to make the best decisions."

Chelsea crossed her arms and shook her head. "This is why I never wanted to ask you before. You don't know how it is. I've been here for over a year. We really aren't getting out. No one is looking to rescue us. This could be forever. Do you want it to suck the whole time?"

I frowned. "Chelsea, we aren't going to live long enough to care if we stick around. We have gifts. I'm a witch. You're a vampire. We're defects to them, and on borrowed time here."

Chelsea threw her hands up in the air. "Yes, I'm a vampire. Who needs blood, so I can't afford to be resistant like you. If I want to get any blood, I have to play along." Her eyes watered, and she looked away. "I tried. Before you got here. But call me weak, I don't want to die."

I moved over to Chelsea and wrapped an arm around her. "I'm sorry, honey."

She nodded and dabbed at the corner of her eyes. "Not all of them are bad, you know. Some are just trying to survive. This world, it's not for regular humans anymore."

I shook my head. "I'm not going to feel sorry for them. I can't go with you, Chelsea."

"Don't you even remotely want to see how the other half lives? If you aren't comfortable, you can leave." She gave me pleading eyes.

I opened my mouth to say no then closed it. Seeing more of the layout of the hospital might be of use for my escape.

I got dressed, and we left my room.

We walked through the familiar part of the hospital, only getting stopped a couple of times by the guards. Chelsea flashed some type of pass, and they let us go without further questioning.

Eventually, we entered a wing I'd never traveled before. It looked like much of the rest of the hospital. White-tiled floors, beige walls with signs listing locations of various specialty areas that were now vacant. Hospitals were typically not the best places to set up any residence, due to the large amount of dead from the Sickness. Then there were the victims of supernatural attacks. And not to be forgotten, those who were already ill or injured from Pre-world misfortunes.

Hospitals, themselves, became nothing more than large morgues and places to raid for medical supplies. Yet, here, the dead had long been removed by those behind this operation to repurpose the hospital. I couldn't begin to imagine how long that ordeal took and how gruesome it must have been. The dead were not contagious, and so the threat of the Sickness was not a threat to our normal human prison guards.

We continued our walk past a pharmacy and a coffee shop and went down an escalator to the ground floor. From there, I followed Chelsea down another hall, and we stopped in front of a cafe that looked like it was once a fancy lunch spot and was now a makeshift bar. Inside, 90s era pop music played from a stereo and men and women dressed in evening attire talked, laughed, and drank throughout the space. Most of the people were our captors, but I saw a few of the gifted people like myself chatting it up with our kidnappers.

The overhead lights were off, and instead, the cafe was lit by string lights and table lamps. Small, circular tables with chairs were placed around the perimeter of the space to allow for a small dancing area.

It was shocking. I turned to Chelsea. "How long have you been coming here?" I asked, loud enough to be heard over the music.

She leaned into me. "Maybe five months," she replied. She grabbed my hand, and we headed over to a table where two men were seated. They were normal humans and, therefore, a part of this whole screwed-up situation.

"Oliver," Chelsea exclaimed. She bent down and kissed a bearded red-head on the lips. He was a handsome, fair-skinned, white guy with smiling brown eyes that lit up when he saw her. Had it been any other time, place, and situation, I would have thought it precious. Instead, it just confused me more.

Chelsea sat down on his lap and looked over to me. "Amina, this is Oliver. And this is Reggie." She pointed to a mocha-colored black man with long, black locks. He gave me a closed-lipped smile.

"Have a seat," Reggie stated, motioning to a chair beside him. "Can I get you, two ladies, a drink?"

"Vodka tonic," Chelsea replied.

Reggie got up and looked at me. "You?"

I remained standing. "Nothing."

He tilted his head. "Come on, relax. Walk with me to the bar, pick out what you'd like."

I looked over to Chelsea, who was now busy making out with Oliver. I tried my best to hide my disdain and followed Reggie to the counter, which was doubling as a bar.

"So, Amina, I think I've seen you around. What are you?"

"Human. Black with a dash of Seminole Indian and Irish on my mother's side. I'm also female."

He chuckled. "Come on, you know what I mean. I'm human. You're," he looked me up and down. "Something more."

I gave a nonchalant shrug. "A witch, I guess."

"Are you pretty powerful?"

I leaned against the bar. I really wasn't up for small talk with this human traitor. "None of us are powerful now, are we?"

He nodded. "Welcome to the club."

Okay, Amina, play nice. You're here to do some scouting, and it might be easier if you didn't do anything to draw too much attention to yourself. "Did you have any family or friends who changed?" I asked with an inquisitive look.

He turned from me and ordered drinks, getting two vodka tonics. So much for letting me pick my own poison. He turned back to me. "No. Everyone I knew either died from the Sickness or were killed by weres or some other monsters," He replied, solemnly.

"Why do you do this?"

Reggie frowned. "I used to be a cop. Nothing I learned from that job helped saved the people I cared about. For half the things that I've seen, bullets don't even work. Regular humans are practically defenseless. I'm not used to that. This serum gives me a fighting chance." The bartender returned with our drinks. Reggie signed what looked like an inventory sheet. Guess that's how they kept track of who owed what since money was only good for burning nowadays.

He passed me my drink. "Look, Amina, right?" I nodded. "You seem nice. And I'm guessing maybe you never hurt anyone. I hope for your sake, things work out for you, and you find your place in this new world. But for tonight, just try to have a good time. You deserve it."

He placed a hand on my lower back, and I stiffened.

31

"Relax," he whispered in my ear. "I won't hurt you. Let's just have some fun."

Geez, guys were still creeps, even in this new and scary world.

"Amina," a familiar voice came from my left. David. Shit. "Very surprised to see you here."

I didn't turn towards him.

"David," Reggie stated in a tense tone. His eyes grew cold.

"Reggie." David's voice sounded tight, as well.

There was tension here. Interesting.

David looked to me. "What are you up to?"

I took a sip of my drink. "Just having a good time." I turned to face the bar, keeping David in my peripheral vision.

"Jealous?" Reggie asked. I think I hated him less than David now.

David looked over to Reggie and then me, before grabbing a bottle of champagne the bartender handed to him. We couldn't get nachos, but we had all of the alcohol we could ever want. New, scary world just wasn't fair.

"Hardly. But I am going to borrow the lovely Amina for a moment. I'll return her to you." David threw out his hand to me.

I looked to Reggie, who scrunched his face and turned away. Guess it was clear who had the power here.

I didn't take David's hand and instead turned to fully face him. "Where are we going?"

"Someplace we can talk and get to know each other better."

My stomach tightened. This would not be good, but something told me I didn't have a choice in the matter. "Let me tell my friend where I'm going, so she doesn't worry. Please."

David waved his hand. "Fine, be quick."

I walked over to Chelsea, who was still caught up in the rapture of love with Oliver.

I tapped her on the shoulder. "Chelsea, I have to go for a bit."

Chelsea reluctantly pulled herself away from Oliver. "Why?" She asked, a look of surprise on her face.

"David's making me leave. He wants to talk," I replied, not hiding my annoyance.

"Are you going to be okay?"

"I don't know."

"Maybe I can get Oliver to talk to him. Does he think you did something wrong? We can cover for you."

"Thanks, honey, but I don't think it's going to be that simple."

Chelsea looked over to David with a glare. "I don't feel good about this, Amina."

"I don't either, but what choice do I have?"

Tears began to form in her eyes, and she blinked rapidly. I wasn't that nervous about leaving with David a minute ago, but now I was getting near panic, based on Chelsea's reaction.

"I'm sorry, Amina," she said. "This is my fault, I shouldn't have told you to come out."

I shook my head. She didn't know this would happen, she just wanted me to have fun. I couldn't blame her, although the petty in me tried. "This isn't your fault. I'm going to be fine. If you don't see me in an hour, find my brother."

She gave an eager nod before leaning towards my ear. "If he tries anything, bite his penis."

I frowned. "I really don't want to."

"Just...fight, do what you have to. Let him know you won't be used. If he thinks he can once, he'll do it all the time."

I nodded and patted her on the shoulder. "I'll fight," I replied before turning and leaving.

David led me to what appeared to be an office a couple rooms down from the cafe/bar.

He offered me a seat, pointing to chairs in front of a large mahogany desk near the wall opposite the door.

"Why do we need to talk?" I asked, remaining standing.

David walked over to the desk and poured the champagne into two glasses. He offered me a glass, and I shook my glass of vodka at him. He shrugged and put the other glass down on the desk.

"You aren't like some of the others. You're tougher. You're more powerful. If you hadn't used your power against my people when they interacted with you, you'd probably wouldn't even have been caught. You don't look like a monster," he explained.

"They pulled guns out on us. *I'm* not the monster."

David made a smug smile before gulping down his glass. "You have a defective gene that showed up when all hell broke loose. You were lucky that it didn't turn you into a four-legged creature."

I'd heard him say this before, so I was now desensitized to his words. "I'm not inferior. I'm more advanced if anything. And you are scared and jealous of us. That's why you're doing this."

He nodded, thoughtfully. "I had a sister. We were twins, actually. I was the oldest by eleven minutes. Her name was Danielle. When the change happened, she was six months pregnant. Her husband was stuck overseas in the military. Air Force." He picked up the second glass of champagne, having finished the first. "We met what I now realize was a fairy. It was a he. No more than eighteen years old. He had these weird orange eyes. I'd never seen a human with eyes that color. He tried to take some groceries from my sister. We'd been struggling to find food, and she had prenatal stuff in the bag. It was several months after everything changed, and we were still trying to find our way. So, this *thing* comes up and even after my sister offered to share, he still attacked. I had a gun and shot it, but it deflected the bullet somehow."

David scrunched his face and I tried to focus on the story, ignoring his use of "it" to describe the boy because I knew where this was going. "Next thing I know, it zaps my sister. Electrocutes her or something. These sparks flew out of its hands and surrounded my sister. She screamed. And burned. Have you ever smelled burnt flesh?" He didn't wait for me to answer, his cold eyes now uncharacteristically pained. "She cried blood. I kept shooting it. But nothing worked. Then it ran. Didn't even take the groceries. My sister and her baby died on the street, in agonizing pain." His eyes watered, and he turned to wipe tears away. "So, yes, you are a defect. You are monsters, even when you don't look like it. This place is helping to keep you from killing innocent humans and helping us to stop others like you."

It didn't seem the time to tell him that this could and did happen with regular humans. There was no monopoly on good people. Those with gifts and without gifts were all free to be good or evil.

"I'm sorry to hear about your sister. What happened wasn't right. But we all aren't monsters. Many of us help people."

David turned towards me, eyes dry. He smiled, but, as usual, it failed to reach his eyes. "You really believe that, don't you?" He walked towards me, and I backed up to the closed door.

"We can help you. It doesn't have to be this way. We can work together. We all want the same thing. To survive. Peacefully." Reasoning seemed silly. David was so far gone into his hurt and anger, but I felt why not make the best last-ditch effort I could? He had never reached out to me in any meaningful way before, and this was probably as much as I would get from him.

David stopped inches from me. I looked down at his right

hand, which was now shaking. "I know of a way you can help me," he said in a low, thick voice. He then grabbed my face and kissed me forcefully. I pushed against him, but he only held me tighter. I punched his shoulder but that only seemed to encourage him. Finally, I kneed him in the groin, dropping my glass. He keeled over, and I reached for the doorknob, but he recovered all too quickly and knocked my hand away.

I knew it was the serum that made him so strong, but it was fight or flight for me now. I had no intentions on being his plaything.

I grabbed the doorknob again and he back-handed me, knocking me out of sorts. I fell to my knees, face in pain, and momentarily stunned.

Amina! A familiar male voice boomed in my head. *Are you okay?*

"What is this?" I murmured.

Don't be alarmed. It's Phillip. I'm telepathic. I felt you might be in danger.

"Who? How'd you know?"

David turned from me and locked the door. I crawled away and rested my back against the nearest wall, my mind screaming.

"Look, I'm sorry I had to hit you, but you did strike first," David said, turning back to me. "I just wanted a kiss."

"Go to hell, you piece of shit."

He grinned wider. "I don't want to take it, so just submit."

Amina, you can fight him. You're strong enough.

I was going mad, hearing voices in my head. However, I didn't have time to focus on that. I needed to use my powers, but the drugs were still in my system, and I only had enough magic to lift a piece of paper in the air. Somehow, I felt a paper cut wouldn't faze him.

"Say, yes." He knelt in front of me and moved closer. He spread my legs apart, and I kicked and tried to resist but failed. He moved between my thighs and grabbed my hands, forcing them above my head and pressing my wrists against the wall in a tight grip.

Fight back, find something to bash your attacker in the head with. Use your powers. The stranger named Phillip persisted in my head.

"I can't," I muttered.

You can! You are strong. Try!

I prayed to God as I searched the room for a weapon. I couldn't have this happen to me.

"This life could be better for you if you would just accept things as they are now. The blood from you with the serum base is beyond anything I've ever felt. And I can't seem to get you out of my head. I don't want to hurt you, Amina. But I can't let you go." David's hands shook again, jerking my hands and arms.

My eyes rested on the bottle of champagne on top of the desk.

"I'd rather die than have sex with you." I spat.

David moved back a fraction, frowning. "If this were any other time, you wouldn't turn me down."

"You aren't my type." I struggled under his grasp and kept looking at the bottle, willing it to move.

It shook.

David grabbed my jaw and roughly turned my face to him. My left hand was now free. "I'm everybody's type," he stated and then kissed me again. I bit his lip hard enough to draw blood, my mind still on the bottle. David drew back and looked at me, a crazed smile on his face as he licked his lip. "Oh, this is going to be fun."

From the corner of my eye, I saw the bottle slide towards me. David squinted his eyes and began to turn his head, but I scratched his face with my free hand. He cried out a curse and slapped me across the face with his open hand. I expected the blow this time and stood against the pain. My concentration didn't falter, and the bottle slid off the desk and floated in the air towards me. I willed it to smash against David's head.

David turned all too late as the bottle crashed into his skull, knocking him sideways. He let go of my other hand. I quickly scrambled away from him ad got up. I raced to the door, unlocked it, and ran out.

I ran down the hallway, unsure of where I was going. I could hear footsteps behind me, but I didn't turn around, afraid to lose speed. The runner was fast and I still had on my heels. I stumbled but regained my footing before hitting the ground. I made a quick right to another wing of the hallway past a gift shop. Still, the feet behind me kept up with my running until I felt the person only inches away.

Someone grabbed the back of my dress and yanked me to the ground. My right knee crashed against the tile floor, and I tumbled, slamming my back against the wall. David appeared over me, a needle in his hand, and before I could fight, he stuck it in my arm. In seconds, I felt like I was floating underwater, and then things went very dark.

CHAPTER 4

When I woke up, the light from the sun was shining right in my face again, and so were Charles and Chelsea with looks of worry.

I frowned and turned away. "Were you looking at me this whole time?" I asked, my voice dry and cracked.

Charles sucked his teeth. "No. I'm not a psycho. I saw you stirring, so I figured you were waking up."

Chelsea leaned in and wrapped me in a hug so tight I thought I would suffocate. I tapped her on the shoulder. "I can't breathe," I mumbled into her chest.

She let me go, and I noticed her eyes were filled with tears. "I should have gone in your place," she cried.

"So, he could do this to you? What good would that do?"

"You're kind of bruised up. He do that to your cheek?" Charles asked, eyes frowning.

I scrunched my cheek and winced at the dull ache. "I'm a little worse for the wear, but I'll be okay."

We heard footsteps outside, and Charles jumped off the edge of the bed. He looked out the door and then came back in. "We can't stay long."

"How long have I been out?"

"Two days," Chelsea said, tearfully.

"Shit."

"They aren't letting you have visitors, but Joanie got us in. Why'd you even go?" Charles asked.

I shrugged. "I thought I could learn something more about this place to help me get out."

"Did you?"

I shook my head, glad there wasn't the usual grogginess I felt after being doped up. Curious. "Just more about the people. Not everyone is what I thought."

Charles grabbed my hand, an odd gesture for him. He looked down at my fingers and shook his head. "I hate to ask this, Mina, but did he..." his voice trailed off in a nervous whisper.

I widened my eyes. "He tried. But I was able to use a bit of my powers and stop him. At least stop him from doing anything while I was conscious. But I don't think he did anything when I was out. He was very adamant about wanting my permission, even if it was fake."

Chelsea let out a deep sigh.

"I'm going to gut him," Charles said, looking up with an uncharacteristically rage-filled face. He didn't have the boyish face at that moment that I'd gotten so used to. We were practically twins, but he was taller and leaner. In that instant, however, he looked more like my father with his eyes so serious.

"Then, you'd get killed, and you're all I have left, so you can't die."

"They're monsters."

I nodded.

"Sam is dead. They drained him," Charles informed me.

I shook my head and sighed. "David said they were helping us. I'm sure Sam had a better chance on his own than being treated like cattle here. Or anyone having to give up their bodies in order to get some extra treats."

Jared stuck his head in. "We gotta go," he said. "Glad you're okay, Mina. Keep fighting." He raised a fist in the air.

I smiled at him.

Charles bent over and gave me a tight hug, and Chelsea swooped in for another air depleting embrace.

They left, and I spent the next several days in lock up with only visits from Joanie bringing me food. I kept replaying the attack and trying to determine how I'd gotten a burst of magic. The magic was still there, to a lesser degree, brimming at the surface.

How?

And how did I hear Phillip's voice in my head? Was I finally going crazy here? I tried to picture him in my mind and conjure him up, but I was unsuccessful. Maybe I was really going crazy.

"Phillip?" I called out loud in my room on day six of solitary confinement.

I was splayed out on the floor, staring up at the ceiling.

No response.

"Well, maybe you aren't real. Maybe I'm getting schizophrenia or multiple personalities. You're one of my personalities, then. So, to the Phillip side of me, thank you for saving me."

Yep, this is how insanity started.

No need to thank me, Amina, said the male voice in my head.

"Well, technically I'm thanking myself since you're just one of my personalities."

Come again?

"You're a part of my undiagnosed dissociative identity disorder."

Is that what you think?

I heard him laugh in my head. "What's so funny?"

I realize this world can make us go crazy, but I'm not an imaginary person. I'm very real. My powers allow me to connect to you for some reason. I don't have the ability to do it on command. At least not now. And I can't say when I first could do it. Probably within the past several months. But I felt you when you were in danger.

"You're real?"

Yes, although I guess you won't believe me until you see me. Look, Amina, you aren't going to make it much longer if you stay there. I'll try to help you the best that I can. Send you energy. You aren't going to get out if you don't have your powers. I was able to send you some strength when you were attacked. I'll keep doing that.

"How?"

I don't know, but from now on, you can't act like you're powerless when you're in danger. You aren't. But try to save your strength for when you are absolutely sure you are ready to leave. Which has to be soon.

"How soon?"

There was a long pause.

"Phillip?"

Sorry, Amina. I have to go. Get out soon! I really want to meet you in person, Amina.

"But where are you? Why are you helping me?"

I waited several minutes for a response but got nothing. I wasn't certain I really wasn't going crazy. However, maybe I was sane, and maybe there was some Good Samaritan paranormal person out there who had run into me in his mind and just wanted to help. Maybe we'd spoken in a past dream like he claimed, and I had told him my story. He wasn't the only one who wanted to meet. A stranger was telepathically communicating with me from who knows where and somehow able to transfer power to me. Yeah, I had to meet him. Or just confirm that I wasn't finally letting this new world drive me crazy.

~

*O*n the seventh day, the door opened and it wasn't Joanie giving me food.

It was David.

I jumped off the bed, steadying myself. I was trapped for a week in the room, but I kept up a workout regimen in the small space, so even if my powers were unreliable, my energy wasn't.

"Have you learned your lesson, Amina?" David asked, walking into the room. He sat down in a chair near my bed.

I didn't reply.

"Sit," he demanded, ice in his voice.

"No," I stated.

"Sit, or you'll never get out of this room, ever again."

I sighed and reluctantly lowered down to the foot of my bed. "What lesson was I supposed to learn? How to let you do whatever you want to me?"

"Amina, the choice is always yours."

I side-eyed him. "Seriously?"

"I'll admit that I was a bit out of character last week." He looked down at his hands, which were much more stable than they had been the last time I'd seen him. Guess he didn't have the withdrawal shakes.

Interesting, assuming that I believed him, that the serum was creating some side effects that were mental and physical. Could that make a person more aggressive? I'd never heard about that happening, but then again, I was pretty sure that wasn't information our captors were willing to go around and share.

"So, what lesson was I supposed to learn if it was your fault?"

"You used your powers on me. How you were even able to still have powers is beyond me. Clearly, you are getting an immunity to our drugs. But we've been putting it in your food every day as well, so that should help."

I looked away. How had I not known I was being drugged? It made sense that they would, but it still made me ill to think about.

"Do you want to get out of here?" David asked, leaning towards me.

"Of course, I do. I want to leave this whole hell hospital."

"Well, I won't be that nice, but I can offer you the end of your solitary confinement."

"In exchange for what?"

"Good behavior. A kiss."

I rolled my eyes. "You're handsome. Do you really have trouble getting women to kiss you?"

"Of course not. But I think you need to understand who has the power here."

"Why?"

"I need you, Amina. Do you know that?" He sat back.

I frowned. "What are you talking about?"

"You are very strong. Some of my colleagues want to pass you around. Send you to other locations."

"There's more than one place like this? How many?"

He gave me a patronizing smile. "More than a few less than a lot. It could be a very difficult life for you, if you were shared with the other stations. You'd never see your brother again. Other places could keep you in a coma and just use you like a juice one keeps in the freezer. As much as you hate it here, just remember, I am the most humane of where you could be. You should be thankful."

I shuddered at the thought of being held in a coma with tubes depleting me of blood. Or being sent to who knows where and passed around carelessly to whoever to do whatever they wanted with me. David was the devil that I knew. And with Charles here, I would at least keep sane. Well, saneish, I thought, thinking of Phillip.

"So, I take it you don't want to send me off," I said quietly.

David chuckled. "And give those pompous pricks a

chance at more power? Let them defeat me and run all of the operations? No. As it is, this base is in a position to take over all of the other ones. With your blood, I can reach levels of power as a human no one has ever seen. I could run this country."

I definitely didn't want to help him with that, but I also didn't want to be put in a coma or separated from Charles.

"This could be a mutually beneficial arrangement for us both." He shrugged. "Or you can make it hard on yourself and suffer. Let me be nice to you, Amina." His tone was softer now, and if I were an idiot, I might think that what he was proposing was desirable.

"What you deem as nice and what I think is nice are two different things. I won't fight you, David, as long as you don't treat me like a whore." If I was going to preserve my strength as imaginary Phil told me to, I had to pick my battles, but I also had to stay out of danger. For me, being some sort of concubine to David just to get better accommodations was dangerous.

David chuckled and stood up. "I would never think you'd allow yourself to be that. Just stay with me, do as I say." He walked over to the door and opened it wide. He then waved his hand as if to usher me out.

I put on my sneakers from under my bed and stood up. David placed an arm out in the air, blocking my exit. He leaned his cheek out. I wanted to punch him, but I was pretty sure that wasn't what he wanted. I held my composure and kissed him quickly on the cheek. My lips itched, but cutting them off would be too drastic.

David laughed again and headed out. "Remember who has the power, Amina. It'll be better if you don't forget that."

Oh, I remembered, but his power was going to be short-lived.

CHAPTER 5

The first thing I did when I got out of solitary confinement was run to the garden. I inhaled the aromas of the flowers and the vegetables. I closed my eyes and turned my head up to the sky, feeling the sun cover my skin with its warmth and the cool spring breeze brush against me. Tears gathered in my eyes. I wanted out of this prison hell so badly. My heart felt constricted. I couldn't do this. I couldn't do what David wanted. However, if I didn't stay on good behavior, he would drain me dry or come for Charles. It was time to leave.

I jumped at a commotion coming from the makeshift farm on the grounds several feet from the vegetable garden. I walked closer, seeing a young white girl, maybe fourteen at most, with her blonde hair in a ponytail, fall to the ground. She had a large trash bag filled with something, probably wheat, and she clutched tightly to the bag. An older Latino male, maybe in his 40s, leaned over her and grabbed her arm. He pulled her, and she dug her heels in the dirt, crying out. I quickened my pace intending to do what, I didn't know. However, the scene felt vaguely familiar to my altercation with David, and I had a sickening feeling that I knew what this guard intended to do.

"Leave her alone, you asshole!" Chelsea shouted, storming up to the guard. "She's just a kid. Go find one of your own women to bother."

Other people in the crowd made noises of support for Chelsea.

"Screw you," the man yelled.

"Leave her alone or—"

"Or what?" the man sneered, letting go of the girl's arm and turning to fully face Chelsea. He put his hand on his baton, which was hanging from his belt. "You want to get the shit beat out of you? Fall back."

Chelsea kept walking up to him, hands on her hips. He was almost a foot taller than her. If she had her vampire strength, this would be no problem, but as is, with our powers muted, he could easily hurt her unless she had some martial arts training I didn't know about.

The guard took out his baton and poked at Chelsea's chest with it. "Fall the fuck back!"

I walked closer to him. If he hit Chelsea, I was going to jump him. Maybe no one else in the crowd was brave enough to defend this girl, but there was no way I was going to stand by and let Chelsea get hurt or that girl be raped.

"Leave them alone!" I called. I walked over to the girl and helped her up. I moved her behind me, and she held on to the back of my shirt tightly, whimpering.

The guard turned and sneered at me. "David's girl."

I bristled at being called that. I was definitely not David's, and I didn't want anyone getting the wrong idea.

"Stay out of this, or I'll tell him," he stated.

" I don't care? Tell him!" I shouted.

He started towards me, but Chelsea grabbed his arm to stop him. The guard wrestled his arm free from her and hit her in the shoulder with the club. Chelsea fell back, and he leaned over and hit her again.

I turned slightly to the girl. "Stay here."

I ran towards the guard and kicked him in the back of the leg. He swung the baton at me, and I ducked. Two other people, an older man, and woman, lunged at him to stop. He swung the baton wildly.

"Get away from me, you fucking animals!" He yelled.

"What's going on?" a male voice shouted behind me.

I turned to see Oliver and another guard, an Asian female with short black hair, standing there.

"This man was trying to rape this girl, and he beat this woman," explained the older man, pointing to the teenager and then Chelsea.

Oliver looked to Chelsea on the ground, and I saw what I can only define as rage in his eyes. He looked up at the guard. "Back the fuck away from her," he demanded before storming over and punching the guard in the face.

The guard stumbled back, covering his nose, which I could see was bloody. He charged at Oliver, but the Asian female guard cut in and hit him over the head with her club, knocking him to the ground. "David doesn't condone rape, you piece of shit," she stated.

I bristled at the lie. If only she knew. I started over to Chelsea to help her up, but Oliver had beat me to it. He picked her up in his arms and walked away with her, probably to the infirmary.

"I have to get out of here," said the teenager behind me between sniffles.

"You and me both," I replied, looking off at Oliver and Chelsea. "You and me both."

∾

48

*I*n the following week, I kept my head low. I got upgraded to a suite, but of course, that came with a price. My blood letting increased, and so did David's presence. He often invited me to dinner. He never tried anything, just seemed to want my conversation. He attempted to remove me from more laborious duties, but I declined. The suite and special dinners were bad enough, any more special treatment, and I'd receive death threats from the other paranormal prisoners.

Others already assumed the worst about me, and my circle became limited to Jared, Chelsea, and Charles.

The four of us sat in a corner of the cafeteria one evening. At night, on the weekends, the cafeteria became our version of nightlife. We couldn't drink alcohol, but we could cook better food and play music, dance, play games, and celebrate birthdays and other special occasions. People were still falling in love and having kids. It was the only enjoyable part of our lives.

I kept looking out of the cafeteria doors leading to the outside, wishing I could teleport away.

"What's out there, Sis?" Charles asked, nudging me with his elbow.

"Freedom," I replied softly.

"Thinking you can just walk out of those doors?" Jared asked before taking a sip of what looked like lemonade but what we all knew was bootleg liquor made by some fellow prisoners.

Security was on high alert whenever we were free, especially on the weekends, so it wasn't as if I could just stroll out of there. The grounds were surrounded by a special magical ward that another prisoner had been forced to make. It kept everyone in and kept the monsters out. There were also snipers on the roofs and cameras, which were turned on by another technology wizard like my brother. Oh, and a nice electric fence. The hospital couldn't have had it before, so they must have built it with paranormal slave labor. I'd tear it down.

I nodded. "I will walk out of here, and everyone is getting out," I said with a feeling of determination.

A group of women walked past us, cutting dirty looks at me. I heard whispers of me being a traitor and slut and how I should be ashamed of myself.

"She's not doing anything wrong, you skanks," Chelsea called out.

The four women stopped walking, and one woman, a tall brunette, walked towards us. "What'd you say, bitch? You're the worst of all," she said. "Snuggling up to the guards."

"It's just one guard," Chelsea replied, standing up.

"Doesn't matter. You're a whore to the humans. You make it worse for us who don't give in!"

"Whore? Because I fell in love? We're all humans here, or has your burly werebear ass forgotten that?"

The tall woman walked closer to our table, and Charles jumped up, standing between Chelsea and the woman. "Ladies, ladies, can't we settle this in a ring with you guys covered in mud?" he cracked.

"I'd pay to see that," Jared said.

The women glared at the two men.

The tall brunette looked Charles up, and down and he gave her a thousand-watt smile. "I'd put my money on you, beautiful," he stated.

At this, the woman smiled at him, and Charles linked arms with her, leading the other women away from us.

"He's good," Jared said, giving an approving nod.

"In here he is," I cracked. "But not in the real world."

Chelsea collapsed back in her seat. "Thank God. Without my vampire strength, she'd have kicked my ass."

"She sure would have, Chelsea," Jared cracked.

"You didn't have to stand up for me, honey," I said, patting her back.

She smiled at me. "You're my closest friend, I'll always have your back."

"Same here, now we just have to get out of here soon, so we don't really have to fight."

"What about me?" Jared asked, scooting in closer to the table. "I gets no love. I think that's the worst part about the supernatural apocalypse."

I laughed. "I feel like there are so many other things that are worse. I also think you are full of shit. Women want the hot werewolf, and you know it."

He leaned back in his chair, folding his arms behind his head. "Well, that's true. I just like to hear other people say it."

I playfully shoved him in the shoulder. "Idiot."

"I really love you guys," Chelsea said, grasping our hands. "I don't know what I would do without you both."

"Same goes for me," I replied, and Jared nodded his head as well.

My eyes teared up. At that moment, I felt like crying. I felt a confusing mix of love and sadness that I let sit with me for a while. It would give me the push I needed.

The rest of the night into most of the next day, I strategized on how we would get out. I lay in my bed that late evening thinking. There was no way we were getting out of here without magic. And we were drugged, but... I couldn't shake the feeling that something had changed in me. I was feeling better and better each day, in spite of the blood draw. It seemed impossible, but I couldn't ignore it.

Phillip's handsome face came back to mind. His knee-buckling eyes. However, it wasn't his eyes; I should be recalling, but rather his words. In the dream, he'd whispered to me in a language that I did not understand. He said he helped me. How? I'd thought at first it was to help me remember the dream. But now I wondered. I was beginning to get my strength back, even though I'd been drugged. There was no logical reason for that. Perhaps I was touched by magic beyond my own. Phillip was the only thing new in my world, even if in a dream. I hadn't dreamed in months. Was he a dream-walker? Could he really have helped me from a dream state?

Only one way to be sure...

I threw out a hand towards my closed bedroom door. "Open," I commanded. And wouldn't you know it, that sucker opened.

My magic was back.

I could sit and decide how the heck that happened or I could act.

Suddenly, things began to seem very urgent. I was wearing jeans and a T-shirt and quickly put on my tennis. I grabbed my jacket off the end of my bed. I looked under my bed and grabbed my book bag of sentimental things that the kidnappers had let me keep. Pictures, articles of clothing, and a few toiletry essentials, supernatural apocalypse or not, my eyebrows were staying tweezed.

I stuffed my jacket in the backpack and ran to the door, stopping at the entrance. Charles and Jared shared a room on a different floor and wing of the hospital, which I felt was purposeful to keep a better watch on us. I was on the third floor in the left wing. They were on the first floor in the right wing. Chelsea was on the same hall as me.

If the guards saw me walking around like I was leaving, they would stop me for sure.

"Unseen," I stated out loud, focusing my mind's eye to me disappearing from sight.

I still wasn't sure how my power worked exactly. I didn't have a specialty like my brother, where I could manipulate an element or thing. That put him in the mage category. Since I didn't have that particular control, I gave myself the general title of "witch." Witches had to use spells, power words, and potions to get their powers working.

I looked in the mirror and saw just my bathroom. I was now invisible, even to me.

I ran to Chelsea's room, but she wasn't there. I'd have to go straight to Jared and Charles' next and then figure out how to find Chelsea on the fly after.

I ran like dogs were chasing me. Down flights of stairs, through halls, pass several people. No one noticed. I finally came to the guy's closed room door and hoped they were in there. I didn't knock and just opened it. Jared looked in shock at me from his bed, or rather, in my direction since I was still invisible.

"We're getting the hell out. Where's Charles?" I demanded.

"Mina?" He chocked an eyebrow, mouth still hanging open.

"Yes, I'm invisible, and we're escaping, so get your ass up. Where is Charles?"

"They moved him this afternoon," he replied, jumping up.

"Where?"

"They wouldn't tell me."

I wasn't leaving without him.

We walked the halls under my cloaking spell, which I extended to Jared. Searching for Chelsea was still on my radar, but I had to admit my brother was first. We searched every room on the floor of that wing without success. The longer it took, the harder it would be to get out. Charles was nowhere that I expected him to be.

Almost twenty minutes into my escape from my room, and I had almost given up hope when I saw Reggie walking towards us. He had to know where Charles and Chelsea were moved, but to get his help, I had to reveal myself and Jared, which put me in danger.

I decided to risk it. They'd realize I was missing from my

room any moment now, and something inside me told me I had to leave tonight or I never would. Trusting Reggie was another thing, but he seemed a bit sympathetic, and I still had my gifts working should anything go wrong.

"Reggie," I said, becoming visible.

He stumbled back, eyebrows raised in surprise. "Amina?" He glanced over to Jared then back to me. "What are you doing out? Over here?"

"I need to find my brother. I need to see Charles. They moved him."

He frowned and looked down the hallway behind him, his long dreadlocks swinging over his shoulder. "You can't be out here."

I sighed. "My powers came back. I'm begging you, Reggie. I need your help. You aren't a bad person. I know that."

Reggie looked back at me. "Did David hurt you that night?"

I didn't want to lie, but I needed as much sympathy as I could get from Reggie. I nodded. Technically, it wasn't a lie. I was sure Reggie was thinking something more sinister when he asked the question, but getting slapped and thrown was painful, so I *was* hurt by David.

Reggie frowned again, a flash of anger crossed over his eyes. "He's a piece of shit. We've taken enough from you all." He looked behind himself again and then back to us. "Your brother is on the fifth floor, room 526."

"Thank you. What about Chelsea? She with Oliver?"

He shook his head. "Just left Oliver, he's on guard duty. I don't know where she is."

"Shit," Jared muttered.

Reggie looked to me. "If you have your powers, then keep going. Get out of here tonight. Leave through the woods, past the parking lot. They won't follow you in there at night. There's something living in the woods. A troll, I heard."

Yikes, that didn't sound good, but I had powers, and I'd

taken on other scaries before. I'd rather risk it than stay here and die.

I reached over and embraced Reggie in a tight hug. "Thank you. I will remember this," I said. Jared and I went invisible again and took off down the hallway.

We ran to room 526 and pushed open the door, again foregoing the courteous knock.

A woman was seated next to Charles's bed, collecting his blood via a tube into the familiar blood bag. Charles was laid back on the bed, eyes closed. The dark-skinned black woman looked up in shock at the now-open door, not seeing us in our invisible status. Charles opened his eyes and raised an eyebrow in our direction. I wondered if he could see us.

"Slumber," I said to the woman, and her head fell forward; body relaxed in her chair. These spells worked easier on non-gifted humans. I didn't even feel any pain.

Charles sat up and tore the needle out of his arm, wincing. "Thank you, sweet baby Jesus," he cried.

"Grab your bag, and let's roll."

He got up and reached under his bed. Like me, he was always prepared. "I won't ask how you got your powers back, but I can't help without my gifts. I don't want to be a liability. They drugged the hell out of me today."

"Say no more." I walked over to him and touched his shoulder. "Heal." I pushed my power from my fingers into his body. I pictured a radiating warmth, red in color to represent the power of witchcraft, flowing from me to him. With my power I could heal his body of the drugs that were suppressing his mage abilities.

Charles turned and pointed an index finger at the TV, which was in the "Off" position, across from the foot of his bed. In the past several years, he had become more expert in the use of his gifts. He could do more than just turn on electricity and get the internet running. He could manipulate all technology, but this was his basic test.

The TV turned on to a bright blue screen. He smiled and blew on his pointer finger like it was a smoking gun.

Jared raised a hand. "Can I get some of that?" he asked, wide-eyed.

I threw some magic on him and he went from neutered dog to scary werewolf. Well, at least his hand he used to test his magic was scary, which looked like a furry monster claw. It was twice the size of his hand previously, with 4-inch, black talons at the end. One swipe with those and I would be maimed for life if I were a regular human or a paranormal with no regenerative or healing abilities. And that was if I survived.

"Great, back in business," he said, checking out his hand with a wicked grin.

"So, we work in sync. We fight and use our powers in the worst way until we are off these grounds," I stated. "If we have to kill, we will."

"I'm all for that," Jared replied, sounding a little too eager.

Charles gave a curt nod. "What about Chelsea and everyone else?"

"I think we're limited on time. It took me long enough to find you. So, we get out, get some folks to help us, and tear this place down. I feel sick saying this, but... I'm not sure we can chance any more time finding Chelsea."

Jared frowned, and Charles shook his head. "That's not right," he said.

"I think Amina's right," Jared stated. "The best we can do is get reinforcements and come back for her."

Charles nodded silently.

"I promise we are coming back for her and everyone else. You ready?" I asked them.

CHAPTER 6

I'm not a cocky person, so I in no way thought getting out of there would be easy. "Whatever you do, don't stop. Just keep running," I stated.

"Are you going to stay invisible?" Jared asked.

I nodded but then forgot he couldn't see me. "Yep, until I need to fight." I wasn't able to use two of my powers at the same time. "Let's go."

And we ran. Luckily, we weren't far from the first floor, and Charles' room was near the exit stairwell.

Naturally, a guard appeared before we got halfway down the hall.

Charles raised his hands upward, and the ceiling shook; plaster cracking and breaking in large chunks. Several electrical wires shot through and wrapped around the guard, carrying him up and into the ceiling.

"That was dramatic," I said, running below the squirming guard.

"Go hard or go home," Charles said, running along-side me; Jared ran behind us, surveying Charles' work.

A camera hanging from the ceiling was slowly turning

towards us. Charles snapped his fingers, and it stopped, the red "On" light.

A blood taker carrying some empty blood packs turned a corner. I put him to sleep like I did the woman in Charles' room earlier.

I knew, as we turned off each monitor and disabled each approaching personnel, that we were alerting attention to our escape. I didn't care; we kept running. We reached the exit door on the first floor and pushed through, undeterred.

We ran straight past a garden on the left and a wide parking lot on our right. At the end of the parking lot was the electrified gate leading to the woods. Still moving, I turned and saw a guard on the hospital roof, pointing what had to be a rifle at Charles.

"Charles, on the roof!" I shouted, now visible.

Charles threw his hand out and whispered a releasing spell. The gun flew from the guard's hand, zooming towards us. I put the guard to sleep; half of his body hanging over the side of the building. Several other guards appeared, and we got in sync to handle them. I made them sleep, Charles lifted their guns, and Jared...scared them, and if they weren't scared, he made them hurt or worse. I tried my best to avoid his monster claws—which were ripping and shredding the chests of guards, releasing blood and intestines—or those giant, furry hands twisting their heads all the way around. Just more images to add to my nightmares since this whole supernatural world became real.

Charles continued to take the weapons until he and I had two. Jared preferred to fight with his claws...and teeth. Although we had powers, having weapons was extra protection in case we faced something we couldn't get through.

We raced towards the fence but were hindered by several guards appearing from our left. They yelled for us to stop.

We didn't.

"Keep going. Charles, get that fence down," I ordered my brother.

A guard aimed his gun at Charles and pulled the trigger.

Charles flung out his left hand, his mouth moving silently as he whispered a stop motion spell, and the bullet stopped in midair, several inches from his chest. The bullet then dropped to the ground. The spell only worked on nonliving things, but it was useful in situations like this or when a car tried to run you off the road.

However, Charles couldn't keep that much power up, and I didn't have the power to

command them all to sleep at once, so I had to think bigger. "Inferno!" I shouted.

A wall of fire a quarter of a mile long and several feet tall, rose from the ground in front of us. It was wild and angry. I pushed it, hands outstretched in front of me, towards the guards who quickly scattered back from the flames and heat.

I felt him coming before I saw him.

David, beyond the smoke and fire and guards. He raced towards us like a possessed man at full speed, arms pumping. His steel-blue eyes, almost otherworldly now, were focused on me.

"Gate's down, Mina, but you got to unward it," Charles shouted.

"Go, I'll make sure no one gets past this fire," Jared stated, his hands out, both fully clawed. He began to shift fully now into a two-legged wolf nightmare that stood over seven feet tall.

I turned to the gate. Aside from de-electrifying the fence, Charles magically made a three-person-sized gap in the links for us to get through. "Stop, David!" I shouted.

Charles joined Jared and focused his attention on the guards and David, while I looked at the ward.

I could see it; a wall of translucent red. I didn't know the witch's spell, but I didn't have to. It was over nine years as a witch now, and I had some experience with breaking wards. I held my breath and touched the magic wall with both hands. The zapping pain was still there as it had been when I touched my very first ward, but I was prepared for it this time. I didn't move my hands and instead pushed into the wall. It was strong and non-yielding. The burning pushed up my arms and spread through my body. I kept pushing; pouring my strength and magic through my fingers. The translucent wall became slightly softened, yet I could not break through. Sweat pooled at my hairline and under my arms as I strained against the ward.

I heard Charles and Jared yelling as they fought the guards. In seconds, David would be on us. I had a feeling that he was doped up on blood serum and wouldn't be stopped by my wall of fire. I also knew that maintaining the fire was weakening me and prevented me from breaking the ward. If I were going to break this ward, I'd have to use a spell and that meant I had to stop my fire spell.

I sucked in a breath and pushed at the wall again. It weakened more, but it still proved too strong to push through. I had to stop the fire. I turned my head towards Charles and Jared, just in time to see David jump over the six-foot-tall wall of fire.

Damn.

He landed on his feet right in front of Charles, who shot the semi-automatic rifle he was holding at him, but David was scarily fast. He dodged the bullet and knocked the gun out of Charles hands, and they began to wrestle.

My options were few now. I had only one hand to play.

I let the fire fade. Since it was magic made, it didn't need water to go away. Just me letting go of the magic, keeping it alive. I turned to the ward with full strength, and I whispered a chanting, barrier-breaking spell to demolish the ward. It broke in seconds, already weakened by my earlier efforts. The witch who made the ward was strong, but fortunately, I was stronger. I thanked God as I watched the ward crack then crumble. I pushed my hands through and felt air on the other side. But I didn't have time to rejoice.

I turned and spotted David grab Charles, who was sitting on the ground, by the throat; Charles clawed at his hands. Jared was surrounded by several guards, and he swiped out at them as they closed in.

"I will kill him, Amina. I will crush his fucking throat. I know you'd hate your brother to die," David shouted.

"Let him go! You know I'm stronger than him. You want me," I yelled back.

"I'm not here to negotiate. You all come back."

I peeked movement from my peripheral. On my left, Jared was now being held down by several guards. Several more slowly advanced towards me on my right. I needed something massive to stop them all.

I put my hands up in surrender and dropped to my knees. "Fine." I stared at Charles, who was giving me pleading eyes. I knew he wanted me to run, but there would be no way I would leave him. I dropped my hands to the ground and felt the earth. I touched the grass and dirt between my fingers. I'd never done this before. I knew no spell, but if I focused on what I wanted in my mind's eye, maybe it would work anyway. "Move," I whispered to the ground. I hadn't used a power word. The ground did not have to magically listen to me. And yet...

A tremendous rumbling erupted from below, shaking the earth. The guards lost balance and fell. They struggled unsuccessfully to get up again, letting Jared go, who got to his feet and used that time to attack them. I grimaced as he slashed the throats and faces of fallen guards.

David fought to maintain his balance, but my mini earth-quake proved too much. He let go of Charles, who then got to his feet and raced towards me, falling midway. He wisely stayed on all fours and crawled to me.

David, still standing in a wide-leg balance, began to move slowly towards me as well. Forcing each step, slowly but steadily; his eyes were locked on mine.

"Get behind the gate," I ordered Charles once he reached me, and he continued to crawl. I got up on shaky feet, pulling at my core to maintain balance. This was my earthquake, it would not get the best of me.

I carefully backed up, trying to beat the pace of David, but he was almost a foot taller than me with much longer legs.

A gun went off close to my left ear. David, hit in the shoulder, stumbled back. I turned around and ducked through the space in the gate. Charles aimed a handgun he had collected earlier at David. He pulled the trigger again, hitting David in the arm, and this time, he fell. Turns out my brother's years of playing video games and fighting real-life monsters these past nine years had made him an excellent shot.

"Jared!" I shouted as the werewolf continued to literally tear through the crowd of guards. He turned towards me, then eyed David. I already knew what he was thinking. "Let it go!"

Jared looked to me again with a heartbreaking mixture of anger and sadness on his wolfen face. He looked back at David, who was now getting up and advancing towards me, oblivious to my friend contemplating ripping his throat out. Jared looked back at me, this time his eyes were calm and resolute. "Go," he shouted in a bass-heavy voice, slightly foreign from his normal tone. He then jumped in the air and pounced onto David's back, sending the man back to the ground. He raised a claw in the air and sliced down.

I turned my head and grimaced.

I needed my full magic, and I released my hold on the ground. "Stop shooting," I ordered Charles.

I needed to make a ward, but couldn't do so if the bullets were passing through, interrupting the ward wall. I had to use this gift that Jared was giving us wisely. I quickly traced three symbols into the dirt where the former ward was placed, my magic pouring through my fingers into the ground. When making wards, I tended to fluctuate between symbols and spells. Neither was better than the other, but I found symbols required less of my energy. This particular symbol would wrap ten square miles around the hospital grounds. Since I didn't have time to cover the exact circumference of the hospital vicinity, I had to guess how wide to make it, and I'd rather it be too large than too small.

I then stood up. I looked to David, who, bloodied, was busy tussling with Jared. Guards came at the pair as Charles tugged on my arm.

"Let's go!" my brother shouted.

David turned to me as Jared raised his hand for another attack across his chest. He didn't speak; just looked at me with icy hate.

I smiled as Jared's hand came down, but the grin failed to reach my eyes. I then gave David my middle finger before turning and leaving with my brother.

We were free.

CHAPTER 7

Six months trapped in that hospital facility treated like cattle, and now I was free again. It felt almost foreign. The air smelled different to me. I felt hope again, filled with possibilities.

"What's the game plan, Mina? We left Chelsea and Jared behind. I don't even know if he's going to survive. It's getting dark, and we don't want to be out in these woods. We gotta find a house, ward it up, and regroup in the morning," Charles stated, walking alongside me as we moved further into woods, putting more distance between ourselves and the hospital.

"We have to keep moving. I don't know how long it'll take for them to get a witch who can break my ward and then they're going to be on us. They have dogs and cars," I replied.

"We should have stolen a car."

"In retrospect, that would have been the smart thing to do. I was in a rush."

"You could have left me."

"Yeah, right, silly."

Charles stopped walking. "Mina, I don't even know how far we are from the road."

"We can't be far. Reggie, who told me where you were, said it was safer for us to go through the woods because we wouldn't be followed in at night. We were in a hospital, and it had to be accessible to communities, so I'm assuming the woods can't be too large."

We continued to walk. We didn't speak, nervous as our surroundings seemed to come alive around us now that it was dark. We were only aided by the stars, moon, and a light from Charles' old magic-powered smartphone he kept in his book bag.

The world had gotten a better grip on living with the supernatural, but we were still hardly where we were before. Between the Sickness and the supernatural, there were certain towns that were abandoned and left to become whatever the new supernatural nature had made of it. I assumed we were in one of those towns since one would assume a filled hospital would draw unwanted attention for our captors.

Charles stopped suddenly. "Did you hear that?" he whispered.

I stopped walking and listened. I heard nothing at first, but then a low growl. It sounded like an injured dog but I was pretty sure it wasn't, which only made it creepier.

There was something staring at us through the trees.

It was about a hundred feet away to the right. It was large. Bright red orbs the size of basketballs glowed at us from about twenty feet off the ground. I didn't need light to know what it was.

A troll.

"I am betting the road is west. The left," Charles whispered. "That's where the hospital entrance faced."

I nodded, but of course, he couldn't see me in the dark.

"Run!" he said in a loud whisper.

We both took off. I stumbled a few times on rocks, but Charles clung on to me, grabbing my hand as he led us through the woods. He was the more athletic one and I hated slowing him down, but my brother was not letting go.

The troll we were running from was silent behind us because I couldn't hear it, and I didn't feel the ground shaking like I would expect from a troll probably the size of a house. Maybe it just wasn't up to chasing us today. Perhaps the troll had enough to eat. Of course, I had no intention of turning around to see if my guesses were correct.

Road. Civilization. Life. Those were my only thoughts.

We ran for about fifteen minutes before we hit road, and then we slowed to a trot. I took a chance to see if the troll was behind us, but I saw nothing, as I expected. I began to wonder if it really had been a troll or rather some creepy-eyed, great big owl perched on a tree limb.

On the road we could find a car, hopefully with gas or electricity-powered Charles was strong enough now to get a car going.

We did see cars. Lots of them. They were moved to the side of the road, I assumed so the kidnappers could come and go easily, making this a dangerous road to be on.

Past the cars, the road was lined with trees from the woods on the right, and the backs of a few dilapidated fenced-in houses on the left.

Charles, who had a knack for finding cars he could get going easily, ran up to a black SUV that still looked in good shape. He opened the door to the driver's side and sat down in the seat. The car started, headlights on. I ran to the passenger side and got in.

"How far should we drive? We really don't want to be moving around here too long in the dark. I'm telling you, we will be targets, especially in an area like this," Charles stated nervously, driving the car off of the side of the road and heading north; away from the hospital.

"We need to get on the highway, find out where we are," I replied.

I looked at the car clock and was surprised to see that it was accurate. Most likely, due to Charles' magic. It was almost 9 p.m. We spotted a sign for interstate I-79 South, leading to Baltimore. It appeared that we were in a rural part of Pennsylvania. Erie to be exact, which was about a six-hour drive to Baltimore. Longer, considering we had to drive at snail speed since the roads were still littered with cars, bodies—both the human and inhuman kind, of various sizes and shapes—and debris.

"First stop on the highway, we pull off and find shelter. You're right, it's getting too dark to be on the road," I stated.

We turned off in Pittsburg, a little under two hours from Erie, to look for shelter. Minutes later, we were cruising down a quiet abandoned residential area with large houses and a lot of land. Not the most ideal, since this was a great location for monsters, but it was the best option for now, and it was dark.

Charles parked in front of a three-story, dingy white house with a large attached garage. We got out of the car on high alert and walked up the front porch steps. The house was still in good shape, all things considered. The grass was waist-tall and weeds had taken over. The windows were a bit dusty, and a layer of dead leaves and dirt covered the porch, but the bones of the house were strong.

Charles knocked on the equally-dingy, white front door. I squinted my eyes at him and twisted my lips. No one was going to be home. The porch was small, only going the length of the front entrance so I couldn't see inside, but the windows were covered with dark curtains anyway.

"I don't think anyone's home," he said.

"What, the grass as tall as trees wasn't a giveaway?" I muttered.

"And the fact that there wasn't a ward, but you never know." He shrugged. "Look, I'm always going to knock. It's rude not to."

I used an opening spell to get in the home. Nine years into this new world and my skills in being all things witch weren't half bad. "Open," I whispered, pushing my magic through the word.

We stepped in and did our usual swipe through the house to make sure there weren't any surprises lurking in corners or under beds. In this case, the only surprises we got were a few bugs. We stayed in the living room because it was easier to escape than going down steps running from a ghost. Yeah, that really happened. Although thus far, ghosts were pretty harmless to us; just unnerving.

Charles, a neat freak, did a cleaning spell to make the place comfortable as I warded us in. He had automatic magic for all things electronic or tech. However, if he wanted to do magic outside of technology, he had to use a spell. Mages were still lumped in the witch category along with wizards, magicians, and warlocks. The basic foundation being that we could do magic with the assistance of spells, prayers, chants, power words, and potions.

Charles recited the two-worded spell in its Latin origin, and the room came alive. The dust on the furniture receded. The sofa, pillows, and linen puffed up, now revived and fresh. Stains diminished, and spider webs disappeared. Even the air smelled like fresh linen instead of stale decay. I felt like spinning around and singing a Disney song as the house went back to showroom new. Every time we did one of these spells, I half expected brooms and mops to pop out dancing and for birds to chirp as they folded laundry. They never did, but I was sure I could do a spell to add that touch.

Charles flopped down on the dark, brown fabric couch, and I sat down beside him. We sat with only the light of one lone candle we found perched on the old-fashioned, wooden coffee table. Of course, Charles could get the electricity going, but that would draw too much attention from any night-time predators or our captors, and we really didn't want to fight, ward or no ward.

"I'm hungry, and that kitchen is bare city," he sighed.

"Not even a rotten apple?" I asked frowning. My stomach was making some hard churns of hunger as well. Using so much power made a gal hungry.

I couldn't make food pop out of thin air, at least I hadn't learned how to do that yet, but I could turn something bad or picked over into something fresh and edible. As long as the ingredients were all-natural. So, sadly, I couldn't turn a pile of Dorito crumbs into a full new bag. Another sadness of the supernatural apocalypse, making junk food, was not a high priority. Of course, I did lose over fifteen pounds in the past nine years, so there was a win.

"Not even a peanut. It might actually have been nine years since someone lived here."

"Well, the place is warded and kind of cleaned up. We can stay here 'til sunrise and go scrounge for food or find a town."

"We don't have anything to barter with, Mina. No one's just going to give us anything."

"Yes, but we have services. Tech mages are rare, and witches are always useful." I shrugged. "I can work in a hospital or something and heal people. You can be an IT person. They need you everywhere. Find a town that can't access outside communication. We'll bounce back, as usual."

"How the hell did this happen, Sis?" Charles asked, putting his feet up on the coffee table. "How'd we get free? I mean, I was there but I still don't understand. How'd you do it? How'd you get your powers back?"

I stared at the black, flat-screen TV in front of us on the entertainment stand. I used to fall asleep with the TV on back in the Pre-world. I found it comforting. I still sometimes found it difficult to sleep without a TV on, even though I knew nothing would be showing. "I don't know for sure. It started with a dream." Then I proceeded to tell him of Phillip.

"Seriously? Okay, so some dude in a dream told you to escape, whispers some words you can't remember, talks to you in your head, and all of a sudden, you fight through the drugs they give us and your powers are back?" He glanced at me sideways in disbelief.

"It sounds crazy, right?" I asked, turning to him.

"Who the hell knows nowadays? I just wanna know who old boy was? Is he real?"

"How else did I get my powers back?"

"Well, go back to sleep and tell dream-walker dude, thanks," Charles smirked. "He must be really powerful if he could use magic in a dream. Never heard of that. But what the hell do I know?"

I nodded.

"Or maybe, Sis, maybe it's all you." He sat up some, excited. "Yeah, so you dreamed about a cute guy, and that gave you some mojo to break through the drugs and get out. You're really powerful. Don't sell yourself short. It was just a dream, and your powers just got stronger because you're strong. We're all getting better, the longer we survive in this new world. The regular humans won't be able to hold us down too long. The hearing voices thing is kinda weird, but maybe it was from stress."

I didn't say anything. I didn't feel any stronger than before I was kidnapped. Yet, I needed Phillip to be real. I couldn't explain why.

"We can't take too long finding help, Sis. They might pack up the hospital and move."

"It'd be hard to quickly move a camp like that. They might do a cloaking spell so no one can see them. I bet my money on them staying and just sending out folks to find us. David was hell bent on getting us. Of course, that's all assuming they are able to break my ward." I crossed my arms, squinting at the idea of David forcing some more magic-wielding people to around-the-clock ward breaking.

"He's obsessed with you, Mina. You were the strongest witch in that place, and there must have been a difference with your blood in the serum than others. Probably why they drained you more. Especially because you recover so quickly." He shook his head quickly. "Nah, we can't get caught again. Let's hope it takes them some time to break that ward. Weeks. We'll have support by then, so we can go back and take them down."

I hoped he was right.

~

*I*t was daylight, and I was outside on a rooftop bar. It was familiar to me; one I remembered hanging out at in the Pre-world. The space was bright with white brick walls near the entrance and white painted railing surrounding the area, which wasn't much bigger than a large living room or den, allowing for a close to 360-view of the city below. Greenery and flowers were strategically placed around the bar, some wrapped around the links of the white railing. At night, bright, elegant lamps and string lighting were lit, spread about the space, adding to a fun and festive atmosphere. Soulful house music played in the background.

I was sitting at the bar near the entrance staring at a glass of what looked like water. I picked it up and sniffed. Vodka. I took a sip.

"I'm more of a whiskey guy, myself," Phillip said from behind me.

My stomach did an excited flip, and I twirled around in my barstool. He was coming from the far end of the rooftop. How had I missed him? I squinted. He looked quite dapper this time. Tailored slacks, tucked in purple button-down shirt with matching tie and black fitted vest.

"You remember me?" he asked, sitting next to me.

I nodded and smiled. "Phillip."

He grinned. "The lady remembers me! I remember you too. Figure I have to ask each time. This is the first time you've said yes," he said, excitement lacing his voice. "Hopefully, I'm less creepy this time around."

"Oh, you weren't creep—you were kind of creepy." I laughed.

"Well, that's not a good look for me. I'll take it as a good sign that you haven't pepper sprayed me." He tilted his head, appraising me. "You look pretty."

I looked down at myself. I was wearing a colorful, halter maxi-dress with a split going up mid-thigh. Sexy but still covered. "Thank you, again," I replied. "So, do you. Handsome, I mean. Nice." I fumbled. Why was I so nervous? Oh, because I was sitting next to a mysterious and super sexy stranger with some crazy powers.

"Thanks," he replied, giving me an adorable lopsided smile.

The teenage girl in me squealed.

"Are you free, Amina?" His smile faded, and his eyes filled with worry.

"Yes, thanks to you. I got my brother, and we got out. We're free." I let out an uncharacteristic giggle and then covered my mouth. "I don't know how it happened. I can only think you had something to do with it. How'd you help me?"

Phillip shook his head. "I don't know. I don't even know how I found you in the first place. You just appeared in my mind one night and kept appearing. It was a dream, so I didn't think too much about it. Honestly, if you asked me to repeat what I said to give you your powers back, I wouldn't be able to. I wouldn't be able to purposefully recreate any of that. Maybe it wasn't my doing."

"No, Phillip. You saved me. What are you? How do you have magic in dreams?"

He leaned in towards me as if preparing to tell me a secret. "You are the only one I can do that with. I have never been able to talk to anyone else in a dream."

"Same. Are you even real? Maybe you're just a reoccurring dream and that's it."

He chuckled. "You keep thinking that. I'm real." He scooted closer to me, his knee touching mine. "But then again, if I were a dream, would I know if I wasn't? And if you were just going crazy and hearing voices, would you know they weren't real? Is a crazy person crazy if they know they're crazy?" He tapped the side of his head, his light brown eyes giving off a playful glint.

I crossed my eyes, showcasing my confusion at his words. "I'm scared to even try to understand what you just said. What are you?"

"Human." He grasped my hand resting on the bar.

He was being cute. I cocked an eyebrow.

He entwined his fingers between mine; considering them. "I'm a witch or a wizard, whatever you want to call it, like you."

I looked down at our fingers as well. My stomach tensed at our closeness, but I didn't want to move away. "What kind?"

"Same as you, I suspect. I believe our powers are compatible."

"What's that mean?"

"Supernatural beings can share their energy to a degree. If you are weak, I can lend you some strength. You healed your brother by getting the drugs out of his system, I assume. He helped with the escape?"

"Yeah."

He nodded. "I did the same."

"But in a dream. That's very different." I raised my eyebrows in confusion.

He grinned. "I stopped trying to make sense of things in this world a long time ago. None of us know how deep this all goes. We don't know the limits. We can only guess the whys. You'll do the best in this world if you assume no limits until you find them. There's no such thing as no such thing." He gave my hand a playful squeeze, and I smiled in response. The touch felt too right.

"Ha. I should hashtag your sayings."

Hashtags had become the number one way to spread information on the internet nowadays. It was a popular method in the Pre-world for social commentary, but now it was the main way to get others to see important information from learning about spells, the Sickness, the government reformation, and more.

Phillip chuckled and looked up at the approaching evening sky. I looked up as well. The sky was now becoming vivid dark blue, and the sun was covered by clouds. A flock of birds crossed above, and the sound of their calls was the only things heard beyond the soft music. We were in the city, but no other signs of life could be heard. Not even a car honk or dog bark or fire engine.

"Amina, do you know you are only using a portion of your powers? You could do so much." He was still looking up at the sky.

"Could I have gotten out of that hell hole sooner? Could I have prevented certain things from happening?"

"Don't ask yourself those questions. It'll drive you crazy."

"Why did you help me? Why do you care?"

He looked back at me. "I wish I could give you some poetic reason, but I just couldn't get you out of my head. Literally and figuratively. I couldn't think of anything else. If I hadn't helped you, I'd have been haunted by it."

I nodded slowly. "I left a friend behind. I feel like shit."

"You did what you had to. We'll go back and get your friend. We'll get them all."

Something large and scary flew into sight. I couldn't see it clearly as it flew in front of the clouds backlighted by the sun. It was a large bird-like silhouette. Vulture sized. Except, there wouldn't be any vultures around here, and its wings looked more like a bat's. I jumped, leaning into Phillip. "What the hell is that?"

"I couldn't tell you." Phillip looked up. "There are a lot of things in this world I couldn't guess at, but this *is* just a dream. It won't hurt you. It's just a reminder." He wrapped an arm around my lower back. I leaned farther into him, feeling comforted by his protective arm.

"Reminder of what?"

"That there are those who don't want us to talk to each other. They are trying to scare us, but they don't have power here."

"Who doesn't want us to talk?"

"I wish I could give you an answer that doesn't sound crazy, but I honestly don't know. It's a presence, a voice in my head. I only hear it when I'm awake. They think it's dangerous that we connect, but it's not. I think they're lying, but I don't know why."

I was quiet. I didn't really know what else to ask. Whoever was telepathically speaking with him was possibly an enemy, and they were threatened by us or me. I wasn't really searching for another enemy, but I had to meet Phillip in real life. I wanted to touch him and see him in person.

I looked up at Phillip, our faces only inches away, and he was staring back at me with intensity. His brown eyes almost glowed, and my heart did this funny skipping a beat thing. "I want to know you, Amina. I want to know everything about you. You have transfixed me. I need to see you in person."

I'd never had a man say that he needed to see me. My desire to see him tripled. "Where are you?" I asked him.

75

"I'm right here." He cocked an eyebrow.

I elbowed him in the arm. "Okay, silly, I mean in real life."

"I'm near D.C. In Silver Spring."

What could only be described as a grumble came from the distance. Like a large, very irritated animal.

Phillip grimaced.

"What's wrong?"

"Nothing."

"That sound wasn't nothing."

"But it's far away."

I shook my head. "Then why are you frowning?" I said, hopping off of my stool. "I'm sorry, I can't keep ignoring this stuff. We should get inside. Dream or no dream."

Phillip stood up as well. "I have to go, Amina." His face looked pained.

"What? Why?"

He pulled me to him and embraced me in a tight hug. It felt right, and I didn't want to let go as my hands rested against his muscular back. I closed my eyes and inhaled a final whiff of his woodsy scent. He rubbed my back, and instant relaxation draped over me, releasing the tension in my muscles. The pressure was gentle, but the effect was profound. I wanted to lay down and rest for days.

When Phillip removed his hands, I tried not to growl in protest.

"Find me, and we'll be able to help you free your friends. Hurry."

He let me go, and I woke up.

CHAPTER 8

I opened my eyes and stared at the living room ceiling from the couch; blinking away sleep and visually gathering my surroundings. Charles lay on the floor, sleeping, a pillow under his head and a blanket covering him.

I sat up, yawning. We needed a plan. There were two concerns. One, we had to stay hidden from our captors. Two, we had to recruit people who were willing to help us free the others. I was more concerned about the latter. This was not a world where we could go to the police, and they would arrest folks. The men and women in blue didn't exist anymore. Even if we went to a community that had a policing system, they still might not be inclined to help people from outside of their town.

After the supernatural took over and many of the non-gifted humans were eradicated from the disease, the United States became, well, less united. The last person in power was the Secretary of State, who became a blood-lust vampire. Such vampires usually stopped being thinking humans and were ruled only by the need to feed. The Secretary killed off his entire cabinet. After that, any semblance of the old government was minuscule. Instead, we were a bunch of self-governing bodies, sharing a continent. Divisions of Canada and Mexico were now irrelevant.

Recently many of the communities were merging, either voluntarily or being overtaken by a larger group; the struggling remains of the former government. Slowly it appeared that we would get back to a country of sorts. Yet, not every community was on board, and the growing government had a fight on their hands trying to recapture what we had before. There were just too many factions that liked their new independence, and those factions had a lot of supernatural power behind them.

Finding a community could be challenging, but... My mind suddenly went back to my time on the roof and Phillip. He'd said his town would help us.

I heard Charles let out a deep sigh, and I stood up, looking down at him as he opened his eyes.

"What's for breakfast?" he asked, stretching.

"Air because there's nothing in the kitchen I can use. Let's check out the neighbors."

We packed up anything of value we could find in the house like jewelry and needed toiletries and headed next door. That house wasn't much better, but by house six, we hit the jackpot. Apparently, whoever was living there had only vacated recently.

"What's for breakfast, Sis?" Charles asked again, smiling as we looked in the fridge.

"Pancakes and eggs," I replied, returning his grin.

"Can I get French toast instead?" Charles asked.

"Sure thing."

I covered my nose as I reached into the refrigerator. I had no idea how long whatever was in there had been marinating. The state of the home wasn't the neatest, but the fridge still was running, so magic had touched it. Once magic from a tech mage touched something, it kept working unless purposefully ended, or the person who was behind the magic died.

So, I wasn't that surprised that there was something redeemable inside the fridge. Anything covered in bugs was my end game. I'm sure I could have made something good even with the rotten meat, but who wanted to pick the maggots out to get to it? And I didn't want to just blend them into the magic meal.

To our delight, the fridge contained spoiled milk, rotten eggs, old shriveled fruit, moldy cheddar cheese, margarine, and hard bread. No viable meat, but that was a rare commodity nowadays since it required hunting. Old meat was the first to get critter-filled.

I looked in the cabinet and found some flour, oil, and several spices.

"And there's some oranges and grapes in here for a little fruit salad," Charles announced.

I did a little dance, and Charles joined me.

"Okay, but first, let's drop a little magic and clean this place up because I can't eat in filth. I'm not an animal," Charles muttered, looking around. He clapped his hands together and recited the cleaning spell again. This time I did do a spin.

Once I'd whipped up the best breakfast we'd had in over six months with my magical food recycling, we sat down at the kitchen table. Charles poured me a cup of tea from some old tea bags he found in a cabinet. We weren't sure about the water here, so it was better to go with boiled water.

"I want a shower and new clothes," I stated before biting into the scrambled eggs. It wasn't as good as the farm-fresh kind, more like a frozen egg breakfast, but it would do.

"I want a fresh haircut," Charles said, cutting into the French toast. We lucked out and found maple syrup in the cabinet as well. "We need to find a town, do some work, and earn some things."

Wherever we went, even to Phillip's town, we'd probably have to ask for credit because we had nothing to immediately barter. I had diamond earrings that my parents gave me when I graduated college, mom's engagement and wedding rings, which hung around my neck on a chain and a diamond tennis bracelet I'd bought myself before the world went to crap that I kept in my bra. Charles had dad's wedding band and a pricey watch. Our jewelry was invisible to the naked eye, due to a cloaking spell, which is the only reason we still had it after being in that hospital prison.

"We need to find more stuff. I'm sure not every clothing store or mall was looted in this country," Charles said with a mouth full of food.

"It's been nine years, Charles. I'm sure they were. Either people stole the clothes or communities moved things to their towns. At this point, people are making new things. There might be clothes here, and I can do a spell to make them fit. If there are clippers, I can shape you up."

"Goal one resolved. Goal two: Find a large community that is strong enough to take out those human hijackers, wants to save others because they have a sense of decency and doesn't hate supernaturals. In theory, that shouldn't be too hard. The question I have now is, how do we go about finding a town?"

"We go to the town Phillip is in, Silver Spring."

"So, we're pinning our hopes on a dream?" Charles frowned before taking a bite out of his French toast.

"A dream that got both of our asses out of that hell hole."

"What about finding a government-backed town nearby? They're probably more likely to help anyway."

"Phillip's town will help."

"Did he say that? And if he did, you trust he will?"

"He knows that helping the others is what I'm doing first. He's a sure thing." I bit into my eggs.

"But why bypass a possible closer town to go practically all the way to D.C.?"

"It's only about four or five hours from here."

"And David's probably already moving camp. Let's not be picky."

I shrugged, unsure. Charles made a good point, but something itched inside of me to see Phillip in the flesh. I couldn't explain why I had so much faith in him.

Back in the car, fully fed, cleaned, and newly clothed in some jeans and T-shirts, we were in search of a computer. None of the houses we'd already searched had computers or laptops lying around, oddly enough. It was possible the owners had taken the laptops with them when they fled if they were able to get them to work. The internet was the only universal way to communicate and learn about magic and the paranormal now.

"Why don't we just go into some more homes and see if they have computers there? We can also get some more supplies. See if there is any food, clothing, toiletries," I said.

Charles turned the car onto a residential street and slowed down as we looked from one cookie-cutter house to another. "This area looks clean but abandoned. Either there is nothing inside, or there is if you know what I mean."

I knew. If the area wasn't damaged, it usually meant people had stayed and eventually left the area for better opportunities. That meant there would be a low chance of finding any supplies.

Trauma in an area meant people probably fled in a rush, leaving behind goods. So, if we saw broken ground, busted doors, or dried blood, there was a higher chance of a payday. There was also a higher chance of finding things we wouldn't want to encounter as well, like ghouls who ate the flesh of the dead or seeing dead bodies.

"We need to get someplace where we can gather more

goods. So far, what did we find from the houses we checked already?" Charles asked.

I thought about all the things we stuffed in two hiking backpacks and trash bags we found in the houses earlier. "Okay, we've got toothpaste, perfume, hand towels, some containers we filled with water, cheese sandwiches, a couple of sharp knives, brushes, extra clothing, and shoes. We still need flashlights, a first aid kit, some type of shampoo or soap, and lighters, clean undergarments, toothbrushes..." I strained my neck to look down another less residential street. I saw a few shop signs and a gas station. "Down this street, make a right. Looks like a main street."

Main Street, USA. Most towns had them. Located in the suburbs, it was a street with a mixture of quaint shops, offices, restaurants, and bars.

Charles turned down the street and parallel parked on the right side in the middle of the strip. The area looked desolate; a few storefront doors and windows were bashed in and broken. From what I could see behind the thick, dark-green plant overgrowth on the buildings, there were deep brownish-red stains of varying sizes on a few of the store porches, streets, and sidewalks. Some of the building signs hung crooked or had long given up the fight and were now on the ground. The street in front of our car was cracked and broken up as if construction was breaking ground before everything went to hell, but no work trucks were in sight. The broken ground stopped right in front of where our car was parked, but that wasn't the disturbing part.

Charles opened the car door and frowned. "Phew, I'd ask what died out here, but I can guess by the broken up skeleton parts."

"Jesus," I whispered, looking out the front car window.

I leaned towards the dashboard and squinted. In this world, I'd seen this scene before. Pass the hole in the ground were skeletal parts covered in dirt, caked blood, and dried skin. There were torsos, unattached legs, arms, and skulls.

"Whatever jacked up the road, did a superman lift-off, right there." Charles got out of the truck and pointed to where the destruction to the pavement ended in front of us. "Because I don't see the stores demolished beyond this broken up area. Whatever did that, if it were going into a building, it pretty much would have knocked it down. And the same goes if it leaped on top of a building. So, it wasn't a gargoyle."

I got out of the truck, looking around. "This must have been done earlier on in the change for these bodies to be this decomposed. These poor people." I let out a cough and covered my mouth and nose with a shirt I got from my backpack.

Charles nodded, surveying the area. "A place like this could have a lot of what we need, assuming no one else has wandered here." He walked over to a clothing storefront that contained a bit of plant life around it and peered in. "I'm thinking the plant life was also a deterrent. It's probably poisonous."

Upon hearing that, I turned to Charles just in time to see a snake-like vine wrap around his ankle. "Don't move, Charles," I shouted. If he did, the vine would grow tighter. I'd seen plants strong enough to rip a limb out of a person's socket.

Charles' body stiffened. "There's a man-eating plant around my ankle, isn't there?" he asked in a quiet voice.

"Possibly. Relax." I moved a little closer and saw the vine tighten. I looked up at the clothing store and saw the second level was covered in moving, wiggly, deep-green leaves, and vines. I hadn't noticed the vines moving earlier, and perhaps it purposefully hadn't. Did I forget to mention that in the new world plant life was smart? "Son of a bitch," I whispered.

"Any day now, Mina," Charles stated through clench teeth.

I could throw magic over anything natural and, like it or not, even the supernatural was part of that now. I recalled how I first controlled the ten-foot monster dog that disrupted my cousin's wedding when the world first went to hell. I'd controlled other inhuman things since then. I usually did so to get them to leave us alone and not eat or kill us. The lesser the lifeform, the easier it was to control. And less painful for me.

I threw my hands up and then balled them into fists; forcing my energy into the plants and envisioning them drying out, breaking off, and dying. I'm not sure if I really needed the hand work, but it helped me focus on what I was aiming my magic to do.

Tiny points of pain pricked my skin all over. Soon after that, the plant life started to change from a bright green to burnt brown, then it crumbled and broke apart. The vine around Charles' ankle fell away and shriveled.

I let out a deep sigh, and my minor pain went away.

Charles turned around to face me, eyes wide. "Took you long enough. Thanks, Sis."

I rolled my eyes again. "You know better than to run off like that."

"I was still in eye range, mom. Plus, the plants didn't look like they were moving. Just poisonous."

"Well, clearly, they were playing games."

"I've never seen plants do that before."

I looked down the street to my left. It was after twelve in the afternoon. Since it was early summer, we still had a good amount of sun left, but we had to watch our time carefully so that we wouldn't be caught out in the dark.

"I think we should know by now that the only certainty around here is that everything is uncertain. All right, let's search this place but stay on your toes."

We searched every establishment together. It took a while, but we were finding a gold mine here. A gory gold mine but a gold mine all the same. We tied some scarfs from a clothing store around our faces to help block out the stench of decaying, dead flesh, and spoilt food and went through the work of gathering supplies.

I focused on practical items. Jackets and gloves for later seasons and undergarments from the clothing stores, a first aid kit from a bar, some non-perishable food, lighters, and a few more toiletries we were in need of for our day to day. We had to build our base all over again. There would be no going back to our old complex, it had been raided and destroyed by David and his gang months ago.

"I think we have enough time to hook up some lunch from one of those restaurants before the plants get to be dangerous, and the sun goes down," Charles surmised, eyeing a barbecue restaurant across the street.

I glared at him.

He shrugged. "What? I'm hungry. You can magically cook us up a meal, and I can get this laptop working and search for a government town," he stated, waving a silver laptop in the air.

While I tried to make a meal out of whatever I could gather in the kitchen of one of the restaurants, Charles made magic happen on the laptop and gained access to the very limited internet. Nowadays, the internet was mostly a ghost town of sites that were abandoned. The only active sites were the informational ones, social media, and of course, what was left of the government had an active site. The only way we even knew of the government's resurgence was by searching the former White House website and Twitter page. From there, word spread from others who had the same idea.

"Okay, so there's a government backed town in Hagerstown. A little under three hour's drive. We go there first. See if they can help. If they can't, we push on to Silver Spring," Charles stated, bringing his laptop over to me in the kitchen.

After lunch, we were on our way back to the highway when we spotted trouble on the side of the road.

A man stood, pulling thin legs out of the ground in front of a tree-lined area off the main road. The legs the man held appeared to be female. The torso attached to the legs was halfway in the ground.

"What. The. Hell!" Charles exclaimed, slowing the car down as we passed them.

"Stop the car," I ordered, straining past Charles to get a better look.

"Why?"

"Clearly, we need to help them. The woman is stuck in some, I don't know, quicksand-like dirt or something."

"What if it's a trap? I mean, that guy looks like he'd swat us like flies. I'm not up for a fight. We have to focus on saving our friends."

I looked to the man. He did look imposing, with a wide and muscular frame. Still, something was telling me to help. "What if it's not a trap? And we're looking for people to help us get our friends. Maybe they'll help us if we help them, so stop the car!"

"Damn it, this is how we got caught last time." Charles came to an immediate stop in front of an opening to a shopping plaza, and I jumped out. "Don't be stupid, Sis! This is bullshit!"

Out of habit, I looked both ways before crossing the vacant street. I didn't bother wasting time asking the man what happened. The situation looked pretty clear.

I raised both hands and focused on the ground around the now thighs of the female. She was getting swallowed up quickly, and I was sure she wasn't able to breathe. If this was a trap, it was a dangerous one.

The man, who looked pretty strong, was no match for

this magical ground. Yet, it was dirt all the same. Like the plants, it was still from nature. However, sinking ground was difficult. Loosening it up didn't help prevent a person from going farther in. Hardening it only made them stuck. All I knew was that the longer the woman was underground, the lower her chances were for survival, as she was not getting any oxygen.

I had to refocus my energy. I needed to try something different. Something I'd never done before, but time was of the essence. Phillip's voice rang in my head, telling me to assume I had no limits unless I found them.

"What's your friend's name?" I shouted, walking towards the action. The man had his back to me, away from the road.

He tilted his head back at me, face strained, and then looked back to his friend. "Can you help?" He asked gruffly.

"She's trying!" Charles yelled, running up to the scene and taking hold of the friend's legs in a fruitless effort to help.

"If I have her name, that'll give me something to focus on to pull her out. I can't move this dirt."

"Lisa," the man replied.

I focused on Lisa's body moving upwards. The woman's body only lifted a little. I needed a better image. "Describe what Lisa looks like," I told the man.

"What? Why?"

"Help me, help her!"

He growled. "Uh, she's tiny, barely over 5 feet, Asian, Chinese background. Looks like she's in her twenties. She has long black hair, well, with some rainbow colors in it too. She's pretty. Oh, she's Fae," he described with what I was noticing was an accent. Australian?

The image of a pretty Asian actress I'd seen on TV years ago entered my mind. I blurred the face a bit to avoid focusing on that actual celebrity and added wings to my faceless Asian female. I'd never met a fairy, but I figured they had wings.

I threw my arms up, hands skyward, and focused on the woman soaring up through the ground.

In my mind's eye, Lisa was lifting through layers of dirt. I could see her rising horizontally backwards. The ground in front of us rumbled, and the dirt moved. Seconds later, a woman burst through; her limp body hovering above the ground. I laid her down on the road, away from the supernatural dirt, with my magic. Charles raced over to her and began CPR. The woman, covered head to toe in dirt, soon started couching and hacking up dirt.

The man scrambled to his feet and took off a backpack that I hadn't noticed before. He brought out a bottle of water and gave it to Lisa.

I turned back to the sinking ground area and encircled it with a ward spell. No one would be able to touch this area and get sucked in again, as long as my ward stood. I turned back to the group, satisfied.

Seeing that his friend would survive, the man turned to me and gave me a curt nod.

That was it?

"What are you, a witch?" he asked gruffly.

Why did he sound mad at me? I looked over to him, finally taking the time to notice him. Not that focusing on such things at this time was appropriate, but he was handsome. He had messy, straight black hair, cut short on the sides and a little longer on the top, and a trimmed beard framing full lips. He was white and tanned, possibly mixed with something else in his lineage, Asian as well? He was also tall, which seemed to make his muscular frame even more imposing. That, coupled with hostile, hazel eyes, currently transfixed on me, made him very scary. I began to wonder if maybe this really was still a trap.

I nodded cautiously. "We both are. Except he's a tech mage. I'm Amina Langston, my brother over there is Charles."

"Ugh, I need a shower," I heard Lisa say in a hoarse voice.

The guy, who I now pegged as being in his late twenties, maybe early thirties, tilted his head towards her. "That's Lisa Xu. I'm Erik Bennet."

Charles looked over at me as if to say, What now?

"So, what brought you guys out here?" I asked.

"Trying to find a place to settle," Erik replied. "Where we were before wasn't working out. You?"

"Same thing. We left a really bad situation and were headed to Hagerstown. It's a government town. Hoping they can help us get some friends we left behind. Do y'all have a destination?"

"Silver Spring," Lisa said through a cough.

I raised an eyebrow and looked over to Charles, who frowned at me.

"Seriously?" I asked.

Erik nodded but didn't say anymore.

"Do you know anyone named Phillip?" Charles asked, looking at me.

Lisa squinted her eyes. "No, why?"

Charles shook his head quickly. "Amina thinks we should go to Silver Spring, too. I talked her into Hagerstown."

Lisa looked to me with wide eyes. "Really? How weird is that? Do you have images of the town too? And an older black lady named Annie Mae?"

I raised both eyebrows now, slightly relieved. If Phillip was popping up in various women's dreams, I'd be done. "No. Someone else."

"Maybe somebody also from the town. Maybe they have a bunch of people there who can dream hop. That's amazing. We should all go together," Lisa suggested, sounding more recovered.

"No," Erik cut in.

We all looked over to Erik, who was putting his book bag

back on. The muscles on his arms strained as he put his arms through the straps of the too-small bag.

"Why not?" Lisa asked, still sitting with Charles on the ground beside her. I could see through her dirt-stained face, striking green eyes that looked mesmerizing against her Asian features. I looked away, not wanting to stare.

"No offense, but we don't know you," he answered, a gruff tone to his husky voice.

"Well, you don't know the people in Silver Spring either. But you know that *we* stopped our car and saved your friend's life, and we didn't ask you for anything," I responded, hands on my hips.

"Yet." He folded his arms.

I glared at him for a beat then shrugged my shoulders. "Okay, cool. Take care. Come on, Charles." I turned and headed to the car. If they didn't want to help us, I didn't need them.

"Just like that, Erik?" Lisa began. "This world is full of assholes, and you're just going to let good people go? The more, the merrier, I say. You don't have to be a jerk. I thought you
were—"

"Fine," Erik barked. "Ana—"

"Amina," I said and kept walking.

"Sorry, Amina. Witches didn't do us any favors where we came from."

"They were into sacrificial magic. Bad stuff," Lisa explained.

I turned back to them. "We don't do that."

"You can control people. That's not a good thing," Erik stated.

I frowned. "What are you talking about?"

"You pulled her body from the ground. That was control."

"That's kind of scary," Lisa said, touching her chest.

"I didn't think about it. I've never controlled a person

before. I was just trying to get you out. I usually have power over natural things, but I couldn't work the dirt fast enough. I didn't mean to scare anyone. Silly me, I don't know what I was thinking, trying to save your life." I put my hands up in mock surrender.

"Oh, I'm not complaining," Lisa added, standing up.

Charles jumped up and helped her get to her feet. He was being super attentive to her. He had a crush. Must be nice to be so cute you attract the attention of a guy even while covered head to toe in dirt.

I turned to Erik. "Look, you have a right to be concerned, but I'm not here to haphazardly hurt people. We were living in a small community, getting by. Then we were attacked by a group of non-gifted humans. They rounded up people like us and held us captive. They found a way to make themselves stronger by taking our blood. We have to go back and save the others we left behind. But we can't do it alone. We were hoping to find a town that would help us. I was thinking Silver Spring, but Hagerstown is closer. We can use all the help we can get."

Erik studied me without speaking. I suspect he was purposely trying to make me feel uncomfortable. Maybe he was a cop in the Pre-world. I shifted on my feet. "And whatever you guys were running from, we might be able to help with that too," I added for good measure.

He cocked an eyebrow. "We weren't running from anything."

I shrugged. "Sure, a guy, who I think has some gifts, and a fairy walking around wooded areas in Pittsburg is normal."

"Some of us don't have tech mages who can start a car."

"Fair enough, but it's clear you guys are moving on from something. And don't act like you don't trust us. If you were that distrustful, you wouldn't have told me Lisa was a fairy. You knew I was good from the start." I gave him a wide grin.

He didn't respond, but something in his eyes softened just a tinge.

I continued. "I think we can benefit each other. And we all have to admit that something big is going on. It's more than a coincidence that we both want to go to Silver Spring. I don't discard coincidences anymore."

"Guys, maybe we want to hit the road," Charles stated, looking down at the new watch he swiped from a jewelry store. I let go of the feeling of guilt from stealing a long time ago. No one was going to arrest us. "We get to Hagerstown, if they won't let us in, then we find some nearby shelter and head to Silver Spring the next morning."

Lisa nodded vigorously. "Come on, Erik, let's just go with them. If they wanted to do something foul, they'd have done it by now. Plus, I'm no weakling. I've got power too. Which reminds me," Lisa began. She closed her eyes and clapped her hands together. A swirl of blue wind, the color of the Fae magic, blew around her like a mini-tornado, and she became a blur behind tinted whirls of smoke. The smoke was odorless and did not affect the air quality. It was actually quite beautiful.

Seconds later, it dissipated, and there Lisa stood, clean, wearing a pair of jeans and a plaid button-down shirt. Her hair, I could now see, was black with highlights of blue, red, orange, and green. Her makeup was fully done, fake lashes, and all. I didn't need to know how she had time to look glammed up. Magic.

"Can I get a makeover later from you?" I smirked.

She winked and nodded. "I got you, girl. That settles it, let's pilgrimage together! Fun times!"

We all headed back to the SUV. Our new friends threw their book bags on top of the stuff in our already-crowded trunk, and we maneuvered into the car. Charles drove, and Erik, due to his long legs, sat in the passenger seat. I sat in the back with Lisa.

Lisa looked at us all. "This feels right. I think we're going to get along and make a difference in this world," she stated, clasping her hands together.

As corny as she seemed, I think I already liked her. Charles looked through the rear-view mirror at Lisa and smiled.

I bumped my elbow to hers and grinned when she returned it.

Erik snorted.

They were strangers, but something in me, like Lisa, still felt they'd be good for us. In this world, that's what we needed.

CHAPTER 9

"*S*o, this is fun, road tripping it with our new friends," Lisa said in a sing-song voice as my brother drove carefully along the highway, maneuvering around obstacles on the road like he had in his old video games. All those times, I used to call him an idiot drone for playing games started to make me sound like the silly one now.

"How'd you get stuck in that magic dirt, anyway?" Charles asked.

Lisa let out a long dramatic sigh. "So, check this. We were walking down the road, and this stupid raccoon thing pops out of the dirt and grabs the bag of food I had in my hand. You guys know how hard food is to come by, so I went after it. And this stupid animal tries to disappear in the dirt. So I grabbed it, and then I got sucked into the dirt with the now-deceased raccoon thing and my now gone food," she explained.

"You...didn't want to let the food go?" I asked eyes squinted.

"Uh, yeah, but by then it was too late. That quick dirt was fast working. Nothing like how quick sand works in the movies. It was like a vacuum. If Erik hadn't gotten to me in time, I'd be gone." She shivered.

"Humph, I told you not to chase it," Erik grumbled from the front passenger seat.

That was his response? His friend almost died, and he just wanted to chastise her. Was he really a nice guy? "How'd you both meet?" I asked.

Lisa gave another dramatic sigh. "Okay, so as you know, I'm a fairy, and I've been trying to find other fairies since this whole foolishness started. Before all this, I was living a sweet life as a makeup artist and stylist in New York, but then this bullshit happened. And fairies or Fae, whatever you want to call them, are so hard to find. The only reason I know what I am is because I met another fairy, but she disappeared before I could even go to the fairy world."

"I'm sorry," Charles cut in from the driver's seat. "Back up, did you say fairy world? I haven't met any fairies yet, so I wasn't even sure you guys were a real thing."

Lisa nodded quickly. "Oh, we're real. Rare, but real. We just have our own separate dimension. Apparently, we always did. Anyway, before she left, she gave me a pretty good recap of what I needed to know about being a fairy to at least survive. Like, who knew all fairies don't have wings? Apparently, some of us don't need them to fly. So anyway—"

"Different dimension? How's that possible?" I questioned.

"Did you think that all of this came out of nowhere?" Erik asked, turning slightly to me.

"Uh, yeah," I replied, shrugging.

Erik shook his head and sat back. "We were always what we are now. When whatever event happened that caused this, all it did was lift a veil. That's how your brother and you are witches. I had family who were werejackals..." His voice trailed off.

Ah-ha, that's what he was.

"But our parents weren't magic. They died of the Sickness," Charles said.

"Maybe your parents had witch genes that may just skip generations, like some diseases," Erik guessed.

"Like sickle cell," I stated. "I guess I could understand that."

"Remember, Mina, you and I used to say Grandma Bea was a witch," Charles stated.

"That's because she was mean," I laughed. "She always knew when we were up to no- good. She'd pop up out of nowhere when we were about to do something we had no business doing. We probably would have set her house on fire if she hadn't, though. Well, Charles would have."

"You're right," he agreed in a low voice.

"Like Erik, I think there was always magic and the supernatural in the world before The Event," Lisa said, making quotation marks around the words "the event." "I think some of us magical beings were strong enough to even use magic in the Pre-world. Definitely some witches. But for fairies, our magic only worked in the fairy world. We never lived among humans. We just visited. But there were some of us who were born in this world and couldn't ever get to the fairy world. Now, in this new world order, we can go between our dimensions. I just don't know how and I haven't been able to find another fairy to help me yet. I wouldn't be surprised if there were other kinds of dimensions too, and not just a fairy one."

"This is so confusing," Charles mumbled.

"Right? So, anyway, there I was minding my business, trying to find some valuables for trade to use in my community, which, side note, I didn't like that place that much. It was so depressing. Anyway, I was looking for things in this abandoned apartment complex, and I got kidnapped by some thugs who brought me back to his camp." She pointed an index finger towards Erik. "They said they wanted to

96

bring females in because they were low on women. But then, when I tried to use my fairy magic on them to rightfully defend myself, they got different ideas." She stabbed Erik in the back. "Tell 'em. Tell 'em what your people tried to do to me."

Erik didn't speak.

"Don't leave me in suspense. Someone tell me," I cried.

"Our pack didn't treat her well," Erik answered.

Lisa made a disgruntled noise. "Didn't treat me well. They tried to tie me on a log and roast me like a pig, to be exact," Lisa stated, crossing her arms.

"This world is some shit," Charles whispered.

"Look, remember, most weres are carnivorous. And when we are in animal form…well, things can be cannibalistic if we are out of control," Erik explained. "I'm not like that. Before all this, I was a bodyguard in New York. I use to be military back in New Zealand before I moved here for work. I help people, not hurt them. Anyway, our pack was changing. We had a new leader who was cracked. He believed if we ate a fairy we'd become more powerful."

"Like those humans that imprisoned you both, but instead of blood, their dumb pack believed the power was in the flesh," Lisa added.

"That was too much for me. I couldn't go from protecting people to preying on them. I tried to rally people up against our alpha leader, but they were either too scared, or they actually believed him."

"And I don't think people liked Erik much. Thought he was too mean," Lisa stated. "In retrospect, Erik shouldn't have been the one leading the resistance."

Erik sighed. "Anyway, some of us grabbed Lisa from her chains, and I got tasked with sneaking her out. We've been on the run for almost two weeks."

"The big grouch has actually been my hero," Lisa said, patting Erik's shoulder.

I wondered if there was anything more between them. Strictly because I'm nosey.

Lisa continued. "Now you guys are my heroes too. I owe y'all some favors, so I'm down to help you set those others free. Us good guys gotta stick together."

"Thank you, Lisa," I said.

"So, tell us some about this, Phillip that Charles mentioned," Erik said.

I really didn't want to, but it felt only fair since we would end up in Silver Spring, and they'd meet him anyway. "He's a guy who keeps showing up in my dreams, and we can speak telepathically from afar. He got us out of prison."

"He was there?"

I shook my head. "I can't explain it. He was just able to give me my strength back through my dream so that I could fight my way out of there."

"Miss Annie Mae never did any of that for me. She just spoke to me in a couple of dreams. She said I'd find my people soon after I got to Silver Spring," Lisa stated. "She told me about Erik too. Said he'd find his place in this world in her community."

"So, what'd this Phillip promise you?" Erik asked.

I looked out of the window. "Other than helping me rescue the others, nothing."

"Why do you want to go then?"

"It's better than the prison and, honestly, since he helped us and has this kind of power, I want to meet him in person. What else is there to do?"

"Was he cute?" Lisa asked, clapping her hands lightly.

I glanced at her. "He's nice looking."

"Well, I guess we really know why you want to go, then," Erik muttered. "Seems like a bit of a superficial reason, but I'm not judging."

"Oh, lay off her, McGrouchy Pants," Lisa said, shaking her head.

"What part of that sentence wasn't judgmental?" I asked, adjusting in my seat. "Fine, since you want to be all in my business, understand this: for the six months that I was contained in that prison for the paranormal, I never dreamed except for when he visited. Why would he come out of the blue to me? Who is he? What drew him to a woman holed up in another state? How was he able to get my powers back? If you were me, would you just shrug and let that go? Maybe a guy like that knows why all this happened in the world. And now that he is probably in the same town as this Annie Mae, maybe this is a pretty darn special town, and I like special towns. That could mean safety, which would be nice in a freaky world like this."

Erik sighed and then nodded. "Fair enough. But you should be careful who you show your magic to. You're a little naive, and I wouldn't want you to get hurt."

I crinkled my nose. "Thanks for the backhanded compliment. How am I naive?"

"Your whole story about this, Phillip, and even you stopping to help Lisa and I makes you a little too much of an easy prey. I'm surprised you've lasted this long. It's probably due to your brother being with you."

"Dude," Charles whispered.

Lisa slapped Erik on the back.

"Hey, Charles," I said in a pleasant tone, leaning forward. "Pull over really quick, so I can scratch Erik like an alley cat."

Lisa let out a cackle.

Erik turned back to me, his eyes all too serious. "I'm just stating facts, Amina. If you were my client, I would tell you the same thing to save your life. Your nature is a danger in this kind of world."

I leaned back.

"He's right," Charles whispered. "Helping and trusting people hasn't really gotten us far in this world."

I wasn't naive. I was hopeful. Hopeful that this world

could still be something good. That we could trust at least some people. If I didn't believe that, then this wouldn't be a world I wanted to be a part of. "If we can never rely on each other, then what are we doing here?" I asked rhetorically.

"You smell like good people. You just have to be more discriminating and find others like you," Erik went on.

I raised an eyebrow. "What do you mean by 'smell like good people?'"

"I'm a were. We can tell good and bad, truth and lies, all through our sense of smell. For good people or truth, it just smells like a nice, natural perfume. Like flowers. It doesn't stand out unless I searched for it. But evil and lies, those smells are strong, and I started encountering it, recognizing it. Still took me a while to put together what the smells meant, but other weres had similar stories, and eventually, we figured it out."

"What does evil smell like?" Charles asked.

"Sulfur."

"Like someone passed gas?"

"Fun. What about lies?" I asked.

"Like body odor. And it was starting to smell like both in my pack."

"That was one funky place," Charles murmured.

"Why didn't you run the pack?" I questioned Erik.

He shook his head. "Not my thing."

I snorted. "Says the man who was former military. I'm assuming you weren't some private ranked equivalent the whole time. What game are you playing? I smell sweaty underarms." I crossed my arms and raised an eyebrow.

Erik glanced at me again with a scowl. "What are you a were-witch?"

I wiggled my eyebrows. "You never know."

The edge of his lips twisted up in a weak smile. Maybe he didn't totally despise me.

"I started out leading when things first fell apart. I think

I've just reached burnout. War can only prepare you for so much. Good people went bad. Bad people went worst. You just stop caring..." he replied, his voice trailing off.

I looked in his direction with a frown. I wondered what he'd gone through since the world changed. Lisa seemed to portray a pleasant disposition, even through all the pain I could only imagine she'd endured. We'd all lost friends, families, ways of life. What had Erik lost to make him so negative?

I looked to Lisa, who had turned away and was staring out of the window on her side. We were all strangers with pasts we wanted to escape.

~

Finding the Hagerstown government town was not a hard task. Government towns were all publicized on the internet. Sure, that was risky, knowing that there were insane people out there looking to take and destroy what was good. It's why the town I'd lived in before I was snatched kept secret. But the whole point of the government reclaiming its role over the country was to let people know they existed. After all, the White House—before it was swallowed into the ground from a large supernatural sinkhole—was never in a secret location. People had to see things getting better.

Also, the only way the government would grow is if it had more people willing to live in its towns and follow its order. Government needed people to get things running and to defend its towns. And by people, they meant all people. As long as you weren't breaking laws, it didn't matter if you were supernatural or a normal human who wasn't sick. And yes, the Sickness was still out there but less of a problem. Many of the non-gifted humans remaining were immune, which seemed like a gift to me.

Each government town was run by someone the equivalent of a mayor. From my limited understanding, they weren't necessarily past politicians. The president and the vice president had perished. Most of government, federal and state, had been wiped out by the Sickness or some supernatural monster. I'm sure some people survived and had gotten roles or were even running the government-backed towns, but most leaders were former non-politicians who'd found the leader in themselves as the world changed around us.

They ran their respective towns and regularly met with the other government leaders in North America. There wasn't one leader, so our former democracy, where we had a president, wasn't quite there yet. I had complete faith that a presidential race wasn't too far away, especially as the government towns looked to expand and battle the "lawless" communities, as they called non-government towns.

I peered out of the front window. There was a large blue sign right off the highway, with wording in black paint telling us Hagerstown was about three miles ahead. When we got off the highway, we drove farther on an almost-cleared street, passing vacant housing, grocery stores, gas stations, fast-food joints, and office buildings.

Another blue sign told us to turn right to get to the town. After that, yet another sign stated, "Slow Down, Approaching Ward." A few years ago, not having such a warning would have resulted in smashed cars at the least, and lives lost at the worst, since driving into a ward was like driving into a brick wall. I felt it before we even stopped in front of the invisible wall.

Charles slowed down, and we approached a final large sign on the left side of the two-way street. It was the size of a hut that stated, "Welcome to New Hagerstown: A United North American Territory." To the right of the street was a bank. There were lights on inside and a car parked in the front lot.

Charles stopped the car on the side of the street in front of the bank.

"There's a camera hanging from the street lamp in front of the bank and pointed at us. They know we're here," Erik stated, glancing out of the window.

"What if we came to the town at another entrance?" Charles asked.

"I don't know how large this place is, but I'd have to assume they have this territory surrounded by cameras with guards scattered about. Probably signs telling people to come here or to particular sites where there are guards. We wait here."

Minutes later, I strained to look past Lisa and saw two men in HAZMAT suits exit the bank and walk towards us. They were armed with automatic weapons.

"Well, that doesn't look very welcoming," I muttered.

One man, a tall black man, walked over to Charles' window. "How can we help you?" He said, his accent sounded very New York.

"Well, we were hoping to get entrance into your town," Charles replied with a smile. "We're all paranormal and don't have the Sickness."

The man looked into the car at all of us. "Cut off your engine and pop your trunk and front hood. Everyone, please exit the vehicle."

The second guard, a shorter Asian man, began checking the engine and the trunk after Charles complied.

"You have weapons in here," the shorter man called from the rear of the car.

We got off of the truck and moved to stand in front of the car.

"Wouldn't you?" Erik replied back, crossing his arms.

The man shrugged. "Well, everything else is clear," he told

the other guard and then looked back to us. "I'm confiscating your weapons for now."

The man then looked to Charles and I. "Open your mouth," he demanded. He took out two cotton swabs and a Petri dish.

I heard the other guard tell Erik and Lisa the same.

"Why?" Erik asked.

"So, we can test you for the Sickness," the black man replied.

"You have a cure?" I asked.

"Not yet," said the Asian man, before inserting a cotton swab in my mouth.

He ran it over my tongue and then rubbed it into the dish. He next took a small vial with a dropper out of his suit pocket and dropped a cloudy liquid in the dish. "Clear," he announced soon after.

They did the same for the others, and we all got clear back.

"Names," said the tall, black man.

We gave him our names, and he hung the gun by its strap on his shoulder. He then closed his eyes and raised his hands. I was pretty sure he was some form of witch. He was trying to determine whether we were good or bad. If we were evil, every bone in his body would ache like he had a severe case of arthritis. That was, of course, if we weren't strong enough to mask our being.

He began mumbling something. I could see through the faceplate that his eyes were moving rapidly beneath closed lids. Finally, he opened them and looked at us. "Your powers are currently under lock, and you will not be able to use them," he said, matter-of-factly.

"Come again?" I asked, eyebrows raised and mouth hanging open.

He gave me neutral eyes. "This is a short spell and will only last twenty-four hours," he replied. "You are free to enter. There will be signs to lead you to our mayor's office. We also have housing if you are allowed to stay. The mayor's office is about two miles down the road. On your left, you will see a glass building. They'll be signs. You can apply for a twenty-four-hour stay at the mayor's and make an appointment to see someone about a permanent stay."

We thanked him, he dropped the ward to the town, and we made our way. During the drive, we passed an active shopping plaza with clothing boutiques, a grocery store, a few other shops, and a couple of restaurants. We also passed a library and a high school. We saw kids playing in the field, running, and jumping. It looked almost like the town was unaffected by the changes in the world.

We finally reached a wide three-story glass building. In its former existence, the building had been your everyday office building. A giant New Hagerstown United American Government sign now stood out of a patch of grass at the entrance of the parking lot.

"So, what's the plan again?" Charles asked, turning off the car.

"We ask for residency. Tell them the truth," I said.

"We tell them we all escaped the prison," Erik replied.

"Why lie?" Lisa asked, looking over to him.

"We don't know if we can trust them. We tell them about Amina and Charles' prison and that they need to help them."

I opened my passenger door. "As long as you guys are good liars, so we don't get kicked out for you lying, then I'm cool," I replied. I didn't like not going with the truth, but I trusted Erik's instinct. He was the former military guy. I didn't know too much about the pack they'd left, but I did know that this world was a suspicious one, and he had the best street smarts of us all.

So, I could go into the tale of us talking to the officials and getting their acceptance, but it was really uneventful. We were split up, and each of us told our stories. I strongly pushed that they needed to help the others in prison and that it would benefit them because I'm sure a lot of those people could bring their skill sets to the town. We were tested with magic of all sorts to determine our truths and questioned about our background to figure out what role we could play in the new society.

My legal background made them curious of my ability to assist with law-making or even teaching, which was a refreshing alternative to just cooking and healing. In the end, I made it through and was told by a local official I'd be on probation for six months. If I did anything immoral or against their rules, they would kick me out, or worse. I was provided with a thin book of rules and town references, given a housing assignment, and told to report to the school to start teaching the next day. Clearly, there would be no rest for the weary. They informed me that they would get back to me regarding helping our imprisoned friends.

When I exited my interrogation room, Lisa was already slouched on a blue couch in the bright and spacious lobby looking bored.

I walked over to her and sat down. I looked through the floor-to-ceiling windows at the parking lot. "Are the others still in?" I asked.

She shrugged. "I guess so. That took longer than I figured it should have. Two hours. I thought these towns were in need of people, especially ones with gifts."

"They still have to have standards, I guess. What job did you get assigned?"

"So, clearly cosmetology is not a job that's of importance now. But they feel me working at the market could be my calling." She crossed her arms. "But they were open to me getting into fashion, which I am good at as well. Clothes are always a need. Maybe I can have my own clothing boutique."

I looked at her with tired eyes. "Save it for Silver Spring. We're only here for a short time."

Her eyes grew wide. "Right. But…" She scrunched her face. "So, what if we go to Silver Spring and we don't like it there? I'm thinking we can just come back here if we like it enough."

"We're going to like it there." We had to. Any place that Phillip was had to be a place I would like to be. That sounded very naïve. Maybe Erik was right about me.

Lisa opened her mouth to speak again, but Charles walked off the elevator with a cocky grin.

"Big surprise, they've put me in I.T. and military. I gots two jobs," Charles said, sounding a bit proud of himself.

"Military?" I asked.

"Well, it's military slash police. 'cause of my control over weapons and technology. Good for defense and tracking."

"I always thought men in uniform were sexy," Lisa said with a shy smile, head titled down.

Charles winked at her. I pretend to gag.

"He worked at an I.T. help desk before all this. Had a pocket protector and everything," I cracked. "Wore glasses and superhero T-shirts."

Lisa widened her eyes and made an O shape with her mouth.

Charles glared at me. "Why do you hate me?"

I gave him a toothy smile, and he rolled his eyes.

"Where's Erik the Grouch?" Charles asked.

"Hasn't come out yet," I answered. And he didn't come out for another thirty minutes.

Lisa jumped up when she saw him exit the elevators. "Finally! Are they kicking you out?" she cried.

"They want me in a leadership role in the government and military," he replied, grimly.

I stood up. "They liked you, didn't they?"

He gave a quick shrug. "More like loved."

"What about helping our friends? They didn't want to act

on anything right now when I mentioned it. Since they loved you, did you talk about it with them?"

He nodded. "I got you a meeting with the governor for tomorrow at four."

"Thanks," I replied. "They really do love you."

He gave another shrug as we exited out of the building and went back to the car.

We headed to a large gated community of garden-style apartments about two miles from the governor's building. Charles and I shared a two-bedroom on the third floor. Lisa and Erik shared a two-bedroom a few doors away from us.

Still not feeling settled, Charles and I left most of our stuff in the SUV.

"This isn't bad," Charles said, looking around. It was a nice apartment, some parts a bit outdated even for Pre-world standards, but style didn't reign over substance anymore.

I leaned on the beige kitchen counter and flipped through the reference book. "Says this place is a 5-square mile radius. That's pretty large. There's even a bar with karaoke and trivia nights. Got a hospital. A grocery store. Mall. A worship space. Two salons. Oh, and a gym...and a bakery. My interrogator said they have around two thousand people here so far. So, I guess this all makes sense. When you have that many people, you have time to make reference books."

"Sweet! We're in heaven!" Charles said, walking back from the bedrooms.

I rolled my eyes. "All right, don't get comfortable; this is just a layover. We earn our keep and their trust. They help us free the others. Then we leave."

Charles shook his head. "You know, Sis if we find this random town in Silver Spring and it isn't as cool as this place, we are coming back. I don't care if this Phillip is real and walks on water. In this world, that's not that damn impressive."

CHAPTER 10

I had to admit, the town *was* really nice. Funny how the everyday things you would find in any small town now seemed like a bustling large city in this new world. Almost fifty percent of the former United States was abandoned, so a town like this with people in it and buildings lit with life was something to be excited about.

That Friday morning, we all reported to our perspective jobs. I was to teach English and History at the local school. I wasn't too upset about that. I enjoyed law, but I always believed I'd one day become an adjunct professor at a college or law school.

I'd done a little shopping at the local mall the day before to prepare for my teaching gig and bought a simple, gray-sheath dress, black ballerina slippers to wear on my first day, and a few other items. Many of the shops in the building were still empty, but several stores were open and running, some repurposed. The store owners allowed me to use credit, which was essentially me working for free to afford the things I got and the local government reimbursing the store for the time that I worked. Capitalism was forming again here. Anything of solid value was the currency. Jewelry, natural gemstones, and gold were products to barter. Although I had some goods, I decided to save them and earn credits working at the school and the hospital.

The high school I would teach at housed all students, which was anyone under eighteen. There was even a daycare. I entered the principal's office and waited in the front area for someone to show. There wasn't a secretary present. I knocked on the closed translucent principal's door located behind the secretary desk but got no answer.

"Okay, how does this work?" I whispered to myself.

"No one's there," came a male voice behind me.

I jumped and faced a large man standing in the doorway. Large was probably an understatement. He was over 6'5 and built like a professional wrestler. He was handsome but looked like he broke people for work. He was olive-colored, maybe of Hispanic origin. He had shoulder-length, loose, curly, brown hair and kind brown eyes. With his khakis pants and white button-down shirt, he looked like a nerdy wrestler, if such a thing existed.

He walked towards me. "Hey, I'm Felix Gonzalez. Math teacher." He offered me his hand, and I shook it. He had a powerful handshake that bordered on constricting. He'd probably break a cat's neck if he petted it.

"I'm Amina Langston. Just came in yesterday," I replied.

He nodded, giving me a game show host smile. "Yeah, I heard. They put you to work quickly. So, right, we don't have a principal here. We've kind of been running ourselves so far. I volunteered to show you the ropes. I can introduce you to the other teachers, and you can shadow them today and get started for real on Monday." He threw out his left arm towards the hallway. "After you."

"So, how many kids are here?" I asked as we walked.

"We got about three hundred kids in the school from ages five to eight-teen," he replied, stuffing his hands in his pockets. "And a good portion of them are orphans, so it's more than just a teach and go."

"Wow," I whispered as I looked inside the classrooms. We came upon one room full of kids looking like they ranged in age from eight to ten years old.

"We have to mix some of the groups of kids up because we're short on teachers. Not everyone can teach everything. Or at all. Had to kick out one guy who kept cursing the kids out every day for misbehaving. It *is* hard work, though. You got special needs kids. Kids with powers and kids without. All in one class together. And the middle school-aged ones are naturally...difficult. Add all this divide, and you can imagine a person going off on a kid."

"I see. What did you do before this?"

"Uh, I forgot. These are the bathrooms." He pointed to the left. "We take turns cleaning, and the students are on shift to help clean as well."

He forgot what he used to do? Something wasn't right here. "How long have you been here?"

"About two years. It's a nice place. I've been in some good places and some not so good ones. This is the best."

"Where are you from?"

He stopped walking and looked at me with those big, almost innocent eyes. "I feel like you're interviewing me." He smiled.

"I'm sorry."

He shrugged. "It's fine. I get it. You want to know about the people in this town. Just because it's a government town doesn't make it a place you want to be. I'm probably not the best spokesperson, though."

He started to walk again in silence.

"Oookay, care to elaborate?"

He looked over at me. "About what?"

Patience, Amina. "Why you wouldn't be a good spokesperson."

He slapped his forehead and grinned. "Sorry. My memory was wiped when the world changed. It's like this wave of the supernatural came, and I just went blank. I remember standing in the middle of the sidewalk. I think I was going for a jog because I was dressed for it. Anyway, I didn't even know how to get home. So, I don't know who I was before the change, and the only reason I know that there was even a change was because people told me. I still forget things that happened since then too." He shrugged.

"Damn. I've never heard of anyone getting amnesia because of this. That's horrifying."

He nodded. "I found my address in my phone. Stayed there for a while before I just had to leave." He started walking again. "So, we have a free period at ten for working out or gym activities. Lunch between eleven and one. We do shifts for cooking and serving for that too. Although a few times a week, the local restaurants will send us food to serve. We also have study period at three p.m. Then, kids are released. Some can stay after for tutoring. We have older people come in for college-level studies a few times a week in the evening as well. Teacher's lounge is to your right, and the cafeteria is to the left. So, my first class starts in ten minutes. You can sit in there and then shadow the English class after that."

I was still stuck on the whole memory loss thing, but clearly, he had moved on. I'd have to file that in my memory bank for later discussion.

We walked towards his classroom, and it was odd to hear the sounds of children giggling and talking. Sure, my old town had kids, and we taught, but it was on a much smaller level, with makeshift classes held in houses. This was so organized. It was a real school. Children's artwork hung on the walls, along with pictures of the student body counsel. There was even a poster advertising the summer talent show.

You really could almost forget that we were living in a

different and dangerous world. I couldn't help but wonder. If we'd gotten to a government town before, would we have ever been captured?

"Are you special too?" Felix asked, stopping in front of a classroom with thirty teenagers gabbing away.

"Do you mean, do I have gifts?"

He nodded.

"I'm a witch. What are you? You said 'too.'"

"I wish I knew. I can heal people, but I'm not a witch or a mage. I can't use spells or anything. No one can tell me what I am and me having no memory before, like nine years ago, doesn't help." His smile faltered a little, and a look of worry passed through his face.

I felt sorry for him and shook my head. "What are you doing after work?"

"Nothing. Well, I got to feed Dexter."

"Dexter?"

"My dog. I've had her for almost five years."

I cocked an eyebrow. "You've been traveling all this time with a pet? And she stayed with you? I opened my front door when I was ten and my tabby cat, Mimi, ran out, and was gone for a week. I only found her when I was out playing with friends. That cat was not loyal."

Felix nodded swiftly. "Dexter's like my best friend."

"Aww, that's…" Sad, is what I was thinking. "Sweet. Well, let's meet at the local pub around six. I have someone I'd like for you to meet."

~

*A*fter my day at school, I rushed to the mayor's office for my meeting with the head of the town. Colonel Foster Robinson was actually former Air Force, and he took his job very seriously. He was a sixty-something, African American man with cropped gray hair and a face set in a permanent scowl. I felt like someone had sent me to the principal's office because I was a little nervous talking to him. I wasn't sure he was even going to care about our situation.

As I explained the past six months of my life, he sat stone-faced, unmoving. Erik sat beside me with a similar look. However, when I choked up and told Colonel Robinson about the death of others drained dry, including children, the usage of sexual favors to get better treatment, and my own assault, Erik reached out and grabbed my hand. I couldn't explain it, but his touch, so unexpected, helped ease the pain weighing down on me. It was surprising that he would be that comforting. It certainly wasn't what I expected from the little I knew of him. I didn't look at him, just held onto his hand as I continued my story.

When I finished speaking, Colonel Robinson let out a deep sigh. "I'm sorry that happened to you, Amina. You're a strong person. A survivor," he stated.

"Thank you, sir. Will you help us?" I begged.

He sighed again. "A place like this cannot exist if we are to become the nation we once were. But we can't haphazardly take on such missions. We have to understand what we are getting into and the risk to the people here. Our world isn't like it once was. Going to battle with another group puts this town at risk. Puts other government-backed towns at risk as well. We're still in repair. Still trying to find survivors and get them to safe towns." The Colonel leaned into his desk and clasped his hands together. "I can't give you an answer right now. I would love nothing more than to find this place and bury those assholes so far in a hole they never see daylight. But I have to talk to the other leaders. Get their support. If we attack this place and they are able to retaliate, they will be coming here or to another government town. We have to be prepared for that. I also have to convince the leaders that this is real and not a trap."

I shook my head, confused. "Who would set up a trap like this?"

"You have to know, Amina, after what you've been through, that there are groups out there that don't want the government to form again. They want to keep us separated with total anarchy. If you've had access to the internet, I'm sure you've seen the streaming reports about such groups and their attacks on some government towns and any towns thinking of combining with us. Did you hear about the ambush in Detroit?"

"I didn't have access to the internet in the last six months. I barely know what day it is."

"Some soldiers from the Detroit government town went to a nearby community that needed medical help after an alleged massive supernatural fire they had a hard time putting out. They were also told the leader of the community wanted his town to join with the government. When they arrived, they were attacked. Most of the soldiers and civilians with them were killed."

"That's awful. And you think this could be like that? That I'm sending people to their deaths?"

"No, but it's the world we're in," the Colonel replied. "Give me time to talk to the other leaders. Then we have to do a bit of reconnaissance."

When we left the Colonel's office, I felt anything but hopeful.

"It's not over," Erik stated, glancing down at me.

We walked out of the building. "We should just go to Silver Spring. They'll help us."

"They'll help you here. This is a large town with back-up across the country. An independent town in Silver Spring, whose location we don't even know and size we don't know, isn't a better bet. The people here will help. I'll make sure of it."

I nodded. He seemed so sure, but I wasn't. My mind was

already focused on next steps. He was right. For all I knew, Silver Spring had just one hundred people, and those people wouldn't all be willing to fight just because a guy in their town asked them to for a woman he'd met in his dreams. And that was assuming that all those imaginary one hundred were in fighting shape and age.

When it came down to it, having a government town was always a better bet in a fight. I had no clue how large David's operation was. There could be another town that supported them. Maybe even a government town. That thought disturbed me the most.

Erik touched my shoulder and stopped me. He turned me to him. His hazel eyes were serious as he looked down at me. "I didn't realize all that happened to you."

I dropped my shoulders and looked down at the tiled floor. I barely wanted to talk about it with the Colonel. I really didn't want to talk about it with Erik and look like some damsel needing saving. I was stronger than that.

"Hey, look at me."

I glanced up at him. "What, Erik? I don't want to talk—"

He put up a hand to stop me. "You're a good person, Amina. I knew that from the

start, even though it seemed like I didn't trust you. When you first approached us do you know what I smelled?"

I squinted my eyes. "I hope something good because I did take a shower that morning."

"You smelled, you still smell, like roses to me, Amina." He looked almost perplexed when he said that, as if he couldn't quite understand how I could smell good.

"I put on perfume," I stated with a shrug.

He shook his head slightly. "I smelled that as well, but I can still get to your natural scent." He leaned towards me and took a deep breath. He wasn't inhaling my scent now, was he?

I shifted on my feet uncomfortably. It was moments like

116

these that reminded me he was part beast because people just didn't sniff each other. "So, good people smell like roses?"

He leaned back. "No. *You* smell like roses. I've never smelled that natural scent on anyone. Most good people smell of flowers but not roses specifically. You're the first with this scent. How is that?" He studied my face as if it, alone, would have the answers.

I opened my mouth to say something but then closed it. I didn't really know how to respond.

Erik straightened up, his eyes returning to their cool demeanor. "When we go back to that prison, we're going to free your friends, and *you* are going to kill David."

I gave him wide eyes. "I don't think I could—"

"You're a badass. At least that's what Lisa calls you." He smiled at me this time. I'd only known him for less than two days, but it was the first time I'd seen anything other than a serious expression on his face. It was strangely soothing. "And I know you can do it. So, say it with me. I'm a badass."

I gave him a questioning smile. "I am a badass?"

He frowned. "Say it like you mean it. I'm a badass." He said it with conviction and I had no doubt he meant it.

"I'm a badass!" I exclaimed, cutting off a laugh. Maybe it wasn't a joke. I was strong, I knew that. I escaped. I survived this long. Maybe I really could take David down.

Erik slapped me on the back, and I bounced forward an inch. "There you go." He nodded his head and started to walk again.

He believed that I could kill someone. How nice. I guessed that was his version of a pep talk.

CHAPTER 11

That night I met the others at the town Irish pub called McFarley's. Outside of the three restaurants, a coffee shop, and the library where they showed old movies, it was the only nightlife in town. The fact that they even had a formal nightlife was still amazing to me. In my old community, we huddled in a house over drinks, food, and an old MP3 player, and that was a party.

In the dimly-lit bar, the four of us sat around a dark wooden table, recapping our first workday and my meeting with Colonel Robinson.

"How long is it going to take them to help us? We passed all the tests," Charles said, with a confused look. "And we got our powers back. We don't have this kind of time to waste."

"It's not going to be easy to get them to just go to a place they don't know about," Erik explained. "Even if they believe us and that it's not a setup, they have to assess the risk. Is it worth starting a fight? Losing people? We have to do this at their pace. We'll have an answer by Monday."

I nodded and sighed. "Thank you, Erik," I said. "Your next drink's on me."

"You don't have to do that."

"I owe you a makeover," Lisa stated, looking at my hair. It was in a high bun, and I could only imagine by her concerned face that she didn't care for it.

"Hey, I have a guy I want you to meet," I said, turning to her.

Charles, who up until that moment had his face buried in a burger and fries, perked up. "Guy? What guy?" he asked with a frown.

I ignored him. "I think he might be Fae like you. He doesn't know what he is. Probably hasn't even tapped into all his powers."

"Is he cute?" Lisa asked, her green eyes sparkling.

I opened my mouth and raised my eyebrows. "If I said he was ugly, would you not want to meet him?"

Lisa gave a light shrug. "Of course, I'd want to meet him. My people are my people. Plus, he can just glamour himself if he's ugly."

"Dear God," I stood up. "Okay, I'm going to go get another drink. Erik, I got your next one like it or not."

"I kid, I kid!" Lisa cried, getting up, and following me. "You'll learn to love me, Amina. I'm telling you now."

I chuckled and shook my head, walking through the increasingly crowded space to the bar counter. Lisa stood next to me.

"I swear I have to slow down. My tolerance isn't what it was," I stated. "Unsurprisingly, they didn't give us alcohol in the lockup, and we didn't have a lot of it in my town before then."

"It's the weekend, sweetie, live a little. For once, we are both somewhere safe. Let's enjoy it for the time that we're here. We deserve it."

"Planning to leave already?" asked one of the bartenders. I hadn't seen her earlier. She had a deep voice that commanded attention. She was white, fair in skin tone, with dirty-blonde, purple-streaked hair cut in a pixie style. She looked around my age, average height, with an athletic figure. Her eyes were deep blue beneath thick, well-shaped, dark eyebrows and adorned with a thin, black eyeliner which was winged out at the edges. The only other makeup she had on was a bright red lipstick. She was mesmerizingly gorgeous.

She rolled up her right sleeve, and I saw a fully tattooed arm and hand. In fact, both her arms and hands were tatted, and more tattoos peeked out of her black collared shirt. "Didn't you just get here yesterday?" she questioned.

"Wow, word spreads fast in a small town," Lisa replied.

"We tend to run through faces quick nowadays." She threw out her hand to Lisa. "I'm Faith Thomas, by the way."

Lisa shook it, and I noticed Faith hold on to her hand, just a beat too long. "Lisa Xu and this is Amina Langston."

"Well, welcome girls," she said, with a slight grin as she shook my hand. "A welcome drink on me. What can I get you?"

"Vodka tonics for us both. And she's getting a whiskey for another friend," Lisa replied.

"Sure thing, sweetie," Faith turned and went to fix our drinks.

Lisa leaned towards me. "She's beautiful. I hate her."

I laughed.

"Amina?"

I turned to my left to see Felix standing there.

"Hey, Felix, glad you could make it." I smiled and gave him a quick hug.

He shrugged. "I didn't have anything to do but feed Dexter."

"So, you said."

"She was pissed that I was heading out. I don't really go out much at night." He leaned his massive frame against the bar.

Lisa leaned into me. "Who's the cute but creepy weirdo?" she whispered.

"Felix," he said, clearly having overheard Lisa's not-so-whispery whisper. Good-natured, as I was beginning to think he was, he leaned over and offered his hand.

Lisa shook it and offered him her most pageant-like smile. "Sorry, I'm Lisa."

Faith appeared again with our drinks. "Here you are, lovelies." She looked over at Felix and gave a look of shock, her eyebrows raised. "I must be seeing a mirage because that couldn't possibly be *my* Felix out at a bar."

He grinned. "Hey, Faith. Amina invited me out."

"I've been trying to get you out forever. All it took was a cute girl to get you out of the house. I should be offended." She leaned over the bar and playfully punched him in the arm.

"How do you two know each other?" I asked before taking a sip of my drink. It was dangerously strong, and the tingle from the alcohol threatened to burn my nose hairs. I would be drunk soon.

"We met each other off base, as I call this place, almost three years ago. Helped each other survive. Well, I wasn't so friendly in the beginning," Faith explained.

"She tried to steal my energy," Felix explained as if saying she cut him off in traffic.

"Say what now?" Lisa asked in confusion.

"I'm a succubus," Faith explained with a sheepish grin. "It's what I do."

"A suck you what?"

I turned to Lisa with a blank face. "I feel like you heard what she said."

Lisa leaned into me. "I think she forgot to put the tonic in this drink."

Faith chuckled. "I'm like a vampire, except I don't need blood. I need life force or energy. I was a bit suspect back in the day, but now I only take from willing men and women. And animals I don't like. Anyway, something about this big guy here set me on the straight and narrow, and I don't steal energy anymore. Now we're like brother and sister. He keeps my control in check, and I make sure he doesn't get too lost."

I shook my head. "I've never run into a succubus before. Awesome."

She winked at me. "Glad you think that, sweetheart. All right, Felix, I'm getting you a whiskey, no objections," she announced and spun away.

"Well, that explains why she's such a flirt. That's how she pulls suckers in and gets their energy," Lisa stated.

"I just wanted a beer," Felix muttered, looking down. For a man built like he lifted trucks as hand weights, he sure was shy.

I clapped my hands. "So, Felix, I invited you out because I think you might be," I looked to Lisa for drama. "A fairy."

She frowned.

"Before you say anything, Lisa. He said he can heal people, but he's not a witch or a mage. What else could he be?"

Lisa shook her head. "I don't know but he's not a fairy. No offense, Felix. You just don't give me fairy vibes. If there is a fairy in the same room as me, I would feel it. We can't hide from each other. It's like a ringing in the ear until we finally meet. I hear no ringing. I've only felt it a couple times before. You could be an elf, maybe?"

Felix's shoulders dropped. "I'm not an elf."

Faith reappeared with two whiskeys and frowned when she saw Felix's hanging head. "Well, what happened?"

"I found out I'm not a fairy," he replied in a gloomy voice, taking his drink.

She looked to Lisa and me, confused. "I don't know how to respond to that."

I explained. "I thought he might be a fairy because Lisa's one, but he's not."

"Erik said not to tell everyone," Lisa loudly whispered. She was drunk already.

Faith stuck out her lower lip and turned to Felix. "It's all right, honey. We'll find out what you are. Don't give up."

Felix took a large gulp of his drink and then looked at Faith. With the way Faith poured drinks, I'd half expected him to breathe out fire, but he was a big guy, so I guessed he could handle it.

"I'm not giving up. I just know more than ever now that we have to leave and go to Silver Spring," he stated with determination in his voice.

"No, he didn't," Lisa said, mouth hanging open.

Faith sighed and leaned back from the countertop. "Not this again. You know I'll go anywhere with you but come on, sweetie, we can't skip a good thing we got here for a dream you've been having."

"I'm blown away. Felix, do you know anyone named Phillip?" I asked.

"Or Ms. Annie Mae?" Lisa added.

He shook his head quickly. "I've seen Annie Mae. People talk about Phillip here, and there but I haven't seen him."

"What people? We both have been dreaming about people from a town in Silver Spring. Actually, communicating with them in repeated dreams," I explained.

"No way," Faith said, leaning on the counter. I heard someone call her name, but she ignored them.

"In my dreams, I see a town. I don't talk to anybody. I just visit like a ghost." Felix looked beyond the bar as if thinking.

"I've never actually seen the town in my dreams," Lisa stated. "What's it like?"

"What's what like?" Felix asked, turning to us.

"Faith!" called a male voice.

I looked to her, and she continued to stare at us, listening to the conversation as if she hadn't heard her name.

Lisa rolled her eyes. "What's Moscow like? Silver Spring, silly!"

Recognition entered Felix's eyes. "It's a bit like here. Big, but more of a city feel. Things are closer together. They live in houses and high-rise apartments. It's like a government town, but they have only supernatural people there."

I heard Faith's name again. She was unmoved.

"High rises," I pondered. "The town has to be in downtown Silver Spring. I know exactly where they are!"

"Faith!" a balding, middle-aged, white man shouted. He was now standing beside Faith. "I've been calling you. Get your deaf ass to the other side of the bar and help people!"

I think I saw literal fire in Faith's eyes as she spun to look at him. The older man, who I was now assuming ran the place, paled and took a step back. Felix reached out and grabbed Faith's arm.

"Chill, mama," he said in a soothing voice.

The scary fire died out in Faith's eyes, and she let out a deep sigh.

"Give me one minute, please, Stan," she said through gritted teeth.

The man huffed and walked away, muttering about how hard it was to find good help. Clearly, he had missed the whole apocalypse, where bartending probably wasn't a high priority.

Felix straightened up with excitement. "Let's go to this town!"

Lisa and I looked at each other. "We can't. At least not right now," I said.

"Why not?" Faith asked, crossing her tattooed arms.

"Well, that's why we're here..." I began.

CHAPTER 12

$\mathcal{I}$ had been in the town for a week before we got in motion to return to the prison for scouting. Colonel Robinson wanted to send out scouts, and we were to go with them as guides. Erik would join. Charles and I gave our perspectives, along with drawing a detailed layout of the facility that we tried to put together from memory. Once Colonel Robinson and his people were comfortable that it wasn't all a set-up, he agreed that they would help us rescue our friends.

Needless to say, I was not looking forward to returning. The very thought of it gave me heart palpitations. Every horrible outcome of our getting to the hospital entered my mind. We get back there, get ambushed and recaptured. We get back there and they have moved. We get back there and see our friends are being treated to worse conditions as a result of our escape. I was ready for this part of my life to be over.

"Doesn't look like anyone is there," observed a soldier, riding in the front passenger seat of the SUV.

The truck, along with several other vehicles, was parked

on top of a hill a quarter of a mile away from the hospital. It was after 10 p.m., and the hospital sat below us, un-lit. We didn't even see any lights from guards posted on the roofs.

"They could all be asleep," I explained from the back seat.

The soldier, a young white guy with a bald head, pulled out goggles from the glove compartment. "Stay here," he ordered and got out of the car, disappearing down the street to a staircase, spilling on to the road in front of the hospital.

We waited in silence for about fifteen minutes. The soldier returned, getting in the truck. "No ones there. Several of us circled the entire perimeter and no heat signatures registered on our equipment," he announced to the driver, a woman with short, curly black hair.

Colonel Robinson, who had been listening in from a speaker, ordered them to go in and search for any clues regarding where David and the others were going next.

We drove up to the gate, which was open, and onto the grounds. Our driver parked near the closest door we came to, and the rest of the trucks parked at other entrances. Charles and I got out from the back and followed the soldiers inside. The doors were unlocked and it was eerily quiet. We never filled up the whole hospital before, but there were enough people there, between the prisoners and the workers and their families, that we should have heard voices and sounds of life no matter what part of the hospital we were in. However, the soldiers ran through the building, kicking open doors, encountering no one.

We did find remnants of recent life. Clothing, partially eaten food, trash, used cigarettes, the garden with most of its produce gone, blood spills...

"The blood is fairly fresh," said a soldier. He wore glasses and had a buzz cut. He shone his flashlight on a spot of red on the floor. He crouched down and sniffed the blood spill, then stood up. He must have been were. "They probably left only yesterday."

I wanted to vomit. While I'd been messing around in Hagerstown for over a week, David and crew had been making their escape. Turns out, my ward wasn't that strong.

Charles let out an expletive and punched the wall hard enough to cause a bruise on his hand. I walked over to him to pat his back, but Charles moved away. "We'll find them, Charles," I said with confidence, although I didn't feel that certain.

He spun around and looked at me with pained eyes. "How, Amina? How? It's not like they left a trail of bread crumbs. In this world, how are we finding anyone? They moved because we escaped. They can go anywhere in this country. They can cloak themselves, so we can't see them."

"We could sense that magic."

"Sense it where?!" He threw out his arms in frustration. "They could have gone north, south, west. We have no idea."

"We can tell our other towns to be on the lookout," said one soldier, looking around as he spoke.

"Half of this country is still uninhabited or with no access to tech. It could be another five years before we are in a place to be able to find them. All our friends could be drained dry and dead by then," Charles said, leaning against a wall, holding his now bruised hand.

"It won't be that long. Things will get back to normal before then. If we have to scout by foot and search this whole damn country, we will." I walked over to him again, intending to heal his bruise.

He moved his hand away from me. "Stop mothering me," he grumbled.

I threw up my hands in surrender and walked away, seeing Erik and a couple of soldiers coming down the hallway.

He looked over at Charles then at me. "You okay?" he asked me.

I shrugged. "I don't know what to do." I crossed my arms, feeling lost.

"Well, we think that these guys didn't operate just here," Erik began. "They have other bases just like this. We saw some names and states on a paper in an office. The closest sites are in New York and one in North Carolina. That helps to narrow down the search."

"Assuming those places don't move too," I grumbled.

A soldier called out that we were leaving.

"We left some cameras around the building, just in case anyone comes back. We're going to do some scouting, settle in a couple of houses for the night, and then head out early morning," the soldier with a buzz cut announced as we headed back to the trucks. "We already pressed our luck being out this late."

He was right. Night wasn't the safest time to travel. Scary monsters seemed to prefer the cover of night to search for food, usually people. Our four trucks ended our scouting in a town outside of Pittsburg and made a stop at an abandoned shopping center to search for supplies.

We broke into groups to check the area with Charles, two soldiers, and myself searching a pharmacy. There was a low chance of finding anything to scavenge, but unless the place looked broken into, we couldn't just ignore the possibility that there might be something worth collecting.

"We shouldn't have left them," Charles muttered as he and I walked down an aisle with shopping baskets. The pharmacy was locked when we got to it, which was a good sign that there may be something inside worth getting. Thanks to Charles' tech magic, we entered without any damage. We kept the lights off to avoid outside attention. Since the store was locked, we could only assume someone had kept it going for a while. There wasn't a full variety of stuff, but there was still more than the usual leftovers we'd normally find.

Whoever left the store probably planned to come back, but everything was covered in dust, so...they weren't returning.

I knocked packages of tampons and sanitary napkins into my basket. Reusable menstruation cups were becoming more popular but were very hard to find.

"What good would we be if we had stayed? We'd we dead, maybe. I'd be raped. Here, we have a chance to set them free," I said.

I stopped walking and turned to Charles, who was staring blankly at several baby items. Diapers were probably needed. New life was still happening around us. I always got amazed when I thought about the children who would grow up in a world like this as their normal. Perhaps the mundane, slice-of-life world that I grew up in would be their new fairy tales.

"You can't feel guilty. Feel blessed. God has a plan for us. That's what mom said, and I believe her. We're going to help them. That's what we do."

"There was a lot of blood splattered," Charles said.

"They were rushing to get out. Maybe they spilled blood bags. There were a lot of people there. And we didn't find any bodies, that's what's important," I replied. I handed him my basket and began to fill his empty basket with various baby items. "Perhaps this is for the best. They're with another one of their operations now. So, when we find them, we have a chance to shut the whole operation down with help from the government. We will help more people."

I gave him a tight hug with my free arm, and he didn't move away this time. "I love you, Charles. You're my best friend. You're all I have. We're going to help the others, but I need you focused."

He returned my one-handed hug and gave a deep sigh. "Love you too, Sis. I'm happy you're here."

We were disrupted from our family moment by loud thuds coming from another part of the pharmacy.

"Sounds like they knocked down a display of items," I said, pulling away from Charles.

"Y'all all right over there?" Charles called.

In response, we heard a female cry.

"That's not good," Charles whispered, moving down the aisle. I followed him.

We made a left towards where we thought the sound came from. Charles stopped abruptly, quietly pointing ahead. I looked around him and saw a male soldier on the floor unmoving. But that isn't who we heard scream. The sound was definitely female.

Charles handed me his basket and pulled out his handgun from his holster. We carefully walked towards the soldier, looking down the aisles on our left as we passed them. I looked to my right, checking the front registers and photo area. I stopped. A dark figure suddenly appeared behind one of the cash registers. Then, he or she disappeared in a blink.

"Charles, there was someone near the register," I whispered, still staring at the front, willing the figure to reappear.

When I didn't hear Charles walking over, I turned my head, but there was no one. Just the down soldier. I spun around, panic quickly taking hold of me. "Charles!" I shouted.

"He won't hear you," said a familiar male voice.

I gasped.

David.

I felt like my heart went into my throat. My legs were weak, and I dropped the baskets. Painful goosebumps appeared on my arms. He was behind me. I could feel his presence. I didn't want to turn. Didn't want to face that nightmare just yet.

"Phillip," I whispered without thinking. I didn't know why I called his name. Perhaps because he had helped me in all my other times against David. However, there was no answer.

"It's good to see you," David said. I heard his footsteps walk closer to me, and I tensed all over. "Looks like you're doing well. You look stronger."

"Where the hell is my brother?" I said in a tight voice.

"Just taking a little nap."

Amina! Phillip called in my mind. *Get out of there. Don't let him touch you!*

"He has Charles," I whispered back. I looked up at David. "If you hurt him—"

"Then, he'll be hurt." He was right behind me now. I could feel his breath on my neck, and I fought the urge to spin around and rip his heart out. I needed to find my brother first. I balled my fist to control my rage.

"We're not going back," I spat.

He pulled my hair back from my neck and leaned in to whisper. "I don't want you both." He kissed my neck, and my shoulders hunched in disgust.

Amina, you're strong now. Phillip said, calmly in my mind. *Kick his ass!*

I sucked in a breath, spun around, and aimed my fist for David's face, but he blocked it with his hand. He was faster and stronger than before. I wondered how many people he drained dry to get to this level.

Use your powers, mi corazon! Phillip implored.

David gave me a tightlipped smile, his ice-blue eyes almost translucent, and dead. I wouldn't be scared. I was stronger too. I was a bad ass.

I focused my mind on pushing his eyes out of their sockets slowly.

David frowned then broke out in a pained cry, covering his eyes with his hands. I smiled as he hunched over now, screaming in agony.

"Where's my brother?" I shouted.

"I have people who will kill him if I don't come back!" David screamed.

I stopped my magic. David ceased screaming and slowly stood up, wiping his eyes. His blue eyes were now bloodshot, and streaks of blood ran down his face.

"You have gotten much more powerful, Amina. Oh, yes. I want you back." He was grinning and his eyes had become wide and crazed.

I felt like throwing up. "I would sooner die."

"And so, your brother will too."

Shit. I wasn't in a position of power here. David was too far gone to value his own life, and I had no idea who else he was with. If I killed him, then they could kill Charles in return. "Fine! I'll go back with you. Release my brother and the prisoners from Pittsburg."

Don't do that, Amina. You can get your brother back. We can find the others. Kill this man.

David laughed, and the sound stabbed at my stomach. "You are the most powerful being I have ever encountered, and I can imagine you have untapped gifts still to come. That is far from a fair trade. You for your brother. That's all I'm willing to do."

This was a chance to try to help the others in the most peaceful way. I had to get David to agree. Even if it was a long shot. "No, for everyone. I'm surrounded by soldiers. You aren't getting out of here alive."

He tilted his head and frowned. "I'm not worried."

Why wasn't he? How did he find us? Had he been in hiding near the hospital and followed us here? Was he not alone? Were the other soldiers and Erik, several stores down at the supermarket, also fighting off these enhanced humans? Were they dead?

The worry made me dizzy. More importantly, without knowing the safety of my brother, I had no real power to bargain with this asshole. "I need to see my brother before I go with you. I need to make sure he's okay."

If you go back with him, you'll never get out. Just hold out.

"How do you know?" I whispered back to the Phillip voice in my head.

"He's with an associate in the back," David replied, eyeing me curiously.

"Take me to him," I demanded, ignoring Phillip's pleading voice in my head.

David smiled again and pointed to the aisle in front of me. I slowly walked down the row of cards and magazines; he followed closely behind me. I would see my brother and say goodbye, but Charles would find me. It would be okay.

I felt magic enter the pharmacy before I saw anyone and prayed it was one of the good guys. Hopefully, David hadn't picked up on it. I didn't believe that the blood potion gave regular humans the ability to sense magic.

Suddenly Erik appeared in front of me, his eyes other-worldly and orange. "Down!" he growled, and I ducked without question as he took a swipe at David with very inhuman hands. His large jackal paws, bigger than my head, held thick claws that were maybe three or four inches long. He missed David's face but connected with his chest.

David cried out and jumped back, putting pressure on the deep gashes as blood poured out between his fingers. With his free hand, he pulled out a gun from behind his back and pointed it at Erik.

The werejackal looked unfazed. He would survive a gunshot as long as it wasn't to the head or heart with a silver bullet. That part of the myth was true. Weres were very allergic to silver.

Erik stepped around me as if daring David to shoot. And shoot he did. He missed Erik's head and hit a wall behind us. David shot again, this time clipping Erik in the shoulder. Erik stumbled back only slightly but kept moving. David shot another time and, again, Erik took the bullet, in this thigh this time, as if it were nothing. However, by this time, Erik was close enough to David to knock the gun from his hand. Erik backhanded David, who only slid back on his feet. A hit like that from Erik would have landed any normal human on their behind and even knocked them out. David cursed and charged Erik, wrapping his arms around his waist and knocking the werejackal to the ground.

David's arm moved in a blur behind his back, and a butcher knife appeared in his hand. He brought it down on Erik, who threw out his arm. The knife stabbed through Erik's arm, and David began to push down the knife, the exposed tip coming closer to Erik's chest.

I threw out my hands. "Stop, David!" I yelled. Pain pricked my body, forcing me to hunch over.

He looked up right before his body lifted off of Erik into the air. His body flew backwards into a front cashier counter and crumbled to the floor. Had I just moved him like I did, Lisa?

Seizing the moment, Erik jumped up and raced to David, practically flying. He bent over David and reared back his clawed hands, ready to cut the man to shreds.

"Don't! He has Charles," I shouted, standing straight. I was suddenly feeling nauseous. A cold sweat drenched my forehead and neck.

Erik paused. "We have him. He was in the back," Erik replied, keeping his eyes on David. "By the way, your partner is dead. Where is the prison?"

David's shocked eyes quickly grew cool, and he looked at me. "'Til next time," he said in a calm voice. Then in a blur, he jumped up and raced out of the building before Erik could bring down his claws. He was as fast as a vampire, but he was still human. I had not sensed him to have magic. The blood serum made humans strong but not at the level of paranormals. Or so I thought.

I didn't have a moment to wonder anymore about that new fact because a sharp pain twisted my stomach, and my knees gave way. I fell to the floor, my vision going blurry.

The last thing I saw and heard was Erik's boots quickly approaching Phillip and me calling my name.

And for the third time in several months, I was passing out.

Damn it. This couldn't be good for my health.

CHAPTER 13

J woke up in a bedroom I didn't recognize. If I were to guess, I'd say it was the room of a senior citizen. The comforter was paisley, and the oak dresser across from the bed had a white doily on the top. On the pale blue walls was a mixture of colored pictures of children and old, black-and-white-and-sepia-colored photos of a couple. The room was lit by a large candle on a nightstand to my left. The room smelled like dust, and I prayed to the heavenly Father above that they had cleaned the bed linen before they placed me under the covers. My right arm decided to itch at that exact moment.

"Did they clean this bed?" I croaked out to the room, getting more and more agitated about my predicament as my other arm began to itch.

"Yeah, one of the soldiers is a witch. She said a cleaning spell over the house and warded it," I heard Erik explain from my right. I turned to face him and found him sitting in an actual rocking chair next to the bed near the door.

He was slightly rocking in the chair, looking like someone's very scary grandmother. I stifled a giggle.

Erik gave me a quizzical look before getting up and

walking to the dresser, pouring water into a glass from a large plastic water jug. I scooted up in the bed and accepted the water when he returned to my bed side. I lay back on the world's fluffiest pillows. Actually, the whole bed was heaven. Grandma had been getting some serious beauty rest.

"It just smells like dust in here. Thank you," I said before taking a sip.

"You want me to ask her to do an air freshener spell?"

I glanced over to him. "Does that exist?"

He gave me a deadpan face. "No. Hell, I don't know. Maybe."

I rolled my eyes. "Where's Charles?"

"In another room resting," Erik answered, sitting back down. "He was knocked out, but he's okay. The witch soldier healed him, but we're keeping an eye on him just in case."

"How about you? Your wounds?"

He shrugged. "Just scratches, I'm fine."

"Scratches? You were shot and stabbed."

He showed me his arm. There was no open cut, just a scar where he was stabbed earlier. If he'd let a witch heal him, there wouldn't be a scar.

"Thank you for saving me."

"You could have handled it. You're a badass, remember?" He smirked at me.

I tapped my forehead. "Ah, you're right." I looked around the room. "What time is it?"

Erik, who I was just now noticing, looked completely exhausted, rubbed his short, brown beard. He looked down at his watch. "Almost 1 a.m."

The two soldiers that were with Charles and I popped into my mind. "The soldiers who were with us, are they…"

"Trisha is alive, Max didn't make it."

I looked down at my hands. "This is all my fault."

Erik shook his head. "You can't think like that. Soldiers put themselves out there to protect. It's a risky thing, but you aren't the one who is responsible. Those assholes who ambushed them are."

I nodded, not really convinced. It was a hard pill to swallow. It was hard to know that these people were here because of me and to save people who weren't even from their town. Max's death was for nothing. How could I go back to Colonel Robinson and ask him to continue to help us?

I looked over to Erik, who gazed at me with a weary frown. "You've been sitting in that seat since we came here?" I asked.

He nodded. "Only been here an hour. It's very comfortable, actually. The soldier who healed you just wanted to make sure we kept an eye on you because you weren't waking up right after we healed you. I volunteered."

I frowned. "Healed from what?"

"You passed out." Erik leaned towards me and searched my eyes. "You don't remember?"

"I remember hitting the floor."

"You were poisoned."

"What? How was I poisoned?"

"Did that guy touch you at all?"

I shook my head and looked up at the ceiling, mentally searching my mind. David kissed my neck. "Yes. How do we know it was poison? What kind?"

Erik sighed and rubbed his weary eyes. "We don't know. They'll test you and your brother, tomorrow back in the town. Assuming any traces of the poison are left."

"He didn't want my brother," I began, replaying the encounter again in my mind. "He just wanted me."

"Well, he's not going to have you," Erik growled with steely eyes. The look was both scary and comforting. "You're safe here. We've got wards up and soldiers keeping an eye out. We're leaving at first dawn."

I smiled at him. "How'd you get so comforting?"

Erik sat back and chuckled. Maybe I was wrong about

him. Maybe he wasn't a grumpy bear. "How should I answer that question? I was raised by two parents who loved me? I served in the military back in New Zealand and was in some areas of this world so horrible I had to comfort my soldiers to keep them going."

I nodded slowly. "So, I forgot to ask. How did you know we were in danger back at the pharmacy? We weren't gone that long."

"I felt it. Something just felt wrong."

"Well, that's amazing. Great intuition. I gotta keep you around," I replied before taking another sip of water.

"That shouldn't be a problem," he replied.

I looked up and met Erik's eyes, but I couldn't read them. They seemed different than before. Maybe it was the candle-light, but they seemed softer, and there was a hint of something flickering behind the honey color of his eyes. Flirtation?

Something changed in me. My stomach was now doing the familiar flip-flops again, confusing me even more. There was a man who I had been dreaming of for almost a month, and then there was this man who I'd only known for slightly over a week. But he was here in person, and I'd seen him every day. He had grown on me. Yep, I was in confusion city.

I gulped down the rest of my water and wondered what to say next. Maybe I was imagining this all. I was exhausted, it was late. I was still in recovery. I was just confused. "Lisa is lucky to have you as a protector," I said, putting the empty glass of water down on the side table.

"She's doesn't need me now," he replied, stifling a yawn.

"You should go rest. Is there a place for you to sleep?"

He shook his head. "No, the rocking chair is fine. Keeps me alert. I doubt David would come around again, but you never know."

"You don't have to be my guard."

He looked over to me with a curious glint in his now human eyes. "Does my being here make you uncomfortable?"

I shook my head quickly, suddenly nervous. "No. I just feel bad that you're sleeping in a chair. I mean, you could share the bed. It's large enough." My eyes were carefully neutral so as not to portray the invitation as anything more than platonic. Not that I didn't find him attractive. He was a beautiful man, but we'd never spoken in a flirtatious manner before. I wasn't sure him telling me I smelled of roses counted.

He eyed the bed, it was queen sized, so large enough but not so large I wouldn't know he was there. He looked back at me. "Are you sure?"

I shrugged. "It's just us sleeping for a couple of hours."

His face didn't betray anything as he rose and walked over to the other side of the bed. I scooted down on the bed, resting my head on the pillow, as I stared up at the ceiling. I bit my lip as I felt the mattress lower as he lay on the bed beside me. Was I really going to be able to sleep next to him?

"So, you're from New Zealand?" I asked in a steady voice, lying flat on the bed.

"Yes," he replied.

"And you're a werejackal. I thought those were only in Africa or parts of Asia. How'd you get to become one?"

He chuckled. "I don't know if the were part is tied to the original location of the animal. But my father *was* Afrikaner, from South Africa. I'm guessing that's the origin if you believe that."

"Is your mom from New Zealand originally?" I glanced over to him. He was lying on his back as well, an arm behind his head. He looked up at the ceiling with a slight smile. Perhaps I was prying, but the nervous energy in my stomach wouldn't let me sleep. He was a man. A handsome man. Lying next to me. In a bed. I was sixteen again, dreaming of Kyle Jefferson, my high school crush.

"You want my family history, I see. Yes, my mother was a New Zealander or a Kiwi, as we call locals. She was white and Maori. What about you? Since this is family history time."

I smiled. "I'm just a local. I grew up in Tampa. My father is originally from Trinidad. He was East and West Indian. My mother was part Creole."

Silence hung in the air. I wasn't sure what else to talk about. His Pre-world life? What had he been doing for the past nine years? Or maybe I should have just drifted off to sleep. I closed my eyes.

"You still smell of roses," he said in a low voice.

My eyes popped open. Nope, wouldn't be sleeping yet.

"Thanks," I whispered, unsure how to respond. I wasn't creeped out and, in a way, it was flattering. I was just overjoyed that my natural scent was pleasant. It somehow reaffirmed something positive in me.

I felt his hand reach out and touch my hair, stroking a few clumps of tight curls between his fingers. That would only make my hair frizzy, but I didn't care. I fought the urge to tense. He wasn't going to hurt me or take advantage of me, but the nerves didn't die quickly. "You're going to give me a big head if you keep saying how good I smell," I joked with a nervous giggle that was very unlike me. Erik had never, in the short time we'd known each other, devoted this much attention to me. Then again, we were never alone together.

"Do you want me to stop touching you?" he asked in a low voice that did something to my stomach. "I should have asked first."

I thought for a moment. "No, I don't mind," I admitted. I closed my eyes again and allowed myself to relax as he ran his fingers in my hair. Moments later, I felt a light breath on my neck. I opened my eyes again. "Did you just sniff me?"

Erik sighed before responding. "I couldn't help myself. I apologize. It's just that this close to you, I'm able to smell more than roses. You smell like cocoa or vanilla. Maybe both."

"Well, as long as you don't eat me, it's okay." I wasn't going to tell him but it was kind of a turn on. Of course, him being someone I sort of knew and being uber attractive made it slightly flirty. If he were a stranger on the street, I'd have kneed him in the groin for sniffing me.

He chuckled, and I felt him scoot closer to me. "Tell me to stop if I'm too close. I don't think I'm able to judge boundaries right now."

"You're fine," I whispered back through my heart, pounding away in my ears. Any moment, I was sure it would burst out of me. I put a hand to my chest as if to keep it in.

I couldn't help but wonder how we'd gotten here. One moment he was the grumpy tough guy I found on the side of the road, and the next, he was lying next to me stroking my hair. I wanted to be near him, there was no doubt in my mind. Yet, I wasn't sure if I was mistaking the stress of the past couple of weeks with me really being into him. I also didn't want to misconstrue his miscalculation of appropriate personal space with meaning he was interested in me beyond anything platonic.

He was a were, they didn't do things or think the same way I did. Granted, he'd only been a were for nine years, but nine years was enough to change your behavior. It'd certainly changed mine. Magic and the use of spells was becoming almost second nature to me. Therefore, my scent could simply be a relaxing agent that helped him fall asleep, and I was in my head, thinking he was flirting.

I turned my head slowly to look at him for some clarity. He lowered his eyes from my hair to mine, and we didn't speak. He was lying on his side now, his hand still playing in my hair. I smiled slightly, still unsure of what I wanted to say or do. Maybe I needed to just go to sleep and get my starved hormones in check. Of course, I was thinking this at the same time I was looking at his lips, and when I looked up at him again, I could now identify the something in Erik's eyes I couldn't place before. Desire.

He grinned at me before leaning in slowly. "Tell me to stop," he whispered.

I didn't, and soon his lips found mine.

His lips were softer than I expected from someone so hard. It had been a while since I'd been kissed, I was not counting David, and a need arose in me that I didn't know existed. I deepened our kiss and felt the warmth from him spread over me and tighten my stomach in desire.

I turned my body towards him, and he moved his hand from my hair to my lower back, pressing me closer. I grabbed his face, trying to fight my sudden sense of urgency to have him, feeling his scruffy beard under my fingers and against my face. I might have some friction burn in the morning, but right now, it was worth it.

He slipped his tongue into my mouth, and his tongue played upon my own. My body awoke as a tingling heat began in my stomach. I nipped his bottom lip, which seemed to set him off. He gave a startling, low growl and leaned in farther, forcing me to lay on my back again.

He pulled away and gazed down at me, balancing on his hands, which were stationed on both sides of me. His normally hazel eyes were again the yellowish-orange color of a jackal. They were distinctly inhuman, and yet I wasn't scared.

"Uh, when's the full moon?" I asked, slightly breathless.

"Tomorrow," he answered, his voice thick and deep. He lowered his head towards my collarbone.

"Your eyes have gone all jackal," I stated, trying to maintain control and ignore the way his lips felt on my skin. Weres so close to a full moon were like animals in heat. I had to be careful.

He was back to kissing me again, this time focusing on

my neck. I closed my eyes, forgetting what exactly I was talking about for a moment as further nerves in my body started to wake up. I let out a soft moan as his tongue coated my skin in tiny circles. I internally screamed with excitement. One of his hands slowly rubbed up my arm. The feel of his hard hands on my skin felt warm and protective.

Guilt suddenly spread over me. Phillip. We weren't a couple. He hadn't professed his undying love, and most importantly, we hadn't really met yet. Still, having sex with Erik would make things way too messy. Especially when I wasn't even sure he was into me or just going for the closest cute gal around. Not to mention, having sex with a man I was just getting to know with my brother in the next room felt kind of inappropriate.

I sighed, tapping Erik on the shoulder.

He looked back down at me again, face questioning. "Did I do something wrong?" he asked.

I shook my head quickly. "Oh, no. You did everything right. Very right. It's just…my brother is right next door with a bunch of other people in the house, and these walls are probably super thin." That technically wasn't a lie. It was a valid concern. Not a huge concern but still the truth. "And with the full moon and all, maybe you aren't making the best decisions… I don't do random hookups, even though dating is dead in the supernatural apocalypse. Although, who are we kidding, it was dying before then too, am I right?" I let out a nervous giggle that annoyed the inner me greatly.

His lips turned up slightly at the corners, and he kissed me on my forehead before moving to lay beside me. "Despite the full moon coming, I have all my senses, Amina. And I want you. Not because you are close by, but because you are you. If I just wanted sex with the closest willing woman, there is a soldier here who was flirting with me earlier. I could have gone over to her," he said.

I elbowed him in the side, a surprising bout of jealousy waving over me. "What's stopping you?" I growled.

He chuckled, moving me closer to him so that I could lay my head on his chest. His well-defined chest with a rippled stomach that felt chiseled from stone. *Get a grip, girl.* "It might be the fact that it's not her that I want," he replied.

He gently grabbed a collection of my curls again and twirled them on his finger. My pulse slowed as I relaxed.

I opened my mouth but had no idea what I would say. I was a bundle of hormones and confusion.

He kissed the top of my head. "Come on, tough girl, let's get some shut-eye,"

We rested for a few hours until a soldier banged on the door, waking us up. As short as my sleep was, it was the most restful sleep I'd had in years.

CHAPTER 14

*I*n the morning, we headed back to town. Thoughts of my night with Erik raced around in my head, bringing a smile to my lips. Charles kept looking over to me in the truck with suspicious eyes, but I didn't care. I felt a little like a teenager who'd found out her longtime crush liked her back.

However, my reminiscing was cut short. The ride to Hagerstown was anything but smooth. Thirty minutes in, and we were stopped on the highway by something big.

It was a troll, to be exact.

The troll was humanoid, wide, and tall. It was large, the size of a monster truck, and almost fifteen feet tall. Its head was the width of its body, and it barely had a neck. The troll was the color of sand with thick, calloused skin. It had dense, bushy, black eyebrows, which almost covered its beady, black eyes. Its mouth took up the length of the bottom half of its face, which held two sharp, protruding lower canines. It wore clothes. I could only assume clothes it made because nothing human ever came in a size that large. On its head grew coarse, spiky, black hair.

I looked over at Charles, who was already looking at me

with a question in his eyes. We both wondered if this was the same troll we'd escaped earlier. I had to believe that it was. There weren't that many trolls in the world, but they typically didn't move locations.

"Anyone got a missile?" joked a soldier over the phone.

"We have to keep shooting it. Only way to get it down," said another soldier.

"How many bullets do you want to lose on this guy?" I asked, leaning towards the front seat. "Or, for that matter, lives."

"He's on the move!" shouted another soldier over the com.

I strained and looked out of the window. The troll had squared up and was stomping towards us. His large hands were in fists. The car shook, and I threw out my arm as if that would steady myself.

Trolls were odd creatures. They were generally territorial and didn't go about seeking out humans. Trolls didn't eat humans for sustenance but would gobble up a person just to be rid of them. We tended to annoy trolls.

Of course, all I knew about trolls was what I learned on the internet, so my knowledge was pretty faulty. Maybe instead of being in a mountain or forest or...under a bridge, this troll thought the highway was his? This was a brave, new world, and it was possible.

"We'll surround him and fire," said a soldier over the com.

"He just wants us off this road," I stated.

They ignored me.

"We have to kill it, Mina," Charles stated. "He's not a big, friendly, giant."

"He's wearing clothes. He's a conscious being who doesn't prey on humans," I replied. "Look at him."

The troll stopped walking and stomped its car-sided foot into the pavement, causing a crack. His face was in a scowl, mouth upside down, bushy eyebrows connected.

"Erik was right, you are way too trusting, Sis," Charles muttered, shaking his head.

"He's angry. He just wants us to leave."

"How do you know that?" the driving soldier asked, looking at me through the rearview mirror.

"Gooooo!" bellowed the troll in a deep, thunderous voice.

I gave the soldier a pointed look in the mirror.

"We should still kill it," said the passenger seat soldier.

I shook my head. "His name was probably Bob nine years ago. He worked as a chemistry teacher at the local high school. He was dating the home ed teacher, Martha."

The three men in the SUV turned to me. "How do you know all that?" the driver soldier asked.

I shrugged. "I don't, I'm just guessing. But not every monster just came up out of the ground or sea or caves. Some were turned, just like us."

The soldiers frowned and looked at each other.

"Let me put it to sleep."

Charles nudged me with his elbow and leaned in. "Remember what Erik said about showcasing too much of your powers," he whispered. "Plus, we've got to help the next people who come around. They might not be able to just sleepy time him."

"Fire!" came a command from the walkie-talkie.

"Sorry," the driver said. The soldiers jumped out with their automatics and commenced to take down the large beast in a blaze of bullets.

Bob, the troll, let out inhuman cries as he was hit. He kicked a soldier, and the poor man went flying far down the highway, like a football. If that soldier was human, he wouldn't survive that.

Bob slowed his kicks and stomping, but he wasn't down for the count. I covered my eyes just as he stomped on a female soldier who was in werebear form. Even in her paranormal shape, I didn't have hope that she would survive such a crushing.

"He's not bleeding out. How are they going to kill him?" Charles asked, hanging his arms off the seat in front of him.

A supernaturally large animal jumped high onto 'Bob's' right side. A jackal. He was huge. Not the size of the troll, but he was probably eight feet tall. His furry body was wide, and it moved on two feet. The fur was a golden beige, and his back had a thick, black-and-white strip of fur. His eyes were a rusted orange color, and they looked almost demonic coupled with a mouth full of monstrously sharp teeth. One bite from him would mean the loss of a limb. He looked almost like the Egyptian god Anubis. Except his body was less human and much larger. He also didn't have any clothes on, so I tried not to peek below.

"Crap, Erik's out there." I opened the car door and jumped out just in time to see Bob the Troll drop to his knees. He sent a mini earthquake down the road, and I fell forward, landing on my hands and knees.

Erik, the Jackal, was struggling with Bob. Thankfully, the soldiers had ceased fire to avoid harming Erik, and a few focused on dragging the injured female soldier away from the troll.

Erik bit into the troll's shoulder, taking out a large chunk. Bob punched him in the snout, and Erik fell back onto the pavement.

I sucked in a sharp breath, fingers itching to help but having no idea how.

The troll got back on his feet as soldiers began to fire again. Erik, the Jackal, looked slightly dazed, but he got back up right before the troll could stomp on him.

"Fall," I commanded in a scream, having no idea if my one-word order would even work. A burst of pain ripped through my head, causing me to dry heave. It felt like the worst migraine ever. But as quickly as it had come, it left

The troll stumbled but seemed to struggle against gravity to avoid hitting the pavement. Eventually, my power won, and the troll fell to his knees, bloodied, and battered.

At that moment, Jackal Erik took the opportunity to punch a hole through Bob's chest. Bob swiped a hand out at Erik and missed as Erik took a large leap in the air, almost soaring. Bob eventually fell sideways, causing another rumble on the ground.

Erik lowered his jackal hand, and I could see him holding what I could only determine was a bloody heart the size of a basketball.

"Damn," Charles called from behind me.

The scary thing that was Erik lifted the heart and...bit into it with his monstrous mouth. My stomach churned.

"Dude..." Charles cried out.

None of the soldiers spoke. Some were in shock, and others were unaffected. A large gray werewolf, a foot shorter than Erik's jackal, walked over on two feet to Erik, who handed him the bloody heart before turning and heading back to the car. The werewolf walked over to the injured werebear and fed the heart to the solider, who was lying on the side of the street with two human soldiers.

"What the fuck..." Charles murmured, sounding as freaked out as I was feeling.

I walked over to Erik's car, where he was now human and standing, a bit bruised and battered, in sweat pants and a T-shirt. He wiped his bloody mouth with a rag, and I bit my lower lip, trying to control my frenzied emotions. It was easy to forget that he was part animal. He ate things that would make me gag or even sick. He kissed me with the same mouth that he used to tear the flesh off of various things.

Do not freak out, Amina. He is still a man. A paranormal man, but you are paranormal too.

Don't make him feel bad, said Left side Amina

But he ate a heart! said, Right side Amina.

Yes, that is a new thing, said Left Side.

I know, right! said, Right side.

"You ate a heart!" I blurted out.

Erik observed me with cool eyes. "Yes," he said, voice neutral.

I paused for a beat. "Is that... Normal?"

He gave me a weary look. Then walked closer, stopping inches from me. My body screamed to step back, but I was a tough girl, and I held my ground. He wasn't the nightmarish Anubis-looking creature anymore. He was hot and moody Erik. He was good.

He reached out and put a hand on my chest above my left breast. "Your power is in your heart. That's the source. When a were eats a heart, we gain strength."

I looked in his eyes, understanding taking hold. "So, eating part of the troll heart gave you more power?"

He nodded and moved his hand away. It now made sense that the soldier werewolf fed the heart to the other were soldier to help her heal. I took the rag from him and wiped at the remaining blood he missed on his face. "I've never seen weres do that before."

He gave a quick shrug. "Some might not know about it."

I nodded slowly and gave him the rag back.

"You okay?"

I forced a smile on my face. I would be. "I'm still learning. Bear with me."

He brushed my face with the back of his hand in a slow, gentle caress, then abruptly stopped as if catching himself. "Damn it, woman," he muttered before turning to head into the truck. "I didn't think I'd care this much."

I frowned. "About what?"

He stopped before getting in the car. "About what you thought of me."

My heart did a silly skip-a-beat thing, and I smiled. "It's because I'm awesome," I called back.

Before he got in the truck, I swore I heard him say, "That you are."

~

When we got back to New Hagerstown, Charles and I were given a clean bill of health to fight another day. We had the full backing of the government to find and end David and his cohorts, now that there was proof that the prison existed.

In the meantime, my thoughts were on Silver Spring.

"We're not going," Charles said two evenings later.

I was in the kitchen, cooking for real. A roast chicken, collard greens, and mashed potatoes from the local grocery store, which was really an indoor farmer's market now. I was feeling quite domestic. We had invited our new gang over for a potluck dinner.

"Come again?" I said, stirring the mashed potatoes.

Charles reached into a top cabinet and pulled out a few wine glasses. "You said we'd leave when we freed the others. We haven't done that," Charles answered, walking to the dining area next to the kitchen.

"I think I said we'd stop at Hagerstown first because it was closer. We did. We got them to help. All we can do now is try to find the others, which the government is doing."

"Right, so why would we leave before then? We can keep trying the locator spells or something."

I stopped stirring and put the lid over the pot, turning off the stove. "Charles, we can go to Silver Spring and then come back. We aren't giving up."

The doorbell rang then, and Charles went to answer it as I checked on the chicken in the oven. I was feeling unsettled. I knew Charles hadn't wanted to go to Silver Spring in the first place, but we had no idea how long it could take to help the others. I had to get at least one thing resolved.

"Hey, Mina," Felix greeted me. "I brought homemade lasagna." He placed two covered containers on the round kitchen table behind me.

"No, you didn't." I smiled at him, hands on my hips.

"And I baked a chocolate cake. Boom!" He threw his hands in the air.

"Aw, shucks. Felix trying to make me gain weight in the supernatural apocalypse." I laughed, moving my neck around.

"I made salad," Faith announced, coming into the small kitchen.

"Aww snap, Faith, trying to make me lose weight in the supernatural apocalypse."

Faith laughed and put her large bowl of rabbit food next to the real people food. "I figure we should have a few more vegetables on the plate tonight."

Lisa called from the dining room. "I brought wine!"

"I brought whiskey," Erik added, also in the dining room

"I brought my love and affection!" Charles cracked.

"I can't eat that," Felix muttered with a frown.

"The food's ready. So, this is buffet style, eat where you like! Happy Friday, we're alive!" I exclaimed, feeling, for the moment, genuinely content.

Faith headed out of the kitchen. "Get me to the liquor."

I smiled. I was surrounded by people I'd only known for two weeks, but we were already like old friends. I couldn't explain the chemistry we seemed to have with each other. Sure, hard times could make people closer, but we all knew there was more to it. We were connected by more than shared dreams of Silver Spring, and I had hopes that by going to that town, we could find out about those ties.

"Felix and Lisa, can you both help me convince Charles to head to Silver Spring now?" I asked, peeking out of the kitchen.

Lisa, grabbing a plate off of the glass dining room table, turned to Charles. "Why don't you want to go?" she asked.

"What if we go, and the place is nothing but trouble? Now we have a new issue to resolve taking us away from our main goal, which is to free our friends. I say we resolve one thing first before going to another," Charles answered, giving a slight shrug.

"But what if Silver Spring can help you find your friends? I mean, it's a town full of supernaturals," Felix pondered, walking in the kitchen with a plate.

"Yeah, Phillip found me and helped me escape. Maybe he can do the same for one of our friends who is still captured," I offered, taking the chicken out of the oven with some mittens I found in the nearby drawer.

"That's a lot of guessing. We know we have a good thing here. And this town could use our help," Erik stated.

I placed the chicken on the stovetop and looked over at Erik with twisted lips. I'd foolishly thought he'd have my back. He looked at me and shrugged, and I narrowed my eyes. We hadn't had any alone time since our make-out session a couple of days ago, and I was beginning to think it was a one-time deal.

"Of course, the Silver Spring town could have helpful information," Erik added. He gave me an arrogant wink as he headed to the dining room, and I pursed my lips and looked away, secretly smiling.

"What about just some of us go," Lisa began. Having filled her plate, she headed out of the kitchen. "It's only two hours away."

Erik entered the kitchen again. Walking past me, he reached out, and his hand grazed the back of mine, which was hanging down at my side. I was still annoyed with him, but the contact gave me instant butterflies.

"A lot can happen in a two-hour drive. And then, what

happens if the place is a setup? We should all stick together," He surmised.

"Well, six of us won't stop that," I said, giving him a tight smile.

He looked over at me. "We're like family now, and we should remain as one." He smiled in return, and it was like sunshine yet again. Secretly. I believed he smiled only for me.

Wait, was he trying to be charming?

I turned away from him and caught Faith's smirking face. I lowered my head. It seemed our secret flirting wasn't so secret.

"I agree with Erik that we should stick together. But we should also head over to Silver Spring," Faith began. "Witches here are trying to use magic spells to locate the prison, but so far, no luck. Even Lisa couldn't help. You either, Amina. So, us taking a quick visit to Silver Spring to see what's going on won't hurt."

"I think that sounds smart," Felix said. "We need to go. They said we have to go now."

Lisa, plate annoyingly filled to the brim for such a tiny girl, turned to Felix and frowned. "Who's 'they?'" she asked.

Felix smiled and tapped his head. "Voices in my head."

We all stopped what we were doing and looked at him.

"Nine years ago, I would have been worried about your mental stability," Lisa began.

"I'm still worried," Erik muttered beside me.

"But now, there actually could be people telepathically communicating with you," Lisa went on.

"Doesn't mean they're good people," Erik surmised.

"We're going. End of story. Either you come with us, or you stay here," Lisa announced before exiting the kitchen.

"I'm with her," I stated. "We have four yeses, one no and one maybe. Yes wins! Let's go."

CHAPTER 15

*T*hree days later, we were heading south to Silver Spring.

"So, where exactly do we head once we get off the highway?" Erik asked, driving a gray sedan, the Hagerstown community let us have.

I sat in the front passenger seat and gazed out of the window as we exited 495 into downtown Silver Spring, following the SUV Charles was driving.

"Felix will know," Faith stated from the back seat.

There were no signs welcoming us to the town. We simply drove straight down Colesville road, but it wasn't long before we saw a tall steel wall a few blocks before Georgia avenue.

"Well, this is new," Faith commented. "What is it, like, twenty feet tall? More?"

Charles made a left down a side street, and Erik followed, circling the circumference of the great wall. It was maybe six miles around, with no visible door or opening and no sign.

"Sooo, I'm going to take a gander and guess this is the Silver Spring town," I said.

"How did they build this?" Erik wondered.

"This is a magic wall, for sure," Faith replied.

Charles stopped his car back to where we first started. Erik followed suit.

I looked around. The street in front of the wall was clear. On one side of the street was an abandoned office building. On the other side, a vacant restaurant. The rest of our surroundings was filled with weeds, tall grass, trees, and a few more side streets.

"Should we honk...or something?" I asked.

"I feel like we're visiting the Wizard of Oz, this is so exciting," Faith said in a sing-song voice.

I shook my head then stopped as, surely by magic, an outline of a door appeared in the smooth, steel wall in front of us. "Whoa," I whispered.

We waited, expecting the door to open and perhaps a man in a green uniform to appear, but nothing happened.

"Do we...knock?" I asked.

Felix and I seemed to have the same thinking because he got out of the car, Charles following, and headed to the door.

Erik leaned over me, opened the glove compartment, and reached in. He pulled out a handgun I didn't realize was in there.

"What are you doing with that?" I questioned.

"Insurance," Erik answered, taking the safety off the gun. He then looked up at the top of the steel wall through the front window. "I don't see any sharpshooters, but it doesn't mean they aren't there. If anything goes down, Charles is going to cover Felix. His magic will better protect them."

"So, you think," Faith said from the back, but I heard her cock a gun behind me, and I turned around to face her.

"Lisa is on alert. If she felt dark magic from the wall, she was supposed to have Charles drive us away and regroup. The fact that we didn't have to leave might be a good sign," Erik added, looking around.

"Hmmm." I turned to him. "Was I not invited to this

strategy meeting? Because I'm sitting here confused," I said with a frown.

Erik glanced over at me, eyes gentle. "I told everyone but you and Felix. Felix was to lead us in, so he had to come pure of thought just in case these people had telekinetic abilities and felt things were a setup. Same with you."

"And not Lisa?"

He turned away. "She is good at sensing magic, even when it's hidden."

If my blood could boil with me living through it, I was sure it would. He had my brother keep a secret from me. If there was anything I had left, it was my brother, and if Charles was willing to keep secrets from me, even if it seemed small to him, then what did I have?

I pursed my lips and turned to look out of the window.

"I'm sorry. I thought I was doing what was right," Erik stated.

I didn't answer.

"Oh, forgive him, woman," Faith piped up from the back. "There are worse things to fight about with your boyfriend."

I opened my mouth to correct her of the fact that Erik and I were far from a couple when the door in the steel wall opened.

Out stepped an unarmed man. He looked late 40-ish, with average height and his dirty blond hair in a low ponytail. I was disappointed there was no green outfit like in Emerald City.

We watched as he, Felix, and Charles exchanged words.

"What is he saying?" I asked Erik. I knew since he was a were he could hear them, even from thirty feet away.

"Felix's telling him we're travelers looking for a community that can help us save our friends. The truth. Basically. The guard, or whoever he is, wants to know how we heard of their community. Felix said he saw it in a dream. He's not going to tell him that you and Lisa also had dre—" He stopped suddenly.

"What's wrong?"

"He asked for you."

"The guard?" Faith questioned.

Erik frowned, eyebrows gathered in concern. "Yeah. He asked if Amina Langston was with him."

I looked on as Felix turned towards us and nodded before speaking to the guard again.

"What's he saying now?" I asked.

"Felix told him you were with us. The guard wants to see you."

"Okay." I reached for the door but Erik grabbed my arm. He gave me a concerned look, but then let go without uttering a word. I opened the door and got out of the car, Erik did as well. I looked over to the guard who was taking out a piece of white, letter-sized paper. He looked down at it and then up at me. I waved. He gave me a curt nod, then said something to Felix and Charles.

"What's he saying now?" I asked Erik.

"He said that we can all come in. We're to follow him in our cars. If we veer off, they will shoot and kill us."

"Well, that does not make me feel welcomed," Faith muttered from the passenger window.

We all got back in our cars, and Charles and Erik drove at no more than ten miles an hour, which was enough to give me a tour of the town as we entered through a larger entryway that slid open around the smaller door space.

I don't know what I was expecting, but all I saw was a town very similar to Hagerstown. There were people shopping in stores, kids playing in a playground, joggers running on the sidewalks, citizens sitting outside, dining at a couple of the town restaurants. There was a movie theater, a gym, a few high-rise apartments, a candy and ice cream shop, a bar. And those were just the things we passed.

"Wonder how many people live here. They can't have people filling all of these apartments," Faith wondered. "Size-wise, it's bigger than Hagerstown, and Lisa mentioned they have, what, two thousand people?"

"Could be using some of these apartments as something else. Hospital, school," I guessed.

The guard's car stopped in front of a high-rise apartment a quarter of a mile away from what I assumed was the center of the town. Charles pulled up behind the sedan on the right side of the street, and Erik followed suit. He put his gun, which had been resting in the cup holder with the safety on, in the back band of his jeans.

"Do we really need that?" I asked.

He looked over at me with steely eyes. "Ask me that again when this meet and greet is all over."

I shook my head and got out of the car.

I walked over to Charles. "I'm going to fight you when this is all over, you know that, right?" I whispered.

He looked over at me, eyes wide. "What did I do?" he asked.

"You didn't tell me about Erik's plan. Family first, remember?" I replied, crossing my arms.

"You!" Shouted the ponytail guard. He was pointing at me. "Amina?" he asked, he had a thick West Virginian accent.

"Yes," I answered.

"Come with me. He wants to see only you first."

"She's not going anywhere alone," Erik said, stepping forward. Another guard that I hadn't noticed before stepped from the other side of another car.

"Who is this *he* you're talking about?" Faith asked, behind me.

"Our leader," the guard stated.

"Can someone come with me and just stand outside of the door of wherever you're taking me?" I asked. "We don't plan to cause any harm. It's only six of us. But as you can imagine, since we're outnumbered, we're a little apprehensive."

The guard gave me dead eyes, head tilted to the side. He then straightened up. "Sure, bring your brother," he replied.

"How'd he know I was your brother?" Charles whispered.

I shrugged and began to move towards the stairs leading inside the building, but Erik stopped me and grabbed my left wrist. I turned and looked at him with quizzical eyes.

He frowned. "I don't like this. How do they know all of this stuff about you?"

I gave him what I hoped was a reassuring smile. "There's probably a telepath around. It's going to be okay. Charles and I made it this far together, we'll be okay in there." I moved up on my toes and gave him a tight hug because, well, I didn't honestly know that it would be okay. This world was just too unsettled for that. Yet, somehow, touching him seemed to bring a calm over me.

His arms wrapped around me tightly. "If you're in there too long, I'm going to knock down every door until I get to you."

I smiled again. "Well, then I better not take too long." I wasn't sure what Erik and I were to each other, but whatever it was, it felt nice to be cared about like this. I moved away from him reluctantly.

"Lisa, do you need a hug to reassure you too?" Charles asked, and the fairy laughed and walked over to him for an embrace.

We then both headed into the building to see the wizard.

"No one gave me a hug," I heard Felix say as we walked through the doors.

Once inside, we were greeted by two guards at the door and security behind the apartment concierge dark oak desk. I only assumed they were guards and security because they were all wearing black. I couldn't imagine that there was much leisure time or importance to make uniforms. I looked up and saw security cameras near the corners of the ceiling that looked very much on.

The space looked modern, with a sparkling clean, light-tiled floor, colorful artwork on the dark gray painted walls, and beige fabric lounge seating.

We followed our hippie guard into the elevator and up to the twenty-fifth floor, one level below the penthouse. We got off and, wouldn't you know it, more guards were around the floor. I had to assume there were a lot of people in the town if the leader could afford to use so much personnel for just watching his building.

We exited to the right of the elevator and walked to the end of the hallway. Our guard guide stopped and turned to us. "You," he said, looking at Charles, "You can sit in our waiting area." He pointed to an apartment across from us with the door propped open.

Charles looked to me, and I nodded before he walked into the apartment.

The guide looked at me. "Knock on the door. I'll be out here," he instructed.

And so, I knocked. A millisecond later, the door opened, although no one stood behind it. I turned and looked at the guard, who was whispering to a female guard already posted outside of the door to the waiting area. They stopped talking and looked me.

"Well, go on in," said ponytail guard.

I sighed and stepped through the doorway, jumping when the door closed quickly behind me.

I walked farther in, past an open walk-in kitchen to my right, and a closet on my left. I entered a great room that looked like an interior design show had taken over. There were dark wood floors, pale-blue walls, a black suede couch covered in tons of pillows, a dark wood and leather dinette set, and gold-framed art on the walls. But that wasn't what caught my attention.

I looked past the living area to the balcony, which ran the length of the room. A man stood on the balcony. There was a small, circular patio set to his right. He rested his hands on the railing, back to me. He was dressed in tailored black slacks, and a pale-blue collared shirt was tucked in his pants. He was around six feet and of average build, although I could see definition in his arms under the fabric of his shirt. His wavy black hair was cut into a low fade, and his skin was the color of caramel. Although I couldn't see his face, I already knew who he was.

I quickly walked through the room and slid open the balcony doors. "Phillip?" I asked, sliding the doors closed behind me. My heart thudded loudly in my ears, and my nerves rattled, threatening to make my knees give out.

The man turned around, and I caught my breath, frozen. It *was* him.

"Amina," He whispered. His honey-colored eyes seemed to glow, and he grinned a toothy smile. Phillip walked over to me, shaking his head. He then wrapped his arms around me in a tight embrace, and it seemed we stood like that for minutes. We didn't say a word.

Finally, he stood back and looked at me from arm's length, his eyes intense. I had never had a man look at me that way. Like I was the best thing he'd ever seen. It was amazing and scary at the same time. "Damn, you're beautiful," he whispered.

"Thank you. You too!" I placed my hands on my cheeks. "I can't believe it's you. I didn't know if it was really going to happen," I said. "There are so many things I want to ask you."

"And I want to talk to you too, but if I don't do this first, I won't be any good," he said in a quiet tone before leaning in and kissing me.

It was soft at first, then deep. He kissed me slowly as if he had all the time in the world. I dropped my hands, and he gently touched the sides of my face and pressed his lips harder on mine. My stomach did backflips. He explored my mouth with his tongue and flicked my upper lip, sending mini-explosions through me. He moved a hand to the small of my back, and I was thankful for that support because I was feeling unsteady.

I pressed further into him and wrapped my arms around his neck, wanting more as he moved me to the patio glass door. My back now against the cool glass, I let out a whimpering moan, tasting more of him. His lips were so soft and warm. He moved his hand under my shirt, his soft fingers brushing my skin. I shivered in response.

How he made me feel like this was beyond me. It was primal. His lips alone stirred things low in me. I wanted to rip our clothes off and press us closer together.

I think I would have, except I did have a tiny bit of my faculties left, and having sex on a balcony in bright daylight with a virtual stranger wasn't my thing. I was no exhibitionist. More importantly, although lust was running the show, my heart was not. I thought of Erik. There was something between us, and I wasn't ready to chuck it all, just because Phillip had been helpful to me. There were other ways to show my gratitude.

I cursed my indecisive hormones. What was going on with me? I didn't behave this way.

I moved sideways, away from Phillip, hands up in surrender, and eyes wide.

He looked at me with similar shock, his hands still out, as if holding me in an invisible embrace.

We stayed like that, in our confused stand-off, for several seconds. I was pretty sure by now that he was feeling as out of sorts as I was. Neither of us could have expected to have that kind of reaction to just touching each other for the first time. It was more than instant attraction and lust. There was a connection that seemed to defy logic. Had we known each other in the Pre-world and simply forgotten? Like Felix? Did

I have some memory blocks since becoming something new? It was certainly possible.

"What was that?" Phillip finally asked, lowering his hands. He sounded a bit breathless, and I understood because my heart was still beating loudly in my ears. "I feel like I've known you for years. But I don't remember you from before. Just from our dreams."

I scrunched my face in thought. "Perhaps we've been communicating in our dreams longer than we think, and subconsciously, we just reacted off of that?" I offered.

He nodded, his eyes slightly glazed. I imagined mine weren't that different. "I'd buy that. Maybe we had a whole relationship in our dreams." He chuckled.

"That would be freaky."

He gave me a lopsided smile that I recalled seeing in my dreams. "We might have a lot to make up for in real life, then." He stepped closer to me.

I backed up. "I don't think that would be very productive. I have friends waiting outside, and my brother is across the hall." Plus, I didn't want to kiss him again. I couldn't. He confused me. There was a man outside professing to knock down doors to get to me who gave me butterflies. I couldn't forget or ignore that.

Phillip paused and nodded. "Would you like to sit? Anything to drink or eat?" He offered.

"Let's sit out here. And nothing now, thanks." I walked over to the table and sat down.

Phillip sat across from me. He reached out a hand, palm up, on the table. "Now that you're here, I don't want to let you go."

I looked at his hand, debating whether I could trust myself to touch him.

"I won't bite," he stated.

I looked up to his face, and he gave me soft, kind eyes. I

put my hand in his. "So, you run this town? Why didn't you ever tell me that before?"

"I didn't even think to mention it. It only recently happened. Our last leader died. Heart attack."

"I'm sorry to hear that. So, is that why I hadn't heard from you in a while? Busy?"

He frowned. "Uh, yeah. I'm sorry to have left you hanging. Is everything okay?"

"Yeah, sort of. First, I want to thank you again for helping me escape. And then supporting me in that pharmacy. I don't know why I keep doubting myself."

"No need."

"My brother and I made friends."

He raised an eyebrow. "And they all decided to follow you here?"

"Something like that. We were in a government town who agreed to accompany us back to the prison to free the others. But the prison moved."

"So, you can't find them. Maybe I can help."

"I don't want to put you out. I mean, you've done so much already. But if there is anything I can do to repay you for setting me free, I will."

"It's not a problem. I want to help you find the others. I only ask that you consider staying here. Are all your friends paranormals?"

I nodded. "Yeah."

"That's great. Part of what makes this town so successful is that we all have gifts."

"You don't want to be part of the government?"

He smiled. "We're doing pretty well here."

"I see."

"Look, why don't you and your friends relax, get freshened up, and meet me and some others for dinner? You can see how we live here."

I nodded. "I look forward to it."

The ponytail guard, who I learned was named Mitch, led us to rooms in another apartment about a quarter of a mile from Phillip's apartment building. We got three apartments on the same floor to relax in and were informed that if we wanted to explore to call a specific number, they gave us, and someone would come to escort us around.

We all crowded into Charles and my apartment, gathering around the living room to regroup. We were surrounded by beige walls and carpets and deep-brown furniture. The barebones apartment was the total opposite of Phillip's fully-decorated place.

"What are we doing here?" Erik asked, pacing the room. "If your friend says he can help us, then we should get right on it."

"Well, he's trying a locater spell, but those things aren't always automatic. They can take time. I gave him a shirt I found in the prison, but it's still work. He says he's putting his best people on it. Until then, there isn't anything I can do but help with location," I explained, sitting on the arm of the couch.

"We can head back to Hagerstown. We don't have to stick around here to do this," Charles stated, looking out of the balcony sliding doors.

"I still need to meet Annie Mae," Lisa said. "And this town seems cool, I'd like to explore it."

"I'd like to meet some of the people I dreamed of as well," Felix concurred. "We can at least stay one night. Maybe we'll find out that we want to stay longer."

"Well, you guys may want to stay here, but I have a good thing going back in Hagerstown," Faith said, crossing her arms.

"You're a bartender," Felix stated, scrunching up his face.

167

Faith cut her eyes at him. "Yes, so? I like doing that. The only thing good about going to a new town is seeing new fa —" Her eyes widened. "—ces. New paranormal faces with lots of energy to share. You know, maybe we *can* stay here for a while."

"Please don't go around draining the locals," Felix implored, eyes filled with concern.

Faith gave a slight shrug. "They'll bounce back. They're all paranormal."

"When we were driving through the town, some of it didn't smell right," Erik stated, face in a grimace. "Like a musky locker room. Means there are some deceptive people here. Possible evil magic too."

"Maybe we can help root that out for Phillip," I stated. "We have to do something to pay him back. Well, maybe you guys don't, but Charles and I do."

"We're all in this together," Lisa replied.

"She's right," Felix said cheerfully. "If this guy helps free your people, then we gotta find some way to pay him back, even if it means staying and helping the town for a while. What else do we have to do?"

CHAPTER 16

*H*er name was Grace Sarin. She was about 5'7, with a toned and curvy build. She had long, waist-length, wavy, brown hair and dark-brown, almost-black eyes. Grace was a deep tan color, highlighting her East Indian descent. She was beautiful, and her smile seemed genuine and inviting. In another life, she could have been a Miss Universe pageant contestant. I was envious, but I liked her from the moment I saw her. She seemed so comfortable as if she didn't have a care in the world.

She wore a bright-yellow sundress under a jean jacket. I rarely got an opportunity to dress so carefree. I was always ready to run. It made me wonder if this town had offered so much security that people could really relax.

"You called for a tour?" she said in a deep voice, almost singing it. I felt like a bird should have flown down and perched on her finger. She was a Disney princess and was smiling so hard I could barely see her irises.

Faith, who had opened the door for her, turned and looked back at us with wide, confused eyes. "Are you part of the welcome committee?" She asked, turning back to Grace, a smirk on her face.

"I guess you could call me that." Grace walked into the apartment towards the living room. "This everybody?"

Faith closed the door behind her and headed back to us. "Yeah, the gang's all here."

Felix stood up as soon as he saw her. "Grace," he stated.

The woman tilted her head and gave Felix a curious smile. "How do you know my name?"

He walked towards her. "You're the woman of my dreams."

Grace chuckled. "Well, that's always fun to hear."

Lisa slapped her forehead.

Faith crossed her arms and chuckled. "I don't think he meant it quite like that, sweetheart," she stated.

Felix's eyes widened in confusion. "I saw you and a lot of people from this town in my dreams. That's what led me here."

Grace nodded slowly, a slight look of confusion on her face. She looked around at everyone else. "So, what brings the rest of you beautiful people here?"

"We heard of the town and wanted to be a part of it," Erik stated, nonchalantly, hands in his pockets.

Grace widened her eyes. "We don't advertise. Except for our steel surrounding."

"How many people do you have here?"

Grace's smile widened if that were possible, and she tsked. "How 'bout you tell me some truths, and I'll give you some answers." Hmm, the girl was smarter than she looked.

"Phillip and I dreamed of each other. Specifically, we were able to communicate through dreams and telepathy, and that's how I found this place," I said.

She squinted her eyes at me, smile still in place. "And how does sweetie pie over there know my name?" She titled her head towards Felix, hands on her hips.

"She thinks I'm cute," Felix whispered to Charles, who was standing beside him.

"I didn't hear her say that," Charles whispered back.

"He has a gift," I answered.

"All of you have gifts, right? What are they?"

"Answer our question first," Erik demanded.

She looked to him, the smile never leaving. "Over one thousand gifted humans here."

"How large is this town, size-wise?"

"Around six square miles. And we've been around for a little over four years. We get bigger over time. There, I gave you two for the price of one." She giggled. "Your turn now. Answer my question," she sang.

"We all have powers. I'm a werejackal. Charles is a tech mage. Amina is a witch. Faith is a succubus. Lisa is a fairy, and Felix...well, we don't know what he is, but he has powers."

I eyed Erik curiously. I hadn't expected him to be so forthcoming. Looks like Snow White was getting Grumpy to follow her. He seemed just as surprised by his sharing because he lowered his head and shook it, eyes confused.

"You won't tell anyone what Lisa is, will you?" I asked Grace.

She gave me a knowing smile. "Of course not. This is a town full of paranormals, but Fae are non-existent. I can imagine why you would want to keep it quiet, and I'll be mum until I can't be."

I lifted an eyebrow. "Okay, I guess we'll have to accept that."

"How'd you get me to talk?" Erik asked, avoiding her eyes.

Grace looked to him. "I'm special. What's your next question?"

He looked like he wanted to argue, but he narrowed his eyes and continued on. "How did your former leader die?" Erik asked.

I turned to Erik. "He had a heart attack. I told you that," I stated. Erik didn't look at me.

"Who told you that?" Grace asked me, a look of concern on her face.

I looked to her. "Phillip."

She cocked an eyebrow and looked away. "Well, that's what happened then."

This time, I narrowed my eyes at her. "That doesn't sound like a reassuring answer."

She looked back at me with smiling eyes. "Why would Phillip lie to you? He seems to like you all, and we don't get many visitors." She clapped her hands excitedly. "So, what are you all interested in seeing?"

She was hiding something which made me uneasy. However, I promised Charles I wouldn't get off track of our first mission, which was to find the others, so I would have to put that mystery on pause. I looked over at Erik who was staring at me. I gave him a questioning look, and he gave me a quick shake of the head and turned away. Well, that wasn't good.

~

*T*urns out, Grace was actually a good tour guide. In our exploration of the small town, we discovered there was also a duckpin alley, which made Felix randomly excited, and a burlesque club run by a vampire group, which made Faith unsurprisingly excited.

Grace explained that she was one of the first to become a part of the town and that they only recently completed building the steel wall with a bit of magic and actual construction. They had a plan in place regarding how to expand as well and move the wall back as they grew in numbers. The town was always looking for more people, but they were set on it being a fully paranormal town. And the steel wall was an extra precaution against monsters and other threats if the ward didn't hold.

The town started as a refuge for those with gifts who were hunted by humans, scared of them or humans imprisoning them. For this reason, she had no doubt that Phillip was honest about helping us free the others. Not that I had any question of that.

"We also have a library, a police station, and a building we use as a hospital, which is headed by the best medicine mage you will ever meet," Grace added as we continued our tour of the town on foot.

"What's your job here?" Erik asked, standing beside her.

"You mean besides tour guide? I run the library and teach. Someone's subbing for me right now. Our school is headed by Ms. Annie Mae. She's like the town mother of everyone," Grace explained.

Lisa perked up. "Annie Mae? Can we meet her?"

"Taking you to her now," Grace said. "You'll love her. She makes the best desserts. I'm trying to learn her recipes."

"Oh, I like the sound of that," Felix stated, patting his stomach.

Annie Mae Jenkins lived on the first floor of garden-style apartments overlooking a beautiful, flower-and-vegetable-garden-filled courtyard. When we arrived, she was sitting in the courtyard at a large picnic table with two pitchers of what I assumed was fresh lemonade, some glasses, plates, utensils, and a large carrot cake and apple pie. I loved her already.

She was whispering something to a small bluebird perched on her index finger. Okay, clearly, she was the real Disney princess here.

Annie Mae was short with cocoa-colored skin and tightly curled, short, black hair. She wore a red, brightly-printed maxi wrap dress and a chunky yellow necklace. She was in good shape for a woman who appeared to be in her mid-50s, although something told me she was ten years older than that. She looked over at us, at me, I thought and smiled. I smiled back without thinking.

"I'll catch you all later. You have my number," Grace stated and backed away through the gates of the courtyard.

I was still amazed they had a local phone system.

We moved through the entrance of the courtyard in awe of Annie Mae and the surroundings. The courtyard consisted of a black stone walkway, mini vegetable gardens, trees, some fruit-bearing, and flowers. Seating areas were scattered about, and there was a mini fountain filled with koi fish in the middle of the space. Surrounding the courtyard were white brick and mortar apartments going up three levels. I swear I heard soothing '40s era jazz coming through some unseen speakers.

A sense of calm fell over me that I had only felt when visiting a spa before the world went to crap. The smell of flowers and pie filled my nostrils, and I felt like skipping over to her.

"Don't just stand there, y'all, come on over," Annie Mae called, watching the bird fly away.

"How'd she know we were coming?" Erik asked as we headed over.

"That's Annie Mae, and she's a seer or psychic," Lisa answered. "She told me in a dream."

"I hope you all have a sweet tooth. I made this, all from scratch, no magic," Annie Mae added. "As easy as it can be, nothing beats old-fashioned cooking."

"You telling me," Felix said, eyeing the spread.

"Well, eat up, honey. I didn't bake this just for it to be seen, chile'," she said, getting up from her chair. "Where's my girl Lisa?"

Lisa, who was behind us all called out. "I'm here!" She quickly walked over to Annie Mae, and they embraced in a tight hug. I felt a twinge of jealousy. We'd all lost mothers, and seeing what appeared to be that relationship in front of us did affect me a bit.

Annie Mae let go of Lisa, who looked a little dejected. "This is a safe space for you all. We can talk freely here."

"We couldn't before?" Erik asked arms crossed again.

Annie Mae shrugged. "In a town full of magic, you never know who is listening to your conversation. Lot of nosey people around. But you can talk here." She clapped her hands together. "I am just so happy to finally see you all."

"Were you expecting us?" Erik questioned, face still in a suspicious scowl. Clearly, he was not buying the good vibrations Annie Mae was selling us.

The older woman smiled at him. "Yes, I was, Erik." She walked over to grumpy bear, reached up, and patted his shoulder.

"Can you be a little nicer, Erik?" I whispered to him.

"I don't mind the questions. You are a born leader, Erik. I can tell. You don't want to be anymore, I know, but you can't help it. It's who you are. You won't be happy with life if you don't stand up. And you have a lot of life left. I am looking forward to watching you make this world better."

Erik softened his face, but he did not say a word. Annie Mae patted his shoulder again.

I smiled and walked over to cut a piece of cake—it was calling me—as Annie Mae moved back to Lisa.

"Lisa, doll. We've talked before, but you know I think the world of you. You are not the lost child you think you are. Your world is about to become much larger. Filled with friends, love, and a strength you've been afraid to find. You are more than what you were."

Lisa gave her a thousand-watt smile.

Annie Mae next moved on to Faith and grabbed her hands. "Faith. You are more than meets the eye. You embody what our future will become in so many ways. Don't be afraid to show all that you are." Annie Mae looked down at Faith's hands and arms. "Love the tattoos."

None of us knew what Annie Mae was talking about, but the look on Faith's face—enlightenment—showed that she did.

Judging by the reactions so far, it was like Annie Mae was more than a seer. It was like she was a blanket of peace. I couldn't wait until she made it over to me. I sat down, ate my cake, and continued to watch the show as Annie Mae walked over to Charles.

"Charles. Aren't you a ball of fun? Don't you ever lose that spirit. I know you've been through heartache, and I wish I could tell you it's all good times from here. But what makes you a survivor is your resolve to be who you always were, even when the world around you isn't. It's admirable, and it's why you are so lovable. No matter what happens to you, don't ever change who you are at your core." Annie Mae gave him a light pinch of the cheeks, and Charles gave her a self-appreciating smile before she moved on to Felix.

Felix stood up and put his pie filled plate down. "Hello, ma'am," he greeted her. "Can I give you a hug?"

Annie Mae laughed. "I was hoping you would." Felix quickly wrapped her in a bear hug, and she chuckled in delight. "You are wiser than people give you credit for. You have heart and intelligence," Annie began, pulling away from Felix. "When these people around you forget about why we are all here still, why God or whatever great power you all believe in has us still living, you remind them. You are the glue."

"Yes, ma'am."

"I can't tell you what you really want to know. What you are, at least not yet, but the truth will come. The things you've lost will return. And with that realization, you must remain the good person you are now. Don't let the truth make you hide from who you are. Embrace it and be better for it." She patted his shoulder.

Annie Mae moved on to me, and I jumped up. She opened her arms and gave me a hug just like I'd hoped she would. My eyes started to water, and again, it made me miss my own mother something fierce. I was going to hold in the tears now, but tonight I'd have a full-on, ugly cry for sure.

"Amina, you have so much work to do." She pulled away and laid her hands on my shoulders. "I hate telling you that because it doesn't sound all warm and fuzzy. But you're a smart woman, and you're used to hard work. And if you remain strong, I really believe that things will work out. You felt alone before, but now you never will be. This new world was made for you. You are going to shine like you never thought you could before. You really are a blessing."

"Wow," I whispered. My heart somehow felt ten times fuller. I wasn't scared by her words. I was going to make myself strong enough to live up to them.

"That was a good one," I heard Felix murmur.

Annie Mae looked at the group of us. "I bet you're wondering what that was about. You must know by now that you were not brought together by coincidence. The six of you are connected by spirit and magic, and it is through you that this world will be able to survive. If you stay strong and united. It sounds easy now, but it won't be. I can't tell you why you were chosen. I honestly don't know. But the stronger you become individually, the more powerful you will become as a unit. You will be able to do things no one else can."

Annie Mae turned to me. "Your ability to dream of Phillip was a showcase of that power."

"Is he part of this too?" I asked.

She tilted her head from side to side. "To a degree. You and Phillip have dreamed of each other for at least a year. He started coming to me often, and he would tell me about a dream he had of you. Each time he never remembered that he had already dreamed of you before; only I knew. Sometimes people come to me to help interpret their dreams. I can even sometimes enter dreams as I did with Lisa. But you, Amina, you seemed to have a profound effect on him. Why he couldn't remember you from his dreams, I didn't understand."

"What kind of dreams?" Charles asked. I gave him a side-eye, which he annoyingly avoided.

I prayed to God Annie Mae wouldn't spill my secrets.

Annie Mae looked to him. "Now that, my dear, is confidential. Although," Annie Mae looked to me. "Maybe we can talk some time about the dreams."

"Then what about the six of us? You said it's not a coincidence we all met?" Erik asked, arms crossed.

Mae looked to him and nodded. "Yes, there is a purpose. I've seen all of you in visions, engaged in battles. You were fighting something very dreadful, but I have yet to see the face of your enemies. I just know that they aren't anything good for humanity. I believe you six were sent here from God to stop whatever is to come. Sadly, I cannot tell you more. My visions aren't always so specific. But if I come to know more, I will share it with you." She suddenly inhaled and clapped her hands together again. "Now eat up, sweeties. I put my foot in this cake."

Evidently, she was done talking about this subject. And here I thought she was comforting.

CHAPTER 17

$\mathcal{P}$hillip's little dinner turned out to be bigger than we expected. There were maybe thirty people in the building. He closed down one of the restaurants, a dark and sexy Japanese restaurant and lounge named Tezuka in its former life. The guests already present were dressed like they were going out to be seen at the club. There was a mix of leather pants, tailored suits, short dresses, and high heels.

My group was a mixture of jeans, cargo pants, tennis, and flat boots. When we packed to go on this little trip, fun wasn't in our mindset. I had on a white T-shirt, jeans with "fashionable" holes in them, and brown hiking boots. I hadn't worn heels in years, which was quite unlike my life before. I lived in dresses and pumps and happy hours then.

We slowly entered the space like a tentative posse ready to fight anyone about to pounce. The inside of the restaurant held black leather couches and chairs in one area, and sleek, black dining furniture in a separate area. Rap music from the early 1990s blared from the speakers. The walls were a deep gray, with black stenciled flowers on top under bright red lighting around the perimeter. Behind the bar was a gigantic fish tank against the wall. With actual fish! Clearly, this community was doing well because between those fish and the ones in the courtyard pond at Annie Mae's, I could have had a fish fry.

"Welcome!" Phillip called with open arms, standing at the bar near the other guests. He was dressed in jeans, a fitted, dark-gray vest over a blue button-down shirt and gray, tailored blazer. He looked amazingly, dapper.

A bartender was busy mixing cocktails, and I looked to my left at the dining space set for a large party. Appetizers were spread out in the center of many of the circular tables, which had been pushed together. This was a real shindig.

"I'm ready for a drink," Charles said as we headed to the bar.

Lisa leaned into me. "I'm so livid right now. We look like we're ready to go hiking in the woods, and they look ready for a photoshoot. I can glamour the six of us and make us look just as hot," she muttered.

I shrugged. "We're fine. We aren't here to impress," I replied.

"But aren't we, though?"

From the corner of the bar and lounge area to my right, I spotted Grace sitting on a couch. She gave me a wave with an ear to ear grin. I waved back and returned her smile.

"Amina, what do you want to drink? Anything at all," Phillip asked. He leaned in and hugged me, kissing me on the cheek. A tinge of welcomed electricity passed between us, and I pulled away quickly. I was pretty sure I wouldn't go all crazy on him again but I didn't trust myself that much anymore.

"I'll have an Old Fashioned if you have the fixings," I replied. I didn't expect him too. Nowadays, access to alcohol was pretty much whoever scored liquor in their scavenging or bartering. Some people made liquor, wine, and beer, but they were few and harder to encounter.

Phillip cocked an eyebrow. "My kind of woman." He

turned slightly to the bartender, a guy with orange, spiky hair. "Old Fashioned for the lady and take care of her friends as well."

I supposed I wasn't surprised he was able to accommodate me. Although the rest of the places I'd been were relegated to simple alcoholic drinks, this town seemed to be prosperous. In a place full of paranormals, I was sure there would be people magically mixing up alcoholic concoctions.

I looked around for the others. Felix was sitting on the couch next to Grace, and Charles and Faith were talking to some other faces in the crowd. Erik was at the other end of the bar, talking to a tall black man appearing to be in his early 30s with a shaved head and deep-brown complexion.

I looked back to Phillip and his people. It was like he was surrounded by an entourage. A woman came up to Phillip, her hand possessively on his arm. She was fair, with almost porcelain white skin, her hair was whitish blond and cut into a bob that was longer in the front than the back. She was about 5'5, and a body-hugging black dress that stopped at the knees covered her slender frame.

"Hi," I said, reaching out to greet her with a shake. "I'm Amina."

"Blake Devlin," she stated, a tinge of a smile piercing her lips, her steel gray eyes looking at me with intrigue.

Phillip moved slightly away from Blake and passed my drink to me. "Blake is the leader of the vampires here," Phillip said.

Ugh, vampires. They were a difficult bunch. They weren't a one-size-fits-all type. Some were pure animals or what we now named blood-lust vampires, having given in fully to the need for blood and losing all control, emotion, and intelligence.

On the other end, were vampires who looked like regular humans and maintained intelligence. Some would still rip your throat out. Others held their humanity and compassion and would ask for a donation of blood, instead of taking it without permission. And still, others would just go for animals and leave us non-vampires alone totally.

The one thing all vampires had in common was that they were not friends of the sun. The stronger they were, the less the sun harmed them and instead just gave them a sunburn at the worst. They were also fast and super strong. Holy water, crosses, and garlic were ineffective, and they did not have to wait to be invited inside your house. But you could still kill them by destroying their hearts or chopping off their heads.

Blake wasn't blood-lust, but that didn't mean she wasn't a threat.

"Are you the one who owns the strip club?" Lisa asked with a knowing smile.

"Burlesque Bar," Blake corrected her, eyes neutral.

"I see," Lisa said with a quick shrug. "Well, I'm Lisa."

"You smell...different," said a man to our right. He looked like the type of guy who would be called Biff or Cal or some football-player-type name. He was an almost 6-foot, muscular white man with short, copper-colored hair and blue eyes.

Lisa moved closer to me.

"This is Seth McIntire, the leader of our weres here," Phillip explained.

"I'm a weretiger," Seth added, eyeing Lisa like she was a steak dinner.

Gold star for you, I wanted to say but kept my mouth shut.

Felix walked over to us, standing between Lisa and Seth, the tiger. Good timing.

"What are you?" Seth asked Lisa, peeking beyond Felix.

Uh-oh. Please don't let this be another were who likes to eat fairies.

"She is not the droid you're looking for," Felix said in his poor imitation of Obi-Wan Kenobi from the old *Star Wars* movie.

"I don't think you have mind control ability," I said in a low voice to him, behind Lisa's back.

Lisa opened her mouth and shrugged, unsure how to answer.

"Throw some magic on the situation," I whispered to Lisa, slightly covering my lips. She was a fairy. One of her strengths was to cause confusion in people.

"Fairy, right?" Phillip asked grinning.

I could kill him. I looked at him with wide eyes and a tight smile, but he didn't catch my face. Had he guessed, or had Grace spilled the beans after all?

"No, I'm an elemental mage," Lisa said, batting her eyelashes.

Phillip nodded slowly, looking slightly…confused.

Lisa turned and winked at me, and I nodded my head in approval.

"Hey, you're a were?" Felix stated, looking to Seth. "My friend Erik over there is a werejackal."

Upon hearing his name, Erik walked over with a woman I had not seen him talking to before. A twinge of jealousy hit me for some irrational reason. I had no right to feel anyway with Phillip being here.

But the woman was pretty, dang it. She was Latina, with collarbone-length, golden-brown hair and dark-brown eyes. She was the same height as me but more athletic in build. She, too, had awesome eyebrows with a perfect arch. Who was doing eyebrows in this town? I used to think I was cute, but I was feeling really subpar compared to these women.

Erik, having assessed the situation, stood near Felix, blocking Lisa as well.

"Yeah, I'm a were. Are you the alpha here?" Erik asked Seth.

Seth gave him a curt nod, briefly looking away from Lisa.

"I was just talking to your second." Erik tilted his head towards the tall black man who seemed to be the only were in the room, not eyeing Lisa. He joined us with a greeting.

Seth gave a toothy smile that came out less than friendly. "Yeah, good ole Carter Banks," he slapped the man's back. "He's not really a were, but he was strong enough to fight his way to second."

"What are you?" I asked. "Sorry, I'm Amina, witch." I offered my hand to him.

Carter looked to me and shook my hand. "I'm a shapeshifter. Basically, I can turn into any living thing."

I dropped my mouth open. "Oh, wow. I don't think I've ever met a shapeshifter."

He smiled at me, and it seemed genuine. "That you know of."

I tapped my head with my index finger and then pointed at Carter.

"Hi, I'm Raya Ortiz," said the woman standing near Erik. We shook hands, and she gave me the slightest smile. It was one of those smiles that could be mistaken for grimaces. Like when you smiled to be polite to someone you really didn't care for. What the hell had I done to her?

I looked to Erik, feeling his hand on the small of my back. I looked back to her, sizing me up like the competition. Well, guess that question was answered. In fact, as I looked around the room, I noticed a few other women not so discreetly staring at Erik. I fought the urge to roll my eyes. He was a sexy, unmated, were. I was not in friendly territory.

We all eventually moved to the dining area to eat, and I met a few other inner circle people. They all seemed pleasant enough but not the warm and fuzzy people that Annie Mae and Grace seemed to be. There was something very pretentious about them all. Money wasn't much of anything anymore, and no one cared about your degrees or career now, but if you were a powerful paranormal, you were at the top. This town had an unspoken hierarchy, and all the cool and powerful kids were at this shindig. Thing was, I wasn't so sure the cool kids were who I liked being around. At least not anymore.

"Everything okay?" Phillip asked me, placing his hand over mine on the table.

Somehow the seating ended up with me near Phillip and Erik far away. I glanced over at Erik seated at the end of the row of the pushed together tables. He was busy chatting it up with Raya, Felix, and Lisa. "I'm fine. Just tired. New faces. Blah, blah, blah," I replied.

"I can imagine this whole experience must be overwhelming. But, I have to say, I'm glad you're here. It's like a dream. I wish you could stay." He squeezed my hand.

"I know, but the others want to head back to Hagerstown tomorrow. We don't want to put you out any more than we have here."

Phillip raised his eyebrows. "You aren't putting us out. As you can see, we have plenty of room and with a group this strong. We could use you."

"I can try to talk to them. Some have lives already set up there and want to be a part of the government."

Phillip scoffed. "The government's a joke."

"The government is becoming more stable, and they have size behind them," Erik stated from the far end.

Weres and their hearing. I slid my hand away from Phillip, feeling as if I were caught "red-handed."

Seth snorted. "We can beat the government. Most of them are human with no powers," he said in a loud voice, mouth full of food. I wished I wasn't seated across from the Neanderthal, so I didn't have to see mushed up food swirling around in his mouth.

"Not to mention that most of the government is still so scattered without the quick ability to connect," Blake chimed in, before taking a sip of what I hoped was red wine.

"And with all those different leaders and infighting, who knows how long they'll stay together," Raya added, placing a hand on Erik's arm. "Getting any larger election formed for a presidency will be a joke. Silver Spring is as safe as it gets. It's better for the people here if we stick to ourselves."

"Is he the leader of your group?" Phillip asked me, tilting his head down to Erik.

"I don't know if we have an official leader," I replied.

"If he doesn't want to stay, he doesn't have to. Everyone is free to come and go as they choose here, but I really would like for you to stick around and get to know this place. Give us a fair shot. I don't mean you any harm. Never have." He leaned towards me, searching my eyes. I couldn't help but think that he looked like a child telling his parents he'd been good all day and could he get the toy he wanted. His eyes looked so pleading and almost innocent.

A calmness tugged at my heart. "Are you trying to use your charm to get me to stay?" I smiled.

Phillip sat back and shrugged. And those puppy dog eyes turned into something more primal as he bit his bottom lip and looked at me. "I'm trying. Is it working?"

I didn't even want to turn my gaze to Erik. He and I had made out high school style on a bed less than a week ago, and here I was flirting with another man in front of him. Not my style. Especially since I hadn't worked out my feelings about him. As charming as Phillip was, I still couldn't get Erik out of my mind, and I wasn't sure I wanted to.

I rolled my eyes playfully. "If the others leave, I'm leaving with them. But I will talk to them. I mean, this town *is* awesome, and it certainly feels safe." Change the subject from flirting. Yes, that was safe.

He nodded. "Remember that dream where we met on that rooftop bar?" He was giving me playful eyes now.

"Uhm, yeah, I do. That was a cool place."

"We have a rooftop bar here that puts that one to shame.

186

It's enhanced with magic by another witch. She is more of an illusionist. Has it snowing when it's not cold. A pond becomes the floor, but you don't get wet. The scenery changes with the music. One moment, you feel like you're at the beach, and the next, you're in a forest."

My eyes widened. "That sounds amazing."

"I could take you there one night. It's only open Fridays and Saturdays."

"I can talk to the group about that."

He tilted his head. "Do that."

"Seems like you have made this town pretty fabulous."

He shrugged again. "It's not all me. My predecessor had a vision, and I'm just finishing it."

"And everyone just falls in line and doesn't complain?"

"Of course, we have complainers, but that's with anyplace. They aren't a problem." He leaned into me. "Your eyes are especially beautiful under this lighting."

Obviously, he had no intention of being focused or talking shop tonight. He wanted to lay on the charm thick.

I smiled, trying to keep things professional in front of the others. "Thank you. I'll have to take this lighting with me wherever I go then." It was just dim lighting upon chandeliers, playing off the red lights. There wasn't anything special about it, so I knew he was finding excuses to flirt with me.

He gave my hand a squeeze, and I pressed my lips together. Faith, who was sitting across the table next to Seth, gave me a questioning look, eyebrow cocked.

"I would love to kiss you again," he whispered.

God, I hope Erik didn't hear that. I gave Phillip a schoolgirl giggle and leaned back in my chair away from him. "So, if dissenters aren't a problem, I guess you don't have much need for policing," I said, hoping this change of subject would stick.

Phillip gave a closed-lipped smile. "We always have to

keep order. No place is perfect. And we have enemies, like the Fairfax town."

"Fairfax, Virginia. That's a government town. Why would they be enemies to an awesome place like this?"

"It's because we run so well, are full of powerful people, and we don't want to bow down to what they tell us. We worked hard to get this place like it is now. And how fair is it for them to come in, take over and do things differently? What we have works. They should take a chapter from us. Assuming we could trust the humans. Which we can't, as you, more than anyone else, should know."

"I do. But there are good regular humans out there. My parents were. Some of the folks in my old town and in Hagerstown are too."

He brushed his pinky finger over the back of my hand, and I fought the desire to shiver again. How had his simple touches made me feel like mush? I was convinced he was very aware of the full situation; of others noticing us and how he was getting to me. I had to get away from him.

"I have no doubt your parents were good, but I have no trust in most humans," he replied.

I frowned. "We're still humans," I stated.

He raised both eyebrows. "Are we?"

I moved my hand and pretended to massage the back of my neck as I looked over to Erik, who was listening to Raya tell him something, but he was looking over at me with not so happy eyes. Shit.

I looked back to Phillip. "Well, I certainly still feel human. I know my metabolism is the same because I still have to exercise to not turn into a beach ball." I giggled nervously.

"You look perfect," He stated, his bedroom gaze back on me.

"Oh, you are way too kind. You know what? I need a drink. Yep, uh-huh. I am going to go to the bar and get another drink. Do you need anything?"

Phillip shook his head and smiled, all too confident of his effect on me. "I can get the bartender to bring a drink to you."

I pushed my chair back and got up quickly. "Nope, I need to move my legs after sitting here eating all that amazing food. The spicy California roll was everything. So good. I don't know how you're getting these ingredients. Magic, right," I rambled and almost galloped away.

I got to the bar and let out a deep sigh. Maybe Charles was right. Maybe this trip was too distracting to our main mission. I ordered a shot of tequila and another Old Fashioned. Pretty sure that was a dangerous combination, but I needed to calm my mind.

I asked the guy behind the bar how much, figuring I would barter something from my purse. He shook his head and turned to service the next person, who happened to be Erik. Erik ordered a beer on tap. They were making beer here, too?

"Hey," I greeted him.

He leaned his back against the bar and looked out at the group on the other side of the room. "And she acknowledges me," he replied.

"Don't do that. I'm just catching up with him. It's weird seeing him in person." I took the shot and winced a bit as the tequila went down my throat.

"I see he's trying to keep you here. We aren't supposed to separate, remember that." Erik looked down at me.

"I haven't forgotten."

"I don't like him. And it's not because he keeps flirting with you and touching you. I think he's arrogant and I don't trust him. Remember what I said about smelling deceit. There's something going on here."

"Well, there are some suspicious people here. Like that Seth guy or Raya."

"I like Raya. She's a werewolf and smart."

I gave him the stink eye, and he smiled at me. "Are you trying to make me jealous or something?"

He raised an eyebrow. "Why would I want to do that? You don't remember our night together?"

A fire grew in his hazel eyes that tightened my stomach. I was affected by him too. Damn you, hormones! As much as Phillip knocked the damn wind out of me with just a touch, one look in Erik's eyes, and I was a puddle on the ground. And to think, nine years ago, I was swiping left on a phone app looking for a semi-attractive, decent guy, and failing miserably.

I lowered my voice, looking over to the bartender, who was busy making a cocktail at the other end of the bar. "Of course, I remember. I just thought it was a one-time thing because we never talked about it again. It was that time of the month for you, and I thought it was all just lust."

He grimaced. "That time of the month? It's not like I'm getting my period, Amina. Yes, I get a certain way when the full moon is close, but if I wanted to just randomly hook up with someone, it wouldn't be you."

I raised an eyebrow. "Well, thanks."

He leaned in. "That's not what I meant. I mean, you are more than some random woman. You are my friend. I wouldn't do something meaningless with you. I kissed you because I am attracted to you, and I like you...a lot. I only backed away because I thought, based on your reaction that night, you wanted to take things slow. I was giving you space. It's barely been two weeks. I understand that isn't a lot of time. Weres can sometimes let our more primal instincts rule us, but I'll follow at your pace."

Well, damn it, that made sense.

"I'm sorry," I said, looking up at him.

His eyes softened, and he gave me a slight smile, head titled back slightly. "So, what are you going to do to make it up to me?"

Good question. There was no doubt in my mind that Raya would wrap her paws, no pun intended, around Erik the moment I stepped away. I craved love, believe it or not. I wasn't going to pretend to myself that it didn't matter. And it had been a long time since I met a guy who had me feeling...special. But I was no fool; neither of these guys were going to wait around for me or fight for me. Erik and Phillip were strong, good-looking men. A girl could dream about a love triangle, like in some sappy romance novel, only for so long.

"I have no clue how to make it up to you."

Erik gave me a devilish look. "I have an idea." He stepped a foot closer to me, grabbed my face, and kissed me.

It was not some quick peck on the lips. It was full and deep, and my knees felt like they were failing. He smelled so good, like clover and wood. His lips had the remnants of whiskey, and I flicked them lightly with my tongue, wanting more of the sweetness.

He inserted his tongue in my mouth, and it danced across my own, pulling me closer to him. I was pretty sure the music stopped as we kissed, but when we pulled away, the hook to a well-known hip hop song was still blaring. Had his kiss made me temporarily deaf?

Public displays of affection were never my thing, and I was very certain that Erik's action was more for Phillip to see than a declaration to me. In some primitive sense, he was marking his territory. However, I wasn't a thing, although secretly, I took some joy out of being desired so much. I really liked this man. His protectiveness and strength intrigued me. His alpha behavior, strong physique, and even his accent turned me on. I had to admit to myself that meeting Phillip hadn't shaken me of Erik's unexpected hold.

I wanted to run out and hide in a room and think about my life choices. Instead, I took a large gulp of my Old Fashioned and willed my heart to slow down, so I didn't pass out.

It was just a kiss, damn it. Just a passionate, knee-weakening, soul-taking kiss.

"Fun party," Erik said, his eyes squinted in a sexy gaze. He grabbed his beer and headed back to the table, leaving me weak and confused.

CHAPTER 18

The rest of the party went as smoothly as possible. After Erik's very public display of affection, I expected Phillip to give me the silent treatment or, worse, kick us out of town, but he didn't. In fact, he looked amused at the whole situation. He was clearly not threatened by Erik. Or perhaps he simply wasn't serious enough about me to care.

I was overwhelmed by it all and called it an early night.

The next morning, most of the gang was ready to return to Hagerstown, having solved one mystery. Well, almost everyone.

We were gathered in Charles' and my guest apartment living room again.

"I can't leave. There's magic here, I heard it," Felix stated.

"You mean 'saw,' sweetie," Faith said, patting him on the back.

Felix shook his head swiftly. "No, I heard it. The voices told me strong magic is here, and I would find my way in this place. Maybe I can find out what I am."

"While I'm still concerned about these voices you're hearing, I don't trust the people here," Charles stated, crossing his arms. "That Seth dude made my butt itch."

I rolled my eyes. "You couldn't pick a better description."

He jutted his chin out. "I said what I said."

"That burlesque bar was everything, though," Faith exclaimed, slouching down on the couch.

"You went after dinner?" Lisa asked with a look of shock.

"Yeah, Blake took me there," she replied, putting her boot-covered feet on the coffee table. "She's kind of fun."

"I don't even want to know," Lisa muttered, putting her hands on her hips as she leaned against the living room wall.

"But Felix's right," I began. "There is incredible magic here. I'm sure they'll be able to help us locate the others. And I can learn some more spells here."

"We aren't staying," Erik said firmly, standing near the balcony sliding doors. "Seth has some barbaric practices with the pack that reminds me of what I left. If Phillip was so great a leader, why would he allow that?"

"Maybe he doesn't know."

Erik chuckled. "Are you being willfully naive?"

I looked over to him and narrowed my eyebrows. "Excuse you?"

Charles jumped up off the couch. "All right, let's pause this lover's quarrel for a moment and remember the big picture." He pointed at me. "And for the record, I'm team, Erik."

"So am I," Felix added, raising a hand.

"Me too." Lisa squeaked, giving me a shrug and an apologetic look.

Faith nodded in agreement. "I kind of want to punch Phillip and everyone associated with him. Except Blake. She's hot, so she can stick around," she said with a lazy smile.

Well damn, so much for a secret love affair. Guess everyone did see that kiss. "Didn't realize this was something open for a vote," I grumbled.

I looked over to Erik, and his face held a cocky grin. Damn his infectious smile. I smiled back.

"Aww, love birds are happy again," Charles stated with a deadpan voice. "Okay, how about some of us stay here, and some of us go—"

"No, if we are this power of six like Mae explained, we have to stick together," I stated.

"I want to stay," Lisa said. "Annie Mae might be able to help me find other Fae with her ability. She could help Felix learn more about himself."

Faith cursed. "I'm not leaving without you, Felix. Maybe we could stay a little while. Blake did offer me a position at her bar."

"And Seth was interested in Erik joining the pack," Lisa said in a sing-song voice.

Erik let a loud sigh. "Let's give it a trial month. See if we like it here," he stated.

"But we're still going to focus on saving our friends, right," Charles said more than asked.

I nodded. "I think we're in a better position to do that here, with all this power around us. We're setting our friends free. This town is going to help us," I stated with determination.

⁓

I awoke to a loud alarm that Saturday morning, but I'd had no reason to set my alarm clock. I searched for the snooze button, but the alarm persisted, and I opened my eyes. The clock read 9:00 a.m., and I slowly realized that the sound was not the annoying chirping birds sound that I had programmed the alarm to blare. It was more of a church bell sound. I shot up and ran out of my room. Fire drill? I raced to Charles' room, and he opened the door right before I could knock.

"Do they have fire drills here?" Charles asked, his eyes still half-closed.

I shrugged. We'd been in Silver Spring for a month now, and this morning alarm was a first for me since being here.

Good morning, citizens of new Silver Spring. Came Phillip's calm voice from seemingly everywhere.

It's a beautiful summer day. Enjoy and be productive. Remember that your leader, Phillip, is here to protect you. I want the best for you. I wish to make this world better for paranormals. Believe in me and follow my rules. Loyalty to me will be rewarded. Disobedience will be punished. Be good to each other. Make it a great day.

What in the entire hell? "You gotta be kidding me," I stated. "What is this?" I waited for more, but the speech was over.

I looked over to Charles. His face was blank and unbothered. Then suddenly, he turned right and walked to his bathroom.

"Hey!" I cried.

He turned to me and raised his eyebrows. "Why are you yelling?" he asked.

"Tell me you heard Phillip's voice coming from some type of loudspeaker."

"Yeah."

I threw out my hands to my sides. "Umm, you don't think that was weird?"

Charles frowned and shook his head. "No."

"Sounds a bit big brother-ish to me."

Charles gave me a sleepy-eyed smile. "Phillip's a good guy. He wants the best for us. He wants to make the world better for paranormals."

I tilted my head and squinted my eyes. Had he just regurgitated exactly what Phillip announced like some brainless drone?

"Don't look for trouble where there isn't any, Mina. Phillip's a good guy."

"Yeah, you said that already. Look, that sounded really weird. Maybe we shouldn't have jumped to move here so fast. It's the end of the trial month. It's time we reevaluate."

Charles smiled. "It's okay, Mina. We're safe here. It's Saturday. Make it a great day." He then turned back towards the bathroom.

Yep, something was definitely up.

~

I decided to make my day great by starting off with a jog around town. After this morning's wake-up message, I was feeling plenty uneasy and I needed to investigate. Everyone in the group seemed to settle in just fine and, unlike a month ago, there was no division about returning to Hagerstown. Even Felix and Faith didn't seem in a rush to go back to the jobs they were on pause from. Not that I was really complaining.

The town was alive, with children playing, people gardening or tending to the farm, brunching at the few restaurants, and shopping. People actually waved and smiled at me as I jogged by, telling me to 'make it a great day.' I said the same thing back out of politeness, but I could have done without it.

I encountered Grace during my jog. She was running as well. At a much more athletic pace than myself. My jog was more of a jog/walk. Okay, mostly a power walk. I waved at her and stopped speed walking.

"Hey," she replied, taking her earbuds out of her ears.

I shrugged. "What's up? Did you hear that message this morning?"

She nodded, smiling brightly. "Yeah, that's the morning message. Play's once a month."

"You know, I can't recall hearing it before. Maybe I missed that day."

She shrugged. "Possibly."

"Doesn't it get kind of annoying?"

Grace frowned.

"Did I say something wrong?"

"No, but I just wouldn't say that again if I were you." She searched my eyes. "The messages are supposed to be encouraging. Phillip wants us to believe that he is here to protect us."

The way she said it seemed so careful and purposeful, but there was no feeling behind it. I was missing something.

"So—"

"I have to go," she started, cutting me off. She gave me a bright smile again. "By the way, is Erik, your boyfriend?"

Random topic change. Why did she want to know? "We're still figuring that out, I think." It was true. Six weeks in and we hadn't exactly claimed each other. I was sure that was mostly my fault, as I was still busy figuring out my feelings about Phillip and then finding our friends, which was sadly still a work in progress.

"Well, you better claim him soon."

I raised my eyebrows. "Oh, are you interested?"

She shook her head. "He's gorgeous, don't get me wrong, but no. See, a guy like that is a prime pick for the women in the were pack. If you can get past Phillip, I'd make a jump on him if I were you."

"So, you're on team Erik too?" I cracked.

She gave me questioning eyes. "I like Phillip and Erik, but from one woman to another, wouldn't you rather make the decision than to let some other woman do it for you?"

I frowned. She had a point. I couldn't keep kicking the can down the road. I couldn't expect them to wait around for me. No man's ego would allow that.

Grace clapped her hands. "You'll know what to do," Grace

started to back away. "Oh, yeah, Annie Mae is usually gardening on Saturdays. Okay, bye now." And she was off jogging at in-shape speed again.

I nodded and looked after her in confusion. Why did I care about Annie Mae's gardening schedule?

I decided to take a hint and pay a visit to Annie Mae. I like to think of myself as a pretty clever gal. Plus, I was looking forward to a one-on-one session with the wise woman.

I walked back to the garden area where I first met Annie Mae, and there she was, like Grace said, on her knees tending to a patch of the vegetable garden.

"Hey, there, Mina, can I call you that? Feel free to call me Mae," she said, not turning around.

"Sure," I replied, no longer surprised at her gift.

"Good. We're going to be great friends. No need to be so formal." Mae got up and wiped dirt off of her jeans. She turned around and opened her arms to give me a hug.

"I'm sweaty," I said.

She wrapped her arms around me anyway. "So am I. I went power walking earlier, then came to garden."

I hugged her back. "I saw Grace just now. She sent me here."

"I see. Would you like some shrimp and grits? I was making some and then had a craving for some fried green tomatoes." She picked up a plastic bag that I assumed held the tomatoes.

"I'm sorry, did you just say shrimp?" My mouth was already watering. "Where did you get them from?"

Mae walked towards the glass apartment door, leaving the enclosed garden area. I followed. "I suppose they came from the sea. A group of folks go fishing and seafood-gathering regularly. It's pretty pricey, getting something like shrimp from them, but I figure it's a nice treat from time to time."

Mae made a left down a brightly-lit, carpeted hall, and I

followed. "I can't recall the last time I've had any seafood other than fish, and even that was rare."

"Well, then you are in for a treat, my dear." Mae opened a door on the left, and we walked through into a spacious two-bedroom apartment. The open kitchen overlooked the dining room, the living room was on the left, and a coat room/laundry room was on the right. She had lovely, light-brown wood floors. Beyond the living room, I could see glass doors leading to a terrace and a view of the garden. "I know we took the long way 'round, but I went straight to the garden after my walk, so I didn't leave my patio doors unlocked. Come on into the kitchen. Want anything to drink while I make the tomatoes? Won't take me long."

"No, thank you. Can I help with anything?"

"No, no, have a seat and keep me company in here."

I took a seat at a small, two-seater, rectangle table in the kitchen.

"So, how's your one-month anniversary going so far?"

"Okay. Except, well, that morning announcement thing kind of startled me. I thought maybe we were under attack."

Mae nodded and rinsed the tomatoes. "He does that once or twice a month."

"Why?"

She moved the tomatoes to a cutting board. "Did it bother you?"

"Yes. It felt odd to me. Charles didn't think it was a big deal and seemed to already have the speech memorized. It was weird."

"Some time ago, I had a spell put on my apartment and the courtyard to block out eavesdroppers. No one knows that, except who I tell specifically," Mae stated, chopping the tomatoes.

I frowned, confused about why she was telling me this again. "Okay, I won't tell anyone. Should I do the same? Is this really like big brother? Grace told me I shouldn't talk negatively about the speech."

"She was right. But for now, I wouldn't suggest you putting a spell up. It would cause early suspicion. Do you know about Phillip's gifts?"

"Only about his telekinetic and dream walker abilities."

She didn't speak and continued to prepare the tomatoes. I was beginning to understand Mae. She didn't like to give away too much information. She wanted us to connect the dots, and for someone who had the power of precognition, I could see how she didn't want to influence us so much to control the outcome of our futures. It was still annoying.

"He can do more than that. So can you. His powers are all mind related. He can influence. It's how you got your gifts back. He was able to trick your mind into believing you weren't drugged. Your magic then broke through whatever drugs tried to block your gifts."

"That's pretty powerful mind control. Especially when we weren't even in the same vicinity."

"It is." She nodded slowly, still cooking.

"Is he controlling the people of this town? Maybe through those speaker messages or whatever they are?"

Mae turned to me and smiled, then turned back to her cooking. "Phillip's a very idealistic man. He wants the best for this town and the people in it. He's been through some things these past nine years. More before that. He had a brother who was unjustly killed by a rookie cop when Phillip was fourteen. He doesn't talk about it with anyone. I counsel him, so he opened up to me."

I shook my head, not knowing what to say.

"Since then, he's had a lot of issues with authority. He felt very powerless. He told me that he went to college and business school so he could get rich and bring wealth to his community. He thought that was what would make him powerful. Then this all happened, and the only way to get power is magic now. And he has a lot of it."

"He doesn't like regular humans."

Mae sighed. "No, no, he doesn't. But that only happened a few years ago."

"Why?"

Mae paused the stirring of her pot. "Someone who was like a father to him was murdered by humans. He was a gargoyle. They change into their non-human forms at night. Some humans found him, were frightened, and killed him. In front of his wife and Phillip."

"So much death," I whispered.

Mae nodded and began to stir the pot again. "Yes. There is." She sighed. "Phillip exerts control because he is afraid of losing control. Afraid of being powerless. But he's a good man, Amina."

"He saved me."

"Yes, he did. He's grown much more powerful in the last two months or so. His ability to control a large group is something new. It happened right before he became the new leader. I assume it has something to do with you."

"How?"

"Oh, I wouldn't know for certain. But when our former leader died—he was a witch named Thomas—things started to really change with him. Thomas taught Phillip everything he knew. He was the one who created this place. He was a politician, believe it or not. A senator. Some super-liberal hippie who had no desire to reconnect with this new government. He wanted something new and different. Thought this new world was our way of making things right that were so wrong. Like a new Noah's Ark. He didn't trust the normal humans, though. That was his biggest flaw. Built that ugly wall around this place."

"How'd he die?"

"He was eighty-one years old. Died of a heart attack alone

in his room at night. With the magic in this town, he could have been saved, but no one knew until the next morning. Then we had an election, and Phillip won. Landslide vote. People really like him. He is a charmer, isn't he?" She turned from frying the tomatoes and looked at me with a knowing smile.

I raised my eyebrows and gave an awkward grin.

Mae turned back to the food, chuckling. "Don't feel embarrassed. He is a cutie. His eyes get you. That stare. Like he means everything he says, and you are the most important person at that moment to him. Makes it hard to stay angry with him."

"But he's not being honest, then?"

"I'm sure, for you, he is. He is quite taken with you. Honey, my power is connected to my mind. I see the future and the past. I can tell what's in your heart. I can tell when you are using magic." She turned back to me. "Phillip needs you. And I certainly would believe that he is quite fond of you, but it won't make it easier." She turned back to the stove. "Okay, food is done. Let's eat."

We prepared the food and sat out on Mae's terrace.

"Hmm, I have to say. I put my foot in it," Mae stated after eating a fork full of grits. She looked over to me. "Not hungry?"

I looked down at my plate. I was feeling too uneasy about things, but I'd regret passing up shrimp, so I dug in, chewing slowly. It was amazing. "This is really good."

"Don't you worry about Phillip. I think with you here, it'll settle him more. Losing Thomas was difficult for him. It was like losing yet another father all over again. Maybe you can heal his heart. You're very much connected, after all. You and Phillip are both mages. You're just a special kind. Probably aren't many, if any others at all."

"What are we mages of? I just thought I was a witch."

She smiled. "Life. Just as your brother has power over all

technology or our head doctor has power over anything healing, you and Phillip have power over living things. Both supernatural and natural. Mammals, amphibians, bugs, plants, nature. Anything that grows or is of the earth."

I frowned. Well, hell, that made perfect sense now. How had I not made that connection? Once again, my college and year of law school had failed me in the new world. That and the fact that I'd never bothered to use my powers to that level until recently, so I didn't have a lot of time to think about it.

"I'm not a witch," Mae began, "But I know a lot about them. We have some very knowledgeable witches here. Every witch has spells and potions, but the higher-level witches have automatic powers over certain things. Those are called mages."

"Right, I knew that. How I didn't connect the dots that me having power over other paranormals or supernatural life without a spell or potion made me a mage, is embarrassing."

Mae shook her head. "Oh, don't bother thinking about that. It wouldn't matter. You made it to where you needed to go."

"So, Phillip and I have the same powers?"

Mae nodded before taking another bite of food.

"Does he know we have the same mage abilities?"

Mae dug into her bowl of shrimp and grits. "No. And I'd advise you not to tell him. Or anyone else, for now. He might not understand as well as you."

Why did I have to tip-toe around Phillip? I thought about his smiling face, the one from my dreams, and the one I met the first time on the patio. That Phillip, the only one I knew, was sensitive and thoughtful. Why would he knowing we had the same power bother him? If anything, wouldn't it make him happy? I sure was comforted by having a fellow mage with my powers. One who clearly knew more about our gifts than I did. He could teach me things. A thought entered my mind.

"Should I be scared of Phillip?"

Mae looked at me with pained eyes. "No. Never."

She didn't elaborate, and I didn't press her.

"Honey, eat up! Shrimp doesn't come around here often, and we best not waste it."

And with that, Mae was done talking about Phillip. But I was just left with more concerns.

CHAPTER 19

*W*hen I left Mae's place, I went to the indoor farmer's market for some groceries and then decided to head home. I couldn't find anyone else, which was odd. Even my brother was no longer in his room. The mystery was solved when I found a note taped to my bedroom door that said everyone was gathering at Felix's place for some very important news. I walked down two flights of stairs to Felix's apartment and knocked on his door.

Faith answered with a somber face.

Oh, shit. We'd only been here a month. What the hell happened?

I walked into the living room and saw Erik, Felix, Lisa, Charles, and Carter spread out around the space.

"Who died?" I asked cautiously.

"Erik's going to fight for a spot in the pack," Felix blurted out from the dining room area.

I raised an eyebrow. "Oh, well, that sounds barbaric."

"It's dangerous."

"Thank you, Felix," Erik growled.

I looked to Erik. "Well, beating each other up *does* sound

dangerous. You didn't want to wait a little bit before jumping in? I thought we were still giving this play a test run."

"It's been a month."

"Sooo, I guess you unilaterally are deciding for all of us to stay?" I looked around at the others. "What do the rest of us say? Are we fine with staying?"

The others gave slow nods and verbal confirmation. I couldn't say I was surprised. Lisa and Faith shared an apartment and had made themselves a large part of the community. Lisa had situated herself as a mage, and no one seemed to be the wiser. Felix and Erik lived on their own, Erik in the pack high-rise apartments, and both Felix and I were doing well teaching at the town school.

"Are you fine with staying, Amina?" Erik asked me.

I looked over to him, folding my arms. I wasn't actually angry. I'd come to like the town and I was learning more in the short time being here than I had in years. I'd made friends, Charles had found love with Lisa, I was enjoying teaching, and I was happy. Well, as happy as I could be while still missing Chelsea and Jared.

I nodded. "I'm good with staying. But why are you so determined to join this pack right now? That's a major commitment."

"I have to," Erik said, solemnly. "They need my help, but I can only do that with a spot."

"What do you mean spot? I thought if you're a were you're already in the pack."

"That's true," Carter began, sitting in a dining room chair. "But if you want a leadership role, you have to fight to get it. The better the fighter you are, the higher you are in line."

I frowned. I was frowning a lot today. "Well, that is a dumb way to pick a leader."

"Power's all that matters, Amina. That's the only way you'll get respect."

I shook my head. "Erik, I thought you didn't want leadership?"

He leaned forward on the couch and rested his elbows on his thighs "I was reluctant to at first, but I can't shake this feeling that I'm needed. Then Mae met with me a few days ago, and she suggested I run for a leadership role. She said I had to be in the top five. She had some sort of vision."

I cocked an eyebrow. Well, that was a bit of information Mae neglected to tell me. Then again, it wasn't exactly information that was for me. "What was her vision?" I asked.

Erik slowly shook his head. "She wouldn't get into it. She just was adamant that the pack needed me. I'm still learning about the pack. It's not perfect, and I've heard some things about certain people, but I can't really do anything if I'm not in a power role." Erik glanced over to Lisa. "I can't just continue to snatch people and run anymore. I need to do some good. And if the town oracle thinks I'm needed, I think I should listen."

I couldn't help myself and smiled slightly. Now I knew what drew me to Erik; his heart. Of course, he'd want to be a protector. It was in his nature. "Fine, fine. But, seriously, Carter, how can you follow someone that allows for this barbaric ritual?" I asked Carter.

Carter sighed. "There are a lot of innocent people in the group. Betas that need protecting," Carter replied. "And I don't want to leave."

I wanted to ask why, but I knew the answer. Phillip's morning messages let people know that this was the best place to be, and they didn't want to be anywhere else. I ached to tell them the truth.

"I think I can do some good for the pack by being in leadership. I'm not afraid of Seth, and so far, he doesn't hate me," Erik explained. "But the only way I'll get any clout is if I fight for a position and win."

I nodded slowly. "Well, I don't like it, but I understand. I can also talk to Phillip about what's going on. So, what, you start from the bottom and fight your way up the line?"

"You can. Or you can challenge a certain spot."

"So, what are you doing?"

"I'm challenging for the third spot."

I raised my eyebrows. "Oh, that's aiming high."

Erik nodded. "I'd go higher, but Carter is number two."

I looked over at Carter and gave him a nod of respect. He returned my nod with a bashful grin.

"And there's something else," Erik stated, his face still all too serious.

Lisa let out a dramatic sigh and turned her head from me, arms crossed. Charles, seated next to her at the dining room table with Carter and Felix, touched her back.

My stomach tightened. Not good. "What is it?"

"It's not like boxing where we fight until someone taps out or gets knocked out," Erik started.

I nodded slowly. "Oookaay."

He paused, and I looked around at everyone's faces for a clue, but they all avoided my eyes. "I don't like suspense."

"It's a fight to the death."

My mind wasn't quite registering what he told me. "No."

Erik raised his eyebrows. "No?"

I shrugged. "No. You're not going to do that."

"Mina, I have to."

"I feel like maybe you guys can just surprise attack this asshole and take him out."

"If we did that, I wouldn't get clout, which is what I need. The only way to get buy-in is to fight."

"Or die, because that could happen."

Erik looked up at me, his eyes filled with determination and strength. "I'm not going to die."

I smiled. "Oh, so you talked to Mae, and she told you that you'd be okay."

"That's a good idea, why didn't we do that?" Felix whispered.

"We can try, but her visions aren't always on-demand," Carter replied.

I nodded my head slowly. "So, I'm back to no again."

Erik smirked at me. "I don't need your permission, Mina."

I huffed and put my hands on my hips. Why'd he have to be such a stubborn ass? Didn't he know that we cared about him? That I cared about him? That I needed him alive? "Then why the hell are we gathered here? You could have sent us all an email. Subject line: I'm gonna die."

He lost his smirk. "Thanks for the faith."

"She's just worried, like we all are," Lisa sniffed, her back still to us.

"Why can't you start with the easiest guy? How many spots are there?" I asked Erik.

"Five. But I don't want to keep killing people. The guy in third is a pretty awful dude. He's done things that he would have been arrested for in the Pre-world," Erik explained. "Like rape and assault, from what's been said."

I put my head in my hands, still standing. This was a nightmare. Why couldn't we have some peace for a little bit? Or at least until we found the others. "When is this happening?"

"Monday."

I straightened up and looked at them, my mouth hanging open. "So soon?"

"That's the way it works, Mina. You make a challenge, so you fight right then and there or within three days," Erik explained.

Lisa sniffed again.

"And the loser is just dead, and everyone goes back to business." I scrunched my face up. "What about helping us get our friends back like you said you would?"

"I'll beat him."

"Who is this guy that you think you can beat?"

Erik jutted his chin out and cocked an eyebrow at me. "That I *know* I can beat. His name is Donte. He's part of the police force."

"What was he before the change?"

Erik shook his head and shrugged.

"He was a pro football player. Quarterback," Faith answered.

Erik gave her a glare, and Faith gave an apologetic shrug in return.

"I don't know what a quarterback does, but I'm betting he's someone who can knock people out. If you get knocked down, play dead," I replied.

Erik's eyebrows furrowed together. "It sounds like you don't have any faith I can win this. I know I'm not a young guy, but I'm still fit. Being a were, we age slowly, so I'm still technically as fit as a late twenty-something. And I was part of special forces in New Zealand."

I was not convinced. I just saw images of Erik dead on the ground in human form, his heart ripped out, and a large—

"What kind of were is this guy?"

"A werepanther."

—a large humanoid werepanther standing over his dead body with Erik's heart in his hand. I pursed my lips and crossed my arms. "What time does this foolishness start on Monday?"

"10 p.m. sharp."

"It's a school night; this is happening that late? Don't people have to work the next day?"

"Well, if I die, work won't matter," Erik replied with a tinge of a smile.

And with that, I stormed out of the apartment full of feelings, mostly anger. I was falling for a man who smiled in the face of death. This seemed like an exercise in pain.

$\mathcal{I}$ decided if no one else planned to reason with Erik, then the least I could do was see if Phillip could get this all to end. It was his town, after all. I took a shower and stormed to Phillip's building.

After getting approval from security, I walked into Phillip's office-apartment and saw him and Blake sitting on the couch, looking at some documents on top of the coffee table.

Upon seeing me, Phillip stood up and opened his arms. "Amina, so glad to see you today," he said.

I hugged him, and that static connection between us was still there, only this time I was prepared for it. My mind stayed focused on my conversation with Mae and what I needed to talk to him about.

I turned to Blake, prepared to give her a handshake, but she embraced me as well. She felt warm like many of the living vampires I'd known. Luckily for her, no one had tried to kill her. As soon as a vampire died a human death, they became the undead. Their powers didn't necessarily change, except all thoughts of procreation were over, and the need to eat regular food went away. They were also more prone to becoming the blood-lust monsters.

"I'm sorry to come unannounced," I began.

"No, *mi corazon*, I want to see more of you. You can drop by anytime," Phillip said.

I looked over to Blake, who smiled up at me. I took a seat on a fabric chair facing the coffee table and the couch.

"I'm sorry I haven't been as available as I'd like this week. Are we still on for Monday?" he asked.

That's right, we'd made plans for dinner Monday. How quickly I'd forgotten. We'd met briefly Thursday, and he'd asked me to dinner for Monday. He had a busy schedule for a man in the apocalypse, but what did I know about running a town of over one thousand paranormal people? Heck, it looked like he was even working on a Saturday.

"Actually, I have to talk to you about that. I need to reschedule," I stated.

Phillip frowned. "What's going on?"

"The pack is going to have a battle for third seat on Monday. Erik is one of the fighters," I explained.

Blake gave a face of disdain and sat back, crossing her legs. "What a waste of resources," she replied.

If she hated the practice as much as I did, then maybe I'd have a better chance of getting support from Phillip to end this.

"Yes, I heard. I understand you wanting to support. We can reschedule for another day," he replied, looking unaffected.

I squinted my eyes. "Sooo, the whole thing doesn't bother you?"

Phillip raised his eyebrows. "Of course, it bothers me, but what can I do?"

"You run this town. You can stop them."

Phillip sat back and balanced an elbow on the arm of the couch. "This tradition was allowed before I became leader. No one has complained to me about it. Namely, because they don't have to do it. You can be a successful, happy person without being in the top five of Seth's pack. And if a person doesn't want to fight another for their spot, they can step down."

Blake snorted, and I looked over to her. "They can step down but they lose all respect. They become betas, which are the weakest members of the pack. A ten-year-old with alpha power has more clout than a fifty-year-old beta," she countered.

"They can become a pacifist, there's no shame in that," Phillip countered.

"Or they get shamed out and leave the pack all together.

213

And unlike the rest of us, most weres need a pack," Blake stated, looking over to me. "The term 'lone wolf' is not a compliment. They're more inclined to go loupe that way, unless they leave town and find another pack." She pointed to her head in a circular motion when she said the word "loupe."

I knew exactly what she meant. A loupe, were was just as dangerous as a blood-lust vampire. Both had lost human thought and became their most primitive and violent selves.

"Be that as it may, a were knows the full ramifications of fighting for a top spot," Phillip stated. "It's not for everyone, but if people didn't want to do it, they wouldn't. Then Seth would have to find some other way to get a top group."

I slid to the end of my seat. "I get it. If people don't fuss about it, we leave well enough alone, but as leaders, shouldn't we do what we must to protect people? Even from themselves? Half the world population is gone, and we're sitting here killing each other unnecessarily. That doesn't make logical sense."

Phillip's eyes remained gentle. "What would you have me do, *corazon*? If I force them to stop something that they want, I could lose their support. Do you think it's easy running a town of paranormals? We have witches, vampires, weres, elves, shapeshifters, incubi, succubi, sirens, gargoyles. And then those groups have their own breakouts like the weres who, incidentally, are the largest paranormal group in town. Being in power is a fragile thing here. There is always someone who thinks they can do better. Better than Blake, Seth, or me. We lose the delicate hold we have, and this could be a town of total chaos."

I clasped my hands together and brought them up to my chest. "I hear you, Phillip, but the government towns are able to do it. Hagerstown has two thousand people, paranormal humans, and regular humans. From what I could tell, they weren't engaging in crazy traditions to keep people happy."

214

Phillip sighed. "With all due respect, Amina, you have no idea what the government towns are doing to keep control. You know what they showed you for the brief time that you were there. We know they don't allow the paranormals to group, which stunts their power. As much as those towns want you to think they are just mini-cities, reminiscent of the Pre-world, they aren't. They can't be. They have to battle each other for power, battle smaller communities that don't want to join them, battle their own citizens who may disagree with what they are doing. And when I say 'battle,' I mean kill. And the ones that oppose them or do wrong that they don't kill, they enslave and call it 'helping to rebuild.' Here, we have found a way to keep the peace. As primitive as it may seem, it works."

I sat back. "So, I guess this means you aren't going to stop it."

"No, I'm sorry, *corazon*. I know I've disappointed you."

I didn't speak and instead looked out of the sliding glass doors leading to the patio.

"Amina," Blake began. "Sometimes we think we have more control than we actually do. Even your worst dictator can't rule without having loyal followers, and you only get that by giving them or promising them something they want. They want violence. We give them that."

I stood up and walked away. "That's not what I want."

CHAPTER 20

*E*very time I thought about Erik's decision, I felt sick. If he lived through this, he would have killed someone unnecessarily. He would also be that much closer to the foolishness that Seth oversaw. What if he didn't change anything but got further mixed up in it all? Carter hadn't done anything, and as a second, I could only imagine that he probably took part in some of the horrors, at least to a degree, to keep Seth happy and off his case. I was sure that Seth didn't tolerate any dissenting opinions.

And if Erik lost and died, I'd be destroyed. Charles morbidly stated that if Erik died, at least my decision making between him and Phillip would end up being made. I threw him out and sent him to Lisa with instructions to tell her exactly what he said to me.

My mind raced with horrible thoughts that wouldn't let me sleep. By 11 p.m. that night, I was still lying in my bed, wide awake. I was reading a horror novel I picked up from the library, probably not the best reading choice, when I heard a knock at the door. I grumbled and got up. I was wearing cotton shorts and a T-shirt, so I figured I looked presentable enough to curse out whoever it was felt the need to knock on my door so late.

I looked through the peephole and found Erik standing there in gray sweatpants and a white T-shirt. His arms were crossed, and he looked annoyed. I backed away. I should let him think I was not home. I didn't want to talk to him and argue.

"Let me in, Mina. I know you're in there, I can hear you breathing," he called.

I sucked my teeth and opened the door a crack. Damn that were hearing. "Can I help you, sir?" I asked, peeking out.

His stern-face softened into a laugh. "Don't be like that, let me in."

I squinted my eyes but stepped back and opened the door wider. For some reason, I didn't think he would leave if I didn't.

Erik walked in, and I closed the door behind him. I turned and he quickly pulled me to him in a tight embrace. I wanted to fight him, to distance myself from someone I might not see again so it would hurt less, but I couldn't. I grabbed his shirt and buried my face into his chest, full of emotion, and willing myself not to show any. It would only make things worse. He stepped back and held my face between his hands before kissing me. It was full of the unspoken emotion we both had. My breath caught, in spite of not wanting to feel anything.

Erik, let me go.

"What was that for?" I asked breathlessly.

"I wanted to get that out of the way before we said anything that we might regret," he stated, leaning against the door, arms crossed again. "I don't take what I'm going to be doing lightly, but I wouldn't do it if I didn't think it was the right thing. I regret not stepping up in my old pack and just running off like some coward."

"You weren't a coward, Erik. You were outnumbered, and you had to save Lisa."

He nodded. "Well, here there are a lot of people who need saving, and I can't grab them all and run out. There's good here, it's just run by a few bad people."

"Is Raya included in that? How does she feel about you doing this?" I asked. Yep, I was jealous. He worked beside Raya on a daily basis in the police force and she was a were, and beautiful.

"She's number four, but loyal to Seth, but she can be reasoned with. And with Carter, and I in the top five, that'll be three of us and if we speak to the fifth spot person, we might be able to get the numbers we need behind us."

"Raya wants you to fight?"

He nodded. "She thinks I'm strong enough to win. Unlike you."

I grimaced. "I just don't want you to change after this. I want us to all be happy, at least for a while." I realized as soon as I said it how childish I sounded. I looked down at my feet. Maybe I was naive like Erik first said, but really, I was just tired.

"Mina, how were you going to be a lawyer? I thought you ate conflict for breakfast?"

I huffed. "I only finished one year of law school."

"I see. Well, as much as I'd like to lay low, I don't think that's why we're here. Mae said as much. Maybe this is one of the things we're here to do. Mina, I'd really like… I need your support."

I looked up at him. His eyes had softened, and he had a slight smile on his lips. I dropped my shoulders. What did I expect? He was a former military leader, and he protected people for a living. You had to get those people to trust you. You had to look them in the eyes and make them believe that everything was okay and that they were important. Showing just the tinge of vulnerability helped to do that.

Well, crap, he was going to do this regardless of what I said or felt. Why make it worse for him by not being supportive? Not that I fancied myself so important, but what if my lack of confidence in him affected his ability to win? He had to know that we were all behind him. And I couldn't let Raya be the one to have faith in him and not me.

I nodded my head. "I support you. You're a good man. This is what you do. It's what you've always done, from what I'm learning." I returned his smile. "How could I expect differently? I'll support you in any way you need me to."

His smile widened and for a moment, he looked like a little boy whose parent just said he could eat ice cream for dinner. I think my heart melted a little at that slight vulnerability from him. Then his smile receded and shifted into something else as he looked me up and down suggestively. I raised an eyebrow and tugged the bottoms of my shorts down a little. They were barely covering half my thighs. I wanted to grab a blanket and throw it over me.

"I know of several fun ways you could support me," he replied.

I raised up a hand to stop him. "Not in that way."

He moved a fraction closer to me. "I'm having a hard time sleeping well. The night that we slept together was the best sleep I'd had in a while. I could really use a good night's rest."

I looked away. Suddenly, I remembered that he was a man. A very attractive man and it was night, and my brother was not there.

"Mina, you in danger, girl," said Whoopi Goldberg's voice in my head, circa the movie *Ghost*.

I stepped back "Are you asking to stay over?"

"So that you can better support me." He grinned, and I let out a laugh. "No, I'm being serious, Amina. This could be our last peaceful moment together. If you turn me away, you might regret it."

I could have kicked him. "You just spent this time telling

me you could beat this guy and now you're guilt-tripping me."

He raised an eyebrow. "Is it working?"

"No," I lied.

He tilted his head and squinted his eyes. He was a were, and of course, he could tell if I was lying. I would love nothing more than to sleep in his arms tonight and forget all our problems, and I knew I might regret it if I did not.

"Fine. Just to sleep." I pointed at him. I wasn't going to be listening to Whoopi tonight, I guess.

Erik followed me to my room, and I closed the door behind him.

Erik walked to the side of the bed closest, to the door and took off his shirt. I tried not to focus on his chest. His distractingly defined chest. He wasn't so buff that he would be competing for a bodybuilding contest, but he was in really good shape. He looked like he'd been chopping wood all day with muscled arms, defined shoulders, and pectoral muscles under tanned skin. His stomach was flat, toned, and hard, only marred by three claw-mark-like scars about five inches long off to the left. I could see the V shape of his pelvic muscles peeking out past his sweats, and I tried not to look lower. On his left arm, leading over the left side of his upper back, was a black tribal tattoo that I'd never noticed before, perhaps because he never wore a shirt with sleeves short enough to show it.

I think I started to drool, and I touched the corners of my mouth with my thumb and index finger to be sure. I imagined I looked like a lecherous pervert just standing there and staring.

"Any significance to the tattoo?" I asked in a feeble attempt to justify my staring.

He looked down at his arm. "It's a Polynesian tat'."

I nodded slowly, still fixated on his chest.

He began to pull at his sweatpants. I threw out my hands

in a panic. "Hold up! Why do you have to get undressed?" I practically screamed through the loud pounding in my ears.

Erik looked over to me with confused eyes. "Most people don't sleep in their clothes, and I don't have pajama bottoms. I doubt I could fit anything of Charles'."

"Maybe most weres don't sleep in clothes, but others do, and you kept your clothes on the last time. Do you even have any underwear on under those?" I asked crossly. And like the pervert I was clearly becoming, I glanced down at his gray sweatpants and quickly determined that he did not. Dear God. There was something very substantial going on down there. I swallowed hard, turned my back to him, but not before seeing Erik give me the slightest of smirks. Oh, he knew what he was doing. I sat down on the bed and clasped my hands together in my lap.

"Sorry. I usually sleep naked. Weres like to be clothes free from time to time. Helps us connect with the animal part of ourselves. And it's more comfortable," he explained.

I nodded quickly, still keeping my back to him. "Uh-huh, keep your pants on, player."

"Not a problem," he replied. I felt the bed lower under me as he laid down. I remained in a seated position. "Is that how you sleep? You don't lay down? I don't recall that from last time."

Get it together, girl. I needed an ice-cold shower, but I wouldn't give him that pleasure of seeing me so distracted.

I turned the bedside light off. "Remember, you're just here to sleep," I reiterated, lying down, my back to him.

"I want to hold you. Is that all right," he said, more than asked, in a low voice.

"Yes," I whispered.

He moved closer to me until I felt my back press up against his chest.

The feel of his arms around me, strong and tender, felt good.

"You're going to win, Erik. I believe in you," I said softly.

He kissed my neck and went to sleep just as I asked.

When I heard him lightly snore, I whispered, "Please don't die."

~

The pack was larger than I expected. As Phillip implied, they were over one-third of the town's population. The town gym was packed. There was something very ancient Rome and all-out sick about people wanting to witness two people beating the crap out of each other. But I suppose that since Monday Night Football wasn't coming on anymore, this was the next best thing. Except football didn't end with the losing team dying.

The crowd spread out among the treadmills and ellipticals that were pushed away from the center of the large gym space. I stayed in the peripheral next to the door. I didn't want to be there at all, but Mae made a visit to my apartment when I was out and told Charles that I needed to go. When Mae says something, I was definitely going to listen, but I didn't mind that most of the pack members blocked my view.

"I smell popcorn in here," Charles muttered besides me. "Who would eat popcorn for this? These people are sick."

A woman with severe blunt bangs turned around and glared at Charles, who avoided eyes with her. I gave a toothy smile to her. She rolled her eyes and turned back to the center of the main gym floor.

I glanced to my right and met eyes with Phillip, who was walking through the door.

"Hey, *corazon*," he said, touching my arm. "How are you holding up? I know you didn't like how our talk ended the other day."

I shrugged. "It is what it is."

"Is that why you're staying in the back?"

I let out a sigh. "I'm staying in the back because I'd rather not watch the bloodshed."

Charles leaned forward and looked past me to Phillip. "So, who are you hoping to win?" he asked.

Phillip gave a cover boy smile. "The best fighter. Ultimately, that's who I need. Excuse me, I need to get to the front." He winked and walked through the crowd.

"He could have at least lied and said Erik," I mumbled.

"You can't be mad, Sis, that he didn't say, Erik," Charles began. "He's known this third guy longer, and things have been working. He doesn't know Erik like that, and Erik's technically his competition."

"I'm just ready for this nightmare to be over."

"Attention, everyone!" Seth shouted from the center of the room. He raised his muscled arms in the air. His tight blue T-shirt strained over his defined chest. Were all alpha weres muscular? Seriously, the powerful weres I'd encountered in the past nine years had all looked like action movie heroes or heroines. "Erik Bennett challenged our third in command, Donte Harris, for his spot. Now, we have all known and loved our guy Donte for almost a year. He's a good guy, but no one can get too comfortable as a top five. Anyone can challenge us for our spots. Even me."

Some people booed and shook their heads. Seemed a lot of people actually liked this guy. I strained to look over at Donte. He was a tall black man with shoulder-length dreadlocks shaved on the sides and in the back. He matched Erik in size.

"Erik here is a strong, standup guy. He's new to town, but that doesn't mean he can't jump in and bring some power to our community."

I looked around as people murmured and nodded in the crowd.

Seth turned to Erik and Donte, who were standing next to each other "Okay, so the main rule here is a fight to the death. There is no time limit unless a person clearly has the upper hand. Then you must go in for the kill in thirty seconds, or you become the loser and die. No one can tap out or take a break. You can't ask to be spared. If you refuse to kill, you die. The fighting is in human form, although you can use your were strength. You can't use any weapons. It's basic hand-to-hand combat. Are you ready?"

Both men nodded, and my heart pounded against my chest.

A horn sounded, and the fighting began. The two circled each other like wrestlers. I didn't know Erik's fighting style. Did he know martial arts? What had the military taught him? As a bodyguard, was he accustomed to only using weapons or did he use his hands? I had no idea about the level of his expertise.

The wait to see who would attack first was too much. As if he heard my thoughts, Donte rushed at Erik, who centered himself and pushed against him, their shoulders connecting. Erik then quickly moved away and gave a hard punch to the middle of Donte's back. Donte arched his spine and let out a cry. I bit my fingernails. Maybe Erik could win.

Before Erik could land another punch, Donte spun around and pounced in one movement on top of Erik, tackling him to the ground. He then lifted his hand, now enhanced with claws, and slashed Erik across his forearm, which he put over his face to block the attack. The cut was enough to need stitches if he were an ordinary human.

"Oh God," I said, turning away. "I can't do this. I can't stay." I touched my chest, feeling my heart threatening to tear through. I felt like throwing up. I couldn't lose Erik. That stubborn, cocky, grouchy jackal had grown on me.

I felt a hand grab mine. I looked down at the hand and then up to see Lisa give me a weak smile. Beside her were Faith and Felix, who had his dog, Dexter, a golden retriever, on a leash. I shook suddenly, hearing the grunts, and cries from the fighting.

"You don't have to look," Lisa said. "If it gets too tough, squeeze my hand."

I looked at her and nodded. My eyes started to fill with tears to match her own. I forgot that she cared about Erik just as much. He'd saved her life.

And so, I turned away. Time passed agonizingly slowly, and I remained unsure of which man on the floor grunted, growled, or cried out in pain. The crowd yelled out in unintelligible excitement, egging whichever man was on top to finish and claim victory. At moments, Lisa squeezed my hand, and I wasn't sure if it was because Erik was winning or because he was getting hurt. My legs were threatening to give out.

"Why don't we stop this? We don't have to stay here. This is stupid!" Faith stated, shaking her head in anger.

With her response, I already knew who was losing.

"At this point, they'll kill him if he taps out," Felix replied. His voice sounded strained.

"He's stronger than this guy. He can win," Charles muttered. I looked over to him, and his profile didn't seem as certain as his words.

They were giving up.

"Not if he has magic to help him," Felix said back.

We turned to him. "What are you talking about?" I asked.

"There's magic in this room, can't you feel it?" Felix asked.

We shook our heads. I frowned.

"There's a lot of magical people in here," Faith guessed.

"No, it feels like magic is being used. There's a difference!" Felix said, growing visibly frustrated. He craned his neck, searching around the room. He was taller than just about everyone in the space, but I was sure any magic-user wouldn't be using magic blatantly.

I closed my eyes and took a deep breath. I focused on my

breathing like I did with meditation. It helped me control my magic and was a tool I tried to perfect when I was locked up. The panic attacking my mind receded. My heart rate slowed. I let go of Lisa's hand, and then I felt it. Hot, thick air; sticky to my skin. Then the smell of lemongrass? I couldn't tell. It wasn't there before. None of what I was feeling was there prior.

"Magic, someone's using magic, and they tried to disguise it," I whispered.

"But it didn't work on me or you," Felix replied.

I let out a deep breath. "No, it didn't." I turned around just in time to see a bruised and battered Donte body slam Erik, who was on the floor and a bloody mess. He had two scary cuts going down the length of the left side of his face, that eye was shut, and his lip was cut as well. He was holding on to his side, so I could assume ribs were broken and there was blood under that hand so perhaps more damage. A cut, bite? Overall, he was in scary shape.

I grimaced and cut through the crowd, moving closer to the center. My eyes avoided the fighting. I looked across the center and spotted a white male in his early forties with thinning, sandy-brown hair. His eyes were half-closed, and his fingers wiggled slowly. His lips weren't moving, but that didn't mean that he hadn't done a spell.

I had no doubt that the magic was coming from him.

I would kill this man. I had no idea how he was helping Donte, but I didn't care. I only needed to figure out how to discreetly help Erik as well. Running back to my room to search for a powerful spell was out of the question. There was no time. Erik could be dead by then

I went farther through the crowd and into the empty weight room to the left. It wasn't hidden away, the room had glass windows but it was dark inside, lit only by the light from the larger gym space. No one could see me doing magic or feel the magic. I didn't know how to disguise it like the man had, but I knew how to cloak, and cloaking would not only make me invisible but also conceal the magic. I quickly whispered the spell and then racked my brain for any spell or power I could use to help Erik.

I looked up at the ceiling. I could control Erik's body with magic, but that wouldn't stop him from getting hurt. I needed to give him a boost of power, the same way I would someone who needed healing. Just as Phillip had done for me. Except I couldn't heal him; that'd be too obvious. Could I control his body to make him stronger? It was worth a shot.

I hid in a dark corner behind a machine and dropped my cloaking spell to use my full powers to help Erik. My mind focused on the vision of a standing Erik. I thought of his muscles, the red ropes under his skin. I thought of his strong heart and lungs. His abs as hard as rocks. His fists hitting like steel. In my mind, he glowed with power.

A sudden wave of wooziness washed over me, and I grabbed on to a weight machine. I'd never tried anything like this before, and it was taking every ounce of my strength. But I couldn't stop. I shut my eyes tightly and balled my fists, imagining a superhero Erik over and over again. I pictured him picking up Donte like a small child and tossing him like it was nothing. The tips of my fingers itched, and my arms tingled with sharp pricks of pain all the way up to my shoulders. I wanted to open my hands and rub my arms, but I couldn't stop. I had to keep this going. Who knew if it would work, but I was feeling something.

I kept going, willing my power into Erik. The longer I tried, the more the pain in my arms intensified, turning into a burning numbness. I felt like vomiting. Until I heard a gasp from the crowd.

I opened my eyes and walked quickly to the weight room entrance, holding on to my head as a bout of dizziness hit me. I pushed through the crowd, the pain in my arm now suddenly gone. I spotted Felix and stood next to him, looking on at the fight. Erik was standing now, and he was lifting Donte up in the air with barely any visible strain. He then dropped the man down hard on the tile floor with incredible force. Donte's elbows hit the floor first, and I heard a loud crack. Bones in both arms were surely broken. Erik, limping, moved to Donte's left leg and stomped down on the ankle, shattering it. Donte howled with a spine-shaking loudness, and I gasped, slightly sickened.

Donte sat up and struggled to stand on his good foot. A normal person would be down for the count but the fighters didn't have the luxury of writhing around in agony. That meant death. If he got up, I didn't know what could happen. Yet, for him to heal well enough to even attempt to stand made it clearer to me that he was being helped by magic. Erik had to finish him before Donte healed even more. My magic assistance was gone now, but I hoped it was the edge Erik needed to win this.

As if on cue, Erik limped over and punched Donte in the face, hard, sending the man back to the floor. Erik's fingernails were now talons, and his fingers were arched out posed to attack.

The crowd, which at one point had been Donte's biggest supporters, were now yelling for Erik to finish him. Donte looked up at him, face swollen, angry, and tired.

"It doesn't have to be like this," Erik said to him.

Donte spits a mixture of phlegm and blood at Erik, and it landed by his boot. "Do it or die!" he croaked out. "And I'll come for your witch bitch as soon as you're gone."

I raised my eyebrows. Was he referring to me?

The crowd was counting down now. Erik had thirty seconds to finish him, or he would die too. But thirty seconds was also enough time for this male witch, or whatever he was, to heal Donte. Erik had to make a move now.

Erik looked down at his feet. His shoulders rose and fell from exhaustion. When he looked up, his eyes were those of a jackal. With a speed I'd never seen from him, he grabbed Donte's hair, forcing his head back, and slashed Donte's exposed throat with his claws. I looked away as the blood began to pour.

I honestly expected the crowd to cheer, but no one did. The room went silent. When I assumed Donte took his last breath, I heard Seth speak. "We have a winner. Erik Bennet is now my third in command," Seth announced, slapping Erik on the back in a less than friendly way. "We will celebrate Saturday. But until then, we mourn the passing of our brother Donte. He was a good man and will be missed."

The crowd agreed. There were cries of anguish and sobbing. A woman, maybe a wife or girlfriend of Donte, was being consoled by Carter, Raya, and a third Hispanic man who appeared to be in his late thirties. I was guessing he was the fifth in command.

I let out a deep sigh, feeling suddenly exhausted as the adrenaline from the battle subsided. I couldn't let anyone see my state. If I fell now, it would be a giveaway that I had used magic. I looked to Erik, who had dropped to his knees and fallen to his side. He looked like he was hanging by a thread. I had to heal him, but if I did, I wouldn't be walking out of here. Yet, another giveaway.

Felix linked his arm with mine and led me to Erik as if knowing I was not strong enough to move on my own. I looked up at him and smiled before leaning heavily on him, thankful that the massive guy could take my extra weight.

When we reached Erik, I fell to my knees and touched his slashed cheek. He winced with ragged breath.

"I'm sorry," I said.

"I can heal myself, Mina," he said in a hoarse voice.

"I know you can, but you'll be covered in ugly scars. I can keep you pretty," I replied.

He gave a faint chuckle before coughing.

I then closed my eyes and pushed my magic down

through my fingers and into him. Since I was weak, his healing was slow; I wasn't going to be able to heal every part of him.

"Hey," Lisa said. I opened my eyes and saw her sitting down on the floor beside me. She laid a hand on Erik's hand, closing her eyes. I soon felt her magic beneath my fingertips. It was cool and feathery. Vastly different from my own heated magic.

I looked back down to Erik and felt another layer of magic, and then another surrounded us in a small cocoon. Waves of coolness, warmth, soft feathers and even a gel-like touch waved over me as the differing magics mixed and combined. Even my own low energy level began to rise. The magic wasn't just healing Erik but me too. Felix sat a few feet from me with his hands hovering over Erik's feet, and Charles sat across me, hands over Erik's chest, muttering a healing spell. Faith sat on my other side and touched Erik's shoulder. I didn't even know she had healing powers. At least not the type of power to heal others. I smiled at them. We really were a team. Maybe there was something to this connection that Mae thought we had. More than ever, I was thankful that she insisted I come.

CHAPTER 21

*W*hen the morning alarm blared through the town that Saturday, I rolled my eyes. The monthly mind control seemed a bit early. I hummed a tune in my head, planning to ignore his words.

"Good morning citizens of New Silver Spring, I am here to tell you that I care about each and every one of you and I am here to protect you and make sure we thrive as a community. There is nowhere else that will be as safe and as prosperous as New Silver Spring. While I am a merciful and wise leader, sometimes I have to make uncomfortable decisions," Phillip's voice blared through the speakers.

This was new.

"It has, regrettably, come to my attention that during a challenge for the seating of third spot for our local pack, magic was used."

I paused my humming. Shit, Phillip knew. But why hadn't he confront me before?

"The perpetrator of this magic broke the rules and assisted one of the fighters. As you know, in order to maintain a peaceful and successful community, we must abide by rules no matter how big or small. Therefore, today at noon, at the town center, we will have

punishment. Everyone over the age of seventeen must attend. Thank you."

I lay frozen. Why didn't I tell the others and have us all get out of here when we could? Mae said I didn't have to fear Phillip. Could she have been wrong?

I showered, dressed, and later made my way to the town center. Since no one came to the door to drag me away, I could only assume that I wouldn't be the one punished. But the thought that they were going to yell out my name when this thing started like the *Price is Right* didn't escape me, so I wasn't exactly breathing easy.

When I got to the town center, it was packed with people. Turns out, the town center was in the middle of the entertainment area. A stage was set up in the middle of the pedestrian-only street bordered by shops, restaurants, and a movie theater. We were standing way in the back, facing the stage where the spectacle would take place. Although we couldn't see anything, Phillip made sure the large TV mounted to a brick wall of one of the shops farthest from the stage showed the event.

"This is bullshit," Felix said, crossing his large arms and shaking his head. "Why are they forcing us to watch some poor dude get punished?"

"Haven't you learned from the pack fight?" Faith began. "This place seems to like outdated practices."

Phillip decked out in a tailored black suit and blue button-down shirt and tie, walked onto the stage and stood in front of a microphone stand. Seth, Blake, Mae, and another older Asian man whom I never met, stood beside him. I was soon coming to believe that they were his top advisors.

"Good afternoon, I'm sorry that we have to be here for this on such a beautiful afternoon so I will be quick. As you know, we lost our brother Donte earlier this week in a fight for pack high position. No matter how we may feel about such things, these are part of the natural being of many were-types and are instinctual. Therefore, when such fights are interfered with by those outside the pack, we take that very seriously. Someone was helping Donte through magic the evening of the fight."

Whispers broke out in the audience.

"I understand everyone's concern. Yet, even with this assistance, our brother, Erik, was able to succeed and win. However, it is with a heavy heart that I must say that Wilfred Flannery used magic and must be punished."

I looked to the right of the stage as we saw two pack members bring to the platform a short, white male, appearing to be in his 40s, with glasses and a receding hair-line of brown hair. The witch from the pack fight.

I turned around to face Grace, who was watching the screen, a hand to her mouth.

"Who's Wilfred?" Erik asked her.

"Wilfred is a witch and was a huge fan of Donte's when he played football. Practically worshiped him. Think it just made him feel normal to have a celebrity around. He's a good guy. Harmless. Guess he didn't want to see his hero die. Or Donte could have asked him to help. He wasn't a very honest man," Grace explained.

"Wilfred," Phillip began, staring down at the man who was now on his knees. "Do you admit that you helped Donte with your magic in the fight?"

Wilfred, who did not look the least bit scared, nodded. Odd. I would be petrified.

"The punishment for such assistance can be as high as death. But I try to be a fair leader, and I don't take killing anyone lightly. Therefore, Wilfred, your punishment shall be the loss of your left hand, and you may not use magic for a year unless requested by a town lead." Phillip nodded over to one of the pack henchmen, a large, bald, white male, who held a machete in his hand. The other henchman, a black man with a low fade, placed a large bucket in front of Wilfred on the ground.

I looked over to Erik, who was staring at me. He leaned in and placed his hand on the small of my back. "We don't do anything," he whispered. He knew from the look on my face that I was getting antsy. "We have to accept this."

I held my breath as a henchman brought Wilfred's arm out over the bucket. Wilfred closed his eyes tightly and bared his teeth. Then the machete came down, and in one swift motion, the hand was removed from the wrist and fell into the bucket. Wilfred cried out in agonizing pain. Blood dripped from the severed opening into the bucket.

The henchmen dragged the crying Wilfred off the stage, while the crowd remained silent and in place.

Phillip began to speak. "Let this be a reminder that rules are in place for a reason. If we break them, this society cannot work. The consequences are swift and real. Follow the rules, and this town will continue to be an excellent place to live." Phillip looked over to me and smiled. "Please enjoy the rest of your day and look out for each other."

The crowd then began to disperse, recovering too easily from the maiming they just witnessed. I, however, remained standing, still in confusion and shock.

"Maybe I can help reattach his hand," I said.

"If you do, Phillip will remove it again," Grace stated, walking closer to me.

"Has Phillip done this before?" Charles asked.

Grace shook her head. "The prior leader did, though. You break the rules, you get broken," she said solemnly. "They've taken people's eyes, fingers, toes, feet, ears. Branded people. We can't afford to have people be unproductive and sit in a prison. So, he does the punishments. It doesn't happen often, though."

"Mae wants us to meet her at her place in an hour," Lisa

stated, suddenly. "Apparently, she is telepathic, and she just sent me a message." She shook her head in surprise.

"Well, does she want to meet about leaving this place?" Faith asked, hands on her hips, and face frowning with anger. "For me, living in a town that chops off people's hands seems like a place I don't want to live."

I was beginning to agree.

~

We met in Mae's apartment, and there was a face I had never met before already there, along with the six of us, Carter and Grace. It was a packed house.

Mae, being Mae, had coffee and tea available and oatmeal cookies sitting on her wooden dining room table.

"Hi, everyone, so glad you all could make it," she announced. "Please grab a cookie or something to drink and make yourselves at home. I know you all are wondering why I asked you to be here." She clasped her hands together and smiled at everyone. There was some excitement in her eyes and considering we all just witness a man lose a hand, I couldn't figure out what it was about. "But first, let me introduce you to my partner, Bill. He's the head med mage, so if your own magic doesn't work to heal, Bill can fix you up as well. He's the best there is."

I looked over to the older man, drinking a cup of tea or coffee, sitting at the dining room table. He was in his late 60s, Native American, with short, gray hair, and kind-looking, almost-black eyes. He had a bit of a stomach threatening to hang over his jeans but was otherwise in decent shape. Bill wore a brown leather vest over a white T-shirt that stated, "Keep Calm and Carry On." Around his neck was a long silver chain with a turquoise feather pendant. He had a pleasant face. I liked him.

Bill gave a nod to all of us with a smile. I had no idea Mae had herself a boyfriend.

Mae grinned at him proudly before turning to us. "I'll bet y'all were a little unnerved by today's events," she stated.

"Grace explained that this is your form of crime control here," I stated.

"This is true. It's not as awful as it seems."

"I beg to damn differ," Faith spat. "You have a prison here, put his ass in there."

"And how productive to the community would that be?"

She shrugged and crossed his arms. "Or he could make people do forced labor to pay off their crimes like in Hagerstown."

"Maim them or enslave them for a period of time. I suppose it's all unwelcome."

I wanted Mae to share with the group what she'd told me. Phillip was a bit more sympathetic if you understood his history with being out of control. Having a witch break the rules without punishment would offend his sensibilities. He hadn't had justice for the death of his brother or mentor, but he would get it in other areas. I was surprised about how much I understood him.

"So, people are all cool with Phillip doing this?" Charles asked.

"It's been this way for a while," Mae replied. "And Phillip has a gift that allows him to keep people in control. Similar to Amina's magic. He uses it from time to time to maintain control. It works on most living paranormal beings that don't possess any mind control powers themselves. Like myself, Amina, or Lisa as a fairy."

I looked to Lisa, and she waved at the rest of us. I'd forgotten that the Fae could make others see things that weren't there, as well as cause people to sleep and be confused.

"Or me," Grace chimed in. "I'm a siren if anyone didn't know."

"Sweet. Wait, sirens control minds? I thought you just sang well and crashed ships?" Charles asked, faced confused as he shook his head and grabbed a cookie.

I eyed Charles with a look of disappointment. I didn't know much about sirens either, but I certainly wasn't going to disrespectfully brush her off as just being someone who sang songs.

Grace lost her smile momentarily and then smiled again, looking to Charles. "You're allergic to cookies, Charles," she said in a sing-song voice that was actually quite sweet and soprano like.

I squinted my eyes. Charles was far from allergic to cookies. I don't think he was allergic to anything, especially if it was edible.

Charles frowned at the cookie and put it back on the plate. "Why am I picking this up? I'm allergic." He shook his head. "What do I have, some type of death wish or something?" he muttered.

We all stared at him. He looked around at the room with wide eyes. "What? Miss Mae, did you make any cake or pie? That was really good last time."

Mae smiled and walked to the kitchen. She was holding out on us.

"You aren't allergic to cookies, Charles," I stated. I crossed my arms. "Ha, Grace made you think that!" I was impressed.

I looked back over to Grace, who looked like the cat who ate the canary. "Beyond what the fairy tales say, sirens are much more than women hanging off cliffs, sending sailors to their deaths. Admittedly we aren't high on the folklore pyramid; therefore, most people don't have a clue about us. Basically, I can sing very well and when singing, what I want someone to do, they do it. Or I can kill them with the sound of my voice. I can even narrow the sound of my voice only to those I want to hear it. And since I have that control, like Mae, I can't be controlled by others who have similar mental powers."

"Does your power trump Phillip's?" I asked, still standing.

She tilted her head back and forth. "Not so much trump but rather works alongside. I can't compel you not to be controlled by Phillip, in general, but if Phillip tells you to do something specific, like sitting down, I could sing to you to never sit down when Phillip tells you. I have to be specific."

"So, we just let Phillip do whatever?" Erik asked.

Mae looked to him, bringing back two plates holding slices of peach cobbler. One she gave to Bill and the other to Charles. "We don't let him do whatever. That's why we are here. And with Lisa and Amina, you both can also make sure he stays on the straight and narrow. And I have faith that you will help us do that. Phillip is a good soul. With the six of you here, I think we're going to all be okay."

"What exactly about the six of us is so special? You alluded to it before, but is there more?" I asked. "I'm assuming that's why you asked us to come? Is there a new vision?"

Mae nodded, sitting down at her dining room table. "I thought you were special. It's why I reached out to you, Lisa. But I didn't want to lead you astray. I've been having visions of the six of you displaying power in a way I've never seen, only read about. You have a connection that's meant for something great."

"Even how you worked together to heal Erik after the fight was very impressive," Bill added before taking another bite of his dessert.

"I understand that magic is new to us all, but it was here even before the world changed. And when it came and took over the world, the magic that was hiding in us all came to exist. Your life is what it is because of the special connection you have," Mae explained.

Erik shook his head. "How do you know this?"

"I've had a weaker version of my current power all my life. I've seen things and connections in the world and studied to understand them. The literature, as I'm sure those with witch gifts are aware, was already out there because of others sensitive to magic knowing of it. After the magic hit us, my curiosity only grew with my visions. I had to understand. There are patterns in history. Special groups of six have changed the world behind the scenes and sometimes in the spotlight. They've ended plagues and wars. They are brought to the world to help humanity survive. And this time is no different." She looked around at the group, her eyes pleading with us to understand. "I just don't know what your purpose is specifically yet. But something dark is coming. You must ready yourselves. What I know now is that magic is ever growing. No matter what type of magic you have, you will be better as time grows. Erik, you are a stronger were-jackal than you were years before. Never doubt your powers. That would have been an easier fight for you if Wilfred hadn't helped Donte."

"Right," I said, throwing out my hands in exasperation. "That's why I helped Erik. To even the playing field." I hadn't told them before because the week became busy after the fight, and it didn't seem like information that needed to be shared, especially since Erik had won anyway.

The group murmured in surprise.

Erik looked down at me with shocked eyes, an incredulous look on his face. I'd never seen that look on him before. "Mina, I wish you hadn't. I could have won that fight on my own," he said a tightness in his voice. "I didn't need your help."

Was he angry? I gave a confused frown, remembering how I nearly passed out, throwing him all my power in that weight room. So much for showing some appreciation. "Erik, you wouldn't have won that fight if I hadn't helped you."

"Aw, shit," I heard Charles murmur.

Several other mutterings ensued by the men in the room. Felix gave bug eyes, Bill lowered his head and shook it, and Carter let out a loud cough.

Erik's jaw tightened, and he looked down at me with a cold stare. "It's always nice to hear, yet again, how little faith you have in me. Next time you think I'm too weak, walk away."

I huffed, thoroughly confused. I didn't understand men in the Pre-world, and in this world, I still didn't. Clearly, instead of learning to fight off crazed gremlins, I should have studied up more on the male sex. "This is why I didn't say anything before. Because of the fragile male ego."

"What the? You don't want to get married, do you?" Charles asked face scrunched up in frustration.

"Even I know she shouldn't have said that," Felix whispered loudly.

"Oh, hell no, I won't be drawn into yet another lover's quarrel!" Faith shouted. She pointed at Erik. "Look, suck it up, dude. Magic was being used for your opponent, and that was an unfair fight. Mina and Felix figured it out, and Mina did what she had to in order to make sure you didn't die out there because she cares about you. I'm sure Mina wouldn't have interfered if magic weren't being used, right?" She glanced over to me, and I nodded vigorously. "And you, Amina." She pointed at me this time. "Some things are better left unsaid. And have faith in your man, woman."

She was so right. I already regretted saying anything. In retrospect, he hadn't needed to know what I'd done. Erik was a strong man, and getting help from someone wasn't going to be something he'd appreciate. I also had to confront the very concern that I was doubting our capabilities. We were supposed to be special, but I still didn't have trust in us or myself. That doubt had been a part of a lot of my troubles in the past. I had to shake it and believe that I could win something. There was too much to do, and none of us had family that we knew of still alive. We were each other's rocks. So far, I wasn't being much support. I needed to get to why.

Erik reached over and grabbed my hand, giving it a tight squeeze. He didn't look at me, but I could see his face was now relaxed. I stifled a smile. Guess we had made amends for now.

"You guys are so damn cute," Lisa squealed.

"Can we get back to the main issue?" Erik grumbled, still holding my hand.

Mae nodded and smiled at me. "I know that I keep saying that the six of you are not only strong but connected. For now, you might have found that you have a good sense of each other's feelings. And a need to touch each other." She waved her hand at Erik and me.

And here I thought it was just were sense and Erik's hidden affectionate nature.

I looked over to Lisa, leaning on Felix, who was propped against the wall and then to Charles, sitting on the arm of the sofa next to a seated Faith, who was resting an arm on his thigh. How had I never noticed the others staying so connected before? Was I so wrapped up in my own thing with Erik to spot it? Of course, I was.

"You work almost like twins would. Don't run away from the natural instinct of what you feel. You are family. Some of you are like sisters and brothers, others are like lovers. But it is meant to be," Mae explained.

I looked over to Charles and noticed him gazing over at Lisa from across the room, who gave him a sweet smile in return.

"You six represent the various forms of power, which is part of this special connection you have. The were's animal connection, mage's earth connection, the Fae's otherworldly connection, the succubus life, and death connection." She looked to Felix. "And you, which I'm still working on figuring out."

Felix lowered his shoulders and sighed.

"I'm here to guide you all to your fullest potential and help you experience your powers in ways you never imagined. I just ask that you be brave, loyal, and love each other."

"That, we can do," Erik replied. He paused. "If one of us dies, does this bond we all have get destroyed?"

Mae frowned and looked over to Bill, who gave her a sympathetic face. She looked back to Erik. "I-I don't know," she whispered, a concerned look on her face.

I hoped we never had to find out.

CHAPTER 22

*S*everal days of normalcy occurred before I was contacted in the middle of teaching a history class to a room of 11 to 13-year-olds.

The African-American female teacher, who I knew only as Tricia, waved her hand for me to leave the room. I asked the class to quickly read over the rest of the chapter of the history book.

"I'll take over your class. You were summoned to the police station by Phillip," she stated with wide eyes.

My heart felt like it dropped to my feet. Had he finally found out I used magic too?

"Did he say why?" I asked.

Tricia quickly shook her head. "I didn't talk to him directly, just someone from his staff. He said it was really important, though."

I nodded in thanks to her and left the building. The police station was walking distance to the school. About a ten-minute walk. Anxiousness made the walk seem more like thirty minutes.

Once I got to the prison, an older white woman sitting at the front desk told me to head back to the cell area. She mentioned that was where Phillip and "the others" were, confusing me even more.

Once I got to the basement cell room, I found my friends, Phillip, Carter, and Seth standing in front of a cell staring at someone. I walked closer, eyebrows furrowed in confusion, and looked inside the cell at a man I'd never seen before.

He was an older white male with thinning gray hair and wire-rimmed glasses.

"What's going on?" I asked.

Phillip smiled at me. "We caught someone who was at the Pittsburg hospital."

I walked closer to the cell. "You're actually from the Pittsburg hospital?" I asked.

The man, sitting on a bench, hung his head, forearms resting on his knees. He didn't respond.

"Answer her," Phillip commanded, slapping the bars.

The man nodded his head slowly.

I looked to Phillip. "How'd you find him?"

"With the help of a couple of my witches. The trace was very bare, so that's why it took so long. I'm guessing these people have a cloaking spell of some sort. One of the witches did her daily locator spell and got a hit. We found him at the Pittsburg prison. He was picking up something he left behind."

I looked back at the man. "Who are you?"

The prisoner didn't respond.

Phillip sighed and looked up at the ceiling. "*Cabrón*, if you don't answer this woman…" he began.

The man looked up. "My name is Mark Flint," he glanced over to Phillip with worried eyes. He was clearly scared of him. What had Phillip done? Mark didn't look particularly beat up.

"What did you do at the prison?" I asked. I wasn't certain I believed this guy was part of the Pittsburg group. He didn't look even remotely familiar.

"I was a chemist. I helped make the serum."

"What?" Charles thundered. "You're behind all of this?"

Mark's eyes went wide behind his glasses. "No, no, no, no," he sputtered, sitting upright. "I just make it from the formula I was given. I didn't invent this. Someone else did. This is bigger than Pittsburg."

"I remember David said that. He said there were more places," I stated.

Mark nodded, scooting to the edge of the bench. "There are a few camps on the east coast. They're like the Pittsburg hospital. We house paranormals, take their blood, and make the serum."

"Then what?"

"Then we-we sell the serum to other humans. It's one of the best things to barter with, out there. People want it to be able to fight you people or take over human towns. A few people think it will aid them in becoming president."

"Of course, they do," Charles muttered.

"How many camps are there? Who's the leader of it all?" I asked, a tightness in my chest. The range of this was much more than I could have imagined.

"You will tell her the truth," Phillip said, leaning against the bars, a neutral look on his face.

"We've got four camps. Well, three, now that we had to close the Pittsburg camp. One in Long Island, one in Charlotte, and a third in Chicago. David is in charge of it all, if one can be in charge. Every base lead is fighting for control, but David has the most control. Long Island is the largest base, but the guy who runs it is an idiot. David controls the scientists who make the serum. The other bases just collected blood and gave out supplies. When David moved our base to another base, he demoted the leader there. He's probably going to have to kill him because the guy wasn't too happy about it and might cause trouble," Mark replied in an agitated voice.

"David didn't say he was the leader," I stated. "Where did you move the Pittsburg base? Where are the other para-normals?"

"Long Island," Phillip answered.

"Okay. Let's go, then," Charles said.

"Let's go scout it out first. We have to know how many we're up against," Erik stated, standing beside me with folded arms.

Phillip shook his head. "I already have people scouting it out now."

"They're already there?" I asked.

Phillip nodded.

"It's only 11 a.m. How'd they get there so fast? How long have you had this guy? You had to get to Pittsburg, then come back here. Then send people to New York."

"I didn't want to disturb you if we were wrong, so my people teleported there."

"What? How?" I asked.

"A spell. We have a large database here of spells we've either found, discovered, or developed and a good number of witches who can make things happen. Teleportation isn't something every witch can do, it takes a certain magic level. I'm sure you can do it. I'll teach you the spell, but it is very draining."

"There are magic levels?" I heard Charles whisper to no one in particular. I had the same question.

"Well, I can't thank you enough," I replied, truly grateful.

"Right, so your people give us the coordinates to the Long Island prison, and we go back to Hagerstown and mobilize. And I'm sure the government town in New York will help us," Erik stated.

"We don't need them," Seth said. He'd been quiet up until now, leaning against a wall near the exit.

"We?"

Seth nodded. "Yeah, we'll help. We've got to support our kind."

"We appreciate the help," I said, looking over to Phillip, "But Hagerstown is coming too. They lost people to this group, and they have an interest in not letting this type of situation go unchecked. It's how they instill faith and support for the new government."

"And this whole town is not going to fight with us. Hagerstown has soldiers," Erik added.

"Although you have gifts, you can't forget that these humans are enhanced with that paranormal potion," Phillip reminded him, voice even. "So, it's going to be more difficult than you may think."

"Which we can fight as well because we have a weapon for that," Seth replied with his cocky smile. We all stared at him. "Come on... I know you want to ask," Seth said in a sing-song voice.

"Ask what? I am lost," Felix whispered to Charles, visibly frustrated.

"Dear God, what is the secret weapon?" Faith asked, shaking her head.

Seth clapped his hands and then pointed at her with both hands. "Glad you aren't afraid to ask. Farrah, is it?"

What could only be described as fire rimmed her eyes. "Faith," she said through gritted teeth. I wasn't sure if she was smiling or snarling, but it didn't look nice.

"Faith! How appropriate. Anyway, we knew about this potion before you guys told us. We've run into some of this David asshole's customers. We've seen these enhanced humans in action. Some of them come from your own friendly government towns. They've been doing this for a year, maybe two. This operation could spread wider than we think. Could be the whole country, maybe the world. You force a tech mage or witch to get you access to a plane or teleport you or you just use a ship, and the world becomes a smaller place again. A place that humans can run and ruin."

"Hagerstown didn't know about this, they're good people," Faith countered, face in a confused frown.

Phillip shrugged. "Maybe they didn't, which then also means the government isn't as together as you'd like to believe. Not all of them are playing by the same rules. Anyway, we decided to fight fire with fire and had our good doctor Bill develop several antidotes. They will, in short, prevent the potions from ever working again, no matter how much they drink. It's not a one size fits all but the blood potions that the humans take aren't either. Certain blood from certain creatures gives certain effects. Of course, we haven't encountered every type of paranormal out there, but we have many here, and the elixirs can, at the very least, temporarily affect the enhanced humans."

"And we put the potions in syringes or syringe guns for up-close battles," Carter added, standing beside Seth. "It just has to get in their system like a vaccine."

"Easier said than done," Erik stated.

Carter nodded. "I was a chemist before all of this, and I've been working with Bill to try to find different ways that are less up close and personal to get the antidote to work. And there's something else to consider." He looked to Phillip, who nodded.

He had to get permission to share information? Phillip had some kind of control over people.

"If you get stuck, it will mute your powers for a while. Not permanently, but it can last anywhere from a few hours to a few weeks, depending on your power level and the type of potion you were stuck with."

"They had a similar serum in the prison. That's how our powers were muted, and we couldn't fight back. We'd get stuck every other day to make sure it didn't wear off. I'm sure they have it in weapon form as well, so we have to be careful of more than friendly fire," I pointed out.

"From what I'm hearing, it sounds like this trip's going to be dangerous," Felix surmised. "Can we have brunch before we go? I fight best on a full stomach."

By the end of our meeting, we'd heard from the scouters sent to New York. They'd determined that between the community and the prison, there were over one thousand people there. Around two hundred of which were prisoners. We decided to set off in three hours. Felix got his brunch wish, Erik was to fill in Hagerstown by email and make sure they were mobilized, and we agreed to teleport there. Seth went to ready the Silver Spring fighters. Carter and some of my group went to prep antidotes. We left Mark in his cell for a later determination.

Finally, we were going to get our friends.

CHAPTER 23

Teleporting felt like one of those amusement park rides where you were shot up into the air and dropped back down. People used to actually wait in lines and pay money to have their insides feel like they were tumbling all around, and here I was, doing it for free. I preferred teacup rides. No stomach-churning moves or soul-snatching drops. Just nice, breezy fun. I knew that I would be taking a car out of New York if, no, when, I survived. They told us we would get used to teleporting, but I wasn't convinced.

We were tossed about five miles away from the prison in an abandoned cul-de-sac far away from the nearest community connected to the prison. Perhaps "tossed" was too strong a word. I did land on my feet, but my insides certainly felt tossed around, and I shamefully retched up what little food I'd eaten that morning. I wasn't the only one so affected, and Charles comically threatened to sue. Who, we would never know.

The Hagerstown soldiers were less than an hour out when we arrived, and the Silver Spring fighters had set up base in a few of the houses.

We attacked in groups. I was left as one of the last waves,

along with Lisa, Felix, and Charles. I didn't like waiting. I was ready to fight. And fighting came soon enough.

By the time my group arrived at the prison, there was no surprise, and we were falling straight into the battle.

The prison was actually a small liberal arts college, and we headed to the dorms where we learned the captured were being held. Most of the fighting was in the other areas of the campus. While we focused on freeing people, the other groups would be fighting off in the distance and, hopefully, distracting the community from what we were doing.

Clearing the area of the guards wasn't as traumatic as I thought it would be. I was able to take out guards without killing them by utilizing a paralyzing spell. Of course, that would make them prisoners, and Silver Spring was more into the take-no-prisoners business. Hagerstown, however, was willing to handle those enemies left surviving.

"I don't see Jared," Charles shouted amongst the chaos. "I don't see any of our friends!"

He was right. I hadn't seen them either. "Maybe they aren't in the dorms."

Lisa ran up to us. "What's going on?" she asked.

"Lisa, can you help the folks who aren't fighters get out of the campus and to safety?"

Before she could answer, the sound of gunshots rang in the air. Several prison guards, positioned down the hall to our right, were shooting at us. Two paranormals fell to the floor, hit. Lisa threw out her hands wide, and a barrage of bullets bounced off the invisible wall of the protective shield she created, surrounding us from the right.

Charles spun his index finger in a circle, and the fallen bullets rose and zoomed back at the prison guards. They attempted to dodge the oncoming bullets but were not fast enough. The guards were hit and killed.

"Don't shoot!" cried a guard walking around the corner. He was a black man with long dreadlocks.

"Reggie!" I shouted.

He frowned. "Amina?" he questioned with confused eyes. "What's going on?"

"We're freeing those we left behind."

He nodded, looking around. "Right."

Charles stood next to me. "Who is this dude?" he questioned.

"He helped me escape the prison. He's a good guy," I explained before turning back to Reggie. "Are you going to help us?"

Reggie nodded. "Of course, I will. Whatever you need from me."

"Good. There's a place for you back in the government town, I'm sure of it."

Reggie shook his head quickly. "I'll do what I can here, but I think it's best I just go on my own way after we get everyone safely out. I don't need to remind these people of what they've been through."

I sighed. "Are you sure I can't change your mind on that?"

Reggie gave me a sad smile. "You're a good person, Amina. I'm glad you got out and could help these people. The world needs more good folks like you."

I walked over and gave him a tight hug. "If you ever need to reach me, here's my email address," I stated. I whispered a basic conjuring spell, and a slip of paper with my email address appeared in my hand.

Reggie looked at it with wide eyes before taking the paper and putting it in his pocket. He gave a nod and then turned to the huddled paranormals, who were looking at us with fear and confusion. "I'll help get you guys out."

I looked to Lisa. "Lisa, please go with them. Can you keep your protection shield up while moving?" I asked.

She nodded. "Yes, I've been practicing with my magic. I can teleport too," she replied, before turning and beginning her teleportation of children and elderly paranormals. "Lock hands, everyone. I'll see how many of you I can get out in one go."

"Take the children first," Reggie stated. "I'll guard the others until you return."

Lisa nodded and disappeared with a collection of children.

"Amina? Charles?" came a familiar voice.

I spun around and spotted Chelsea coming down the hall with a few other freed paranormals. I rushed over to her, and we embraced in a tight hug.

"I'm so happy you're okay!" I cried, pulling back from the hug.

She nodded a look of relief on her face. "Did you do this? Did you bring people to help us?" Chelsea asked, tears threatening to fall down her pale cheeks.

I nodded. "Charles and I."

Charles appeared to my right and rushed to hug Chelsea.

"I didn't think we'd see you again," she said in a choked voice.

"I'm so sorry we left you behind," I said, grabbing her hand.

Chelsea quickly shook her head. Her frizzy reddish-blond curls framed her face almost like a lion's mane. It was long and tangled, and for the first time, I noticed her clothes were dirty along with her face and hands. She looked even skinner than the last time I'd seen her. It was clear they were punishing her for our escape. Guilt stabbed me even more.

"No, I understand. You probably wouldn't have made it out if you came looking for me. I'm just so grateful you came back. And with reinforcements. I thought when we moved, it was over for us."

"Do you know where Jared is?" Charles asked.

Chelsea looked over to him, her eyes suddenly filled with sadness. She shook her head. "He didn't make it. They... They killed him. When you escaped, he was murdered as punishment for trying to get out and to set an example for us to stay in line. They were saying if we escaped or tried to escape, then someone close to us and left behind would be killed."

I put a hand to my mouth and shook my head. I felt like I was gutted. I pictured Jared's jolly face in my head. His laughter when he told inappropriate tales of his life in the Pre-world with groupies, his scowling at the injustices around him, and most importantly, his selflessness on the day that Charles and I escaped. I would never be able to repay him now. We had to free everyone. His life would not go in vain.

"I'm sorry, Amina," Reggie whispered. "I tried to get him to reconsider killing him."

I shook my head. "You could only do so much without getting implicated."

Charles closed his eyes and leaned his forehead against the cement wall. "Let's end this."

I nodded.

"Where are we going?" Felix asked. He came up beside Charles and patted him on the shoulder.

"You should go with Lisa," I stated.

Felix narrowed his eyes in confusion. "Why? I'm not useless."

"I didn't say you were."

Felix lowered his head, and his shoulders rose and lowered quickly. He looked like he was hyperventilating, only he wasn't. I looked over to Charles, who glanced at me with a worried look.

Chelsea leaned into me. "What's wrong with him?" she whispered.

"Good question," I replied. "Felix, honey, we have to get moving. You can come with us. I don't mean to make you angry." I looked around at the others. "Is that what I did, did I make him angry?" They shrugged, and I looked over to Felix again. "We have to get going." He didn't acknowledge me, just kept doing that Lamaze breathing thing.

I looked to Charles, who pointed at his watch and tossed his hands outwards.

Felix suddenly looked up at Charles, and his brown eyes seemed brighter than before; the whites of his eyes were clearer. "They killed your friend as punishment. We have to stop them, and I can help with that." His voice was deeper and stranger like there was more than one voice coming out of him. It was scary.

"The hell," Charles said in a barely audible voice.

Felix turned and walked out of the dormitory. Charles, Chelsea, and I followed along with a couple of other soldiers.

"Where are you going?" I asked him.

"To David. I assume you want to kill him," Felix replied in the same creepy voice.

"Does he sound like he's possessed to you?" Charles whispered.

"That's not his regular voice?" Chelsea whispered back. "What's his power?"

"We don't know what his power is," Charles replied.

"I think we should just be quiet before he looks back at us. I'm a little nervous," I stated.

"Should we be following him?" Chelsea asked.

"He seems to be on the way to the fighting, and the soldiers are with us, so I guess it can't hurt," Charles answered.

We followed Felix the rest of the way in silence. From the sound of it, the fighting was spread throughout the campus. We walked to the middle of a long, white building on our right and entered the building through double glass doors. Once inside, we faced an open space leading to an auditorium.

"Do we want to go in there and help out?" Charles asked. He pointed to the auditorium doors, a few knocked off the hinges, where lots of shouting and shooting could be heard.

It would be chaos inside. We could help.

Felix kept walking to the left of the doors down a wide, open hallway. "No," he replied.

I looked back at the two soldiers, who looked like they were seriously considering ditching us as they stared into the auditorium beyond some open doors. It was all-out war in there. With the bodies being thrown around, it was hard to tell who the good guys were, except for the fact that Hagerstown and Silver Spring folks were wearing green bands around their arms.

The soldiers accompanying us whispered to each other but kept walking. There was something about Felix now that made us believe he knew where we could be most useful. I couldn't explain it, he just had a new aura around him that we wanted to follow. And we had to get to David. And kill him.

We walked a few minutes more, entering a linked walkway, taking us into another building. One side of the walls were ceiling-to-floor windows. The other side held display cases with trophies and several closed classroom doors. Felix stopped and turned in front of another set of double doors. It was the cafeteria, and I could hear a serious rumble as loud as the one in the auditorium.

"Here," scary-voiced Felix stated before walking through the open doors.

We followed. Once inside, we were greeted to what looked like several wrestling matches happening all at once. To my left, I spotted Faith grabbing a weapon-holding capturer by the face with both hands. She kissed him. "That does not look like fighting," I said aloud, moving out of the way of our soldier teammates, who rushed into action.

However, Faith's make-out session was anything but that. Within moments, to my horrified eyes, the male prison guard thinned out. Fat disappeared from his body until he was only muscle; thin skin stretched tightly over muscle and skeleton, leaving an emaciated figure. His eyes bugged out, and cheeks sank inwards. His skin dried, looking as fragile as paper, and paled, taking on a grayish tint. Soon all life left his eyes, and only a frozen look of terror remained on his mummified face. This all took a matter of seconds before he died. Faith dropped the corpse, and I could see her eyes were now ruby-red circles, taking on a terrifying, otherworldly look. A wicked smile crossed her lips.

Charles leaned into me. "Remind me never to kiss her," he stated, before bending down to grab a gun out of the hands of a deceased soldier.

"Watch out!" I screamed right before seeing a guard shoot Faith in the shoulder from behind. She bent forward and then straightened up quickly as if she had only been shoved. Milliseconds later, I saw a blur grab the guard's rifle, and he fell to the ground, grabbing his stomach, shot. Faith stood in front of him, pointing the now-smoking rifle at the guard. I hadn't even seen her move. She wouldn't be needing my help.

I moved my attention further into the crowd, searching for David. Instead, I caught sight of an eight-foot furry nightmare known as jackal Erik. Jackal Erik grabbed a guard who shot at him and ripped out his throat with his razor teeth, tossing the dead man to the side.

I covered my mouth and turned away. My friends were scary monsters.

I walked farther past the door and to the right, keeping my back to the titled cafeteria wall. More guards poured in from a door across the room, leading to an open outside eating area. I spotted Grace near that door, her arms open. Her eyes turned a brilliant gold, and she opened her mouth and...sang. It was something in another language and sounded like opera. Her voice was amazing, but...she was singing. The guards and unfriendly soldiers from New York battling around her stopped moving and gazed at her; swaying to the sound of her voice. It was melodic. I was tempted to walk over to her, but I held my position. She looked down at her audience, and they actually began to smile at her, hands reaching out to touch her, as if in worship.

She continued singing, reaching an impossibly high note.

Then their bodies exploded.

I let out an involuntary scream as I stared at the now-bloodied woman, looking less like a Disney princess and more like a horror movie scream queen. She was surrounded by blood, guts, and body parts. Grace gave a satisfying smile as she stepped over the mess to find new victims.

What...the...hell?

Something slammed into the wall next to me on my right. I jumped back and saw that it was a guard who had rammed his head into the wall and knocked himself out. Thick blood splattered the concrete wall, and the guard crumpled to the ground. I looked past him and saw Phillip walking towards me.

"Gotta be alert, *corazon*," Phillip said, a twinkle in his eyes. I think he liked this.

I snapped to attention. "Thank you. Grace was singing."

He nodded quickly, "Fun ability, isn't it?" He didn't wait for me to answer. "We're getting outnumbered, we must have miscalculated or underestimated their strength. I need you to do something drastic. Open up the ground."

I frowned. "What? I can't do that. I can shake the—"

He grabbed my arm gently. "Amina, you are stronger than you think. Crack open the ground. Now," he said in a measured voice.

"What if good people fall in?"

"They will move. And they know the risk of this mission. We're short on time."

I didn't like that answer, but I closed my eyes anyway.

Splitting open the ground didn't sound like it was in my bag of tricks, but then again, I never had occasion to do such a thing. I focused on the linoleum floor in my mind's eye and saw it breaking apart and splitting down the length of the large cafeteria. My fingers itched, and a sharp heat raced down my arms from my shoulder. My head throbbed, and a dull pain grew in the base of my skull. My legs grew shaky. I touched the wall behind me for support, and soon after, I felt a crack under my fingers. I opened my eyes and saw the wall separating.

Screams drew my attention back to the action in the middle of the cafeteria as a large gap appeared in the center of the floor. It was like a sinkhole with depths I could not see. It grew by the second. People were running towards the walls and exits while still shooting and attacking each other. But not everyone. To my amazement, some guards were actually walking and leaping into the hole. Their faces were blank, and they walked with purpose, not even pausing at the edge of the massive hole before jumping in.

I turned to Phillip, whose gaze was fixed on the guards as he moved his fingers in the air as if swiping a touchscreen computer. I turned to my left and saw two crying women huddled in the corner under a table. They looked like support staff. Much like nurse Joanie, who helped us stay alive in between draining's. I briefly wondered where she was now. I turned back to Phillip, who continued to swipe the air, and I had no doubt that he was controlling these guards and sending them to their probable deaths. Mind control was clearly his gift. I had way too many questions for him if we got out of this, namely why he kept his gift a secret.

I sensed movement from the corner of my eye and saw the two female support staff walking towards the hole with purposeful movement. I turned to Phillip. "Stop them!" I yelled.

He ignored me. I grabbed his arm and tried to lower it,

but the women kept walking. "They are support staff, don't kill them."

"They are part of this," he said through gritted teeth.

"Then we detain them. They aren't attacking us." The women were close to the edge now. My heart pounded loudly in my ears. Fear pricked at me, and my headache showed no signs of leaving.

"No one is going to waste resources, keeping these people alive."

"Stop!" I screamed, yanking at his arm. The women stopped in mid-stride, each having one foot hovering in the air over the sinkhole. The pain in my skull grew; dizziness accompanying it. "Get out of here! Run!" I commanded. They turned and ran out of the backdoors, away from the fighting.

Whoa! That was new. I hated to say it, but— "Did I do that?" I asked. I controlled supernatural primitive creatures before but never humans—gifted or otherwise—not until Lisa when I pulled her out of the ground. I thought maybe it was a fluke with more to do with the supernatural ground than her. Seems I was wrong.

Phillip looked over at me, mouth open, eyes frowning.

"I'll take that as a yes," I replied to myself.

Phillip suddenly smiled. "You've been holding out on me, *mi corazon*." He then turned away and stood two guards to attention with his mind control.

They began to walk away from each other. One of the guards had red hair and a beard. He looked familiar. I quickly recognized him as Chelsea's guard boyfriend, Oliver. I turned to search for her and found Chelsea across the room, backhanding a guard with her full vampire strength. I waved my arms and called to her. She eventually heard me and turned to my location, leaving her guards to bleed out and die.

Phillip clapped his hands together.

I turned to Phillip. "That guard with the red hair is my friend's boyfriend, so stop whatever you're going to do."

Phillip ignored me. I turned to see the guards raise their guns to their temples and pull the trigger.

Chelsea ran over to Oliver in lightning speed, but it was too late. The red-headed guard and his companion fell to the ground, dying instantly from the forced self-inflicted gunshot wounds. Chelsea let out a gut-wrenching scream.

I turned to Phillip and shoved him. "Why?"

Phillip looked down at me with confused eyes. "They're the bad guys."

I shook my head quickly. "Not everyone, Phillip. He was kind to my friend."

I turned back to Chelsea, who was now on her knees in front of the fallen Oliver, crying. She looked up at us in rage, her hazel eyes darkening. In a swift and supernaturally easy movement, she rose and stormed over to us. "Who did this?" she shouted.

Phillip looked down at her with a cold stare. "I did," he replied in an even tone.

"I didn't recognize him at first, Chelsea. When I did, it was too late. He didn't mean it," I lied to keep the peace. We had to remain focused on the greater mission and not fight each other. And, to be honest, Oliver wasn't totally innocent. He *was* part of the problem.

Chelsea looked to Phillip and considered him. He wasn't helping his case by maintaining a cold and uncaring look. "You don't look so sorry," she said in a steely tone.

"I am," Phillip said in a deadpan voice. "But he was a human, and if he were really good, he would have been the one to let you go instead of us." He *really* wasn't helping himself.

I spoke up. "Chelsea, this is the guy. He's the one who helped me escape. He's the reason we found you all."

She looked back over to me, hate and tears still in her

eyes. "Watch who you surround yourself with." She turned back to Phillip. "You are lucky Amina is here, and there's more to do. But I don't care what you did. Don't think this is over. The monsters aren't just the humans, Amina." She turned and stormed out of the chaos.

"You'd think she'd be appreciative," Phillip stated, unfazed by Chelsea's threat.

"Things aren't so black and white, Phillip. What you did was wrong. Even I don't understand," I said, placing my hands on my head to unsuccessfully stop the pounding in my skull. I was in pain and disappointed in Phillip. He wasn't exactly the gentleman that I saw in my dreams. Or had his seeing me imprisoned angered him enough to act so recklessly and cruel? Was I to blame for his behavior?

"It'll stop hurting soon. Teleporting can bring headaches when you go on to use more magic after, but the more you teleport, the less it happens."

"Thanks for the warning," I muttered. I turned my head away and witnessed Jackal Erik rip the arms off of a guard who shot him. I get shot, and I'm down for the count. Erik gets shot, and he mutilates a person.

I'd had enough. I didn't see David. It seemed Felix was wrong to lead us here.

CHAPTER 24

I headed to the door, leaving Phillip behind, but Felix was blocking the entrance battling a guard. Another guard, built like a sumo wrestler, rushed at Felix and tackled him to the ground. Felix pushed the palm of his hand against the man's forehead, and like that, the man fell to the side off of Felix, unconscious.

"You knocked him out with magic?" I asked, wide-eyed.

Felix looked up at me with those same strange glowing eyes. "No. I killed him. Get down!"

I didn't turn to see, I just dropped to my knees as the sound of bullets raced above me. I risked looking up and saw Charles to my right. He stopped them in mid-air with his hand outstretched in front of him. The bullets changed direction and returned to our attackers, killing them.

I glanced back to Felix, but he was gone; just the dead guard remained. "What?" I whispered. I crawled out of the cafeteria and looked in both directions down the hallway. No Felix. Was he that fast?

I got up on my feet and turned to my right, then left, jumping back as Felix stood in front of me with a blank, almost robotic face. I yelped.

"David was in that room, but then he ran out," Felix stated. "They say he's down this way." Felix pointed behind him.

"Seriously, man, what are you? Who is 'they?'"

Felix pointed to his head. "Azrael says you are not focused."

"Azrael is the voice speaking to you?"

Felix nodded.

"Azrael sounds really old school. Like old testament. Where is Azrael?"

Felix pointed his index finger to the ceiling. I looked up and saw nothing. "Upstairs?" I asked.

"Higher."

I thought for a beat. "Azrael's in heaven. He or she's an angel?"

Felix nodded again. "He says we have to go right now." Felix backed up as he talked before turning away from me and jogging down the hall. I ran after him, full of questions, but knowing it would have to wait.

We didn't run far before Felix stopped beside a door and held up his hand to stop me. "He knows," Felix whispered.

"Who?" I asked in a low voice.

"Come in, come in," a male voice called from behind the door. "I think we'd like the company."

Felix pushed the door open wide. I grabbed his shoulder, gently moving him out of the way. "Me, first," I said, my heart pounding in my ears.

My body tightened, and I balled my fist as I walked around Felix and entered the lecture hall. Rows of chairs went at a decline upon wide, tiled steps towards a podium at the lowest level of the room. David sat in a chair on the wide podium with an unconscious Lisa lying on the floor to his right. Damn it, why didn't she stay with the others?

David crossed his legs and waved me down. "Come on down. I've missed you," he called. He reached his hand in his pocket, and took out a syringe full of what I assumed was the blood potion and stuck it in his forearm. I grazed my hand over my pocket where my antidote syringe lay as I walked down the steps slowly, not sure of my next move. I looked over to Lisa, hoping she was just knocked out and not dead.

David followed my gaze. "Don't worry, your friend is alive. She's different. What is she?"

"None of your damn business."

"I'd hate to drain her. I mean, I still will. I'd just hate to. She's quite beautiful. Perhaps maybe we can...get to know each other first."

I reached out my hand and balled my fist again, envisioning his throat constricting. It still hurt my head to use my power, but this would be worth it. David's eyes widened, and he clawed at his throat, mouth hanging open as he struggled to breathe.

"Pois—" he gurgled out.

I frowned. Pois? Was he trying to say poison? I thought of his attack on me in the pharmacy and let go of the magic strangulation I had on him. "What?"

"I pumped her full of poison. Worse than what I gave you before."

"I can heal her." I clawed my hands out again, ready to restart my attack.

David threw out his hand in a stop motion. "But if the poison is magic based..."

"Someone will have the cure."

"That someone is me. And you can tell your friend waiting in the hall to not even bother, he can't get in. I had your friend here ward the entrance, which only allowed for you to come through."

I turned slightly to Felix, who was banging at an invisible wall. I had wondered why he didn't follow me in the room but was too focused on David and Lisa.

"Let her go, and I will follow you out of here. Leave the cure."

David stood up, jumped down from the podium, and stepped up the levels towards me. Every bone in my body wanted to back away, but I didn't. I thought of Phillip. Surely, he was strong enough to break the ward. Why didn't I bring him with me?

David was now at my level in the middle of the room, right in front of me. He gave me that icy, soul-freezing smile, and I grimaced, leaning back. He grabbed my face with both hands and kissed me. It was rough and hard, and I pushed at him, but he was too strong. He bit my lip hard, drawing blood. I cried out and hit him in the face with my fist, but it was as if he didn't feel me. He shoved me back, and I lost balance, falling to the floor on my bottom.

He licked my blood off of his lips. I rolled over and dug my hand in my pocket, touching the syringe and wrapped my fingers around it. David grabbed my legs and flipped me over. He got on top of me, spreading my legs on either side of him, and grabbed my syringe-holding hand. I clasped my fingers tightly over the syringe.

"What do we have, here?" he asked, prying my fingers open. Why had I not bothered to learn a strengthening spell? "Silly girl."

He grabbed my closed hand and raised it high in the air and then slammed it down with inhuman force to the hard floor.

I cried out in pure agony. Sharp, hot, stabbing pain attacked me. I momentarily gagged as agony washed over me. I had never broken a bone before, and there was no doubt in my mind that he had broken many of the bones in my hand. I could already see that it was misshapen, and a few bones broke through my skin, releasing blood and throbbing pain. My breathing increased as I sucked in quick bursts of air to control the pain.

David took the now-broken syringe away from me, the liquid spilling over my hand onto the floor. Bits of the syringe stuck out of my palm, and I stared in horror at it as a welcomed numbness began to spread over my hand.

"Now, that was uncalled for. I really hated to do this," David said, sounding nothing close to remorseful. "What was this?"

I didn't answer him. I just wanted to kill him. Problem was, I wasn't sure how. It became glaringly clear to me at that moment that I should have spent more time learning how to kill people. Killing wasn't my thing, and I was told it drained the heck out of you.

David leaned down towards me. "If you don't answer me, I will slam your head into this ground like I did your hand and gut you. I have containers. I will drain you and save your blood in my freezer."

I scrunched my face in anger and pain. "Antibody for your potion."

"Ha. Well, aren't y'all clever? And here I thought you all were a bunch of idiots just relying on your powers."

I closed my eyes and prayed. I had to focus through the pain and control myself. I wanted to rip David to shreds, but he had control over Lisa's fate.

"You know what?" David announced. "I think I'm just going to take you and your friend, both."

I felt something sharp stab me in my arm, and I opened my eyes. David tossed a now-empty syringe behind him. I instantly felt nauseous. I was drugged with the same mix of chemicals they had used on us back in the prison to suppress our powers. My magic wouldn't leave instantly, but they were getting weaker by the moment. Every part of me, including my mind, felt heavy, as if a load of bricks was balancing on my head.

I looked back up at Felix. He pointed to something behind me and gave me the thumbs up. I frowned and looked to the front of the room again, and Lisa sleeping. What did he want me to see? I looked back at Felix. This time Phillip stood beside him. He was mouthing something in slow motion. Get him? I couldn't think. I mouthed the words, "I can't, Lisa."

Phillip closed his eyes and touched the ward. I frowned and turned back to David, who was hovering over me, smiling. Probably plotting what horrors he would do to me next. I wouldn't be able to kill David, but at least these prisons were over. I would talk David into forgetting about Lisa. She didn't ask for any of this.

"Kill him, she's okay!" Felix cried from behind me. My face froze, and I looked back. Phillip was still pressing at the invisible wall, but I could now hear Felix banging against the ward.

David looked up and frowned. I had just a bit of my mind left alert. I hadn't made it up that Felix had said Lisa would be okay.

That's all I needed.

I looked back at David just in time to see him slam his fist down towards my face, and I pushed my hand out, sending him flying off of me and into the air. I sat up and felt the world spin around me; my head throbbed as if a jackhammer decided to do some work on my skull, but I pushed through. I dropped my hold on David, and he fell to the ground. Before David could get up, I waved my hand at him, as if swatting a fly, and knocked him against the nearest wall. I was pretty sure that I wasn't going to be getting much strength to stand up, so I remained where I sat.

Sadly, the force did not knock David unconscious. I was beginning to understand that I had no real concept about how much strength the serum gave normal humans. He should have at least blacked out, but instead, he only rubbed the back of his head as if it was some minor ache.

"You killed Jared. You aren't going to hurt anyone else," I yelled.

"Ah, your friend," David crossed his arms, giving me an amused look. "After you and Charles escaped, we had to make an example of a prisoner. Let them know what happens to others when they escape. And he did help you. Actually, we still have some of his blood in storage. We laid his body out on display, just to prolong the reminder. A bit barbaric, I know, but I don't think anyone was even dreaming of escaping after that."

He laughed.

"How can you do that to other humans? What kind of monster are you?" Anger overpowered any physical pain. I needed to focus. He had to die.

"You are an abomina—" He began before suddenly disappearing.

It wasn't like the teleportation. There was no elaborate affair when we teleported. That wasn't the case here. An array of what I could only describe as glitter encircled his body, and a few feet of the space surround him. It appeared like a tornado of colorful confetti, and soon, I could not even see him anymore. Then, as suddenly as the glitter appeared, it was gone, and so was David.

"The hell?" I shouted.

I looked over to Lisa, who was sitting upright with her hand in the air, aimed in the direction that David had been.

"Did you do that?" I asked.

She nodded, her eyes looking slightly glazed over, face devoid of emotion. "He was going to hurt you more," she said in a quiet voice.

"Did you kill him?"

She shrugged. "I don't know. I didn't think. I just didn't want him to hurt you. He had a gun, he was pulling it out from behind his back. I sent him away."

"To where?"

"In my mind, I was sending him to hell."

"Does that really exist?" The pounding wooziness in my head grew.

"Does anything not exist anymore?"

She had a point there. I hoped there really was such a place and that David was burning away now. However, I needed to see his cold, dead body before I'd be fully sure. I closed my eyes and laid back down.

I heard footsteps from behind me and saw Phillip and Felix, shouting my name. I cracked open my eyelids slowly. They felt sore and stung. Exhaustion washed over me, and I couldn't sit up even if I tried. I felt like my body was made of Jell-O and wondered if I had levitation powers so that I could float to the car. I couldn't even crawl at this point. Well, at least I didn't feel pain anymore.

"You okay, Mina?" Felix asked, face full of concern. He knelt in front of me, his large frame blocking my view of anything but him. His eyes were different now, the bright light had gone, leaving him with normal brown eyes, and his voice was back to normal.

I gave him a weak smile. "I'll live. Go check on Lisa."

"Yes, help," Lisa called. "I may have woken up, but I feel like my head is being spun in a blender. He's in hell, Mina. I know it."

He nodded and rose. "He lied to you about having the only cure for Lisa," Felix said, walking over to the dazed fairy. "Azrael told me. I can heal her. Azrael also confirmed that this David guy is, indeed, in hell."

I let out a thankful sigh.

Phillip came into view, perched on my other side, inspecting me. "Who is Azrael?" he asked.

"An angel," I replied.

He cocked an eyebrow. "I won't ask...for now. Where are you hurt?"

I looked to my damaged hand, which I could begin to feel

again, and Phillip followed my gaze. He lightly placed his hand on top of mine, and in seconds, I felt a wonderful heat radiating through my hand, and just a mild ache as bones quickly reshaped and cut skin drew together. Moments later, I was able to flex my hand without so much as a cramp.

I looked up at him. "Thank you."

He smiled. "How do you feel?"

"Same as Lisa. We should go find the others. Think I'll be able to sit up without passing out?" I asked Phillip with a slight smile.

"You have to stay back with the others, *mi corazon*," Phillip stated. "I'd heal you all the way, but I'll need to preserve powers." He gave me an innocent smile with raised eyebrows. "I can carry you to safety."

I struggled to sit up, and the stabbing head pain came back. Looks like I was very much not out of the woods. I sighed. "Leave me here with Lisa and Felix. We'll meet up later. Go kick ass and shit."

Phillip reached over and wiped what I would assume was blood from my lips with his thumb before leaning towards me and kissing me. It was light and quick. As if he were giving me a quick kiss goodbye before heading off to work. He moved back and winked at me before getting up and walking away.

Before I could ask him why he kissed me or ponder how odd that act was, my body began to relax. A blanket of soothing comfort came over me. I wanted to relish in it and fall asleep. It was like I had just come in from the cold into a heated room. It felt cozy and inviting, and I wanted to stay in this feeling. I lay back down on the floor, feeling my eyelids grow heavy, and my body almost float. A welcomed sleep soon took over.

I woke up back in my apartment in Silver Spring. No place felt exactly like home, but this was becoming close to it. I sat up, yawning, and stretching. I felt surprisingly good. Like I could get up and go for a jog if it weren't raining outside, which I could tell it was by the beating of heavy water drops on my bedroom window to the right of me.

I smelled pancakes and bacon. I was alive, comfortable, and about to eat that great-smelling breakfast, I hoped. All was right with the world because breakfast meant that things were okay. It meant that Charles was fine and that we had won the battle and rescued everyone. I put a lot of pressure on breakfast.

Getting out of bed, I walked to my ensuite bathroom and took an equally inviting hot shower. I was already clean, and I could only assume either someone had done a cleaning spell on me or washed me in my unconscious state. For modesty's sake, I was hoping for the former. I let my curly hair air dry and threw on some jeans, a red T-shirt, and black high-top Converse sneakers before leaving my room.

I found my brother in the kitchen with Lisa, making breakfast.

"Hey, love bugs," I stated.

They turned to look at me with smiles on their faces.

"Charles, I won't even ask how you got bacon," I said, walking into the kitchen. Meat of any kind was super expensive in this new world, and due to the popularity of the pig, bacon was always a special treat. There was a small farm in town, but still, meat was scarce. Humans weren't the only beings that liked to eat pigs, cows, and chickens now.

"Hungry?" Charles asked, putting a stack of pancakes on a plate and passing it to me.

I accepted the plate. "Thanks."

"Wait up." Charles turned and used tongs to gather several strips of bacon off of a plate on the counter and faced me again, dropping the strips on my plate.

My mouth drooled. "You're my hero."

He winked at me.

"I made fresh orange juice too," Lisa stated, carrying a pitcher of juice into the dining room. Charles filled more plates, and we followed Lisa out of the kitchen.

"How long have I been out?

"Just since yesterday afternoon."

"Hmmph. I think Phillip put me under a sleeping spell."

"Oh, I know he did," Charles snorted. "He claimed it was to help you heal. Which, I guess it did. You look better. If you didn't, Phillip and Erik wouldn't have left here."

I cocked an eyebrow as I cut into my food. "What do you mean?"

"They've been in and out of here since yesterday. They only just left an hour ago because they had to take care of the influx. Talk about tension in this place. They both really like you, Amina," Lisa replied before taking a sip of juice.

Thinking about that made me a little light-headed. I was

not up for the challenge of telling someone that I could not give them my heart. I didn't want to cause that kind of pain.

"You mentioned an influx? What's that about?" I asked.

Charles put his fork down. "Most of the folks we rescued from the prison came here. After being imprisoned by humans, the thought of going to a supernatural-only town was enticing, I guess. I don't blame them, although the Colonel is good people. Except, Chelsea's not going."

I pursed my lips, remembering how Phillip cruelly murdered Oliver. I wouldn't make light of that, regardless of how I felt about the man. Oliver had been Chelsea's love, and Phillip had flat out ignored our pleas.

I grabbed a piece of bacon and chewed it in mini bites. It wasn't over. We could work together with Hagerstown to find the other prisons. And with teleporting, I could easily see Chelsea, although a two-hour drive wasn't too bad either, assuming no trolls or other scaries showed up.

"So, which guy are you picking?" Lisa asked, a look of excitement on her face.

"I feel like there are so many other, more important things to talk about. Such as finding the other two prisons or honing in on this power of six."

"Probably, and we'll talk about it later but romance talk now, please, and thank you," she stated, wiggling in her seat.

Charles shook his head, and she gave a little giggle before tilting her head on his shoulder briefly.

I rolled my eyes. "They're both good guys." I began.

"Phillip's fine," Lisa cut in. "Like he seems cool, and he's super cute. But Erik really likes you. He's a great guy and he's been through so much. He deserves happiness."

"What has he been through?"

"He had a daughter. Seven years old."

My mouth fell open in shock. I'd only known Erik for a little over a month and a half, but how had I not known about a family? "What happened to his daughter and, I'm assuming, wife?"

"He was divorced."

"Damn, how old is he?" Charles asked with a mouthful of pancake.

"That question wasn't urgent enough for you not to finish chewing," I responded.

Lisa sighed. "Yeah, he got married and had a kid young. He was in his late twenties when the world went to hell, so he's 30 something now. I love this age delay for paranormals thing. That's my favorite part, I think. He still looks like he's in his 20s, so you wouldn't know how old he is. Anyway, I think the ex-wife died of the Sickness or something. His daughter died too. She was a werejackal like him, but she didn't survive the change." Her voice took on a hushed, saddened tone. "Apparently, children don't fare well with the change. Like fifty percent don't make it."

I shook my head slowly, feeling an overwhelming sadness. I couldn't begin to imagine what it would be like to lose a child. That pain had to be unimaginable.

"His daughter got stuck in mid form, and it was very painful. He didn't tell me any more after that, but I think he helped her transition on if you know what I mean."

I touched my chest, feeling nauseous. He had the right to be angry forever. To see your child in a permanent state of pain and then to have to take her life as her only way out... My eyes began to water, and I touched the corners of my eyes to prevent the tears from falling.

"Don't tell him I told you both of this. He only told me because we were on the road together for a while. I didn't trust him at first, and I think he opened up to me to calm me down. And in case you're wondering, he and I never had a thing. He's a beautiful man, but we aren't each other's types."

"I figured that out when you fell for my unmuscled brother," I cracked, dabbing at my eyes with a cloth napkin.

"Hey!" Charles cried. He reached for my plate of pancakes, and I moved it away.

Lisa shook her head. "I'm only telling you because Erik deserves good. I wouldn't want to see him getting hurt," she stated.

I stared at her. "He won't get hurt by me," I said with confidence.

~

*P*hillip asked me out to dinner a few nights later, and I decided that since he'd help free my friends and heal me, dinner would be all right. Dinner with Phillip turned out to be dinner at his apartment with a personal chef. I was nervous about the location at first, but then thought better of it as anyone, namely Erik, seeing us out might get the wrong idea. Of course, I hadn't told Erik that I was even going out with Phillip, but I would tell him as soon as this was over. As I promised Lisa, I had no plans to hurt Erik.

"You look beautiful," Phillip stated when I walked in. I had on a black wrap dress that I'd purchased with credits at the boutique where Lisa was employed. It was a dress she'd made herself with her fairy magic. The dress fit me like a glove. In fact, that was becoming her claim to fame in town. Men and women were overjoyed with how she could make clothes for them that fit them well and highlighted features they loved while hiding those they didn't. She was really beginning to become my fairy godmother.

Phillip looked nice as always in a pair of black slacks and a gray button-down. He leaned in to kiss me, and I turned my cheek towards him. He didn't miss a beat and showed me the way to his separate dining room area. Two walls of his penthouse living space consisted of windows overlooking the town. Inside, the space was lit with candles, outside lighting, and dim recess lighting. It made for a romantic setting.

He offered me a seat and poured me a glass of red wine. Phillip sat across from me at the dining room table. We spent the time before our meal arrived with idle chit-chat. I let him lead the conversation, for now, curious about anything he would divulge.

Dinner came, and it was seafood risotto with tiramisu as dessert. I had no idea how they even got some of the ingredients, but I supposed that with teleportation and magic, the sky was the limit.

"Dinner was fabulous," I stated after eating. I adjusted in my seat, readying myself for the big discussion.

"I'm glad you liked it. I only want to make you happy," he replied with kindness in his eyes.

I sighed. "About that. I think we might have a disconnect."

Phillip nodded swiftly. "I agree. I feel like you, and I haven't grown closer. I thought actually seeing each other in person would be an instant bond for us, but instead. I think we've grown farther apart these last two months."

I had to tread carefully here. Phillip was a shrewd man, and I wasn't ready to, nor did I want to, make an enemy out of him. On the one hand, I wanted to be honest with him about my feelings for Erik so that I could move forward with that growing relationship. On the other hand, I had no idea how Phillip would react. What if he tried to mind control me into loving him? I couldn't do it, and he'd know that I wasn't under his spell. If he knew that I was immune, how would he react? He could kick me out. Lock me up. Or maybe he wouldn't care? Perhaps he wasn't as horrible as I was starting to wonder. Mae did say he would never hurt me.

I looked down at my half-eaten tiramisu. Finding the right words was harder than I thought. "I care about you, it's just that—"

"You've fallen for someone else. Erik," Phillip cut in with a tight voice. "He's falling in love with you."

I looked at him with wide eyes. "How do you know?"

Phillip shrugged. "Got him to tell me the truth the night I put you to sleep."

I narrowed my eyes. "You mean you did your mind control on him."

Phillip took a sip of wine, his eyes cool. "You can't blame me for trying to check out my competition."

I frowned. "I think I can. That's way more than checking him out. That was unfair and cruel." Heck, Erik hadn't even told *me* he loved me. He probably wasn't ready to, yet Phillip had forced the words out of him before he had time to even come to terms with them. With all that Erik had gone through, I felt protective of him and didn't want anyone harming him. "Your power is scary, Phillip. And using it the way you do…" I stopped myself. I was saying too much. Mae told me to keep quiet.

"What do you mean, Amina?" He held my gaze, not saying a word, his eyes cool. I started to panic. What if he was exerting his mind control on me now? I wasn't susceptible to it, so I wouldn't know, and I'd give myself away.

"I'm sorry if I sound judgmental," I began. "You're a good guy. And you mean to protect us." I was elated. I remembered his speaker speeches. "It just makes me a bit nervous. But I know you mean well."

He smiled. "Glad you know that. As for this Erik thing—"

I cut him off. "Phillip, I'm sorry. It came out of nowhere, but I just can't ignore the feelings I have for him."

He nodded. "I get it. You want to see how it plays out. You're scared of what we have." That was one way of putting it. "I understand. But, see, some time ago, I met with Mae, and she told me that you and I were going to do great things together. That we were connected. And would make each

278

other better. When I found out I was able to help you get free, I knew for sure she was right."

Interesting what information Mae decided to share with Phillip and what she decided to keep hidden from me. I had a strong feeling that I wasn't getting the whole truth from her.

"So, you see, letting you go wouldn't make sense."

I scrunched my eyebrows together in concern. "What does that mean? You would force me, with your mind?"

Phillip grimaced. "Making a woman fall in love with me with magic seems ...pathetic. I'll convince you, the old natural way."

I looked at him with disbelief.

He chuckled. "You'll see, I love a challenge, and I believe you are worth that fight."

I relaxed my eyebrows. "Phillip, if Erik and I have something like I believe we do, I would never betray him."

He smiled and lifted his wine glass again. "We'll see."

His tone was condescending and arrogant as if I were a child just telling him that I'd seen a unicorn, and he was the parent nodding his head saying, "sure, you did sweetheart." Ignoring the fact that unicorns were actually a possibility in this world, he was wrong to be so confident.

*E*rik opened his door and looked me up and down in my dress and heels. He'd clearly been headed to bed, dressed only in black sweat pants and a white T-shirt. "You aren't just coming from school, are you?" he asked. He looked down at his watch. I already knew that it was after 10 p.m.

I shook my head and bit my lip, not looking forward to telling him where I had been. Why had I decided it was important to come to his place right after meeting with Phillip? Perhaps it was Phillip's words that set me off. I wanted to tell Erik now how I felt. I didn't want him to get the wrong idea about dinner or Phillip and me. It was time to declare my decision and if Phillip was going to kick me out of town because of it, well, then, Hagerstown would have me back.

"I just came from dinner...with Phillip," I replied in a mutter.

He started to close the door. "Wait!" I cried, pushing my hand out on the door. "It wasn't like that! Let me in, and I can explain instead of putting my business out in the hallway for everyone to hear."

He eyed me suspiciously but opened the door wider for

me to walk inside. Once in, he closed the door behind him and leaned against it, arms crossed. "Amina, I care about you, but I won't share you."

I smiled and walked over to him. I uncrossed his arms and placed them around my waist before leaning into his chest. "That's good to hear because I told Phillip that I couldn't see him romantically because I'd fallen for you."

He gave me a gentle squeeze. "And what did he say to that?"

"That he was going to try to win me over."

A low growl began in his chest. "I'm going to have to kill him."

"Please, don't. We have enough things to worry about."

"What about maiming him?"

I pulled away from him and lightly punched him in the arm. "I don't think that'll work either."

"Can I bash his car windows in, then? Sounds like my only resort now is to be petty. The guy rubs me the wrong way. He wouldn't leave your side the night of the raid. Why he thinks he has claim to you, just because you spoke to each other in a dream confuses me."

I suddenly thought of Phillip's words about Erik confessing his love for me. I wondered if Phillip was telling the truth.

Erik squinted his eyes and looked at me. "What's wrong? I was just kidding about hurting him...for now." He grinned, and my heart skipped again.

Every time he smiled, I melted a bit. His ability to still smile even in the face of his past pain made his smiles even more special to me.

I shook my head. "Nothing, just allowing myself to be happy for a moment."

He reached out and touched my cheek. I leaned into his hand, resting my cheek in his palm.

"I think you must have bewitched me," he said in a low voice.

I chuckled. "I didn't use any magic on you."

"Then, I really am falling for you." I thought of what Lisa said, then Phillip. They were both so sure Erik wanted to be with me.

"Good," I whispered back.

"Woman," was all he said before leaning down and kissing me.

I loved his lips, the taste of him. I pressed into him, hungrily exploring his mouth with my tongue. My hands rested on his chest, feeling the definition and heat of his body through the thin fabric of his shirt. He seemed to run extra hot compared to me, and I sought out more of his heat, even in the warmth of the summer evening.

His hands moved away from my face and rested on my hips, pulling me closer to him. I moved my arms to the back of his neck to get closer. Even with me in my four-inch heels, he was still towering over me. My chest mashed against his as I tried to clear the space between us. He let out what sounded like a frustrated growl before moving his hands to my rear and lifting me up.

I let out a yelp and wrapped my legs around his hips, my dress bunched up in an unladylike way around my waist.

He looked into my eyes, a look of restraint on his face. "Do you want to go to sleep?" He asked in a low voice.

I shook my head quickly. "But I want to go to your bedroom," I whispered, my own voice thick.

He then began to slowly walk us to his bedroom with me wrapped around him like another article of clothing.

Way to make a girl feel light as a feather. I think I liked him more in this moment.

Somewhere between the front door and the bedroom, I lost my heels. He carefully lowered me on the bed and took his shirt off, revealing the wonderful cuts and defined lines of his body that I had drooled over not too long ago. He lowered my dress off of my shoulders carefully, although the fire in his eyes made me think he'd really wanted to rip it off. I laid back down on the bed and lifted up as he took the dress and my panties down the rest of my body and gently placed them on a chair beside the bed.

I unhooked my bra without his assistance, and he took that too. He placed it with my other clothes and looked me over. The room was lit only with the light outside of his window behind open blinds. However, I'm sure his were vision allowed him to see just fine in the dark. I couldn't say I didn't feel vulnerable at that moment.

He leaned over me, his hands balancing on the bed to hold his weight. "You're beautiful," he whispered before kissing me again. He moved a hand onto my waist and slowly moved it up my side until it reached my breast. The heat of his hand on my skin made me let out an involuntary gasp as his fingers lightly played over my nipples, bringing me to attention.

I grabbed his face, deepening our kiss, and sucking his tongue as he continued his massage of my chest. Something lower in me stirred for him, and I raised my hips, wanting to feel him between my legs. He moved from my lips and grazed my neck, marking me with his teeth in a gentle bite. The pain bordered on pleasure, but it would leave a mark, and I didn't care.

I clawed my hands over his back, feeling the muscles bunch under my fingers as he continued.

He moved back and gave me a devilish grin. I could see, even in the dark, that his eyes were now fiery orange and in their jackal form. He rose up and removed his pants in a literal blink of my eye and was over me again, positioned between my legs.

He lowered and kissed me again, and I ran my fingers through his short, silky hair, wrapping a leg around his waist.

He moved to my ear, licking at the lobe. "Can I have you?" He whispered.

I'd never had anyone ask me that before. I wasn't sure what an appropriate response would be, but at that moment, I wasn't in a state of mind to want to give it much thought. "Yes," I replied in a whispered voice.

Apparently, my "yes" meant just what I thought it would because he entered me agonizingly slowly. I wrapped my other leg around him, my arms falling lazily over the back of his neck. He played a game of fast and slow in a show of absolute control, adjusting his angles to hit my pleasure spots.

The heat within me grew, and he sent me over with waves of met desire. That seemed to set him off because his control shifted, and he moved within me rapidly before succumbing to his own gratifying release.

A growl escaped from him before he lowered halfway on me and moved beside me so that we were still facing each other, one of my legs trapped under him.

He leaned forward and kissed me, slowly and lazily. The fire in his eyes remained, and I sucked in a sharp breath as I felt him move again. One of his hands went to the small of my back as he continued steady movements.

This time there was no calculated control, just an easy rhythm, and I enjoyed it just as much. As he sped up his pace, for the second time that night, I cried out, and he soon followed.

We stayed still for a long moment, interlocked and quiet. I felt the rapid beat of his heart as my head lay against his chest. His skin was damp and hot, and I snuggled closer to him, unperturbed.

I wanted this man more than I had admitted to myself, and for some reason that scared me.

CHAPTER 26

$\mathcal{D}$ ue to the rescue, the pack celebration welcoming Erik into his new position was delayed, so that Saturday night, Seth finally held a party. The shindig was also a welcoming of the several new members they'd received from the Long Island prison raid.

"Did I tell you how amazing you look tonight?" Erik whispered in my ear, hand on the small of my back. We'd been practically inseparable, except for work. I was sure Charles didn't mind since Lisa was spending more time at our apartment anyway.

Erik's breath on my neck sent a ticklish delight down my spine, which sent my mind back to the night before. I would definitely want more, but before, that I had to get through the celebration.

Apparently, this event was supposed to be a snazzy affair, although it was in the pack's Irish-styled pub, which was anything but fancy. The weres, or anybody for that matter, didn't have many opportunities to dress up, so when we found an inkling of a reason we did it up.

Lisa styled me in a royal-blue, fitted, off-the-shoulder dress that stopped just below the knee. She did my hair and makeup, sweeping and pinning my coily hair to one side of my head. I wore a costume golden choker that I'd found in my prior scavenges to finish it. I did feel like a pretty, pretty, princess.

"Well, you don't look so bad yourself," I whispered back. He looked more than not so bad. Erik looked hot, in fact. He wore a tailored black suit, white shirt, no tie. His hair was slicked back, still shorter on the sides, and his beard was neatly trimmed.

"I much rather be at home with you, taking that dress off." He smiled, and his hand lowered, grazing my rear-end. I smacked his hand away.

"Inappropriate," Felix said behind us.

I turned to him and smiled. He was handsome as well, wearing a navy-blue suit fitting well over his wide frame, and his long, black hair was combed back in a low ponytail. Faith, Lisa, and Charles stood behind him.

"Well, that was fun. Looking at my sister getting groped in public," Charles said with an exaggerated disgusted look. He was equally dapper in a charcoal-gray suit.

"If it helps, I can grope you too," Lisa smirked. She was wearing a short, gold bodycon dress with nude heels. Her hair was parted down the middle in a long bob, short in the back and reaching her collarbone in the front. She had streaks of gold throughout her hair. "You look so good, Mina, and you're welcome, Erik." She gave him a wink.

I rolled my eyes. Inviting Lisa to a majority were party might have been risky, but her magic cloaking seemed to be holding up.

"Now, I'm the third wheel." Felix frowned.

Faith raised her eyebrows and shrugged. "You can be my date tonight," she said, patting him on the shoulder. She looked unusually feminine with her short hair set in a deep right part and smoothed back. She wore a black wide-legged, one-sleeved jumper with a cut-out, exposing her flat stomach. On her feet were red stilettos. I gave her an approving nod, and she winked at me.

I looked back to Felix. "Erik and I aren't a couple," I said, playfully.

Erik removed his hand from my back, and I felt an instant coldness hit me. It was most likely from the air conditioner blaring above me, but the heat from his touch seemed to be enough to warm me. Fortunately, it wasn't gone long because I soon felt him clasp my hand in his.

He leaned into me and whispered. "After the other night? Who are you fooling?" he whispered. "You're mine."

"I don't remember us having a discussion about me being yours," I whispered back.

"Remember, when I asked if I could have you? You did say yes."

I narrowed my eyes. At that moment, I would have said yes to darn near anything. Also, I thought he'd just meant sex.

"Well, that wasn't very romantic."

"Do you need a formal declaration?" He looked amused.

I nodded jokingly.

He bent forward as if preparing to get on his knees, and I grabbed his shoulders, pushing him upright. "What are you doing?"

He looked up with a playful smile. "I'm just doing what you asked. Do you want an old-fashioned courting? I can do that too." He grabbed my hand and kissed it.

Oh, he was laying it on thick. "That'd be nice." I grinned at him.

"Oh, look at you both," Lisa said, clasping her hands together. "Two beautiful people in love, lust, like. Who knows? It's just so damn cute."

Crap, they were still there the whole time watching our exchange?

Charles looked like he had just ingested something that

wasn't sitting right with his stomach. "I think I'm going to be sick. I didn't survive the magical apocalypse to watch this."

"Oh, grow up," I said, squinting my eyes at him.

Felix looked confused. "So, am I a third, no, fifth wheel or not?"

"We'll find you someone, Felix. Meanwhile, there's Seth," Faith muttered, looking behind Erik and I. "I really don't like that dude."

I turned and looked through the crowded bar, past the band on the stage area, and both packed bar counters. I spotted Seth sitting at a large table surrounded by women with bottles of alcohol and beer on the table. He snapped his fingers, then wiggled an empty glass in the air. A man soon rushed to him with a pitcher of beer. Apparently, Silver Spring had its own brewery that a few people decided to bring back to life; enter a new local magic-infused beer that tasted like whatever type of beer you liked, even flavored. Blueberry beer was becoming my personal favorite. Hagerstown didn't even have a stake in the beer game yet. Not that beer alone made a town better. I'd give up beer any day to live in a real democracy without corruption and with jelly beans.

I shook my head. "I really don't care for your boss," I mumbled. I was in a space full of weres with great hearing, so I knew that a whisper didn't keep my words private, but I really didn't care.

As if hearing me, Seth spotted us and waved us over.

"Come on, put on a fake smile and play the game, woman," Erik said, leading me away by the hand. "We'll catch up in a minute," he told the others.

"We'll be at one of the bars," Charles replied.

"Why do I have to come with?" I asked.

"You're right, having you there might be a block to Raya," he replied, looking ahead.

I stopped walking, and he stopped as well, turning to me,

a smile on his face. I tried to yank my had back, but his stupid were strength wouldn't let me go. "You just promised to court me. I don't feel courted," I grumbled.

He moved closer to me and put his hands on my waist. "I'm sorry. Raya is not on my radar. I just love seeing you pout. Now come on. I need arm candy I can trust to help me deal with this guy." He stepped back and held out his hand.

I grumbled some more but took his hand.

We reached Seth and crew, and I put on my best neutral face. I did some acting in college, so I was just going to have to tap into that and act like I didn't want to high kick the arrogant S.O.B. in the face.

"Hey, Number Three, good to see you," Seth stated with a big, teeth-baring grin. He looked over to me. "You fill out that dress nicely, A."

Do not cast a spell on the pack's alpha. Do not cast a spell on the pack's alpha.

I grimaced slightly as Erik's hand grew tight around mine. He was going to have to find another way to hold his anger in before my fingers got bent up.

"Take a seat and join us." Seth nodded to two women seated on a couch opposite from his, and they rose without protest. One stood behind him and began to rub his shoulders, and the other stood beside her, waiting her turn, I guessed. I was appalled.

"They didn't need to get up," Erik stated. "We were just coming over to say hi."

"Oh, no. You and your lady have to have a drink with me. The others in the top five are around here somewhere."

Erik nodded and motioned for me to sit down on the couch opposite Seth's. I took a seat next to an overly-done-up redhead with glassy eyes. Erik sat on my other side.

A waitress appeared, and I ordered an Old Fashioned. Erik just poured a beer for himself.

"So, who is everyone?" I asked.

Seth threw his arms around two women seated next to him. "These are my wives."

I pouted. "Say what now?" I thought weres were monogamous creatures, but apparently, Seth and his harem of five women were exempt from that.

"This is Tasha and Jessica." He pointed to a black woman with a short pixie cut beside him and a blonde, white woman to his other side. "Darla." The redhead next to me. "Kiki and Beth." The women he made get up; a Latina with honey-blonde curls and an Asian woman with long, burgundy red hair. Well, at least he was an equal opportunity chauvinist pig.

"I thought weres were monogamous?" I asked.

Seth shrugged. "I am, to my wives."

I cocked my eyebrow. "Do they have other husbands?"

He shook his head, grinning. "Perks of being a leader in the pack. Anyone in the top five can have similar arrangements."

I let out a puff of air in shock. I really, really didn't like this guy.

"Of course, having a pack member, especially a top five, with a non-were is not preferable," Seth began, eyeing me. "Erik, you can keep Amina, but you'll need to add a were wife to balance it all out."

I bared my teeth and looked at Erik, whose eyebrows were furrowed together.

Seth drew his hands up in surrender. "Don't mean to ruffle feathers. I'm just saying pack sticks with pack. That's the way it is everywhere. We're just starting out, and we want to preserve our kind. Hey, Amina, we could turn you. A quick bite. I mean, you aren't a regular human but I'd think a witch would still be susceptible to catching our gifts. We don't have any other werejackal's. Maybe you get Erik here to bite you, and you can be Mrs. Jackal." He looked pleased with his idea.

I wanted to knock the glass out of his hand and backhand him a few times. "Thanks, we'll consider it." I could be diplomatic.

Erik looked at me as if I'd lost my mind, his eyebrows raised. He looked back to Seth. "I think the pack is going to have to get over it. I'm not getting a second girlfriend or turning Amina into a were. They will take her as she is, just as I do."

There he went, claiming me again. Except this time, I wasn't going to fight it. If I was looking for a romantic declaration from Erik, this would do just fine. I smiled at him. Seth's sister wives all looked at Erik with sad puppy eyes, as if they were watching the cutest thing in the world. I supposed compared to being with Seth, Erik was a nice distraction.

Seth, looking unconvinced, shrugged and took another gulp of his drink. "Don't say I didn't warn ya."

I'd had enough. I scooted forward on the couch. "How about I let you guys talk shop? I'm going to see what the others are up to." I leaned over and kissed Erik on the cheek. "Behave," I whispered.

He smiled. "Always."

I walked through the crowd, searching for Charles and the others. I passed Raya. She gave me a stare down as she headed over to Seth and Erik. I was tempted to follow her, but after Erik's defense of me, I let it go. Her charms weren't going to work, even if she *was* a were.

I eventually spotted the others at a corner table with Carter. I pulled a chair from a nearby table and sat down. "I just had a nice conversation with Seth in which he inappropriately commented on my body and then told Erik to get a were girlfriend or turn me into one. He clearly is not trying to win me as a fan."

"I don't think he has many fans period," Carter said in a

lowered voice. "He's just the strongest. But maybe Erik can change that."

"Oh, no. I need for Erik to chill out on the whole challenging people to death bit."

Carter nodded. "Fair enough. And Seth's a good fighter. He used to be a professional MMA champ."

I widened my eyes in shock. "Well, that's fun. Carter, please make sure Erik doesn't make another challenge."

He gave a curt nod with an all too serious face.

A sudden force slammed me into the table, cutting into my stomach. I turned, ready to right the world. A thin, white man of average height with a buzz cut, who was obviously inebriated, stood behind me.

Felix jumped up. "Hey, man," he yelled.

The drunken fool looked around at the table with half-open eyes. "You got a problem?" The man slurred.

Faith rose up as well. "Yeah, man. You bumped into the third's girlfriend. Apologize," she stated.

The drunk looked down at me and scoffed. "This bitch? She ain't pack. And no one cares about Erik. That piece of shit killed my friend."

My fingers itched to do a spell.

Charles and Carter got up as well.

"Luke, apologize and get out of here before you get hurt," Carter announced.

"Fine," he said with a screwed-up face. He looked down at me again. "Sorry... Bitch."

"I can turn him into a rat. Let me turn him into a rat," Lisa cried.

"I was thinking cockroach," Faith stated, fire rimming her eyes. This would not be good.

"Or a gnat. Then we can swat him," Lisa went on.

Drunk Luke looked over to Lisa and sniffed. "What are you?"

Uh-oh. She should smell like a regular human to him.

"You human? I thought only those with powers could live here. Only thing we need from plain old humans is food." And before I could stop what was happening, he lunged at Lisa and bit her arm.

I screamed in shock. It was getting close to a full moon, but even so, while in human form, he wasn't supposed to just try to eat a person.

Felix pulled him off of Lisa and tossed the man in the air to the nearest wall in one swift motion as if pulling a miniature dog off of her. I moved to Lisa, but Charles was already near her, whispering a healing spell over her shredded right arm as Lisa whimpered in pain.

"Oh, shit," Carter yelled, looking past me.

I followed his eyes and saw Drunk Luke, impaled through the heart by the antlers of a stuffed deer head mounted to the wall. He was not alive.

Everything stopped in the room. The band stopped playing. People stopped talking.

"He killed him!" A woman screamed from a nearby table. "The big guy threw Luke into the wall!"

And that was it, there would be no hearing of Felix's side of the story. With this one act in defense of Lisa, Felix was doomed.

Pack members growled and started to surround us. They would see a pack member they knew, who was allegedly murdered by a non-were who was on the side of the new third in command they weren't sure they liked yet, with the non-were girlfriend. No one would be taking Felix's side.

Except for Carter, who jumped in front of us and held out his arms. "Fall back. He was defending this woman, who Luke attacked," he pointed to Lisa, whose arm Charles had just about healed. Which, of course, didn't aid to the cause of her being a victim. "Luke bit her! He tried to eat her. He wasn't in his right mind."

I looked around the crowd, and no one looked convinced

of Carter's explanation. I locked eyes with Phillip, who I had not noticed earlier. He was leaning against the bar and looking disturbingly amused. What was he up to?

"One of ours was murdered by another pack member," Seth shouted, walking through the crowd. "We don't stand for violence against our own unless it's a challenge, and this was not. This does not go unpunished. Take him down!"

"If anyone lays a fucking hand on him, I'll rip your throats out," Faith shouted. She kicked off her heels and stood beside Carter.

"Seth. Carter told you what happened," Erik replied, standing next to the pack leader.

"Move, Carter," Seth shouted. Ignoring Erik. "Now!"

Carter sighed, shook his head, and reluctantly moved to the side. Faith steadied her position in front of Felix. Several pack members charged at Felix, who took a wide-legged stance to hold his ground. He was built like a wrestler. I still didn't understand what Felix was, but after seeing him in action at the prison I knew that I didn't want to be on his bad side.

I had no idea what the pack members were going to do. Beat him up, take him into custody, or kill him. I wasn't willing to find out. The six had to live and stay together.

I threw out my hands, and the charging pack stopped in mid-stride. Several people who were approaching, close to ten, froze like statues. An explosion of pain ripped through my head, bringing me to my knees. I fought back the urge to vomit. I wanted to control the attackers, but I still wasn't prepared physically or mentally for it to happen.

Phillip walked from the bar. "Now, now, *mi corazon*, can't interfere. This is pack business," he stated his tone chiding. He stopped beside Erik, who looked like he was suppressing a growl.

"I'm not going to let them hurt my friend. He was saving Lisa from that monster. He took a chunk out of her arm," I replied, still on my knees. Charles knelt down beside me and helped me to my feet. I leaned heavily on him, still feeling extraordinarily weak.

Phillip lowered his head. "Amina, do not use your power. This is not your business."

I knew he was exerting his mind control. If I listened, I preserved my secret that I couldn't be controlled by him. But then they would hurt Felix. We were family, and I couldn't let family get hurt.

I could already see Erik with clenched teeth and balled fists. He would fight this whole bar to prevent them from hurting Felix. I didn't have to turn to look at Lisa and Charles to know they would do the same. I had the best chance out of all of them to stop this without getting anyone hurt. We could still rebound if Phillip knew I wasn't controlled. This didn't hurt the bigger plans.

I looked at Phillip. "No."

He frowned. "Amina, leave this bar."

"I will not let them hurt my friends."

Phillip tilted his head and considered me. He then sighed and smiled. "I should have known."

"Should have known what?" Seth asked, looking over to Phillip, body ready to charge at Felix and myself. "Tell this bitch to fall back before I make her."

I felt like folks knew my name. "Bitch" was not going to be my going nickname.

Erik flexed his hands. I foresaw a bloody Seth and the whole pack pouncing on Erik. Or worse, him getting carried away with the moment and making a challenge against Seth.

The crowd grew restless and antsy. Some other people shifted closer, and I stopped them too. I'd freeze this whole damn bar if I had to.

Phillip continued to look at me. "Erik, remove Amina from the premises."

I looked to Erik, whose eyes suddenly went blank and

devoid of emotion. His back went straight, and then he looked at me with laser focus before walking over to me and grabbing my hand. I yanked it away. He grabbed at me again, and I moved back before he could touch me, bumping into the table.

"Erik, stop!" Charles shouted.

"Erik, pick her up and carry her out of here," Phillip stated in an annoyed voice.

Without missing a beat, Erik scooped me up like some damsel in distress and started walking to the front entrance. I was horrified. Once I left the building, the action would start again, and who knows what would happen to Felix or even Charles, Faith, and Lisa.

"Erik put me down on this floor or I will kick your ass!" I yelled, kicking my legs.

He ignored me and continued to walk.

"Put me down, Erik! Now!" I cried.

Erik stopped walking just as we reached the door. He looked down at me and gently lowered me to my feet.

I looked up at him with wide eyes. Had he just listened to me? *Act now and question later*, I told myself.

"We need to go back and stop them from hurting Felix."

He looked at me with the same blank eyes he had before and nodded. He followed me back through the frozen crowd to stand in front of Felix.

"This is the second time you've broken my magic. You're the same as me, aren't you?" Phillip asked me, visually unsettled.

I gave a slight shrug. I wasn't telling him a thing.

"Phillip, get her to unfreeze my people. We can't let this asshole get away with murder," Seth shouted.

"You can't kill him," I stated, glancing over at Seth. "I know you knew Luke longer, but Felix is a good man, and this was a mistake. Luke was drunk and out of control. Felix reacted quickly to save our friend."

"Lock him up if you have to until we figure this all out," Erik began. I looked back to him, and his eyes were filled with life again. "But he doesn't get hurt for defending someone. If Luke had attacked one of your wives, you'd want Felix to react the same way. Any of you would want Felix to defend your loved ones the way he did. Lock him up and give this a fair investigation and trial if you have to. We're not animals."

Seth looked unconvinced, but the crowd seemed to shift, even while locked in place. Their faces became less certain. If I had any mind control power, now was the time to test it out. I looked at Seth. "Seth, Felix is a good man. He deserves a fair trial. He would never hurt anyone on purpose. You know this," I stated in a steady voice.

Seth squinted his eyes at me. "We lock him up. He hasn't shown himself to be a menace. Let's give him a chance to tell his story," he stated in a monotone voice.

I sighed and released the crowd from their frozen positions. I looked over to Felix. "Don't worry. I'll represent you. We're going to have a fair trial and get you out of lockup."

Felix looked sick, and I felt like crying for him. "If you say so, Amina," he said in a low, pained voice. He was a gentle giant who had only ever protected us. He didn't deserve this.

Faith turned around, and they embraced. I knew she loved Felix like a brother, and he loved her like a sister. I wasn't sure anyone would be able to break them up without a fight.

"It won't be a trial like you're used to," Carter whispered, moving closer to me. "But I'll make sure it's something as fair and humane as possible."

I shook my head as two guys I didn't know roughly grabbed Felix by the arm.

"Get the fuck off of him!" Faith yelled, still hugging Felix.

"Hey, little mama," Felix said gently. "You gotta let them

take me away. I'm going to be okay. I don't want anyone else to get hurt."

Faith, who I had never seen cry, reluctantly released him. Her face was wet with tears. "I will come and visit you in lock-up," she said before raising her voice. "And if he has even one scratch on him, I will hunt you, people, down and end you."

"Don't threaten me, bitch," said a foolish pack member holding one of Felix's arms.

Faith kneed the male were in the crotch, and the man bent forward. She leaned down and grabbed him roughly by the hair. "I will do what I want to do, you piece of shit," she said in a tight voice.

The man looked up at her with pained eyes and then paled as he looked at the fire burning in her own. Faith let the man go and then backed away with her hands up in surrender as a couple of other pack members inched towards her.

The man recovered and went back to Felix, walking him towards the door...with a limp.

"Where are they taking him?" Lisa asked, eyes full of tears.

"To the police station," Erik answered. "There's a cell."

"Amina," Phillip began, suddenly appearing beside me. I jumped slightly and backed into Erik, who balanced me. I hadn't seen Phillip move through the crowd. "You've been holding out on me, *corazon*. Mind control?"

"I didn't know I could."

He gave me a smile that failed to reach his eyes. "Really? And I take it you don't respond to my monthly messages either."

I didn't say anything.

"What do you want, Phillip?" Erik growled, moving between Phillip and me.

Phillip chuckled and walked around him. "Amina, you

have some very strong gifts that I just can't ignore. Most likely, you are the same as me. But you see, what makes this town so successful is order. You have shown here tonight that you are willing to break any rules or processes we have and that you have the strength to do it."

I frowned. "I haven't caused any problems here."

"I think you just did." Phillip gave a dramatic sigh. "I hate to do this, but I need to confine you for now. Until I decide how to handle you. I hate to say this, but you're a threat, *mi corazon*."

"To who? You?"

"To everything. If you'd picked me over…" He looked to Erik with disdain. "This would not be a problem. But as it is, I can't trust you. I'm sorry."

"What? So, you're putting me under house arrest?" I continued.

"Confinement. I will put you in another apartment." Phillip quickly reached out and grabbed my hand. "Time to go." And then we vanished. Teleporting away from the bar and Erik.

CHAPTER 27

My confinement turned out to be a studio apartment in Phillip's building that I believe was previously owned by a woman. This particular woman loved bright colors because I was staring at a yellow wall behind a sofa bed, probably meant to be energizing. The sofa bed was forest green, with bright-yellow pillows covering it. I'd been in lesser lockups.

I sighed and sat back down with a book I'd found in the bookcase next to the bed. Some cheesy-looking romance novel. It had been almost a week in confinement, and I was nearing rage. Since Phillip had stuck me in there, he hadn't bothered to visit me, and I couldn't find a way out; the place was warded beyond my powers or my understanding, so I couldn't break it. Some stranger came to drop off food, toiletries, and a change of clothes. There was no laptop or computer to watch streaming movies or surf the limited internet. The TV worked, and I found a few old DVDs to watch but that excitement ended quickly since the former owner really didn't have many.

The apartment didn't have a balcony, so I stared out of the window like a nosey cat for most of the day. I read, I ate, I did some exercises, I prayed, and I slept. Rinse and repeat. Days passed. There were no visits from Erik, Charles, or the others. I could assume Phillip was preventing them from seeing me. No one visited me, except to give me food. And that delivery person didn't say one word to me, even when I tried to talk to them. I had no clue what was going on in the town. I didn't know if Felix was still locked up or if there'd been a trial. Phillip was trying to break me.

My door opened, and I expected it to be a food delivery person, but it was Phillip. I remained on the sofa bed, book in my hand, motionless. He walked in with a container of what I assumed was food and headed to the dining area. He placed it on the table and sat down.

"Sorry, it's been so long since I could come. As you can imagine, it's been a busy week," Phillip said, looking at me with sad eyes.

I snapped my book shut, jumped up, and slapped him across the face. He had left me there for a week in solitary confinement. I had no clue how anyone I cared about was doing. I didn't know if he had kicked the others out or convinced Seth to change his mind and kill Felix.

Phillip froze momentarily. His eyes grew wide, his shoulders raised, but then he relaxed, seemingly unaffected. That only angered me more, so I slapped him again. He didn't do anything. He just took it. He gave me no words and made no face of anger or apology. He just gave me neutral eyes. I lifted my hand to slap him again but stopped in mid-motion. Hitting him was no longer satisfying.

"I fucking hate you," I spat, forcing back tears of anger. I spun around and sat back down on the sofa bed, resting my tightly balled fist on my thighs.

"It pains me to hear that, *mi corazon*. I certainly don't hate you. I know you don't understand why I'm doing this, but you will one day." He sighed. "Felix is fine. He's still in lock-up. We're going to have the trial in a week. Mae will defend

301

him, and Tyler, one of my other top advisors, will prosecute." He looked at me, expecting a response I assume since I was the one who was supposed to defend Felix. "And Lisa is fine. She didn't catch anything from Luke's bite. Apparently, fairies are immune. And your students miss you. Looks like you made a good impression already. Or it could be your mind control." He grinned slightly.

"I want out of here," I replied in a tight voice.

"I know, but keeping you here is for your own safety. People got scared off by what you did back at the restaurant. Keeping you here makes you under my protection. No one will touch you."

"You won't even let me see my friends or my brother."

Phillip nodded. "Amina, this situation is serious. The pack is…challenging. They aren't going to believe a newcomer over someone who has been a part of their family. They want blood. Keeping Felix in lock-up is only proper. It's what the police would do a decade ago…if they weren't crooked. And keeping you here keeps people from thinking you'll try anything."

"So, you're helping me?" I asked with a sarcastic tone.

"That's part of it. The other part is that I have to keep control here and understand what you are. Which seems to be a lot like me."

"So, you don't really care about me?" I said it more as a statement than a question.

Phillip frowned. "Of course, I do. I would love for you to be by my side in all of this. It's you who stopped caring about me."

I didn't respond, just looked away.

Phillip walked closer to me, and I took a step back. "I am but one man. We can't work as some fluffy, happy, day camp. This world doesn't allow for that, it never did. It's rule or be ruled. Demand respect or be overrun. Weapons don't work in a town like this. Jails only work for so long on people with power. People will only follow you nowadays if they think they can't beat you. And I wouldn't want to do anything like what happened at that prison. We need as many people as we can get to rebuild society. Judge all you want, but what I say makes sense."

I turned to him and glared. "I don't like your style, and I think it's harmful."

Phillip nodded his head slowly. He looked out of the window in the living space, face in thought. He sighed. "I would do just about anything for you, *corazon*, but it won't matter if we lose control here. I've been helpless. I've seen when those who shouldn't have power exert control. I can't allow for that again. I can't keep someone like Seth in check without making some allowances."

"You're trying to make yourself sound innocent, but I'm not buying it. You find us a threat. We could have worked together, but you want things done your way instead. Did you kill the former leader, Thomas?"

Phillip looked at me. "You think I'm the devil, don't you? Everything bad that's happened, you blame me."

"I've been in isolation for a week. I had a lot of down-time to figure things out."

"If I said no to everything you just accused me of, would you believe me?"

I shrugged. I didn't know. Some part of me still wanted Phillip to be good. Still wanted him to be the man that I remembered from my dreams.

"Amina, we're not meant to be enemies," Phillip said in a quiet voice. "I'm a good guy. We got a lead on the other two prisons. We're still working with Hagerstown, and we're going to check the towns out."

I perked up. "I can help."

Phillip frowned. "Not locked up, you can't, and I can't let you out."

"Look, I won't get in your way, Phillip. Just let me out. I

can help free the other paranormals. Let me see my friends. We can leave, or they can leave if you want me to stay."

Phillip chuckled, "Always sacrificing yourself, Amina. You're more than that. But you're right. You can't stay here."

"Thank you." I got up.

"You can stay with me."

"Say what now?"

Phillip smiled and walked over to me. "You'll stay with me."

I backed away. "Uh, I already have a place."

"Not anymore."

"Excuse me?" I placed my hands on my hips.

"I'm not saying I don't trust you. Buuut, I don't trust you. You don't want to get in my way. Fine. Prove it. Let me keep an eye on you. I have a guest room."

I sighed and rolled my eyes. "I'll stay here."

"I just want to make things better, Amina. You may not agree with my methods, but it works. I don't know why you fight this connection we have. You know we're meant to be together. We have become better people because of each other." He reached out and touched my cheek.

I could have pulled away, but I didn't think fighting with him would get me out of there. I just needed to get away, free Felix, and then we'd all leave.

"Plus, if you stay here, you won't get to leave this apartment. With me, you can come and go as you please. So, what do you say? Roomies?" He smiled.

I smiled at him in return. "No." David had kept me in solitary confinement. I wasn't new to this, sadly.

Phillip sighed again. "You are a tough one, *mi corazon*. I hope you change your mind," he stated before leaving.

I could handle this. At least until the trial. Even if it meant I wouldn't see the others. I was as strong as Phillip assumed. Maybe stronger.

$\mathcal{I}$ woke up in the middle of the night to scratching at my window. Had this been the Pre-world, I would have ignored it. In this new, scary world, scratching in the middle of the night was actually something terrifying. I once woke up to a vampire staring at me through the window. He was clawing at the glass trying to get in but, due to the ward, was unsuccessful. I screamed and slept in the windowless bathroom for the rest of the night. Moments like those made me super hate this world.

So, when I heard the scratching this time, my imagination went straight to scary baddie at my window. I'd closed my blinds, so I hoped the scary monster couldn't see inside. I pulled the covers up to my eyes, foolishly hoping the fabric would shield me.

"Amina!" came a familiar male voice. "Amina, open up! It's Charles."

"Charles?" I cried, jumping out of bed. I paused at the window. It could be a trickster. There were many creatures that could imitate someone else, even beyond the shapeshifter.

"Dude, it's me. Open up," My brother called.

I peeked through the blinds. My brother was at the window, hovering in the air. "How? How are you floating, and how are you able to touch the ward without getting zapped?" I asked, eyes wide.

Charles gave me a cocky smile. "Fairy dust, Sis. Lisa threw some on me, and I'm flying like freaking Peter Pan. And she was finally able to break the ward with her magic. She's on lookout below. Open the window and let's get out of here. It's my turn to help you escape now."

I nodded, drew up the blinds, and opened the window. I pushed the screen out with my magic, Charles gave it to me. I put it on the floor before backing away. "Let me at least put on some tennis," I stated before bending down to put on my shoes. I only had on some stretch pants and a large T-shirt, but I didn't need anything here.

"Okay, hurry up," Charles grumbled.

As I tied my shoelaces, a wave of cold air blew over me. It was summer, and the evenings were beginning to be just as hot as the days. This was not a gust of cold air from the air conditioner. This was something else, something bone-chilling.

"Amina," said a raspy voice from behind me.

My insides turned to ice.

David.

I looked up towards Charles, who had been half perched on the windowsill. His eyes were wide with shock.

I slowly rose, keeping my eyes on Charles, who was still staring at David.

"Stay the fuck away from her," Charles spat.

I heard the shuffling of feet behind me. I took a step towards Charles, and the footsteps behind me quickened.

I spun around. "How the hell are you back?" I said through gritted teeth.

He was alive, and he looked like he had clawed his way from hell to return. He was covered in dirt and caked blood from head to toe. His clothes were tattered, and his eyes were bloodshot. Cuts and bruises ran across his face and body.

If he'd been to hell, how did he get out?

"You're supposed to be in hell," Charles growled.

David let out a snort. "Seems I have friends in high places," David replied.

"Like who?" I asked.

David shrugged. "I don't know, but when I find out, I'd like to thank them. They brought me right to your door."

Who would do that? What kind of enemies did I have that would help him? I instantly thought of Phillip. No, I didn't believe he was that powerful or conniving. He already had me where he wanted me. Someone from the pack? No, they weren't powerful enough to break someone out of hell.

I frowned at David. He was free now, but he was still human. I couldn't imagine he had enough magic serum left in his system to be a match for me.

"The prisons are gone now, and we have your scientists. The few who survived. You were better off turning around and leaving."

David looked at me with hatred in his eyes. "You are an abomination." He continued moving towards me. "You are not humans. The world is safer without your kind. I can make it great again...with you gone."

David lurched towards me, and before I could react, Charles leaped from the window and flew towards David. Charles wrestled David to the ground, and the pair tussled on the carpet floor for a few moments as I looked on, trying to figure out how to stop the fight without hurting Charles. I threw out my hands and flung David's body across the room and away from Charles. His head banged hard against the wall, knocking him unconscious.

I stomped towards David, intending to end this once and for all.

"Amina?" Charles croaked.

He didn't sound good. I turned to my right and gasped.

Charles lay on the ground, a hand covering his bloody stomach area. Charles coughed, and blood trickled down his chin. Tears were streaming down his cheeks, and a pool of blood began to gather around his torso. He looked at me, his eyes full of fear.

I ran to my brother. "No, no, no," I cried.

How had I not seen a weapon in David's hand?

I hovered my hands over his wounds, pouring healing magic in him, but nothing changed. He wasn't getting better.

"Lisa!" I cried.

She didn't come, she hadn't heard me. I reluctantly got up.

"Don't leave me," Charles whispered. "I don't feel good. It's burning." He writhed in apparent agony.

I felt his forehead. It was cold and clammy. "I need Lisa's help. It's going to be okay, Charles. I promise." I raced for the window. "Lisa!" I shouted.

She looked up from the street.

"I need you. Charles is hurt!" I shouted and then ran back to my brother.

One second later, Lisa was in the room. She cried out upon seeing Charles and ran to him.

"What happened?" She cried.

"David stabbed him. I didn't know. He's not healing from the stab wounds."

Lisa hovered her hands over Charles, and I joined her again. We poured our magic into him, but nothing changed. I looked to Charles' face, but he wasn't moving anymore. His skin was already ashy, lips dry.

"Charles?" Lisa called. "Baby?"

Charles' eyes were seemingly fixated on the ceiling, and his chest did not rise and fall. I touched his neck; no pulse. "Shit, no."

I put my hands over his wounds, willing my magic into him. I stared at his face again, nothing. I continued, straining my magic.

"What's going on? Why won't he wake up? Why can't we heal him?" Lisa cried.

I shook my head, my mind growing numb. He wasn't dead. He was hurt. We could fix him.

"Supernatural poison that I brought with me from hell. They pump it in us. Kills us, but of course, in hell, they bring us back just to do it all over again. One of many tortures," I heard David explain behind me.

Lisa sobbed but continued to pour her magic. I lowered my hands.

"Keep going, Mina. Don't stop!" Lisa shouted.

"You're monsters. And you all deserve to die," David spat. I heard him rise up.

David, although still human, was the real monster here. I wanted him dead. I wanted him gone with no trace of his existence left. I wanted him erased away, even if it killed me. I would give the last of my power and life to make David disappear.

I turned to him with rage in my eyes. I raised my right hand to the ceiling, outstretched, and pictured him disappearing from this world. As if he never existed. My power tore through me, and searing pain brushed every nerve in my body, causing me to cry out and bend backwards.

My eyes watered, and my breath caught in my throat. I didn't hear anything, and my vision blurred until all I could see were shapes. I felt like I was dying. The pain remained but I forced myself to focus it into my remaining power. I thought I would explode from the pressure. Sweat dripped into my eyes, further compromising my vision. I could vaguely make out David's form only a few feet away from me, and I continued to focus on David, willing his heart to stop. I wouldn't send him to hell. I wanted to see him die.

And, as if part of some cosmic joke to my sensitive stomach, David's body exploded. Bits of his blood, muscle, skin, and other things of which I had no clue, flew everywhere including on me and Lisa, who shielded Charles' body from most of the gore.

I collapsed back to the carpeted floor; my body stretched out and unmoving. Nothing would work, no matter how much I willed my limbs to move. I was paralyzed. I could hear Lisa screaming for me as she tried to heal my brother. She needed my help, but I could not move. I could not even turn my head to see her or Charles.

The next moments became a blur. I heard the voices of Faith, Carter, and Erik. They sounded muffled as if someone was talking through a covered phone receiver. Movements seemed irregular. People walked at a slow pace, yet suddenly appeared from one spot to another. Erik and Faith tried to move me to get my body to wake up, but it would not. Lisa shouted for them to help her heal Charles.

Phillip poured magic into him. Bill, the best med mage in town, soon appeared. He gave every effort he could. Phillip moved to me, seemingly having given up the fight for Charles. He touched my forehead and closed his eyes, and a warmth spread through me. Feeling returned to my limps with a warm tingle. As soon as I was able to get my body to function, I crawled to Charles to help. I tried to pour my magic into him, but nothing came out. It was as if I was tapped out of any powers.

I screamed in frustration. My brother was dying, and I could do nothing to help.

The growing group of paranormals soon stopped their efforts.

We knew already before starting.

Charles was dead. We simply weren't powerful enough to heal an evil magic sent from hell or the wounds that had sliced into major arteries, along with the massive blood loss. But I couldn't stop. Wouldn't stop. I couldn't lose him. My brother. My family. He was all I had left.

"Amina," Erik said softly. He put his hands over mine, which were still on Charles' chest. "He's gone."

I swatted his hands away, continuing on. I willed in my mind's eye for Charles to wake up and make a funny comment. But he didn't. He just lies there, unmoving, eyes still aimed at the ceiling and unfocused.

"No, no, no, no, no, no," Lisa cried over and over. She grabbed Charles' face. "Wake up, Charles. Wake up. We gotta go. Come on, come on. Please. Please."

I sat back. Nausea swept over me. Erik wrapped an arm over me, and I tore away from him, getting up and running out of the crowded room. I raced to the bathroom and vomited in the sink until I could bring up nothing more.

I fell to the tile floor and cried until I couldn't breathe. I didn't want to breathe ever again.

*P*hillip was sorry. He'd reasoned that if I hadn't been in lock up, Charles wouldn't have been there to free me, thus wouldn't have been there to fight David. Of course, that would mean I might be the one David stabbed with the poisoned blade instead. However, I'd gladly exchange places with my younger brother if I could.

I wanted to blame Phillip, but I was still level headed enough to know that it hadn't mattered where I was. If I were back in the apartment that I shared with Charles, the same thing could have happened. And it wasn't Phillip's fault. It was David's, who I'd killed in the most gruesome of ways.

When I was able to get up off of the floor, I left the apartment and went back to my own, walking the street covered in David's bloody remains. I felt Erik walking at a short distance behind me but didn't acknowledge him. He followed me inside my apartment. I went straight to the bathroom for a shower, and when I got out and dressed, I went to Charles' room and laid down on his unmade bed. More tears sprang from my eyes, and I let out a guttural cry, hyperventilating in the process.

Strong arms surrounded me, and I felt Erik's chest

against my back. He didn't speak, just held me the rest of the night until I fell into a restless sleep.

When morning came, I heard voices in the living room. Erik was no longer in bed, and I got up and headed out of the room.

Phillip stood in the center of the living room, speaking in a low voice to Erik. Phillip turned to me, and his eyes actually looked pained.

"I'm so sorry, *mi corazon*," he stated.

I sat down on the couch, feeling weak. I didn't speak and looked down at my feet.

"I came by to check on you and let you know that we were able to free the Chicago paranormal prisoners. Some of our people are on the way to the Charlotte one as we speak. We, well, Hagerstown and us, thought it best not to wait around and risk camps relocating again. David had the largest base, so the others were easier to attack."

I nodded slowly, feeling foggy. "Thank you," I said in a weak voice. "Who let David out of hell?"

Phillip walked over to me and lowered to my level, balancing on his toes and resting his arms on his thighs. "We don't know. Did you have any other enemies besides David?"

"Only the people who worked the prisons."

"The remaining leaders couldn't have been powerful enough to do something like that."

"They could have forced a powerful witch to conjure him up."

"That would take one powerful witch. Or a collective of them. I'll question everyone we bring in from Chicago and Charlotte."

I nodded again. "Why did my powers leave me?" I asked him.

"I think it's because you used your mage magic to kill, instead of just control. It happened to me once when we fought that nearby town. Bill was able to bring me back, but he was the only one. Before he got to me, I was paralyzed for an hour. It took several hours before my magic returned," Phillip explained.

"So, she can't kill someone?" Erik questioned.

"Of course, she can. However, it's best you use a spell or power words like other witches or do it the old-fashioned way. If you don't want to temporarily become paralyzed and lose your gifts. You can still do it indirectly, though. Like through mind control."

"If I hadn't killed David the way I did, maybe I could have saved Charles," I whispered.

Phillip shook his head. "He was dead before we got there, *mi corazon*. There was nothing you could have done differently. That piece of shit had to die."

"He's right, Mina," Erik chimed in.

"I also came because I want you to know that you don't have to stay in confinement anymore. You can go wherever you like in town. No one will bother you. The leaders of the various groups will be sending their condolences," Phillip stated.

"What about Felix?"

"He's still in lockup. I can't change that before there's a trial. I'm sorry."

I looked up at him. "Anything else, Phillip?"

He frowned and shook his head. "We're going to find the people who helped David. Charles was a good man. Despite our differences right now, *corazon*, I don't mean you any harm. We'll find out who helped David, and if there is anything else you need, I'll make sure you have it."

He then stood up and left the apartment without another word.

"Mae said we were special. That there was a connection between the six of us for a greater purpose," I stated to Erik. "But Charles is dead now, so how can that be? Did Mae see this coming and not tell us?" My voice cracked, and I felt a sharpness in my chest. I rubbed at it, but the pain would not go away.

Erik sat beside me and wrapped me in his arms. "I don't know, Amina. I think she would have told us if she'd known," he replied.

"It's related. I know it is."

"What's related?"

"Whoever brought David back to kill me. They want to get rid of the six. Stop us from doing whatever it is we're meant to do. And they're winning. Felix is locked up. That trial won't set him free. They're gonna kill him. Charles is dead. They are trying to pick us off."

"They're not going to win, Mina. We're going to get Felix free and find out who was behind it all."

"I'm going to get stronger," I sniffed. "No one I care about is going to get hurt again. When we find out who did this, I'm going to destroy them. Just like I did, David."

I had a power now that I didn't understand. However, I wouldn't take it for granted. I would grow in strength. I would find whoever our enemies were, and I would kill them.

Continue Amina's journey to find her enemies in
Mystic Journeys

If you enjoyed Mystic Bonds, please leave a review on Amazon and Goodreads.

ABOUT THE AUTHOR

C.C. is originally from Baltimore, Maryland, and has actively written fiction since the age of eleven. She's an avid "chick lit" reader and urban fantasy fan. During her days, she works in Civil Rights for the federal government. In her free time, she sings karaoke, travels the globe, and watches too much TV…when she's not writing, of course.

To keep updated on future books and C.C.'s travel and lifestyle blog go to:
    www.ccsolomon.com
    www.free2livegroup.com

You can also reach C.C. at the following social media sites:

ALSO BY C. C. SOLOMON

Standalones

The Mission

Paranormal World Series

Mystic Bonds, Book One

Mystic Journeys, Book Two

Mystic Awakenings, Book Three

Mystic Realms, A Novella